Pandora's Box

Wesley Brian Williams

Whimsical Publications, LLC

Florida

To purchase the authorized electronic edition of *Pandora's Box*, visit www.whimsicalpublications.com

Cover art by Shyanne England
Editing by David Walker

ISBN-13: 978-1-940707-72-3

Published by
Whimsical Publications, LLC
Florida

"So?" Athena asked, unfazed.

"So?" Remus repeated incredulously. "So I don't think anyone, regardless of the offense, deserves that."

Athena blinked before smiling slyly, her grey eyes hiding her thoughts. "Sorry. It's your go."

It was time to stop dancing around the issue. "If they found you once, they might be able to find you again."

Athena had lifted her fork to take another bite, but at his words, she slowly lowered it. "I know."

"Then why are we here and not running?"

Athena paused for a second. That second became ten seconds. "Damn you, Remus." She said it with a grudging smile, and Remus got the feeling he might have won this game. "We're here because we want them to attack."

"Why?" Remus blurted. "Why not keep driving."

He was afraid Athena would take this as a separate question, but she answered with a quote. "To be prepared is half the victory. If they have a way of tracking us then it's not *if* they will attack, but *when,* and we want that 'when' to be on our timetable. Not after we've both been up for forty-eight hours in the middle of nowhere."

She sure was throwing out the pronoun "we" awfully freely. To give himself time to think, Remus absently jabbed his fork in his spaghetti for another bite, but when his fork scraped plate, he looked down to find it empty. Athena's plate was empty as well. The pot with the last little bit left was directly between of them.

Athena's eyes sparkled with mischief. "Three..." she said. What was she doing? "Two..." she counted down, glancing meaningfully at the pot. *Oh crap.* Remus reached over to grab the pot. "One..." Athena finished, leaning over, her hands snapping out quicker than Remus' eyes could follow. She grabbed the pot's handle and dragged it out of Remus' reach at the last possible second.

"Mine, mine, mine!" she sang, shaking the last portion of spaghetti onto her plate.

"Not fair!" Remus protested. "Of course you would get to it first!"

"I gave you a three second head start!"

"Yeah...but without warning." He was smiling, despite himself. Despite the fact she had just told him in all likeliness they would be attacked again. He should be cowering in a corner, not competing for spaghetti.

"My go," she said, after taking a bite of spaghetti. Remus noticed she was now waiting until after she chewed to speak, which meant his words had gotten through to her. "Don't read too much into it," she warned.

"Don't read my mind." Before today, he'd never had need to utter those words.

The corner around Athena's eyes tightened and Remus wondered if he had annoyed her again. "In all likelihood, there will be another battle." She took a sip of soda. "If you leave now, there's a decent chance of escape. So...what are you going to do?"

She was looking at him anxiously. Why was he so important? Why did she want him to stay so badly? He would use his next question to figure that out. "I won't...I won't leave," he said, his voice coming out as a barely-heard whisper. It was hardly the most encouraging statement, but the way Athena grinned ear from ear, you would think he gave a rousing speech

"Excellent!" she exclaimed, standing straight up so that her chair toppled backwards. "Well, best to get prepared."

"Wait," Remus cried. "I had one last question!"

"Uh-uh. We started with you so the last question is mine." It was a decent point, but Remus knew she was using it to prevent him from asking his last question. "Besides, we have measures we must take..."

"Measures," Remus repeated, trying the word on his tongue and deciding he didn't care for it. "What type of measures?"

Athena was in the other room, though her voice carried. "Measures to stop us from being murdered by a band of meticulous killers with advanced weapons and tactics," she explained, her voice far, far too cheerful.

"Is it too late to change my mind?" Remus asked hopefully.

Athena stuck her head out of the room, grey eyes alight with righteous indignation. "Yes!"

"Thought so," Remus sighed. "How can I help?"

Acknowledgements

To my mom and dad...for believing in my dream even during the times when I had given up on it. To my brother...for the many thankless nights you spent editing my work.

Chapter 1

"Don't get near them, avoid eye contact at all cost, give precise instructions whenever speaking to them, and make sure your answers to any question are short but polite."

Caleb glanced back at the two newest recruits. He hadn't bothered to memorize their names as there was a high chance they wouldn't last the week. Caleb himself had seen seventeen years at Pandora's Box, ten years longer than the closest runner-up, making him somewhat of a legend.

"With me so far? Good. Now, the most important thing you need to remember is—don't give them anything unless sanctioned by me or the higher-ups, and if you value your lives, do nothing to antagonize them. Any questions?"

Recruit Number 1 cleared his throat. By his stance and the way he conducted himself, Caleb figured he was ex-marine. "Sir, I understand we are restricted from using lethal force?"

"That's what I said, ain't it?" Caleb had gone through a half hour explaining that very fact and he hated to think he'd wasted his time.

"But, sir, what if we're attacked?"

Caleb stopped in his tracks, beginning to fear the newest employee might be stupid. Stupid didn't last long in Pandora's Box. "If that's the case, son, you better hope you hit them with one of those tranquilizers the company gave you."

"So you expect us to combat these...creatures...with tranquilizers?"

Caleb made a mental note to keep a closer eye on this recruit. Too often, they got young upstarts who thought they could come in and whip the Residents into order. These were always the first ones to die—usually not a quick and painless death—and often times would get others killed with their foolishness.

"No, I expect you to get along with the Residents and avoid combating them at all costs. Anything else you want to ask?"

Recruit Number 1 didn't look satisfied, but said nothing else.

"Good. Now, I figure we start you boys off easy, so you'll be helping me escort Athena to the director's office. Be careful not to—"

"Why?" Recruit Number 2 asked.

Caleb gave him a withering glance. "I reckon she'll be seeing the director."

"No...I mean...you know," Recruit Number 2 stammered. "You said you were starting us off easy, so I thought that means...that meant... Is Athena not dangerous?" He gave a weak smile.

Caleb didn't return the smile. "By the age of eleven, she'd killed seventeen guards and maimed thirty-one more. She's perhaps the most cunning person in here, and as the story goes, she once convinced a man to take his own life."

The recruit's face turned a chalky white, and he seemed to be having problems breathing. "She's considered easy?" he gasped.

Realizing he'd gone a tad overboard while trying to make his point, Caleb softened his tone. "Well, she's mellowed out since then. Her last victim was two years ago, and she has a new habit of giving warnings to all the people she's thinking about killing."

"So what happens to the guards she gives warnings to?" Recruit Number 1 piped up.

"Athena never sees them again. Sometimes they're delegated to other duties, but most of the time they're terminated."

"So, you let her decide who works here?" Recruit Number 1 demanded. "Have you ever tried calling her bluff?"

Caleb slowly counted to ten while wondering who the hell was interviewing these idiots. "One of the Residents, Lamia, cracked a guy's head open and licked up the blood. Typhon killed a man and laughed the whole time while doing it. When one of them takes the time to warn you of an upcoming attack, you damn well believe we take the time to listen."

They walked in blessed silence for another five minutes before Recruit Number 2 spoke up again. "You said she mellowed out at eleven. What changed?"

For the first time that day, Caleb cracked a smile. "She found a hobby."

Last Stand, or its more common name within its halls, Pandora's Box, was a maze of twisty halls and corridors designed to frustrate the average human to the verge of suicide. It had taken a solid year before Caleb could navigate its halls without getting lost, and even still, he occasionally ended up on the other side of his destination. The walls were metallic, making it easy to look in multiple directions at once, and more difficult for a Resident to sneak up from behind to strangle an unsuspecting victim. The floor was metal also, and every footstep clanked loudly, announcing one's presence to those around him.

With Caleb leading, he and the two newest recruits walked past multiple identical doors, abruptly stopping at one that looked no different from the others. Before knocking, he examined the two recruits. Recruit Number 2 was a nervous flop who was constantly wiping sheens of sweat from his forehead. There was a difference between respecting Residents and cowering before them; Recruit number 2 was doing the latter. *Athena might bully him a bit, but she should leave him in one piece.* Hell, she might even be sympathetic once she found out it was his first day. Recruit Number 1, on the other hand, was practically oozing aggression. That would not sit well with the young girl. Caleb briefly considered ordering him to back away, but thought better of it. If he was going to pick fights with Residents, best to know now, and against one who might let him live, depending on her fancy.

He knocked loudly on the door twice, then took a step back. A few seconds passed, and the recruits glanced at each other. Finally, a melodious voice came from within the room. "What is Fame?"

"The advantage of being known by people of whom you yourself know nothing, and for whom you care little," Caleb answered. "May we come in?" He waited for the recruits to back up before pressing a number into the control panel, the door sliding open a second later. Instead of a simple lock, all the doors were outfitted with control panels, with the codes changing daily. Pandora's Box insisted this was somehow safer than regular doors, but Caleb just figured someone who loved sci-fi crap and who had had a ton of money architected the whole building. He couldn't count how many incidents they'd had because a guard had forgotten a code, or worse, a Resident had discovered it.

Athena's room consisted of a bed, a table, and a chair; the rest of the space was scattered with stacks of books. Books of all shapes and sizes filled every corner of the room, with some of the piles threatening to touch the ceiling while others looked dangerously close to toppling over. The stacks drew the eye, so Athena wasn't immediately noticed until she coughed. A teenager with a slender frame and long blond hair, she sprawled across the bed, a book propped up on pillow, casually flipping through the pages.

Caleb waited a second before clearing his throat. "It's about that time, Athena." Whenever he entered this room, his left arm always ached in remembrance of when she had stabbed him with a piece of mirror.

Without glancing up, she responded, "Reading is to the mind what exercise is to the body." Translation—she wasn't finished with her book.

"I'm sure it's a good one, but the doctor is waiting, and if I ain't mistaken, you're the one that wanted to meet with him." That wasn't entirely true and they both knew it. Athena's only response was the flipping of pages.

Recruit Number 2, who Caleb was beginning to think was a bit dim, took this unfortunate moment to speak up. "This looks nothing like a prison cell."

The girl's eyes abandoned the book and traveled the length of the room to fix Recruit Number 2 with a paralyzing stare. "Real knowledge is to know the extent of one's ignorance." Recruit Number 2 paled when he saw the feral lights in her unblinking grey eyes.

"He's new," Caleb quickly intervened. "Just began today. Athena, I'd like you to meet..."

"Nick Hensley, ma'am," Recruit Number 2 said, his tone extra polite. "It's a pleasure to make your acquaintance. I was in the army for four years before they...before I quit."

Athena nodded for him to go on, which was unfortunate because Nick seemed to be at a loss for anything else to say. Caleb opened his mouth to speak, but she silenced him with a passive glance. She was testing the recruit's mettle.

Nick cleared his throat. "As long as I'm here, I promise to do my duty to the best of my abilities...and also to protect you with my life." Athena raised an eyebrow. "That's not to say you need my protection," Nick hurried on to say. "Just to say...you know...just in case." He trailed off sadly, but his bumbling was rewarded with a gentle smile.

Caleb struggled to keep a straight face. "So, what do you think?"

"Welcome anything that comes to you, but do not long for anything else," Athena answered.

Nick looked questioningly at Caleb.

"She's says you're okay," Caleb told him.

Athena added, "Respect commands itself, and it can neither be given nor withheld when it is due."

"She also says to watch what you say from now on. She might not take offense easily, but other Residents ain't as nice."

Nick nodded vigorously. "Yes, ma'am. Thank you, ma'am."

Caleb nodded, so far so good. "And this fine young fellow on my left would be..."

"Mycheal Lawyer, black ops, seven years," Recruit Number 1 said crisply.

After studying Mycheal for a minute, she diverted her attention back to Caleb. "If one does not know to which port one is sailing, no wind is favorable."

Caleb shrugged. "Don't have a clue. They told me to fetch you and that's what I'm aiming to do." Then, he added casually, "I *did* hear that Mr. Titanos himself was making an appearance. I reckon he heard about your request."

Athena's face broke into a smile that brightened up her whole face. Hopping off the bed, she stretched, giving Caleb and the new recruits something to look at. "Occasionally in life there are those moments of unutterable fulfillment which cannot be completely explained by those symbols called words. Their meanings can only be articulated by the inaudible language of the heart."

Caleb nodded, relaxing slightly. "Martin Luther King, if I ain't mistaken? Thought so. Well if you're ready to go—"

He broke off abruptly as Athena headed towards him. Upon reaching him, she thrust both hands at his face in a move so quick it had both Mycheal and Nick reaching for their guns before realizing what was happening. Athena grinned wickedly at their response.

Caleb proceeded to cuff Athena and lead her out. Arriving at the door, she paused to glance back at Mycheal. With a steely smile, she recited, "If the desire to kill and the opportunity to kill came always together, who would escape hanging?"

Mycheal looked affronted. "What was that? What's it mean?" he demanded.

Without looking back, Caleb answered. "That was Mark Twain, and it meant your termination."

Chapter 2

Remus Sylvia was cursed with the worst luck ever. Why the universe had chosen to target him with such appalling luck was anyone's guess, but it had. All his attempts to achieve happiness only made him more miserable. All his attempts to get friends made him more despised. Eventually, Remus stopped trying to fight the inevitability of his cursed luck, which was why he wasn't surprise to find himself in his father's study, nursing a bloody nose, while facing the behemoth that was his dad.

"You tripped," his dad said slowly. "And hit your head on a rock?"

Remus sniffed and applied more pressure on his dripping nose. Bad luck had also cursed him with the natural appearance of a clown. Tall and lanky with red hair and sharp features, he looked ready to perform in any big top.

"Tripped and hit head. Yep, sounds like me."

His father shook his head in disgust. "You're pathetic."

Remus knew Maris Sylvia was talking more to himself, but answered. "Yes, Father."

"Spineless coward."

"Completely spineless," Remus agreed. He had learned from past experience not to contradict his father when he was in mid-rant.

Maris sat back in his seat with a heavy sigh. "Did you even bother to defend yourself?" he demanded suddenly, a hint of pleading in his voice.

Remus shrugged, knowing what his dad wanted to hear, but also knowing he would immediately spot the lie. "What can I say? The rock had a sharp left hook."

He instantly regretted his words as his dad gave him one of his patented glares. If Remus looked like a clown, Maris Sylvia looked like a bulldog in a suit. A big man with wide shoulders and rough features, his father liked to boast he was a successful politician and at one point had even held an office, though that was years ago. Of course with Remus' extraordinarily bad luck, his father could be nothing else but a corrupt politician with little respect for his son.

"When do you graduate?" Maris demanded.

Remus sighed. He knew the next song and dance. "Two weeks from now."

"And what have you accomplished in your four years of high school?"

"Absolutely nothing, sir"

Maris shifted in his seat. "Really? No clubs, no sports?"

"No, sir."

"So, you spent the last four years doing nothing?"

"Yes, sir."

"You spent your entire life doing nothing."

"Yes, sir."

"No talents at all?"

Actually Remus *did* have one talent. He was a whiz in the kitchen and could cook more splendid dishes than anyone in the city. If Remus had it his way, he would enroll at the Culinary Institute of America in New York. Of course, with Remus wanting to be a chef, the universe ensured that Maris was a male chauvinistic pig who found cooking to be a woman's job. Thus, Remus' amazing aptitude for the culinary arts went untrained.

"Why are you such a screw up?" Maris wondered.

"No idea, sir."

Maris sat back in his seat, surprising Remus. Usually, his father's list of his inadequacies would go on for much longer, gradually growing louder and angrier. Rubbing his temple as if the sight of Remus was enough to induce a migraine, he said, "Even though you don't deserve it, I do have some good news for you."

Learning from past experience that good news from his dad rarely meant good news, Remus opted to remain silent.

"Seeing how you have no plans for the future, I have secured you a job. Once you graduate, you'll be working under me as my assistant."

WHAM! Remus felt like he had just been punched in the gut. The staggering news that he wouldn't be taking his car after graduation and driving as far away from Maris Sylvia as possible was heartbreaking to say the least.

"A job!" Remus gasped. "Wouldn't a job of this caliber be better suited for Romulus?"

"Your brother doesn't need my help. He's not a screw up like you, remember?"

"What exactly will I do as your assistant?"

Maris shrugged. "It doesn't matter."

Remus pondered this for a moment. The universe had also burdened him with a high I.Q and intuitive skills so he would always know exactly how unlucky he really was. It was absurd to think his father would offer him a job simply out of concern for his welfare. A more plausible explanation was that his father worried he might embarrass him if left to his own devices. He would make sure Remus stayed in a dark corner while also projecting the image of a family man who gave a job to his struggling son.

Maris looked expectantly at Remus, clearly waiting for him to speak. The ringing phone saved him from mumbling false words of gratitude.

"Hello?" By the way Maris' eyebrows scrunched together and the way he tightened his fist, Remus could tell he despised the person on the phone, which wasn't a surprise, seeing how his father despised most people.

Remus contemplated the idea of working for his father the rest of his life, and found the prospect unbearable. The only reason he kept on stumbling forward through the many months of misery was the thought of escaping and living a mediocre life, but now it seemed even that small dream was above his grasp. The universe obviously hated him and wanted to see him suffer.

"Yeah....of course your support is valued. I understand...won't be a problem." Maris snapped his phone shut. He looked ready to scream, but after a moment of struggle, seemed to calm down. Without looking at Remus, he spoke. "I got your first assignment, son."

Remus felt a sinking feeling in the pit of his stomach. "I thought I started *after* I finish high school."

"Shut up. "You start whenever I say you start." Maris paused as if waiting for Remus to argue, and seemed to hope he would put up a fight, but when Remus kept his silence, Maris continued woodenly. "There's an envelope that needs to be delivered tomorrow."

"And there's no one else who can deliver it?" Remus demanded. It seemed extraordinary that all of Maris' cronies had tomorrow off.

"I don't want them to deliver it; I want you to deliver it. Will that be a problem?"

Remus gave the only answer he could. "No, sir."

"Thought so." Maris started scribbling on a notepad. "The delivery will take place tomorrow, five p.m., at that mall on Lexicon Street." Maris tore off the sheet and handed it to Remus. "To be honest, son, I'm sick of looking at you. Leave."

Remus left the office with thoughts of his bleak future running through his mind.

Chapter 3

Dr. Ahab Pluck wiped his sweaty hands on his pants and took a deep breath.

"You're okay?" Mr. Titanos inquired.

"I still think you're making a dreadful mistake, sir."

Mr. Titanos smirked and glanced down at his notes. In his late twenties, Matthew Titanos was the youngest and most powerful man in the room. His rusty hair was cut neatly, and the barber was probably paid more than what Dr. Pluck made in a month. His money, intelligence, good looks, and cavalier attitude made him into the perfect businessman. Dr. Pluck, being fat, dumpy, and miserable, hated everything about Mr. Titanos.

"It seems you're the only one who has a problem with her," Mr. Titanos observed. "Everyone else finds her the easiest to work with."

"Because they don't know her," Dr. Pluck insisted. "They haven't been inside her mind like I have. She's a sick twisted monster, just like the others. The only difference is she's better at hiding it."

Mr. Titanos shifted through some papers. "Do you have a vendetta against her, Dr. Pluck?"

Dr. Pluck paused. "Why would you say that?"

"You had an argument with her three months ago?"

Dr. Pluck nodded stiffly, not liking where these questions were leading.

"And since then, she's refused to do any of the tests?"

"Until she talked to you. Yes, I'm quite familiar with our conversation."

Mr. Titanos scratched his head like he was just so helplessly confused. "So, you had an argument with Athena. Athena asked to see me. I get all that. Now what I want to know is, why wasn't I contacted?"

Dr. Pluck waited a beat. The real answer was that he had been the director of Pandora's Box for a number of years, and simply didn't need the input of a silly young man who had never made contact with a Resident, nor knew the horrors they were capable of. "I didn't want to bother you with it."

"Our most promising Resident refuses to cooperate until she meets with me and you don't think to call?" Mr. Titanos frowned, shaking his head in disappointment. "Seems like poor thinking on your part."

"Who did call you?" Dr. Pluck demanded, trying to sound assertive, but failing miserably.

"A concerned employee, dissatisfied with the way you were running things."

The good doctor was finding it increasingly hard to remain respectful. "I was thinking of your safety, sir." He added the "sir" as an afterthought. "It's obvious she wants you here." He struggled to keep the slight edge out of his voice. "This could be an attempt on your life."

"Do you think I'm stupid?" Mr. Titanos sneered and Dr. Pluck had to work very hard not to answer that question. Mr. Titanos gestured towards the guards, who all stood up a little taller. "Four highly-trained guards are more than adequate to deal with a teenage girl, regardless of any enhancements she might be hiding."

"It's not enough," Dr. Pluck whispered. "Not nearly enough."

"Really, Dr. Pluck, I believe you're exaggerating."

"You don't know her like I do!"

Dr. Pluck jumped as a loud knock at the door interrupted their conversation.

Matthew gave him a million dollar smile. "In that case, it's time I knew her better."

Dr. Pluck sat opposite of Athena with his desk being the only thing separating them. She was staring at him. He knew it, could feel her intimidating grey eyes, like lasers, digging into his skin. She wanted him to look at her, but he refused to give her the satisfaction.

The one good thing was that the guards appeared to know what they were doing. After Athena entered the room, they had spread out accordingly. One was behind Pluck, while two others were behind her in different corners of the room. Caleb was standing directly behind Athena and would be the first response if and when she decided to act up. Dr. Pluck had always thought Caleb looked like he'd missed his calling to be an actor on Walker Texas Ranger. About six feet tall, he was never without leather boots, cowboy hat and black sunglasses that he wore even inside the facility. There were even rumors that he occasionally ate and slept, but it couldn't be verified.

Mr. Titanos was sitting several feet behind Dr. Pluck with the last guard by his side. Even with Athena's capabilities, there was no way she could get all of them without someone putting a bullet in her. It also didn't hurt that Dr. Pluck insisted she be chained to the chair.

Athena finally made eye contact with him and gave him that damn smile. The one that showed off all her teeth. The smile that held the promise of immediate violence and death. He had to strive to keep his hands steady.

Mr. Titanos coughed and Dr. Pluck realized everyone was waiting on him. "And how are you doing today, Athena?" he said, giving a smile that was every bit as insincere as hers.

Athena raised an eyebrow. "To live happily is an inward power of the soul."

He'd always had a hard time deciphering Athena's quotes and she knew this. He suspected that sometimes, during their sessions, she said quotes with no meaning just to exasperate him. "That's good to hear. Athena, we have a very important guest with us. This is Mr. Titanos." She looked past him to Mr. Titanos, her gaze carefully blank. When she didn't say anything, Dr. Pluck cleared his voice. "Mr. Titanos, this young lady is Athena."

"It's a pleasure to meet you," Mr. Titanos said warmly. "I've heard so many things about you, and please, call me Matthew. According to Dr. Pluck, you're a very talented young woman."

"A talent is formed in stillness, a character in the world's torrent," Athena quoted.

Mr. Titanos nodded his agreement even though Dr. Pluck was absolutely positive he had no clue what she meant. "So true! And from what I hear, your progress has been most promising. But sadly," he continued, letting out a theatrical sigh, "Dr. Pluck has informed me you have been most uncooperative these last couple of months."

He paused to give Athena time to respond, but she just sat chained to her chair, looking bored. When it was apparent no response was forthcoming, Mr. Titanos carried on. "It has also come to my attention that you will no longer allow Ambrosia to be administered." He stopped to stare at Athena like a concerned father staring at his rebellious teen. "Is this true?"

"Men's minds are too ready to excuse guilt in themselves," Athena explained serenely.

Mr. Titanos appeared to be picking up on Athena's unique way of speaking. "So, you're saying the problem is with Pandora's Box?"

Athena nodded encouragingly and Dr. Pluck watched as Mr. Titanos swelled up with pride. *She already has the fool eating from her hands.*

"What specifically is the problem?" Mr. Titanos asked.

For the first time, Athena looked unsure of what to say. She glanced almost accusingly at Dr. Pluck.

"Do you have a problem with Dr. Pluck?" Mr. Titanos inquired.

Dr. Pluck gritted his teeth. It was obvious Titanos wanted to swoop in, find an easy scapegoat, and still have time for a round of golf.

"Nothing in the world is more dangerous than sincere ignorance and conscientious stupidity," Athena answered.

No one needed a translation for that quote, and it brought a smile to seven out of the eight people in the room.

The doctor decided to reinstate his authority. "Regardless of your feelings for me, you must respect my wishes," he said firmly. "You will do as I order or consequences will follow."

Athena's smile vanished, her grey eyes piercing, leaving the good doctor short of breath. "It is only too easy to make suggestions and later try to escape the consequences of what we say." Translation—*If I don't, what are you going to do about it?*

Dr. Pluck realized his dreadful mistake. By challenging Athena, he had given her room for defiance. Now the whole room was waiting in anticipation for his reaction. Worst of all, he had the sinking suspicion that Athena had planned this from the start. The monster, once again, had that damn smile slapped across her face.

"Dr. Pluck, it really doesn't seem like you have things under control," Mr. Titanos observed. "You can't even get her to take her shots?"

"It's not my fault!" Dr. Pluck protested. "I told Caleb to restrain her and administer the Ambrosia."

"And I told him he could go to hell," Caleb growled, speaking up for the first time. "Ain't no way I'm going to waste my men's lives to give her a drug she don't want."

Focusing his attention on an enemy he had some degree of power over, Dr. Pluck responded. "You're paid to enforce security and settle problems. If you're too much of a coward to give her the shot when she's free, then give it to her now while she's chained up!"

"And have her take it out on me and my men later?" Caleb countered. "You want to bring back the bloodbath of five years ago? Because if you force her to take the injections against her will, that's exactly what you're going to get." Then, through clenched teeth, he added, "And if you dare call me a coward again, I'll put my foot through your ass!"

"Enough!" Mr. Titanos demanded. "Both of you."

The two men shut up, but continued to glare with contempt at one another. Dr. Pluck knew he was acting childish but couldn't help it. It was Athena; she always brought the worse out in others.

Mr. Titanos whispered to his closest bodyguard and the bodyguard's guns subtly moved in Dr. Pluck's direction, who almost laughed at how absurd the whole thing had become. Athena was three feet away, yet Mr. Titanos thought he was the greater threat.

"Athena?" Mr. Titanos asked. "What would happen if the shots of Ambrosia were forced on you?"

Athena, who had watched the whole scene unfold with a look of boundless pleasure, was now forced to consider the question. "For murder, though it have no tongue, will speak with most miraculous organ."

Dr. Pluck recognized the Shakespeare quote, and like before, it needed no translation. Mr. Titanos was looking increasingly troubled and Dr. Pluck hoped he was realizing it would take more than a stern lecture to get Athena to tow the line.

"What do you want, Athena?" Mr. Titanos asked. "Why am I here?"

Athena nodded in approval. "Nothing is cheap which is superfluous, for what one does not need, is dear as a penny."

It took Dr. Pluck a beat longer to get the meaning, Mr. Titanos figuring it out before he did. "A deal," he simplified. "I'll do something for you, and you do something for me." He pondered for a moment. "We can talk of a deal, but you need to stop talking through quotes."

Athena cocked her head to the side like she didn't quite understand, but Dr. Pluck knew it was a ruse even as Mr. Titanos tried to clarify.

"Come on, Athena, we both know you can talk normally if you were so inclined. Your roundabout way of speaking will ensure it would take forever to iron out the details of a deal."

Dr. Pluck leaned back, confident now that they were on familiar ground. For years, he and the top specialists at Pandora's Box had been trying to stop Athena from speaking in quotes, and at one point, had even refused to feed her until she asked for the food normally. Of course, that move had backfired and led to the death of two of Dr. Pluck's closest colleagues.

Athena still didn't look convinced, so Mr. Titanos tried a new tactic. "I want to help you out, Athena. I want to be your friend, but we have to deal as equals."

She raised an eyebrow and shook her hands, rattling the chains that bound her to the chair. "The only way to have a friend is to be one."

Mr. Titanos appeared to mull it over. Dr. Pluck hated the way Mr. Titanos had taken over. He also abhorred the idea of making any type of deal with the monster in front of him.

"Release her," Mr. Titanos ordered.

Dr. Pluck's heart skipped a beat. "What?" he whispered. Surely he wasn't suggesting releasing Athena? In a blink of an eye, he had gone from being on the verge of unemployment to being on the verge of death.

"I said release her,"

Caleb looked uncomfortable, and even Athena looked surprised she was getting her way so easily.

"Sir, are you sure that's wise?" Caleb asked.

Mr. Titanos threw his hands up in exasperation. "Good grief! If the five of you aren't adequate enough to deal with one girl, then I'll find five that are. Now for the last time, release her!"

Dr. Pluck watched with great trepidation as Caleb bent down and, after a moment's effort, unlocked Athena's chains before taking a quick step back. Athena scanned Dr. Pluck's desk, as he knew she would, probably looking for a pen or a stapler, anything that could be used as a makeshift weapon. Finding none—he always made sure to clear his desk before starting a session with a Resident—her gaze traveled around the room, noting the distance of the four guards and Caleb. Dr. Pluck was sure two behind her and two in front of her was too much for her to handle. He hoped she would reach the same conclusion.

"Well, Athena?" Mr. Titanos inquired, his voice holding the slightest traces of nervousness.

Athena looked over at him and smiled. "Thank you."

A stupid grin emerged on Mr. Titanos' face, and it looked like he wanted to do some fist bumps for good measure. Dr. Pluck knew he had to defend his lack of progress with Athena, but at the moment, he was at a loss. Athena had given up her greatest annoyance just to appease Mr. Titanos. It didn't make sense.

"You're quite welcome, Athena," Mr. Titanos said grandly, as if he had done a humongous selfless act for her. "I'm so glad you've chosen to talk to me, but if I may ask...why haven't you spoken like this before?"

Athena shrugged. "No one ever asked."

Again, all eyes managed to find Dr. Pluck, who refused to acknowledge the unspoken question. That liar! He had asked, pleaded, threatened. Had practically gotten on his knees and begged her to talk normally.

Mr. Titanos shook his head pityingly in Dr. Pluck's direction before focusing his attention back on Athena. "Miss Athena," he said, and she blinked, thrown off by the title but not seeming to mind it too much. "I believe you wished to discuss something with me?"

"My name is Athena and I'm sixteen years old," Athena started, picking up a little steam after Mr. Titanos nodded encouragingly. Her voice was oddly melodious. It sounded like she was constantly singing, but it was in no way annoying, nor did it take away from her words. "I've spent my whole life on the grounds of this compound and the one thing I want, the only thing I wish to experience, is an hour of freedom away from this prison I call home."

The bomb hit, and Dr. Pluck was the first to react. "Don't be insane!" he yelled, leaping out of his chair so fast his feet actually left the ground. "You can't seriously be thinking about it. She would escape first chance she gets!"

"Sit down and shut up," Matthew demanded, stunned but trying desperately not to show it. He had known she wanted something, but this was ludicrous. The thought of letting a Resident walk around in public was an unfathomable nightmare and not one his father was likely to consent to.

"I assure you, there will be no escape attempt," Athena stated calmly. "I give you my word."

"Yes, her word," Dr. Pluck sneered. "The word of a psychopath. How honorable."

"Shut up!" Matthew roared, his patience snapping at the toad that had somehow gotten to be in charge of Pandora's Box. "The next time you speak, I'll throw you in Lamia's room."

That shut Dr. Pluck up and he covered his mouth as if afraid an errant word might escape his lips. As scary as Athena was, she was nothing compared to Lamia, Pandora's Box's most monstrous Resident. Athena looked so serene and detached that Matthew wasn't sure she knew the full weight of her request.

"When you say an hour of freedom..." Matthew began.

"I mean an hour at a public place with minimum guards," Athena elucidated, as if talking to a small child. "Riding in a van for an hour with a barrel stuck in my face doesn't count."

Matthew had to laugh at the image, and Athena responded by winking at him. Despite the recent trouble she had stirred up, he found himself quickly growing fond of the young girl, but reminded himself that charisma was a more potent weapon than any type of gun. "Well, Athena, you do set your hopes high." He leaned forward in his chair and stared deep into those grey eyes. Even though she was only sixteen, Athena was a breathtaking sight. "So tell me, what do I get out of this arrangement?"

"The promise I will be a good girl and take all my medicine," Athena said sweetly.

Matthew snorted in derision before catching himself. "You know I need something better than that for the price you're asking."

Athena nodded good-naturedly, probably realizing her first offer would fail, but feeling the need to try anyway. Like any ordinary teenager testing her limits. "The Residents of Pandora's Box have been lying about their capabilities ever since your father constructed this facility. What we allow you to see is only a fraction of what we're truly capable of." She paused to let that sink in. "Surely you have seen some evidence to support this?"

There was proof to support this claim. Pandora's Box had a sister organization, Ragnarok, and the Residents in that facility flourished with boundless abilities, easily overshadowing the weak improvements the Pandora's Box Residents had shown. One of his father's biggest agonies was his inability to gauge how effective the Ambrosia drug was, due to the obstinacy of the Residents. Somehow, with minimal contact, the Residents at Pandora's Box had organized enough to agree on being as uncooperative as possible. If he could solve the problem, then maybe his father would finally recognize him for the man he was.

"Let's say I do believe you," Matthew started off slowly. He saw the hope flare up in her eyes. She wanted this more than she cared to admit. "What can you do about it? Are you suggesting you, and you alone, can call out to your fellow Residents and make them comply with our wishes?"

"Not at all," Athena admitted. "I'm listened to, but not necessarily followed. Not well liked, but not disliked either. My influence is minimal."

"You don't know how to sell yourself, do you?"

She acknowledged the hit with a quick nod. Despite Dr. Pluck's reports of a volatile temper, she came across as easygoing. "That being said, I can show you my own unique skill set. My own abilities and, for lack of a better word, powers."

"Sounds interesting," Matthew concurred cautiously. Glancing down at his watch, he saw that he had fifteen minutes until he needed to check in with Ms. Yang, or else the busybody of a secretary would report him to his father. He looked up and saw Athena staring at his Rolex in fascination. Perhaps if things worked out, he would buy her one to celebrate. "I'll be the first to admit that a fully functional, fully cooperative Resident would be a major step in improving efficiency at Pandora's Box. However, you must realize, being the exceptionally bright girl that you are, I require more on the table if an agreement of this magnitude is to be reached."

Athena looked bitter, and Matthew wondered what he said that had offended her.

"It takes a truly exceptional man to make bartering for one's freedom sound no more interesting than a simple business transaction," she remarked. Caleb inched forward, but by then Athena had bounced back and was smiling again. "I believe you fail to grasp what I am offering. I bet Dr. Pluck and your people would give anything to see me at my best. Also, there's a chance if I cross the picket line, others will as well."

How disappointing. "No," Matthew said flatly. "Your offer is weak at best. I'm supposed to take a risk of this scale on the off chance you might be able to show off more talent? So you can maybe convince others to show off their talents?"

Athena's smile never left her face, though her eyes became unreadable. "Well that's a real bummer," she said mildly. "Just to satiate my own curiosity, Mr. Titanos, how exactly do you plan to get me to cooperate with the numerous tests and Ambrosia shots you wish to administer to me if you turn down my demands?"

"If you refuse to complete the tests, or if you refuse to take the shots, then I'll be forced to take severely drastic measures." His time was about up. He nodded to Caleb standing directly behind Athena. "I'm afraid this meeting is over."

"Don't be stupid," Athena said brightly, suddenly in high spirits. Though she didn't move, something fundamentally shifted in the young Resident and Matthew felt a wave of fear. "We're just getting to the demonstration part of the meeting."

Moving abruptly, and with stunning strength that far exceeded what a normal girl should be capable of, Athena kicked the desk and sent it hurtling into Dr. Pluck and the guard standing beside him. Because Matthew was at an angle, the desk missed him, but it was close enough to get his heart racing. Athena was already up and moving in a blur before the desk could come to a standstill. Picking up the chair and spinning around, she clobbered Caleb, who had reached out to grab her. Caleb fell awkwardly to one knee, a long gash on his temple, and Athena spun around once more before releasing the chair in the direction of the guard stationed in the right-hand corner behind her. Matthew heard the sickening crack as it hit the guard squarely in the head, and he slumped to the floor, blood oozing from the wound.

Matthew couldn't quite believe his eyes. Being his father's son, he had lived his entire life knowing about the existence of Residents, had seen a dozen of them in action, but none quite like the sight before him. There was a terrible beauty in Athena as she trounced his unprepared guards, her blond hair dancing with the ferocity of her movements. Her smile never left her face, in fact it seemed to grow brighter. None of them, except Caleb and Dr. Pluck, had ever worked with Athena before. They believed Dr. Pluck's warnings to be exaggerated, and Athena's sweet nature had made them lower their defenses. Thus, they were almost helpless against her fury.

Caleb staggered to his feet and went for his gun, but was stopped by a flurry of punches all aimed at the human body's vital spots, the last blow being a jab to the crotch that made Matthew's own groin ache in sympathy. Training finally snapped in, and the remaining two guards reached for their weapons. Athena wrenched Caleb's gun from his hand, and after casually shoving the Texan to the ground, she fired two shots into the guard standing closest to Mr. Titanos. Matthew yelled as the guard staggered back from the impact before collapsing. Before the guard's body could even think to hit the floor, Athena reached down, grabbed Caleb's arm and, once again revealing her amazing strength, threw the hulking man at the lingering guard. The last guard managed to get off two shots before Caleb's body slammed into him and the two smashed into the wall, ending in a jumble of tangled limbs.

Finally, she turned her attention on Matthew, who had just managed to pull out his .45 and was trying to look like he was still in control.

She gave the gun a dismissive glance before meeting his eyes. "Was that good enough?" she asked, sounding slightly winded.

With great effort, Matthew managed to keep his voice even. "Was what good enough?"

"My demonstration, of course." At his uncomprehending look, she went on to explain. "I assumed at some point of negotiations, I would be forced to give a small display of the skills I've been holding back."

"So all this was a...demonstration?"

"A small one, yes."

"You couldn't have given me a warning?"

Athena smirked at the question. "Come now. You're saying you wouldn't have tried to stop me if I did?"

"Yes!" Matthew looked around at the sheer destruction of her attack. The guard whom she had shot let out a loud groan, and Athena eyed him critically.

"You know, that's one of the reasons Pandora's Box only allows tranquilizer guns," she commented, her eyes devoid of anything even closely resembling compassion. "It's child's play to take them away from the clowns you have working here. Your man should be okay. I shot him through the right rib cage, and the bullet barely grazed the lower quadrant of his right lung. His lung will eventually collapse, but we have a good three hours before that happens. More than enough time to complete our negotiations, though I suggest we hurry. The rest of your men won't stay down for long and I would just hate to have to kill any of them."

For someone who only spoke in quotes up to now, she sure is a chatterbox. Matthew smiled and nodded in agreement while secretly wondering where the rest of the guards were hiding. Someone had to have heard the gunshots. Why was no one rushing in after hearing the attack?

"Stop thinking of it as an attack," she advised, accurately guessing his thoughts. "Can you honestly look around and not recognize the potential I have?"

As he studied the damage she had wrought, Matthew's terror gradually gave way to elation. She had kicked a desk with enough force to bowl over two men; thrown a chair with enough accuracy to knock another out. And this 115-pound girl managed to throw a man twice her size across the room. Adding the fact that she'd managed to do this all in less than 10 seconds...it was indeed impressive. Perhaps not as powerful as the Residents in Ragnarok, but indeed there was raw potential here that could be exploited. If he could get her to showcase these talents to his dad, he could prove that Pandora's Box was not just a huge waste, that he deserved to be in charge of the facility, exclusive of the toad, Dr. Pluck. Speaking of Dr. Pluck, Matthew saw the man groan loudly from his position on the ground and open one eye to survey the damage. Upon seeing Athena free, he quickly shut it and pretended to be unconscious, but Athena's mocking giggle informed she had not been fooled.

"One hour?" Matthew asked, drawing her attention.

"One hour," she agreed. "One hour of unrestricted freedom, and then I willingly become a prisoner again." Of course, he had to consider with her abilities she would try to escape. "I told you, I won't try to escape," Athena said impatiently, spotting his expression. "You have my word."

"Your word?" Matthew repeated with perhaps more skepticism than was prudent.

For the first time, Athena looked offended. "Breach of promise is a base surrender of truth," she quoted, the melody in her voice now taking a sinister quality. "I make few promises, but the ones I do, I always keep."

Matthew was going to ask if she could verify this. *"She can be trusted."* Blinking as a sudden headache formed in his mind, he realized Athena was probably the most trustworthy one in the room, certainly more so than the doctor. "You'll get one hour at the mall," Matthew declared. "You wear an ankle bracelet, and a dozen guards will be watching, so if you try anything—"

He broke off as she came dashing towards him. Heart in his throat, he tried lifting his gun, but was no match for her...hug?

"Thank you, thank you, thank you!" she gushed. "You won't regret this!"

"You're welcome!" he gasped, trying to pry her off him.

Of course, this would be the time guards finally came bursting into the room. And, of course, he got more than one raised eyebrow as he tried in vain to explain the situation they'd stumbled into. They treated Athena with caution at first. But when it became apparent she would give them no resistance, they quickly handcuffed her and proceeded to lead her out.

Matthew surveyed the aftermath and sighed. This would take some explaining to his dad, and Dr. Pluck would eventually have to be fired for his incompetence, but he would have a week or two to find a capable candidate for his job. Matthew was practically pushed to the side as a medical team came in to look at the guard Athena had shot. In concurrence with Athena's assessment, they said he would most likely live if he got treatment immediately and whisked him away.

Ms. Yang, his secretary/babysitter had already called a half-dozen times. Whether it was because it was time to check in or because she had heard of the incident, Matthew didn't know, but there was one thing he wanted to take care of before answering her call. He walked to Dr. Pluck, who was glaring his way. Matthew opened his mouth to tell Dr. Pluck he was done, that he was an incompetent toad, too stupid for the job he had.

But before he could, Dr. Pluck fixed him in an uncharacteristically fierce gaze. "She's going to destroy everything!"

In the weeks to come, Matthew would look back and wonder how the doctor could have possibly known...

Chapter 4

Remus' bad luck ensured each day was atrocious for a variety of reasons, but today was particularly gruesome. His car broke down in the middle of the road and he had forgotten his cell phone at home so he was forced to walk the remaining four miles to school. Along the way, he managed to step in a steep pile of poop that the universe had left for him. He got to his first period late and stank up the room so bad his teacher asked him to leave.

He took a shower in the gym only to find upon coming out that his clothes had mysteriously vanished. It was only natural that the only other clothes he had was his band uniform, which was bright red and gold. Second period consisted of kids snickering at him and making whispered comments behind his back. It was doubtful they were praising him on his attire. At lunch time, his brother, Romulus, managed to catch up with him.

"What do you want?" Remus asked warily. His brother would never voluntarily agree to talk to him; their last in-depth conversation had been in eighth grade. Romulus was blessed with good looks that any male supermodel would kill, slaughter, and maim to have. His hair was a golden-brown that seemed to attract girls like moths to a flame. Both of them were tall, but even though Romulus was the shorter, the way he carried himself made him seem infinitely taller. His skin was a shade darker and every feature on his face was flawless.

As he took purposeful strides towards Remus, several heads craned to see him walk by, not all of them females.

Maris' ancestors emigrated from Rome, and the father of

the year saw fit to name his two sons after the two brothers in Roman Mythology. As the bloody story went, Romulus killed Remus to secure his right as king.

"Dad wants to speak to you," Romulus said, his voice a husky baritone. "Why don't you have your phone?"

Remus grimaced. "Left it at home."

Romulus shook his head. They used to have a closer relationship, but it all changed when Romulus started dating Delilah. Remus knew Romulus didn't understand why Remus was distrustful of her. Remus didn't have the courage to reveal her secret, nor did he think he would be believed.

"Take my phone." Romulus tossed the phone at him. "Give it back after school," he ordered, never really saying anything but the bare minimum to Remus.

Not five seconds after his brother left, the phone started buzzing. Remus sighed. There was no point hoping it wasn't his father. The universe would find such a notion laughable. Snapping the phone open, he offered a feeble, "Hello?"

"Where's your phone?" Maris demanded. "I've been trying to reach you the whole day!"

"Good to hear from you too, Father."

"Don't be a smartass."

"I left my phone at home."

Maris muttered something unpleasant under his breath. "You have the envelope?"

Remus was fairly sure it was still in his book bag, unless some thief had stolen it. In Remus' world, this was a very real possibility. "I still have it."

"Good. Maybe you're not a complete waste of space."

"Glad to hear it, Father."

"Stop being a smartass! Now you're going to drive to the mall after school and meet your contact at the food court. Deliver the envelope, then leave."

Remus winced. "Yeah. Um...problem." An ominous silence over the phone as Maris waited. "My car broke down on the way here. I have no way to get to the mall."

Maris mumbled something else that would have made any sailor cover his ears in shock. "Take your brother's car then."

"But what about Romulus?"

"Your brother will get his own ride home. He actually has friends, remember?" There was a distinct click as Maris hung up the phone.

Remus put the phone in his pocket, fighting to remain calm. His father had once again managed to slip under his armor and leave him feeling depressed and broken. *After seventeen years of abuse, I should be used to it.* He took a breath as a sudden streak of defiance ran through him. Why should he allow his father to dictate his life? Maris Sylvia was a powerful man only on a local level. If Remus ran far and fast enough, he could escape him. They were dangerous thoughts, but the alternative was too much to handle.

He spent his last two periods contemplating his plan. Graduation was less than two months away. Remus wanted that diploma, but as soon as he got it, he would leave, driving as far and fast as a full tank of gas would get him. Maris or Romulus would never see it coming; both thought he was too craven to act on his own. As soon as they realized he was gone, it would be too late. Maris would be angry, but he would only do a cursory search before giving up. As long as Remus stayed away from him and out of the public eye, his father shouldn't care. Might even be relieved his reject of a son was gone. But the whole plan hinged of him playing docile until his chance came, which meant Remus would have to follow Maris' orders until then. It meant delivering the envelope.

After class, Remus cornered Romulus and asked for the keys to his BMW. Romulus wasn't happy, but he knew better than to contradict Maris' wishes. Remus spent the ride to the mall hoping it would be uneventful. Of course, the universe would never miss an opportunity to throw him a curve ball.

Romulus loved her jet black hair, her pouty lips, and her generous bosom. But most of all, he loved Delilah's smooth skin. He could caress it all day long and, in fact, he was content to do just that in the backseat of her car when his phone rang. Coming up for air, he answered his phone and instantly wished he hadn't.

"Where's your brother?" Maris demanded.

"I thought he was doing a job for you," Romulus answered, trying to slow down his breathing.

There was silence for a moment, and Romulus wondered

if his dad had forgotten. "I'll need you to go to the mall and check on him."

Delilah gave him that pouty expression and tugged at his arm. "Hang up," she whispered.

Romulus shook her loose. "You think he needs checking up on?"

There was a snort over the phone. "What type of question is that? He's your brother! Of course he needs someone to hold his hand."

"What's the job?"

"Delivering an envelope"

"What's in the envelope?"

It was doubtful that Remus had thought to ask that question, for if he had, Maris would have ripped him in half. Romulus, on the other hand, was allowed certain leniencies.

"Five thousand dollars."

It was a decent bribe, but certainly not the biggest Maris had ever delivered. "Who's it going to?" Romulus asked, instantly regretting the question, as Maris' leniency only went so far.

"Stop being so nosey! Get to the mall and make sure he doesn't muck it up!"

"If it's that's important, why give him the job at all? Why not let one of your guys do it?"

"Because I need to figure out what to do with your brother."

"Meaning?"

"Remus is a pain in my side," Maris explained. "He's been one his entire life. I've tried to instill in him the values needed to succeed in this world, like I did with you."

Romulus knew better than to contradict him.

"If Remus can't handle a simple task like this, then I'll have no more use for him."

Romulus felt a chill. He knew what happened to people who were of no use to his father. Ignoring Delilah, who was now giving him the evil eye, he said, "What would happen to Remus if he failed?"

"Make sure he doesn't."

Romulus heard the click that signified his father had hung up.

Delilah tried to snuggle in close, but he held up a hand. Delilah stopped. "What is it?"

"I have to go to the mall."

"Why?" Delilah demanded before Romulus could even fin-ish. He took too long to come up with an excuse, and Delilah crossed her arms. "It's because of *him,* isn't it?"

"Delilah..." Romulus warned.

Delilah pouted, something she excelled at. She was the perfect image of seduction. Her slightly pale skin would glis-ten in the sunlight; her amber eyes promised sensuous pleasures; her alluring smile could bring a man to his knees. As cheesy as he knew it sounded, Romulus would gladly give his life for Delilah if he thought it would make her smile, and one day, hopefully soon, he would marry her. No one in his family was invited to the wedding.

Delilah fluttered her eyelids at him. "You don't have to save him, Romulus. Whatever it is, he can handle it. Wouldn't you rather spend more time in the backseat with me?"

The offer gave him pause. Why did it always fall on him to save his brother from his own screw-ups? His ungrateful brother who seemed to resent him because he refused to let life roll over him. A brother, always lost in his own world, who wouldn't even look at Romulus nowadays.

With a heavy sigh, he grabbed his shirt and threw it on. "Can you please take me to the mall?"

Delilah took it as a personal rejection, instantly straight-ening up and becoming distant. "Of course," she said stiffly. "You'd rather be with your brother at the mall than with me in the backseat of a car."

"It's not like that."

"I understand. I really do," Delilah said in a tone that suggested the exact opposite. She fished for her keys. "Re-mus is so messed up that he needs constant saving." Finding her keys, she hopped into the front seat. "You must really hate him," she added petulantly.

Romulus slid into the passenger seat. "I don't hate Re-mus." He thought to say something else, but decided against it. Something had happened between Remus and Delilah, but try as he might, he couldn't figure out what. Whenever he asked her, she would turn nasty, and asking Remus only made his brother shut down completely.

Delilah sniffed and started up the car. "He really doesn't deserve a brother like you," she said, refusing to let the topic drop. "What has that idiot ever done to earn your respect?"

There was no way Delilah would understand; living under Maris Sylvia had been and would always be a nightmare. If Remus hadn't been there, Romulus didn't believe he would have survived, but there was no way to put into words all Remus had done to protect him when they were children. Even if there was, Delilah wouldn't be receptive of it.

"I said what has your brother ever done for you?"

"Drop it," he snapped, but changed his tone as Delilah looked on the verge of mutiny. "Look, we go to the mall, check up on Remus, and then I'll take you someplace nice for dinner."

"Promise?"

"Promise. Shouldn't take more than a couple of minutes." After all, it was only a simple hand-off. Not even Remus could mess it up.

Chapter 5

It was an extremely tense situation inside the van, the air saturated with the stench of fear and hopelessness. Chris Burlington tried to keep his hand close to his gun without appearing threatening. Athena appeared to recognize his effort and gave him a smile.

None could call themselves Athena's friend, although there were a few who came close, and Chris was among the selected individuals who had developed a pleasant rapport with the gray-eyed Resident. For the past couple of years, he'd been sneaking in sweets and junk food for her to sample. Three years of Pop-tarts had made them as close to friends as anyone was liable to get.

The one word that could sufficiently describe Chris was "average." He wasn't tall, but wasn't short either. Not good-looking, but in no way was he ugly. Nothing except his horn-rimmed glasses would distinguish him from the next Average Joe on the street. His was a face immediately forgotten after seeing it only moments ago. In his former line of business, it was a useful trait to have.

He cleared his voice. "Twenty guards will be stationed at the mall. If you don't see them, that means they're doing their job. You'll be free to go wherever you want as long as you stay within the parameters of the mall. If you leave the parameters at any point, you will receive a shock of 80 volts from your ankle bracelet. Failure to move back into the target zone will result in an even greater shock."

Three guns flashed out as Athena moved but then relaxed when they realized she was simply scratching her nose. Her only reaction to their hairline reflexes was a slight twitch of her lips.

"The wristwatch on your arm will count down from an hour," Chris continued, trying to blow past the awkward moment. "At the two minute mark, the watch will beep, indicating you should head back to the rendezvous point. If at any point you feel distress, then press the left button and someone will get to your location as quickly as possible. Any questions?"

Athena smiled. "If worry were an effective weight-loss program, women would be invisible."

Chris hated that Caleb wasn't here, as he was the best at deciphering Athena's literary references. A handy ability, especially since Athena was known to hide death threats in her quotes. However, Chris was relatively sure she was poking gentle fun at the anxious looks on his men's faces.

"Can't blame us, ma'am. We never done this type of thing before, and Caleb isn't here to keep us in line."

Athena wrinkled up her nose at the mention of Caleb. Come to think of it, Caleb now had a bruised arm because of Athena, so perhaps they weren't as close as everyone thought. There had always been gossip and rumors swirling around the enigmatic young girl, but the newest information suggested she had taken out a room of armed men and threatened Dr. Pluck until he agreed to this outing. Thinking like a soldier, an hour at the mall was a strategic nightmare; too many unforeseen variables to control, too many places where Athena could leave line of sight, and way too many potential hostages. For the life of him, Chris could not believe anyone was so stupid to agree to this. This could be the biggest disaster ever to happen.

"You can either feed negative thoughts or you can starve the suckers." Athena was looking right at him as if she could sense his doubts.

"Excuse me?" Chris said politely.

Her grey eyes continued to burn into him. "You must trust and believe in people, or life becomes impossible."

He got the gist of it. "Of course, I believe everything will work out. I am confident..." He trailed off as Athena shook her head.

Raising a hand, she wagged a finger at Chris. "Liar, liar, pants on fire," she sang, her eyes glittering eerily.

His mouth was dry as Athena singled him out. Her attitude was making the men around her very nervous, but fortunately, the van lurched to a stop, signifying their arrival. Six men and one girl came clamoring out of the van, scaring an elderly couple half to death.

"Remember, you'll get one hour," Chris reminded Athena. "The rest of your security personnel should have already spread out within the mall. Your ankle bracelet has a tracer and a shock of up to two hundred and fifty volts, so I wouldn't try escaping."

Athena smiled. Quicker than he could react, she gave him a quick peck on the cheek before cheerfully skipping to the entrance of the mall.

Remus hated the mall. There were just so many places that the universe could strike. It could make him slip on the escalator and break his hip. It could cause a thief to pickpocket his wallet. He could get massive food poisoning from a Cinnabon. God forbid he should ever walk into the priceless antique store.

"You can do this," he murmured. "Get to the food court, find guy, give envelope, leave. It's all so simple. What could possibly go—" He stopped, almost cursing out loud as it hit him. He had no inkling on what the guy looked like. He didn't think to ask his dad, and his dad hadn't volunteered the information.

It was okay. He would just call his father and ask him... The second realization almost brought him to his knees. He swayed sideways, barely missing a family of three, which earned him a dirty look from the dad as they passed. He had given Romulus his phone back and had left his at home. He could either try to find a payphone, borrow someone else's phone, or simply head to the food court and hope he was recognized.

He thought it through, and began heading in the general direction of the food court. It would be okay. Once he got there, if he wasn't recognized, he would borrow someone's phone. Or perhaps the contact would be so obvious that he wouldn't have to call his father and have an unpleasant conversation.

Remus sent a prayer to the universe asking, just this once, if it could mind its own business.

Romulus scowled and glanced at his watch for the fifth time in ten minutes. It had been over an hour and there was still no sign of Remus.

"When can we leave?" Delilah whined from the seat across from him. When Romulus didn't immediately answer, she asked the question again, this time with a hint of rebellion coloring her voice.

"I already told you," Romulus softened his voice as Delilah looked outraged. "When Remus delivers the envelope."

"But it's been over an hour!"

He swiveled around in his chair to face her. "You want me to buy you another corn dog?"

"I don't *want* a corn dog! I want that nice dinner you promised. How do you know Remus didn't already deliver the envelope before we got here? We could be waiting here for nothing!" Delilah's voice was steadily rising.

He grabbed her hand in an effort to quiet her down, but she slipped out of his grasp. "Listen to me for a second. You see the man on my far right? The one wearing the red cap?" Delilah glanced around and nodded. "That's the guy my brother is supposed to meet. You can see he's looking around, just as frustrated as we are, which tells me Remus hasn't showed up yet."

Delilah grumbled, "Stupid Remus."

"Any restaurant you want to go to, I'll take you," Romulus promised. "Just wait ten more minutes."

She sighed. "You're lucky you're so cute."

"Thanks. You're the greatest." He was just about to suggest the unthinkable. That they actually got up and look for Remus when...

"What's wrong?" Delilah asked, noting his frown.

"Not sure," he wheezed. He used his sleeve to wipe at the perspiration that had materialized on his forehead. An intense and deeply uncomfortable feeling had settled over him. Not exactly pain, but the next closest thing. He peered at his corn dog with newfound wariness, suspecting the three dollar item of being the source of his woes. "I think I might have eaten some bad meat."

"Some bad meat?" Delilah repeated skeptically.

"Yeah." The feeling was growing more intense, and he shifted in his seat, trying to get comfortable.

Delilah stared past him. "I don't know what you ate," she remarked. "But I do know who's checking you out."

Romulus followed her eyes and found a girl on the other side of the mall looking intently at him. Only slightly taller than five feet, she had long blond hair that fell past her shoulders. Her clothing was grey and bland, but despite that, her beauty shone through. Romulus was not attracted to the girl and, instead, he felt an instant panic as soon as he laid eyes on her. Something about her was off. She had the indefinable air of a villain up to no good. The same air one might find from kids planning to shoot up a school yard. Added to that, the appraising look she was giving him was making him exceedingly unnerved. He felt like a piece of meat being examined for flaws.

Delilah wrapped her arms around him to signify possession, but the girl didn't seem to see her. She slowly made her way towards them.

Athena made it a point to never panic. It didn't benefit anyone and it lead to bad decision-making. However, today she had to confess that she found herself a tad perturbed. She had already wasted forty minutes of her time and she still couldn't find the specimen she needed..

She had spent her first five minutes of freedom studying and researching the humans swarming around her. It was enjoyable to understand the significance of a first date or the pleasure of eating something sweet. The frustration of working a minimum wage job and the anger over a recent breakup was also welcomed, for they offered experiences that she would never have a chance to partake in firsthand. Athena could stand in the middle of the mall the whole day and soak in the thoughts of people passing around her, but there simply was not enough time. She had to find a specimen, preferably a guy, in her age group with the right thought process. Four years of planning hinged on this detail, except no one fit the criteria. The few whom she might have considered were lacking on the inside; what she needed was a streak of chivalry. From the books she read, the world was supposed to be full of humans with this trait, but she was having difficulty locating a single one. At this point, she was growing desperate, ready to accept just about anyone.

She passed a couple with a small child who were angry about a drunken kid almost running into them and her interest piqued, despite her upcoming deadline. She stopped, hoping to catch a few more stray thoughts, when she saw him. Tall, with light brown hair and wide shoulders, he sat at a table with a female companion beside him. He was a magnificent sight. Almost too pretty to be a guy and even from where she stood, she could feel the Resident gene vibrating within him.

The female spotted her first. She said something to the male, and he turned around. Their eyes clashed and Athena felt her heart quicken. It was possible he had the qualities she required, but there was no way to be certain without reading his thoughts. The female misunderstood her intentions and hugged the guy, marking her territory. Athena took a couple of steps forward and concentrated. She was about to find out if he was an acceptable fit when someone attacked her from behind, tackling her to the floor.

Chapter 6

Remus quickened his walk. He only had six minutes left to get to the food court and deliver the envelope. He might have gotten there sooner if it hadn't been for his uncanny lack of directions. He had walked to the other side of the mall before realizing he was nowhere near his destination. What would happen if he wasn't on time? Would the contact leave? He broke into a jog while glancing at his watch.

The universe struck again! Remus was so busy looking at his watch, he didn't see the blond girl step in front of him. The collision was brutal. He slammed into her, knocking them both face down on the ground with him on top of her. Before he could offer an apology, her elbow snapped back, hitting him viciously in the face.

"Christ!" he yelled, finally getting on his feet. He felt the tender remains of his nose, still brutalized from the last beating he had received. The girl was still on the ground and, on silly impulse, he reached down to help her up before remembering she had just reshaped his face.

The blond stared coldly at his hand before springing to her feet in one fluid motion. Although blessed with good looks, she gave off the impression of being unkempt. Her hair was ruffled in desperate need of a good combing, and her fingernails were ragged, probably due to her biting at them. Though only a bit taller than five feet, she gave the impression of towering over him. The most unusual thing was her piercing eyes, which seemed to be an unnatural shade of bright grey.

"A clumsy fool claims his knife is blunt," she stated icily.

Remus was so transfixed on her eyes that it took him a

second to realize he had just been insulted. "It was an accident! I didn't mean to knock you down, and it doesn't give you the right to break my nose!"

"Show me a good loser and I'll show you an idiot."

"What?" It was just his luck to bump into a psycho chick this close to the food court. "It was an accident," he stressed. "I'm sorry. Now let it go."

"Never attribute to malice that which can be adequately explained by stupidity," she continued relentlessly.

It clicked that she was speaking with quotes. "Bitterness is like cancer. It eats upon the host," he retorted, remembering the Maya Angelou quote from middle school.

For a moment, she seemed stunned, and Remus was deathly afraid she was going to scream for help. The last thing he needed was mall cops asking inconvenient questions like "why are you here?" or "what's in the envelope?" Then, cocking her head to the side, she fixed him with an inquisitive stare.

"On Monday mornings I am dedicated to the proposition that all men are created fools."

Recognizing a challenge when he saw it, he responded. "Better to remain silent and be thought a fool than to speak out and remove all doubt."

"There is nothing more frightful than ignorance in action."

Drat! She was quick. He wracked his brain for more quotes and came up empty. She was waiting patiently, head still cocked to the side. Then in a sudden flash of inspiration, "I'm rubber, you're glue. Everything you say bounces off me and sticks to you."

He was rewarded with a musical laugh that sent goosebumps down his arm. "Brilliant!" she cried, startling him by clapping her hands together.

She had gone from being cold to having excessive energy in under two minutes. He wondered if she was bipolar.

"Sorry for jumping down your throat," she apologized, as if reading his thoughts. "You caught me by surprise."

"And that was a reason to break my nose?"

"I said I'm sorry. Now let it go!" the girl mocked, reciting his previous statement. She tossed her head, causing her blond hair to ripple. "What's your name?" she demanded.

"I'm the one with the crushed nose, you go first."

She blinked as if unaccustomed to people not following

her command and then smiled, showing off two rows of perfect white teeth. "Athena. My name is Athena."

"Grey-eyed Athena. Goddess of wisdom, war, and heroic endeavors," he remembered. At least it explained the choice in contacts.

Athena gave a sardonic bow. "And your name?"

"Remus."

"Remus, doomed brother of Romulus. Slain so his brother could be king," she quoted, then smiled.

Remus couldn't tell whether she was mean-spirited or merely playful. Everything she said was either an insult, or of the mocking variety, and for some reason, she made him nervous. There was a predatory aspect to her movements and tone; the way her eyes glittered was especially disconcerting.

"Crap!" he yelled, remembering his task. He grimaced when Athena raised an eyebrow. "Sorry. I just remembered I have to be somewhere." If he didn't deliver this envelope, his father would kill him. Probably literally. And he still didn't have the faintest idea as to what his contact looked like.

"I'm afraid I must depart as well," Athena said with a heavy sigh. "I have to find some dope with an envelope."

His pulse quickened. "You're looking for an envelope?"

"To be more precise, I'm looking for a dope with an envelope." She beamed at him. "You wouldn't happen to be that dope, would you?"

"Probably not." He had to be sure before he handed over the envelope. If he gave the envelope to the wrong person, Maris would rip him apart *before* killing him.

"Well I hope the guy comes soon." She shuddered. "I would hate to see what Maris would do to the man that fails him."

"You're expecting an envelope from Maris?"

"Isn't that what I just said?" Athena said snippily, hands on her hips. "Now do you have an envelope for me or not?"

Remus hesitated. Something was wrong with the situation. Maybe it was the fact that she seemed to answer every unspoken question he had. Maybe it was the gut-wrenching sensation, which had been intensifying every second she was in his company. Or perhaps it was just too convenient. He just so happened to bump into the contact who just so happened to innocuously reveals herself as the contact? The universe would never allow him to win so easily.

"The universe?" she asked, eyebrows arched.

"What?"

"You said the universe would never allow you to win so easily."

"I did?" One of the betraying signs of insanity was the habit of talking out one's thoughts without realizing it.

"You must have or else how would I know?" she snipped, as if he was an idiot. "I must say, I didn't know I bumped into a celebrity who was on first-name basis with the universe. What's your problem with him? Mr. Universe, I mean."

Remus glared suspiciously, but though her lips were still quirked with mockery, it seemed she genuinely wanted to know and, for reasons unknown, he genuinely wanted to tell her.

"I don't have a problem with the universe; the universe has a problem with me."

"I'm sure the universe has a problem with a lot of people," she responded dismissively. "Seems like a real prick like that."

"But I'm a specific target," he insisted. "The universe has a personal vendetta against me."

"How so?"

Up to now, he had gotten the feeling she had been taking this as a gigantic joke, but at this insistence, a small frown was forming on her lips. He knew he should quit at this point and play the whole thing off, but his mouth continued to run without his permission. "Everything I do is destined for failure. Everywhere I go, bad luck follows. The universe has it in for me, and I have no idea why. I would trade a kidney for a week of good luck." He shut up, realizing how immensely self-pitying and pathetic he really sounded. Expecting a sharp retort or a sarcastic comment, he was surprised when he received an understanding smile.

"The universe can be a cruel mistress at times," Athena allowed, acting like she accepted his convoluted theory. "I myself have suffered most unceremoniously because of fate and other people's dealings." A flash of resentment crossed her face, but was quickly chased away by her natural smile. "But you can't quit, and you can't give up, or else the universe wins."

"You don't get it. You can't fight the universe. It's too powerful! Anywhere I go, it finds a way to do me either bodily or mental harm. Like today, for instance. I accidentally collided into this blond and she proceeded to try and break my nose."

"Are we still on that?"

"And at some point today, I fully expect to break my hip while riding the escalator."

She looked deeply perplexed. "Escalator? Are those the mobile steps?"

Remus matched her confusion. "You've never seen an escalator before? Where are you from?"

For the first time, she looked embarrassed, her cheeks reddening. "Stop changing the subject!" she yelled, unnaturally loud and beginning to attract attention. "We're talking about you, not me. Now, I think you're letting the universe have too much dominion over you."

"But—"

She stuck her finger in his face, forcing him to lean back so as to not have his eye poked out. "No buts! If you're afraid of breaking your hip on the escalator, then ride the blasted contraption all day long!" She was practically vibrating with energy. "It's you against the universe and it needs to recognize you're not going to take any more crap! You must shove off the universe's yoke of oppression!"

It was impossible not to laugh at the imagery. She sounded like a hyped-up motivator on steroids. "You're insane," he complimented. Again, his mouth running ahead of his brain.

He was afraid she might take it as an insult, but all she did was nod as if he had said something profound, before holding out a hand. "Envelope," she instructed.

Hesitating slightly, he withdrew the envelope from his pocket and handed it to her. She had called Maris by name, and knew an envelope was supposed to be delivered at this time. She had to be the contact.

She glanced at the envelope with curiosity, briefly weighing it in her hand before nonchalantly sticking it in her back pocket. "Thanks."

"So, I guess this is goodbye," he said gloomily.

Athena sighed and shook her head in disgust. He had annoyed her, but he didn't know how. "There you go letting the universe trample all over again. If you want to see me again, say it!"

Thunderstruck, he stared at her. He'd never met anyone quite as eccentric as Athena. "I want to see you again, gray-eyed Athena." Only having one girlfriend in his entire life, he knew he was woefully ignorant in the ways of flirting. He didn't have an inkling if his words came across as being touching or tacky, though he suspected the latter.

Her eyes shone with an unnatural light. "You want to see me again, doomed brother Remus? What happened if I told you your earlier assessment was correct and I am, in truth, insane?"

Remus was taken aback by the bizarre question, but recovered quickly. "If you were insane, would you even know you were insane?" he mused. "In any case, it doesn't matter. Insane or not, I still want to see you...so will I see you again?"

Athena beamed. "I promise, and I make those so very rarely. You really should be honored." She broke eye contact to check her watch, which was beeping manically. "It seems my time is up," she said regretfully. For a moment, she seemed to look past him. "But we'll see each other again."

Without warning, she embraced him in a passionate kiss. He had only been kissed once before and it paled in comparison with Athena's. It was sensual, compassionate, and literally shocking, seeing as a charge of static electricity passed between them. She broke off after a couple of seconds. "I'll see you later."

And with that, she was gone. Remus sighed deeply. He was happy for the next three seconds. Until he turned around and faced an enraged Romulus.

Chapter 7

Delilah laughed unpleasantly as Remus collided with the blond. She practically squealed with delight when the blond elbowed Remus in the face. "Okay, this was more fun than I thought it would be," she confessed. "Now can we go?"

"Soon. Just wait until he puts the envelope in the contact's hand. Then we can go."

He watched as Remus awkwardly got to his feet, and couldn't resist a small smile. Now all he had to do was apologize, find the contact standing 50 feet in front of him, and deliver the envelope.

The girl stood up and said a few short words. Whatever she said, it wasn't an apology. Remus looked cross and said something insistently to her. They had a heated exchange that looked like it was growing more volatile by the minute.

"Maybe she will hit him again," Delilah said hopefully.

"Why do you hate my brother?" Romulus had asked this question many times in the past and had yet to receive a satisfactory answer.

Delilah shrugged, more tolerant than usual whenever this question came up. "He bugs me."

He wanted to pursue the issue, but his attention was diverted when the blond started to laugh.

Delilah clucked her tongue, disappointed that the girl showed no intention of plummeting Remus to the ground and stealing his lunch money. "He must have told her about his love life."

"Be nice."

"Can we go now?"

"Wait until he delivers the envelope."

"That will take forever!" Delilah whined. Romulus' future wife had a shrill voice that, when used, could be heard in three different counties. Not for the first time did Romulus consider forking over the money for earplugs. "He's too busy chatting it up with that slut!"

It was true. Instead of apologizing to the blond and moving on, Remus was now in deep conversation with her. Lots of smiling and laughing.

"Oh my gosh," Romulus whispered as the truth dawned on him. "He's flirting with her!"

"Your brother? He chooses now to go through puberty?"

Romulus watched with growing horror as Remus took out the envelope and handed it to the blond.

"What the hell is he doing?"

"I thought you said the guy with the red cap was the contact?"

"He is!"

"Then what is he doing?"

"I don't know!"

He leaped out of his seat. "Stay here," he instructed Delilah. Ignoring her cries of protest, he began running. *Remus!* he thought hatefully. *Always have to mess things up!* For a second, the blond looked past Remus, straight at him, as he quickly approached from behind.

In a brief instant their eyes clashed. *Who are you?* Romulus thought. The girl smiled cynically in his direction. She grabbed Remus and planted a kiss on his lips and then left, moving at speeds that seemed to be inhuman.

Romulus skidded to a stop to avoid colliding into Remus. His brother turned around, surprised. "Romulus? What are you doing here?"

"Watching you be an idiot!" he snarled. "What the hell were you thinking?"

Remus looked like a kicked puppy. "I wish you wouldn't yell like that."

"Do you realize what you just did?"

Remus sniffed, offended. "You know that wasn't the first time I kissed a girl."

Despite their differences, it really wasn't that often that Romulus felt like punching his brother. "You gave the envelope to that girl!"

"I know I did. Maris asked me to deliver the envelope to

her."

"Maris told you to deliver the envelope to the contact!"

"And I did."

Romulus pointed to the man wearing the red cap. "That's the contact."

"There're two contacts?" Remus was blinking in confusion, and the urge to hit him was growing stronger.

"No, you idiot!" Romulus shouted, pointing crazily. "He's the contact! The one and only contact!"

It was unfortunate that Romulus raised his voice, and it was even more unfortunate that the man about whom they were speaking heard the word "contact," saw Romulus pointing at him, and started to amble over, probably assuming they had the envelope.

"Fuck," Romulus groaned.

"So, you're saying the girl I just handed the envelope to was, in reality, *not* the contact?"

"Yes!"

"And the man now coming towards us, that *you* in fact attracted, is in reality, the contact who will now be expecting us to hand over an envelope?"

Romulus stared at Remus. "Correct."

"That's unfortunate," Remus remarked, seemingly unruffled.

His brother was saved the barrage of insults Romulus was about to unleash by the contact.

Scowling, the rugged thug looked them both up and down. "You know how long I've been waiting?" he demanded in a deep, lugubrious voice. He was a big man with arms that looked like they could crush a piano. "I don't like to be kept waiting, he added helpfully.

Knowing Remus' track record for handling people, Romulus felt it better if he took the lead. "I apologize for the inconvenience, Mr. ..."

"Bob," the man supplied. "And you don't need to be sorry. You just need to hand over the package."

"That might be a problem."

Bob's face was expressionless. "Why is that?"

Romulus hesitated, and Remus stepped in. "The package was stolen." There was no way to put the information in a good light, but there had to be a better way than blurting it out. Furthermore, while Remus sounded appropriately nervous, his voice lacked the respectful pitch that was very much needed in this circumstance.

"Who stole the package?" Mr. Bob asked.

"I don't know." There was too much rebellion in those three words.

"You don't know," Mr. Bob repeated, taking a step forward while looking around as if checking for witnesses. The mall was too crowded for violence, but the fact did little to alleviate Romulus' fears. Their father often times worked with people lacking impulse control. "What did he look like?"

Remus looked down. "I didn't see him."

He was a poor liar; Mr. Bob took another step forward, now close enough for Romulus to tell he was in tragic need of a shower. "What did he look like?"

Remus raised his eyes to meet Mr. Bob's, and Romulus was shocked to see a streak of defiance in his posture. "I didn't see his face."

"It was a woman," Romulus intervened before Remus could take a beating. He had thought Remus was trying to save himself from admitting he was stupid enough to give the envelope to the wrong contact, but it now looked like he was trying to cover for the blond, and if he was indeed that foolish, then it would be up to Romulus to salvage this mess. "Blond hair, blue-grey eyes, about five-four. Around our age." Remus gave him a frantic look, but Romulus ignored it. She went running in that direction." Romulus pointed.

Mr. Bob didn't even glance in the direction Romulus was pointing. "You saw her run off?" he asked. "You saw her running off with my package?"

Remus cringed, forcing Romulus to entertain the notion he had made a mistake. His brother might be an idiot, but he was a perceptive idiot.

"Yes, I did," Romulus slowly admitted, trying to spot the trap.

"You saw her run off...a blond girl no older than you two, with my envelope...and you didn't bother to give chase?"

The question stopped Romulus cold, his mind racing for an appropriate answer that did not exist.

"No," Remus said loudly, his voice only wavering a little. "I gave her the envelope because I thought she was the contact."

His brother was taking the heat. While it was touching,

Romulus would have been further moved if it wasn't his fault in the first place.

Mr. Bob's eyes narrowed at the preposterous statement, his mouth opening wide to reveal yellowish teeth. "You thought we would send a blond girl to pick up twenty thousand dollars?" Maris had lied about the amount, but it didn't come as a surprise. "Did she ask for the envelope? Did she approach you?" Mr. Bob asked, his bafflement clear. "Why on God's green earth would you give our money to a random girl?"

Remus needed to answer. Needed to spew forth an excuse, no matter how unbelievable, but instead, he remained silent.

Mr. Bob sighed, his breath enough to make Romulus nauseous. "What was her name?" he demanded. It was Remus' best and only hope to avoid a grueling punishment.

"I don't know," Remus answered, not even trying to make the lie sound believable.

Mr. Bob's hands clenched up, as if fighting the impulse to hit him, but then they slowly relaxed. "Wait here," he instructed before walking away and pulling out a cell phone.

While Mr. Bob was distracted, Romulus took the opportunity to glance at Delilah, who was still sitting at the table where he had left her. She was also talking on her phone, her eyebrows knitted in worry. Romulus hoped she wasn't calling the police, as that would only make matters worse. He turned to his brother. "Who was she?" Remus acted as if he didn't hear him. Romulus grabbed his arm, spinning Remus around to face him. " Do you know what you have done?"

Remus stared. "Why *didn't* you go after her?" The words were said with curiosity rather than accusation. "Instead of stopping by me to tell me what an idiot I am, why didn't you chase after her?"

The truth of the matter was Romulus' first instinct had been to go after the girl, but he'd been too afraid. Everything about her, the way she moved, the way she smiled, even the way she laughed, seemed alien. The girl terrified him. He was afraid to chase her because he was afraid he might catch her.

"It's not my job to chase after women! It *was* your job to deliver the envelope to the right person!"

Remus nodded absently, his mind somewhere else when it should be dedicated to surviving the night.

Mr. Bob was just finishing his conversation. "I'm serious. He claims a blond girl stole the envelope. Boss, I wouldn't make this crap up." A pause. "I understand." He pocketed his phone and began ambling over to them. "Here's what we're going to do," he said during his approach. "We're going to take a ride over to my boss, so he can personally asked you two a few questions. If either of you gives me a hint of trouble, I have permission to tear one or both of your limbs off. Understood?"

"Screw it," Remus said.

Chapter 8

Remus had once again been outmaneuvered by the universe, but instead of his default mode of desperation mixed with apathy, he felt something new. An intense concern that made it difficult to breathe, but not for himself, and not even for his brother. Athena wasn't the contact, but she had to be involved in Maris' operation somehow. It was the only way she could have known about the time and place for the meeting, and if Athena knew about Maris, chances were Maris could find out about her. Romulus had already given a fairly accurate description of Athena, but Remus had spoken to her. He knew she liked speaking in quotes, and that she was a fan of Greek mythology and literature, as Athena was most likely an alias. And try as he might to resist, he would eventually give the information up; Remus had a healthy respect for the "interrogation" techniques that would be employed to find answers.

Maris and Mr. Bob's employer would utilize this information to track her down. They would do terrible things to her, and not because of the money, as 20,000 could easily be replaced. They would make her suffer to prove a point—*this is what happens to those who steal from us.* After the point was proven, she would most likely die, but even if she didn't, she would never be the same smart-mouthed, demanding girl as before.

Mr. Bob took another step forward and grinned. The arrogance and cruelty of the grin prompted Remus into answer, as he imagined him grinning at Athena the same way. He grabbed Romulus by the hand and broke off into a run.

"What are you doing?" Romulus cried.

"Do you want to answer his questions?"

It didn't take long for Romulus to decide on an answer. "Let go of me! I'm faster without you holding on."

Mr. Bob looked stunned that someone would have the nerve ignore his commands, but he quickly got over it. "Come back!" he thundered, chasing after them.

"I wonder if that ever works," Remus mused. "Yelling at people to come back."

Romulus was indeed faster than Remus. He quickly gained an early lead over him. On the other hand, Bob was quicker than he looked. He was steadily catching up to Remus. They blew past startled shoppers or, to be more accurate, Romulus blew past startled shoppers. The universe, which was immensely enjoying Remus' suffering, made sure to place every single fat person it could find in Remus' way. He was forced to dodge and weave, which increased the distance from his brother, but decreased the distance from Mr. Bob.

It occurred to Remus that there was a better way to deter Mr. Bob. At this point, they were causing too much of a ruckus and had attracted too much attention for Mr. Bob to feel comfortable abducting them. Logic suggested that all he need do was to stop and maybe yell a little, and the man with the generic name would be forced to retreat. He was about to implement his plan when, upon glancing back, he saw how dire his situation was. The look on Mr. Bob's face was a mask of murderous intent. The guy, whom Remus had understood to be a professional, was nothing more than a hyped-up thug. A man who wouldn't think twice about beating Remus senseless, even under the supposed protection of a public mall, and if he caught him, there was a very real chance Mr. Bob would try to kill him. And how sad would that be?

Romulus was heading towards the escalator. Of course, the parking lot was downstairs, and without the escalator, they would be stuck running around upstairs until Mr. Bob caught them or until they ran out of energy. Remus remembered his words to Athena about falling down the escalator and wondered if his words were prophetic. As they headed towards the steps, he could feel the universe's anticipation. Could feel it practically salivating at the mouth at the thought of him trying to run down the escalator unscathed. Romulus rounded the corner and galloped down the escalator. Remus was four feet away when he felt icy hands at the back of his neck.

"Got ya," Mr. Bob growled, pulling Remus towards him. "Kid, I ain't happy having to chase you down."

Remus, remembering Athena's move, snapped his elbow back, hitting Mr. Bob squarely in the solar plexus. Mr. Bob grunted and loosened his grip, Remus tearing free of his grasp. He hopped on the escalator and started running before realizing something was horribly wrong. The escalator was going the wrong way! Instead of going down in the direction he was running, it was going up towards Mr. Bob and he wondered how he could have been so stupid.

The only good piece of news was there was currently nobody on the escalator. Mr. Bob was waiting patiently at the top, ready to grab him once Remus reached him. Remus did the only sensible thing left in a situation this bizarre—he started running down the ascending steps.

"You're really starting to step on my tits, kid," Mr. Bob grumbled as he followed Remus down the escalator. What Mr. Bob planned to do once he caught up to Remus was anyone's guess, but Remus had visions of being thrown off the escalator...and breaking his hip. Halfway down and Remus was already gasping for air. Mr. Bob was drawing steadily nearer when it happened.

Mr. Bob lost his footing, and with a surprised grunt, toppled head first down the escalator. He picked up momentum and started to roll down the escalator, looking like a human bowling ball. Remus looked back just in time to see the peril he faced. With surprising agility he didn't even know he was capable of, he hoisted himself onto the side railing and watched as Mr. Bob blew by, landing with a sickening thud several feet below him. With Mr. Bob now past him, Remus jumped off the side railing and ran *up* the escalator.

He made it up the escalator and looked back to see if Mr. Bob was following him. That's when the universe proved that it wasn't done with him yet. With a grunt of surprise, he ran into a woman, knocking her down. That made the second woman today he'd knocked down. Except this woman was accompanied by her humongous, overprotective boyfriend.

Remus saw the fist coming, and could do nothing but brace for it. The fist connected with the side of his face, mercifully missing his much-brutalized nose.

"What do you think you're doing?" the boyfriend asked.

"Right now, getting a concussion," Remus answered, rocking back and forth, covering his eye. He knew it would be pitch black within fifteen minutes.

His answer must have been too cheeky, for the guy made to hit Remus again, but that's when the mall cops, who couldn't be bothered when a kid was being chased by a man with murder on his mind but could magically appear when a guy accidentally knock a person down, arrived.

"Is there a problem?"

"This punk knocked my wife down."

"It's all a big misunderstanding!" Remus panted. "I can explain."

The escalator chose to profusely disagree with this statement by depositing a now-unconscious Mr. Bob at the top of the stairs.

"Jesus! Is that a body?"

"It's this kid's fault! I saw him leave the escalator."

By now, a crowd was forming. Lots of yelling and pointing as people recalled that, yes, they did see this crazed young man running desperately down the mall and boy, did he look suspicious!

"Sir, may I see your ID?"

"Of course." He reached into his pocket...

"Sir, your ID?"

Remus reached in his other pocket. Also empty. Someone, most likely Athena when she was kissing him, had pickpocketed his wallet.

He grinned meekly. "You're not going to believe this, but someone stole my wallet."

Remus was woefully right; they did not believe him.

Chapter 9

Chris couldn't believe his good fortune. When told of this mission, there had been a lot of resentment, for everyone knew Athena would try to escape and her attempt would lead to a hostage situation with several bodies in her wake. So it was a fantastically pleasant surprise for all involved when she walked into the mall, hung out for an hour, and then came back like she was supposed to, with only a few small hiccups. The one moment of real panic was when a lanky teen bowled her over. She rose to her feet, furious, and every one of the guards, including Chris, expected retribution up to and including the guy's head on the floor. But, somehow, the kid managed to talk himself out of death and actually made her laugh. They carried on a conversation without difficulty and without Athena using quotes. The whole conversation was recorded through the speaker on the watch and later, would be carefully dissected and analyzed for hidden code.

"Did you have a good time?" Chris asked her on the van ride home.

Athena sighed. "It was simply magical." So she had officially abandoned speaking in quotes. "I had a good time," she added, as if verifying his thoughts. "More productive than I thought it was going to be."

"How so?" Chris asked, very much suspicious. It had not gone unnoticed that she had basically promised the young man she would see him again.

Her face broke out in a wide smile. "Souvenirs!" she said brightly, holding out her hands, showing off the items she'd collected. None of the guards, particularly Chris, was happy with this development, but it was a compromise made ten minutes earlier.

One of the rules was Athena could bring no mementoes back with her. It sounded harsh, but for a girl who could make a paper clip into a weapon of mass destruction, it was hugely appropriate. So, it was natural that a skirmish would erupt when Athena first walked to the van carrying a wallet, a half done crossword puzzle, and an envelope.

Chris had firmly but respectfully asked her to toss out the items. Athena had firmly but respectfully told him, in her own way of speaking, to go to hell. The argument escalated; Chris had thought about using the electric ankle bracelet, but to do so would erase all the goodwill of today and so, he had conceded the wallet and crossword puzzle weren't a threat. However, he did have an issue with the envelope, and flat out refused to let her keep it unless it was checked. Athena had reluctantly agreed.

Upon opening the envelope, he found it to be stacked full with money. Chris counted twenty thousand dollars.

"That's a lot of money," one of the guards had said.

"It is," Chris had agreed.

"It's not like she needs it."

Chris leafed through every bill. "I'm only checking for dangers that might compromise the security of Pandora's Box. If you want to take the money, I won't stop you...I also won't attend your funeral."

The guard didn't mention it again. They all piled into the van and left, Athena's treasures held securely in her hands.

"I also met someone," Athena added.

"Who?"

"A boy named Remus," she said dreamily. Then she frowned. "Or is he considered a man? He looked around my age."

"Culturally, around these parts, people consider eighteen and above to be an adult. Of course, it depends on the boy."

"Oh well, I'm guess I'm still a girl then." She squinted suspiciously. "By your tone, Mr. Burlington, I daresay it sounds like you don't approve of my Remus."

Her Remus? Chris chose his words carefully. "He seemed like a nice lad. I'm just wondering if he's right for you."

The other guys grinned and shook their heads in bemusement. They all knew it was unlikely she would ever see that boy again and wondered why he was trying to pick a fight. Chris had a 13-year-old daughter and would have been horrified if she was infatuated with someone as shady as Remus.

Athena responded as if he had asked a question. "He's funny. A little clumsy, as you say, and he can be a bit depressing at times, but he has intellect. I need more people who can keep up with me."

There was an insult there, and her teasing smile said she meant for them to get it. Athena wasn't like the others. Half of the Pandora's Residents had obvious physical deformities. The half of them that looked normal enough often said and did ugly and abhorrent things that set them apart from humanity. Athena was one of the few who could blend in to human culture; talking about Remus, she looked like any other smitten teen gushing over their first crush. Four years ago, it had been easy to spot the monster hiding inside of her, but now, glimpses of her darker personality were rare occurrences, and Chris sometimes felt bad she would never do the things a regular girl should do. Still, sympathy for her could not factor into his job. She had made ominous statements to this Remus kid, and Dr. Pluck had to be informed for the safety of Pandora's Box. *A troubling development.*

Chris winced as a headache hit him. Athena gave him a cursory look of concern before opening the wallet and pulling out an ID. "Remus Sylvia. Interesting name," she mused. "Don't you think so?"

"It is a name. Analysis of it will prove to be a waste of my time and effort." The words came from the man sitting beside Chris, and it was alarming, as it seemed he was purposely picking a fight with Athena. Chris tried to rebuke him, but his thoughts were muddled.

She sighed. "Poo, you're never any fun." She leaned back, eyes closed. "I made a mistake." It was impossible to tell if the words were a statement or question.

Another soldier, sitting closest to Athena, eventually answered. "You have made several crucial errors that give credibility to two theories—one, the level of your intelligence is significantly lower than previously estimated. Two, you yourself do not desire to see your plan fulfilled. Both theories are disconcerting." Chris could no longer speak or move. He knew he should have been terrified, but found himself strangely disconnected with the events happening, like it was happening to someone else on a movie screen. Athena was up and moving, which should have been impossible, as her seatbelt had a custom-made lock to keep her still. With a smirk, she waved her hands in front of a soldier's face while he stared blankly ahead.

"Athena!" This time it was Chris who yelled out her name, but without his mind's consent. Someone else was using him as a puppet and the thought jolted him out of his indifference. It was like waking from a dream, his sense of self returning along with a growing sense of horror. Athena glanced his way, but she wasn't looking at him. No, she was looking at the puppeteer.

"Are you aware of your offenses?" A guard behind Athena spoke these words. "Your inane promise to see that human again, along with your recent comments underlining the same statement, has caused unease among your wardens. Several had intentions of telling Dr. Pluck, which would further complicate your already perilous plans."

Athena was amusing herself by honking the noses of two of the guards, paying the puppeteer the minimal amount of attention. The puppeteer had to be controlling the driver, yet the van continued to speed down the road, implying the puppeteer was capable of complex instructions. "Instead of scolding me, why don't you take care of it?" Athena asked.

"I am currently attempting to erase their memories of the incident. However, this task, along with my other undertakings at your bequest..."

Athena laughed—a musical tinkling. "You did all this to tell me you're overworked?"

Chris had to do something. Whatever Athena and this mysterious puppeteer were planning, it could not mean anything good. He concentrated his entire will into moving his arm, but all he managed to do was make his finger twitch. That was it; a finger twitch. It should have gone unnoticed, but instantly Athena was staring at him with an intensity that didn't bode well for a long-lived life.

"I am endeavoring to explain how each of your mistakes requires my intervention and each intervention requires energy." All eyes followed Athena as she walked over to Chris. "Since my energy is limited, you have a finite number of mistakes before your scheme becomes impossible."

Athena nodded, her two grey orbs continuing to stare a

hole into Chris' head. "Are any of these guards aware?" she asked.

"No. All of them are in a sleep-like state."

Athena rubbed a cool hand across Chris' stubble. The only way for Chris to survive was to pretend to be a puppet, so he kept his body still even as he felt life return to his limbs. "Why didn't you contact me privately?" The question was more of a rebuke.

The guard directly behind Athena answered. "I was already in the process of conditioning their memories. This seemed the most efficient way of speaking." Athena's hand moved across Chris' chest, her eyes narrowing as it passed over his pounding heart. "Athena, he is not aware."

"You're sure?" she asked softly. She reeled her hand back and struck out towards Chris' face. Chris, acting on instinct, raised his hand to block the attack. When the blow never came, he lowered it to see Athena gazing at him with an unreadable expression. Suddenly, she emitted a harsh laugh that must have hurt her throat. "People who live in glass houses shouldn't throw stones. So intent on telling my about my mistake, you have made one as well."

"A grievous miscalculation," the soldier on the left observed. Chris felt his limbs go rigid though his mind was still aware. "Manipulating the humans' minds for the events of tomorrow has proven to be a tiring ordeal."

Athena's mouth twitched and Chris was able to guess her thoughts. The puppeteer had admitted there was a mistake, but at the same time, had placed the blame of the mistake on Athena's scheming.

"His mind is proving unusually resistant to my ability."

All mirth from Athena vanished, leaving behind a cunning predator. "You're saying you can't erase his memories?" she asked. It was terrifyingly easy to see where this was leading. If Chris' memories couldn't be erased then a more permanent solution would be implemented.

"I can briefly erased his memories, but am unable to ensure they will not return to him," a man on the right stated. "If he happens to be outside my range when he remembers, he can call and warn Pandora's Box and I will be helpless to prevent it."

Athena frowned.

"Another solution is available," the puppeteer offered.

"Within Pandora's Box, I can initiate an accident that will cause the death of this human."

Chris' heart leapt to his throat. They were discussing his death as if talking about the weather.

"His death would instigate tighter security, but the risks should be manageable."

Athena twirled a strand of blond hair, looking up at the ceiling. "You hear that, Chris?" she said, too amused for Chris' liking. "Your death for my schemes. Sounds fair, doesn't it?"

"You won't," Chris said, surprising himself. He didn't know he had regained the ability to speak. He tried to say something else, but his mouth locked up as the puppeteer tightened control.

Athena looked at him, grey eyes dancing. "What an incredibly optimistic view you have! Do you really think I won't, or are you desperately praying that I'm a decent principled individual?" Her hand drifted uncomfortably close to his neck. "Of course, you're not supposed to lock up decently principled people," she reminded him, gaze unblinking. "Caged like an animal because some nameless person deemed it okay." She blinked, the air of menace vanishing. "Oops, I was ranting, wasn't I?" She withdrew her hand. "I'll take my chances. Leave him be."

There was silence. Chris got the sense that the puppeteer was shocked. "I do not understand," one of the guards confessed. "The cost of one life versus the failure of a plan that required four years of preparation."

"I know," Athena agreed with a casual flick of her hand. "But this happens to be one out of the five humans that I like, and as such, I won't have him killed."

"Your reasoning lacks logic," snapped the guard beside Chris.

A second passed before another guard spoke up. "If you fail because of this decision..."

"I'll still owe you your favor," Athena promised. She sat back in her seat, strapping the seatbelt across her chest. "The decision is on me."

"Very well," one of the guards responded.

Athena smiled, even as she sat back and strapped the seatbelt across her chest. "Chris Burlington," she addressed, cocking her head to the side. "I did so love all the sweets you smuggled for me over the years. I used to look forward to my next delivery of chocolates."

Chris blinked, rubbing his head to alleviate the forming migraine. "You're quite welcome," he said, even as some of the guards gave him dirty looks. It was against the rules to sneak in any outside substance to the Residents. Undoubtedly, some of them would snitch on him, but if that was the worst thing to come out of this outing, Chris would gladly accept it. The van began to slow down, surprising him. The ride back seemed to have been unnaturally quick.

"It seems my break from Pandora's Box is over," Athena sighed. None of the guards offered an opinion, afraid to annoy her, and Athena wrinkled her nose up at the vacuum of silence. "No fun. No fun at all. I'll go back to speaking in quotes at this rate." Again, there was silence, and Athena fell into a sullen mood, seemingly annoyed no one was playing along. The rest of the procedure passed in silence as the driver called in the van's ID and waited for the large doors leading to the outer perimeter to open.

There was a moment of escalating hostility when Athena barked at the guards trying to take away Remus' wallet and the envelope full of money. They looked to be on the verge of violence when someone had the good sense to call Caleb, who told them to leave her the hell alone, and that he would tell Dr. Pluck and take responsibility.

Another moment of concern came when it was time to handcuff her. She was supposed to have already been handcuffed on the way back, but the original fight over the money had put her in a bad mood, and Chris didn't want to risk antagonizing her further with the handcuffs. However, in Pandora's Box, it was a strict rule. She looked at the handcuffs with disdain before eventually sticking her hands out. She then walked with unnatural slowness to her room, forcing the guards around her to match her pace. One of the guards close to her made a remark about "hurrying up," and a second later, he had "tripped," ending up face-down on the floor. Athena looked around innocently as if another culprit would present itself. She wrinkled her nose when Chris politely asked her to behave, but afterwards moved at a normal pace. Still, by the time they got to her room, nerves were frayed and Chris decided he could handle the rest by himself.

He dismissed the other guards and unlocked the handcuffs around Athena's wrists. "Thank you," she said, looking him in the eyes. He noticed she had been staring at him lately. He didn't feel threatened, but he did feel watched.

Athena entered her room. "Dr. Pluck asked me to tell you that a round of Ambrosia is scheduled for three o'clock tomorrow," Chris said, looking for her reaction. He knew she hated the Ambrosia shots.

"Of course," she said smoothly, not looking back. "It's what was agreed on." She grabbed a book that was resting on her bed and began flipping through it. Eventually, her eyes lifted to Chris, who was still standing in the doorway. "Problems?"

Chris shook out of his daze, wondering what was wrong with him. It felt like he was missing something crucial. He smiled an apology. "Nothing is wrong. Have a good night, Athena."

"And to you as well," she dismissed, already refocused on her book. Chris slid the door closed, made sure the locks were in place, and left.

Chapter 10

Romulus had been sitting in the lobby, waiting for several hours for Remus to come home. Their father was in an enraged state; his only words to Romulus were to inform him Remus had gotten picked up by the police. He had then marched into his office, slamming the door shut as he did so. He didn't officially tell him to wait, but Romulus knew the consequences of leaving. He hated the lobby...hated the whole house for that matter. Most of the walls were decorated with pictures of important figures glaring furiously at an unknown target. Occasionally, there would be a bookshelf of unused books to make Maris appear scholarly, but it was a wasted effort, as no one would use "scholarly" and "Maris" in the same sentence.

The lobby was the worst. There was a giant portrait of Maris and Romulus with eyes that seemed to follow you. Romulus had called Delilah, who claimed she had to get off the phone because an important matter had come up. More likely, he was being punished for leaving her. He called a few of his friends, but eventually had to settle with having a staring contest with the portrait of Maris. He was just on the verge of winning when Remus slunk in silently, plopping down tiredly in the chair beside him.

Remus' nose looked off-center, and his movements lacked any type of energy, but otherwise he looked okay. Romulus waited for him to speak, but it seemed his brother was content to stew in silence. That was too bad, as Romulus had questions that needed answering before they saw their father.

"What happened?"

Remus raised his head. "Was stuck in a jail cell for three hours. They were about to process me when Maris' attorney came in. Five minutes later, I was walking out the front door." A yell from Maris' office made both of them flinch. "I might have done better in jail," Remus added sardonically.

Romulus agreed, but wouldn't say so, in case they were being listened to. A couple of seconds passed. Why?" he asked. Remus blinked, acting like he didn't understand. "Why give that girl the envelope?"

"I don't know. I made a mistake."

Romulus pursed his lips. Not good enough and not believable. Remus wouldn't give it to a random girl without having some sort of verification she was the target.

"Maris isn't going to believe that." Romulus paused. "Scratch that. It will be the worst-case scenario if he does believe you. If he thinks you're stupid..." He let the statement hang, hoping Remus' imagination would prompt him into answering the all-important question. "Why did you give her the envelope?" Remus ignored him and Romulus felt his temper snap. "Tell me! Now!"

He expected Remus to shut down like he usually did when someone raised his voice at him. He hoped his commanding tone would make Remus answer truthfully. Instead, something entirely different happened. Remus' eyes shot up to meet Romulus, his back straightening up into a challenging posture. The fact that he was meeting Romulus' eyes for longer than a second was amazing enough, but what came next was nothing short of miraculous. "No," Remus said steadily. "Leave me alone."

Romulus couldn't think of anything to say. The moment stretched until the door to Maris' office slammed open and there stood Maris in the doorway, literally trembling with rage. "Get in, now!" he yelled. Maris sometimes pretended to be enraged to bully others into doing what he wanted, but Romulus could tell this was the real deal.

Romulus stood up; he was almost afraid his brother would refuse, but Remus also stood and followed him into Maris' office. Maris moved to the side of the doorway so that each of them had to pass uncomfortably close to their father in order to pass. Romulus took the seat to the right while Remus headed to the seat on the left. It was funny, but that's how they always sat in any occasion, whether it be thanksgiving dinner, formal event, or in Maris' office. Remus on the left, Romulus on the right. Maris waited until they were seated before heading over to his desk and pouring himself a drink. Romulus opened his mouth to speak, but Maris silenced him with a glare. Maris proceeded to drink the whole glass before pouring himself another one.

"Explain," Maris instructed after taking a sip. His icy gaze was turned to Romulus, as if Remus wasn't there. "Don't leave anything out."

In the end, Romulus stuck with the truth. He told Maris about the blond girl. When explaining how the girl elbowed Remus, Romulus thought he saw his father's lips twitch, but whatever amusement Maris had quickly vanished when Romulus detailed how Remus gave up the envelope. He left out their kiss, and Remus momentarily glanced his way with an expression of puzzlement mixed with relief. He ended with the sprint away from Mr. Bob where he eventually lost track of Remus.

Maris looked at Remus, tapping his fingers on the desk as he did so. Romulus knew the point was to have Remus' fear escalate in this interval, and it should have worked. However, Remus just looked back at their father, waiting almost impatiently

"Why?" Maris asked. It was asked the exact same way Romulus had asked, and Romulus was not happy with the knowledge that he and Maris were alike in that regard.

Remus paused, and Romulus' hopes soared as it looked like Remus might finally tell the truth. But when he answered, there was a shrug in his voice. "Because I thought she was the contact. It was my mistake."

Maris sneered. "Stupid, I know it was your mistake. I'm asking why the mistake was made." He took another gulp of his drink. "What did this woman say or do to make you think she was the contact?"

Remus took a deep breath. "Absolutely nothing." He said it with a straight face, managing to look Maris in the eye and keep his voice from wavering. It was still dreadfully obvious he was lying.

Maris' hand tightened around the glass, and for a second, it looked to be in danger of breaking. "So, you really are a fool."

"I guess so." Remus' lying was enough to invoke Maris'

wrath, but Romulus knew his caviler attitude would see him in the hospital.

"She's not worth it. No piece of tail is worth it. You already know every single dame will betray you in the end."

Romulus was surprised, but managed not to show it. Not at his father's words—it was very much something Maris would believe—but his tone was almost that of fatherly advice. Remus didn't respond.

"Last chance. Why did you give her the envelope?"

"I thought she was the contact."

"Why?"

"Because I'm an idiot."

A vein was bulging on Maris' temple. "What is her name?"

Romulus held his breath and prayed to every deity he could think of that his brother would give in.

Remus opened his mouth. "Little Miss Muffet." It was a stupid joke, one a five-year old would find funny, but Remus grinned all the same, too proud of his own defiance. Maris nodded, filling up his glass. He raised it to his mouth, but in a violent motion, threw the whole drink into Remus' face.

"You're not leaving," Maris stated, as Remus spluttered and wiped the droplets of liquid from his face, "until you tell me who she is."

Remus regained his composure, his face carefully bland.

"We're going back to the beginning," Maris said. "Tell me what happened upon first entering—"

Remus stood.

"Sit down!" Maris ordered, his words losing some of their bite because of surprise.

Remus, acting as if he didn't hear him, turned around and walked out. It seemed so simple; Maris told him he couldn't leave, which meant he shouldn't have been able to. Maris' word was law; going against it was unthinkable.

For the first time in Romulus' life, Maris seemed at a loss for words. He stared at the doorway where Remus had left as if expecting him to return with an apology on his lips. Then, very slowly, his gaze slithered over to Romulus, his lips curled back to reveal his teeth. "Explain," Maris instructed, the one word packed with a promise of pain if Romulus didn't immediately comply.

Romulus didn't know what his father wanted to hear. "It was a blond girl about—"

"Did they know each other?" Maris interrupted.

Romulus paused. "I don't think so. Remus knocked her over and—"

"Was it possible the whole event was staged?" Maris interrupted again.

Romulus finally got what his father was implying. "I don't think so. It looked real enough. And when I told Remus she wasn't the contact, he seemed honestly surprised."

"If she stole the envelope and his wallet, why would he protect her?" Maris mused. It was almost funny that Maris couldn't comprehend someone committing a selfless act. The more Maris thought on it, the more it looked like he was going to explode, and Romulus dared not move a muscle for fear of setting off the detonation. Finally, Maris spoke. "I don't want you going home tomorrow. Spend the night at your girlfriend's house. What's her name? Debra?"

In truth, it was Delilah, but now wasn't the time for corrections. "Yes, sir. Why am I spending the night at Deli...at Debra's house?"

"Because I need to take care of some stuff with your brother, and I don't want you barging in."

Romulus hesitated a moment too long

"You have a problem with that?"

"No, sir," Romulus said quickly.

Maris reached for the bottle. "You don't want me angry at you, do you?"

"No, sir."

"Good. You're excused."

Romulus didn't move, as the need to know outweighed the fear of punishment. "You're going to torture him."

Instead of looking angry, Maris looked surprised. "It's a rare day when your perception is better than your brother.."

Romulus tried not to let the implied insult bother him as Maris took another swallow from the bottle.

"Just going to rough him up a little. Nothing permanent. Actually, this is a good learning experience. Once I find this girl, I'll have her beaten and killed in front of him. Should toughen your brother up a bit."

Looking at Maris now, watching his warped smile and the casual way he spoke about his brother's torture, Romulus was fully able to believe that, not only did a tangible evil exist, but it flowed deeply in his family's bloodstream.

The Sylvias family tree sat near the gate of hell. Instead of feeding on nutrients from the earth, their family tree fed on insanity, chaos, and acts of evil. Romulus' great grandfather had killed his wife and two children because dinner failed to arrive on time. His grandfather was responsible for the rapes and deaths of three women, and just because his dear old dad had yet to be convicted of a crime didn't mean he didn't have many sins stashed under his belt. Romulus' biggest fear was that one day he would look in the mirror and find the same malevolence he saw in his father's eyes staring back at him. He left knowing the evil would soon devour Remus.

Chapter 11

Athena lay on her bed and stared at the ceiling, the same ceiling she had looked up at for 16 years. Her thoughts flashed to Chris, and she felt a pang of regret. He was one of the few decent men she knew. However, if all went as planned, his life could be in danger. She had been monitoring his mind along with Selene; there had been brief instances in which his memory threatened to come back, but so far, they had stayed dormant. Selene had reinforced the erasure so that there was only a small chance of him remembering.

Her next thoughts were of Caleb. The arrogant Texan was the closest thing Athena had to a friend. Caleb was the one who had introduced her to reading. The one who had given her her very first book, *Romeo and Juliet*. Her books were the only things that kept her sane.

She imagined he wasn't happy with the whooping she gave him, but he would eventually get over it. Without him lurking around, the other guards were a lot more nervous of her movements, and that was a must for her plan.

She thought of the next component of her escape—Remus. In truth, he was the wild card preventing her from sleeping. If her plan was to fail, the breakdown would most likely involve him. His mind was also the most intriguing she had ever encountered; even with her abilities, she still couldn't figure him out. Despite her deceit, his first thought had been of protecting her instead of himself. But what at first looked like an extreme sense of nobility might be something more worrying, like a low sense of self-worth or self-preservation. Another problem was that he'd had ample time to reconsider and now probably hated her, which was troublesome, because her whole plan hinged on his cooperation. In order for her brilliant plan to succeed, she and Remus would have to become the best of friends. It would be difficult, but fun.

Athena sighed. She needed sleep, but couldn't turn her brain off. She had plenty of books to read, but wasn't in the mood. So, she diverted to an exercise she hadn't done in months. Closing her eyes, she allowed her mind to wander, trying to capture the thoughts of those around her.

The first mind she encountered was the guard directly in front of the door. *Screw this AA crap. I'm a grown man! I'm old enough to have one drink and be okay.*

Wrinkling her nose, she moved past him and found her first Resident. Aletheia seemed harmless. However, all the guards who worked in close proximity to her quit after weeks. A fourth of them committed suicide. Wary of Aletheia's mind, Athena passed by without diving in.

The next mind she stumbled across was Teutates. *Thirsty... Hungry... Thirsty... Hungry.* Knowing she wasn't going to get anything more substantial from his mind, she moved on.

A guard was handling himself in the bathroom, and she quickly backtracked in disgust.

The next resident was Thor, and Athena plunged into his mind, knowing he would feel her presence. "*I daresay someone's in my mind,*" Thor thought, seeming amused. "*Is that you, goddess?*"

Athena couldn't communicate. She was gifted with the power to receive thoughts, but the gift of sending thoughts was one only Selene had. However, Thor and Athena had long since worked out a way of communicating. Athena left Thor's mind, waited three seconds and then reentered.

"*So it is you. It's been a while. I would ask what you were up to, but I already know the answer.*" Thor's disapproval was clear. "*Is it true, girl?*"

She left his mind, and then quickly reentered.

"*I was afraid of that. This leaves me with only two conclusions. Either you've finally lost your mind, or you're finally about to pull off your escape plan you keep babbling about.*"

Once more, Athena left than reentered Thor's mind.

"*That's my girl!*" Athena heard the pride in Thor's thoughts. "*I was beginning to think this fabulous plan didn't exist. You better not fail!*" Thor's thoughts became unusually somber. *"If you do fail, I doubt you'll get the chance to try again. There are those who aren't happy with you, goddess. If you fail, you die. Do you understand?"*

Out then back in Thor's mind.

"Good. Now leave my mind and stop wasting your strength! You're going to need it."

Athena left, but couldn't return yet. She needed to verify what Thor said. Needed to make sure that Selene was still willing to help her after everything that had happened. A sense of frustration overwhelmed her. Her perfect plan was now looking fragile. She hadn't expected a response from the other Residents so fast.

Athena felt her mental self weakening. Lamia! Suddenly terrified, Athena twisted and narrowly avoided an encounter with Lamia's mind. Lamia was one of the most destructive Residents and even a brief encounter would destroy her mind.

Shaken up, Athena was about to reenter her body when she sensed her.

"You have been searching for me," Selene pronounced, forgoing pleasantries. *"Why would you risk yourself in this way? After all I've done, all I have risked to clear the path for your escape."*

"I appreciate it," Athena responded. Like Athena, Selene was a mind reader, but unlike Athena, the stoic Resident's main weapon was the ability to control others and send her own thoughts, thus the conversation became more fluent than with Thor. *"However, in order for my escape to work, I must constantly check the variables, and to that effect, I have a couple of questions."*

"I will consider answering them," was the brusque reply.

"What happened this afternoon? You didn't know Chris was aware?"

"You desire for me to repeat myself? Chris' mind is unusually resistant and I was already overtaxed. That being stated, I should have been more attentive of the minds under my dominion."

This was the second time Selene admitted to some degree of fault, and Athena knew better than to push her luck. *"How's everything going?"*

"You wish for an update?"

Athena just wanted to talk, but the notion would be lost

on Selene.

"*Everything is proceeding within the set parameters. Hermes and I are coordinating in an effective manner and, besides the anomaly with Chris, there have been no incidents worth noting. Do you have a specific inquiry you wish to make?*"

If Athena continued to circle around the issue, Selene would eventually cut contact. "*Thor says there are those who are displeased with my actions.*"

"*If you replace 'displeased' with 'murderous rage,' then yes, this is true.*" If Athena didn't know Selene better, she could almost believe that was a joke. "*I do not comprehend your surprise in this matter,*" Selene confessed. "*If you are not intelligent enough to realize this would happen, then you are obviously not intelligent enough to pull off your plan and I have wasted my time aiding you.*" There was no anger in Selene's thoughts as she had long ago renounced all useless emotions like anger, sadness, or happiness.

"*I knew there would be trouble, just not this quickly. To hear Thor speak, I should expect a full size mob at any moment, equipped with pitchforks and torches.*" Athena felt Selene's confusion, and remembered she had never read any of the classic monster books.

"*You put too much faith in Thor's words. Residents are developing a plan, but it will be weeks before you see a response. Nothing but I, and your own shortcomings, can impede your plan for tomorrow.*" A pause. "*You do remember the deal we had? My payment for the crucial assistance I am giving you?*"

"*Really? Gosh darn it all, I completely forgot!*" Sarcasm was wasted on Selene, which didn't stop Athena from trying. If anything, it boosted her efforts, for she was determined to find a crack in Selene's emotional armor. "*Of course I remember your payment. Relax, I made you a promise and, being the honorable Resident that I am, I would never go back on a promise.*"

"*I agree you will not go back on your word, but not because of some misguided sense of honor. You enjoy the game of manipulation, but it tends to be easier for you since you are a telepath, and so you put regulations on yourself to even out the playing field. You love it when you keep your word and yet the other party still ends up with nothing.*"

For some reason, Selene's comment greatly annoyed her and she could have sworn she felt a puff of satisfaction arise from the other Resident.

"Get some sleep, Athena. You will require it for tomorrow."

Athena opened her eyes and winced at the throbbing of her head. Blood flowed freely from her nose, and she cursed herself for her stupidity. Thor and Selene were right. She needed her strength; she needed to sleep. She closed her eyes and dreamt of Remus.

Remus laid in his bed, bathing in the feelings of exhilaration and fear. However, the more he thought about it, the more the fear began to win over. He heard footsteps outside in the hall. He tensed up as they stopped at his door. A minute passed, and then the footsteps began again, growing fainter and fainter as the unknown person drifted away. Remus let out a breath, trying to calm his racing heart. What he'd done was so beyond stupid. Even if he wanted to protect Athena, he should have lied instead of using boldface defiance. He would have eventually been found out, but at least in the delay, Remus would have had a chance to implement a plan. His only option was to escape.

The realization sent his heart racing again. So often he had dreamed of running. In his mind, he had always left in a flurry of dramatics, slamming the door in Maris' face. That definitely wouldn't. He needed to be out of the state before his father even knew he was gone. Maris' connections only extended so far. In a distant state, he would be helpless to locate Remus. Maybe Florida. There were no unhappy people in Florida, right?

Remus shifted, the bed creaking as he did so. With only 350 dollars to his name, he wouldn't be living a life of comfort, but it had to be better than this existence. He needed to pack...no, that would tip Maris off. He needed to go to school, and then leave around noon. His father wouldn't be home until four, giving Remus plenty of time to pack and leave.

Earlier, upon entering his home, he had seen his car parked innocently in the driveway as if it had never broken down. Maris must have had it fixed, which meant he now had transportation.

Remus would not miss Maris, but it did sadden him to think he would never see his brother again. Maybe he could convince Romulus to go with him? It would be thrilling, but terribly lonely to embark on this journey by himself. He didn't have many friends, so if Romulus wouldn't go, who else would? Athena flashed in his mind, but Remus quickly dismissed the thought. No matter how interesting she was, she had callously lied and stolen from him. Hadn't cared if her action brought him pain or not. He closed his eyes, trying to shake her from his thoughts, but found the task to be impossible.

Chapter 12

Nick Hensley wanted to quit. He had worked at Pandora's Box for a total of two and a half days, and he loathed the place with his entire existence. The employees were cruel, the Residents were scary, the only one who had shown him a shred of kindness was Athena. And today no one had bothered to show up! Pandora's Box was operating with little more than half of its usual staff, which meant everyone was working overtime.

It might have been semi-acceptable if he was risking his life to stop monstrous creatures from wreaking havoc on the unsuspecting public, but the meaningless tasks he was assigned made him feel no more important than a babysitter.

"Deliver the toilet paper to Thor's room," his supervisor, Edward Gantz, instructed. He was a short man from El Salvador with a thick, bushy mustache that he must have started growing when he was still in diapers. "Make sure you're very polite. He has a short temper and won't warn you like Athena will. After that, come back. Janus needs his time in the yard and you don't want him growing restless."

Nick scowled. "Toilet paper?"

Edward matched his scowl. Nick knew Gantz didn't like him because most people didn't like him. "I really don't have time for your complaints. I'm overworked because, unknown to me, today is hooky day. I'm scared shitless because I know there's no way everyone here will make it to the end of the day alive, and I can only pray that I will be one of the ones who does. I'm annoyed because, if I happened to make it out in one piece, I have to call the families of the ones who didn't survive the day and give them a worthless speech about how their loved ones died for a noble cause. Do you think I have time for your wisecracks?"

"I was just commenting!" Nick exclaimed, his face growing warm with humiliation. Edward didn't seem to hear him. For a man who didn't have time to listen to Nick's complaints, he sure had time to voice his own.

"There's nothing glamorous about this job. We're not guards, we're babysitters. It's our job to keep these monsters happy in the hope that they won't kill anyone while they're happy. Of course, some of them are only happy when they're killing someone."

Edward's accent steadily became more pronounced the angrier he became. So much so that by the end of his rant, Nick could only understand a few wandering words. One of the words was monster and Nick repeated it inside his head.

"Sir, I thought these people were human. Caleb said we should never refer to them as monsters or creatures."

Edward glared hatefully at him. "Deliver the toilet paper," he ordered. Then, unleashing an unpleasant smile, he added, "And then you can feed Lamia. We'll see how you feel about these *monsters* after that."

So, off Nick went, accompanied by several other guards. Normally, he would have laughed at the prospect that it took several armed guards to deliver toilet paper, but his colleagues' faces said otherwise. Every single one of them wore the same identical expressions, each one suggesting they were all heading for an extended trip to the gallows. On the way, the other guards lamented about the dire state of Pandora's Box. On a normal day, their job was risky. On a day with half its staff gone, it was downright suicidal. They soon arrived at Thor's door.

"So, who's going in?" a guy with shifty eyes asked nervously.

Another sighed. "Make the newbie do it. It will be good experience for him."

In an instant, Nick was being pushed towards the door, all the while being peppered with helpful advice.

"Make sure you give eye contact."

"Be extra polite!"

"Don't get too close."

"Can't we just open the door and throw the toilet paper in?" Nick asked desperately.

"And risk offending Thor?" one of them scoffed. "He'll just kill you the next time he sees you."

"Residents are notorious for holding grudges. Come on, man, it's time to either sink or swim."

"What happens if I sink?"

"Then you drown, don't you?"

"Deliver the toilet paper and get out of there!"

"But don't run out. Just walk quickly back."

The lead guard knocked on the door.

"Who is it?" a voice cried out sharply.

Upon hearing the voice, most of Nick's new buddies took a step back, as if Thor's voice alone was a powerful weapon that needed to be feared.

"It's Simon Hern. You requested more toilet paper?"

"Come in."

Simon swiped his keycard and the door opened. Toilet paper was shoved in Nick's arms and he was pushed in. He stumbled through the doorway and heard the door click as it locked behind him.

"Leave the toilet paper on the desk and leave," Thor instructed.

Nick could only stare. Thor looked to be in his mid-40s. His hair was balding and his nose threatened to bring shame on Pinocchio. His snout was so big that it covered the majority of his face and was mere inches away from being unbearably freaky. His humongous honker wasn't the only quirk in his appearance. Thor wore all pink. Shirt, jeans, socks, everything was a vibrant pink. However, what caught Nick's attention was the fact he was painting his toenails.

"What's your name, boy?" Thor asked without looking at him, in a surprisingly normal voice.

Nick snapped out of entrancement. "Nick Hensley, sir."

Thor chuckled. "Well, Nick, you're a lucky man."

"Excuse me, sir?"

"I had planned on killing you for the way you were staring at me. However, Athena asked me to give a Nick Hensley a reprieve."

Nick was confused. "Athena's protecting me?"

Thor finished off the big toe and moved on the next. "Yes, unless there's another Nick Hensley working here. Lucky you. However, her protection only extends so far, and on that note, I suggest you leave."

Nick left quickly and returned to his colleagues, noticing that some of them looked suspiciously disappointed.

"Athena's protecting you?" Simon asked in awe and what sounded like jealousy. "How'd you manage that?"

"Can't tell you," Nick said pompously, secretly wondering that himself.

Simon shrugged. "Whatever. I got word that Edward wants to see you. Something about you feeding Lamia." He grinned nastily. "You better hope Athena's protection is solid, because if it ain't..."

Nick returned to the supervisor.

"Still alive," the supervisor said brightly. "Good. Now I want you to go the kitchen and find the food for Lamia."

Nick was struck on how much he disliked Edward. For some reason, the man wanted him to die, and it was unfair because he'd never done anything to him. Why was everyone so mean?

"It's only ten-twenty-four," he said, stalling for time. "Didn't she eat breakfast with the other Residents?"

"Lamia needs to be fed seven times a day. Now, go to the kitchen and gather the food. You're going to have to make several trips, so I suggest—" He broke off with a scowl as a female guard came strolling up.

"I have a message," she declared without introduction.

"I'm busy!" the supervisor snarled. "Can't it wait?"

"It's a message from Athena."

The supervisor hesitated. Snubbing any Resident was dangerous. Snubbing the Resident who had Mr. Titanos' ear was deadly. "I guess I'll hear it," he said begrudgingly, as if he had choice in the matter.

"She requested that Nick Hensley be sent to her room immediately. She said she had important business she wishes to speak to him about."

"That's preposterous," Edward stammered. "There's no way... She doesn't have the authority to..."

"She also has a message for you."

"And what's that?"

Nick watched in muted amazement. He might be spared Lamia's room and be sent to Athena's instead. Surely this was a good development.

The guard said, "She says that a man of your status should know better than to call Residents monsters. She says you can go feed Lamia while she chats with Nick." There was a moment's hesitation. "She also gave a quote, and had me memorize and recite it back before I was allowed to leave." She looked at Edward, and there was a trace of pity in her eyes. "If you have to kill a snake, kill it once and for all."

The supervisor's face turned a chalky white. For a second, he looked like he was about to argue. Than he swallowed and said to Nick, "You shouldn't keep the young lady waiting. Go and see her, but come back as quickly as possible. There is work that needs to be done."

Nick couldn't believe his luck. Athena had saved him twice! Is this how Caleb felt? Was that why he was always so confident? Because he had Athena's protection hovering above his head? Then again, the rumor was Caleb was in the emergency room, perched between life and death, and the thought sobered Nick up.

"Sir, what about backup?"

"Is Athena's golden boy scared?" Edward sneered, although it didn't appear his heart was in it. Athena's words must still be on his mind. "I don't have enough men to send you, let alone send someone to hold your hand. Go ahead and go see that *monster*. I don't care what she says!" he exclaimed after Nick looked at him incredulously. "There's nothing she can do to me." It seemed he was trying to convince himself as well as Nick.

Nick left, feeling superior. *Serves him right for trying to mess with Nick Hensley!* It was about time some of his enemies got their just deserts and he wished he'd had Athena with him when he was serving in the army. He hoped she found a way to kill Edward in the most excruciating way possible.

Nick sighed blissfully at the thought of Athena decapitating all his adversaries, and promptly bumped into the last person he expected to see.

"Watch it," Caleb growled, shaking his bandaged hand in Nick's direction.

Nick stared at the battered reminder that Athena liked to turn on her so-called friends. "Sir, I thought you were taking some time off."

"I was until some jackasses decided not to show up. Dr. Pluck called me in to sort the whole mess out, although I don't reckon it will do much good. I made a couple of calls, pleaded to a couple of Residents. You might be okay, but me...I'm heading home." Caleb eyed Nick before looking beside and then around him with a scowl. "And how come you by yourself, boy? You never go anywhere unless accompanied by at least one other person. You looking for a short career at Pandora's Box? You know it takes thirty days for your health premium to kick in."

"Athena wants to see me, and there aren't enough men here to give backup," Nick said rather smugly. There, he'd said it. Let's see how Caleb took the news that he no longer held the title of Athena's favorite.

"Athena asked specifically to see you?" Caleb repeated, his scowl deepening. "Be careful of her. She's a tricky one."

Nick was suddenly nervous. "Am I in trouble?"

"Did she threaten you?"

"I haven't talked to her since my first day when me, you, and the other recruit delivered her to the doctors."

"In that case, you ought to be okay. She never kills without warning."

Nick glanced at Caleb's bandaged hand.

"I said she doesn't *kill* without warning. Roughing you up is an entirely different matter. She and I have had our share of scraps over the years, and I no longer take it personally when she tries to jam her fist down my throat. Just the way her kind is wired. Now you best be going. She doesn't look too kindly on folks keeping her waiting."

Caleb left and Nick continued his walk towards Athena's room.

Chapter 13

"I'm glad you could make it," Athena said, eyes never venturing from her book. She casually flipped a page. "Did Macbeth give you much trouble?"

"Macbeth?"

"The supervisor."

"Oh... I thought his name was Edward."

Athena shrugged and smiled mischievously. Nothing out of the ordinary here. Just a plotting teenager. "I call him Macbeth and he always answers for me."

Nick laughed dutifully. "So what can I do for you today, ma'am?"

Athena shrugged again. "Nothing I can think of. I called you in so you could avoid feeding Lamia. Hope you don't mind, but I thought it cruel that you would have to deal with a Resident of her caliber on your second day."

"How did you know that Edward...Macbeth...called the Residents monsters?"

"This isn't the first time. Macbeth has always been careless about tossing out the word 'monster' in reference to my kind."

"What about Lamia? How did you know he planned on sending me to feed her?"

Athena threw her hands up in mock exasperation. "Good grief, you're just full of questions! I can't be telling you all my secrets, now can I?"

She was still in a playful mood, but why push it? Nick moved on. "Yes, ma'am. By the way, I talked to Thor today."

"Yes, I heard of your encounter with him. Oh Nick, it seems you're destined to get under people's skin!"

"He said you told him not to attack me."

"Not true," Athena corrected. "I *asked* him to give you a break. It's probably going to cost me something down the road. That's the way it is with us."

"How were you able to ask for a favor? As far as I know, you two are never in contact. And how did you hear of my encounter with him? It just happened."

"Asking too many questions again," Athena admonished.

"Sorry. Um…" Nick hesitated. "Can I ask one more question?" Athena's nod was too slight for comfort, so Nick waited until she nodded again with an air of impatience. "Okay. Why did you ask for me in the first place?"

Athena sighed and set the book to the side. "Is it strange for me to want a friend? I've been here all my life, Nick. Half the people here want to kill me. The other half are afraid I want to kill them. It's no way for a lady to live. You seemed like a nice guy and I was hoping…"

Nick's heartbeat accelerated. Athena was a beautiful young girl and only 12 years separated them. Was that what she meant? Dr. Pluck wouldn't like that.

"Of course, things will have to start off slow," she said quickly. "After all, we don't want Dr. Pluck finding out. He would kill you and the other Residents would kill me."

"Of course, ma'am," he croaked. "Is there anything else?"

"Tell me about the other Residents you visited today."

"Well, I visited Thor, and I was supposed to accompany some guards to let Janus have his time in the yard. That was before the supervisor switched me to Lamia. I think I have to take Selene out at some point too."

"Okay, listen carefully," she instructed, and he almost wished he had a pen and paper so he could take down notes. "Even by Resident standards, Thor is strange. However, he wants to be treated like one of the guys. Look him in the eye while you're talking to him, and avoid staring! Of course, it goes without saying that anything resembling a gay joke will end with instant death. Janus is the opposite. He enjoys the fear he gets from guards because he equates it with respect. Do not look him in the eyes! And work on your cowering. As for Selene…moon pies."

"Moon pies?"

"She's a sucker for moon pies. Make sure you have one handy every time you see her. It won't guarantee your safety, but it will certainly help your friendship along."

"And if I have to see Lamia?"

"Don't," Athena said flatly. "There's nothing you can do for Lamia. No way to gain her friendship or respect. Avoid her at all costs."

Nick nodded, feeling dizzy. He had the keys to surviving this job! And to think, just this morning, he had planned on quitting. But now, with Athena's help, he would rise through the ranks. He would use Athena, and reward her by teaching the young girl the ways of romance.

For a split moment, a look of deep and utter disgust crossed Athena's face. As if she'd spotted something truly vile. Something so revolting that the mere sight of it caused a gag reflex.

"Is there something wrong?" Nick questioned, fighting the urge to sniff his armpits. Was it him? Did he smell? He knew he'd taken a shower this morning, but couldn't recall if deodorant had been utilized.

"No," Athena said, smiling, though it seemed forced. "Well, there is one little thing you could do for me."

"What's that?" Eager to prove his loyalty, he would have agreed to almost anything

Athena fished under her pillow and pulled out a half-finished crossword puzzle. "I seem to have lost my pen in this mess I call my room. I've been looking for it the whole day to no avail."

"You do crosswords?"

"Helps keep the mind focused. I don't suppose you happen to have an extra pen on you?"

He searched his pockets. "Got one right here," he declared proudly, taking it out. Then he frowned as a thought occurred to him. He had never seen this pen before. Had no idea how it ended up in his back pocket.

"Great!" Athena exclaimed with an eagerness that seemed out of place. "Can I borrow it?"

Nick stared at the young Resident's lustful expression and then back at the pen. No one would ever accuse him of being the reincarnation of Einstein, but even he realized that the situation was odd. This pen that he had never seen before was huge. Something you would buy as a gimmick or for someone with poor motor skills. Not an item he would have any use for, and certainly not something he would carry around. And the way Athena was fixated on it was very odd.

Something inside him screamed at him to leave as quickly as possible, but if he did, who would protect him? He quelled the voice in his head and, after a brief hesitation, tossed her the pen. After all, they were now friends. Athena caught the pen, and for a second, she looked triumphant. Her mouth split into a cruel smile and her eyes looked rabid with excitement. It was like looking at a different person. Nick blinked, and that Athena was gone.

"You really shouldn't hand pens over to Residents," she chided gently. "However well you think you might know them. Dr. Pluck would fire you on the spot if he knew you gave this to me. He really is dedicated to his paranoia. He would think by handing me this pen..." Athena twirled the pen in her left hand, tossed it in the air, and caught it. "I could cause countless deaths and orchestrate the destruction of Pandora's Box. Can you believe it?" She shook her head in amusement. "He would think this pen is the only weapon I need to accomplish some sinister plan that I've been hatching in the back of my mind. Oh, the absurdity of it all! Of course, he would call you a spineless idiot for giving me the pen in the first place. Isn't that funny?"

Nick smiled uncertainly, and admitted to himself that Athena wasn't all there all the time. Still, she was a hell of a lot better than the other Residents he'd met. "I should be going now, ma'am."

"Yes, you should," Athena agreed, sounding bored. Her mood changes were dizzying. "You've been here a long time, and there's bound to be some guard whispering about it. Whispers become rumors and rumors become facts and facts lead to problems."

"Yes, ma'am." Nick turned to leave.

"One last thing."

"Yes, ma'am?"

"I forgot, when is my first round of Ambrosia?"

"I believe Dr. Pluck scheduled it for three o'clock today along with a round of tests."

"Excellent. That will be all, Nick."

"Yes, ma'am." Nick left, shaken up.

Chapter 14

Romulus didn't see Remus or his father the next morning. He went to school like usual. He pleaded for Delilah's forgiveness like usual.

"You left me," she yelled, the walls around her shaking with her anger. "And I never did get my dinner!"

"My brother went to jail!"

"So? You should have left him there to rot!"

In the end, it took the promise of a fancy dinner and another trip to the mall, where she was guaranteed anything she wanted, for her to calm down. His wallet screamed in protest as he made the promise.

All day long, his thoughts churned in turmoil. The problem was elegantly simple—what was the best way to protect Remus without throwing his own life in peril? The answer was equally simple. Have Remus beg for Maris' forgiveness while giving up all the information on the blond girl. Remus was being unusually stubborn in this regard, but if Romulus could convince him, then he could prevent Remus from losing a toe. Compared to his family, Cinderella had it easy.

"Romulus!"

Romulus turned around and saw Remus streaking down the hall towards him, all the while waving his hands like a fool. Unpleasant laughter followed in his wake, but Remus didn't seem to hear, or more likely, had just given up caring.

"What are you doing?" Romulus hissed when Remus got within hearing distance.

Remus paused to take a breath before answering. He was badly out of shape, and Romulus had yet to figure out how he had escaped Mr. Bob. "Needed to talk to you," Remus was finally able to gasp.

"Me too, but can we not do in the middle of the hallway?" Romulus asked, plastering on a grin as he looked around. Remus did as well, eventually noticing all the attention he had drawn.

"Sorry," he said sheepishly. Remus' eyes scanned the hallway, eventually settling on the bathroom's entrance. "Shall we—"

"I'm not following another guy into the bathroom while everyone is watching," Romulus interrupted.

Remus gave an uncertain grin as if he wasn't sure Romulus was joking. "We're brothers!"

"Doesn't matter." The bell rang, scattering the onlookers like cockroaches. Romulus waited until everyone's interest in them dropped before addressing Remus. "The best way to avoid Maris' anger is to give her up."

"No." Remus was almost cheerful in the way he said it.

"She's not your friend. In fact, she played you for a fool. Probably laughing at you now."

There was no disagreement in Remus' face. He must have thought all of this out and had already accepted this to be true. "If Maris gets his hands on her, she won't survive."

"So?" Remus' expression didn't change, though the atmosphere around him did. It was clear that Remus was disgusted with Romulus, and that enraged Romulus. "It's your life or hers," Romulus explained. "You can't have both."

"Yes, I can."

"No, you can't."

"I can if I run!"

The words stopped Romulus and the two of them stared at each other.

Remus seemed to regret the way he blurted it out. He licked his lips nervously. "This isn't about her. I have been dreaming of running for the longest time. This is as good a time as any."

"And you're telling me because you need money?"

"I want you to come with me." Remus' smile was full of hope.

Romulus' fist impacted Remus' chest, forcing his brother back with a wheeze. He quickly looked around and found himself lucky that no teachers were around to witness it. He also spotted Delilah heading their way; by her expression of concern, he knew she had seen the punch and was heading over to intervene. As helpful as she thought she was being, her presence would only make his brother flee, as she and Remus couldn't breathe the same air for very long without disaster striking. Remus had recovered. He also spotted Delilah coming and his face went slack.

"You ask me to abandon everything I have here because of your mistake," Romulus said in a lowered tone. "How selfish are you?"

Remus nodded. "Sure, I get it. My bad, man, I didn't think."

He made to leave, but Romulus grabbed his shoulder. "Apologize, give her up, and this will be over."

Remus shrugged him off, but not in an angry fashion. "You're right. Yeah, I'll see you later." He was still a very poor liar.

Romulus might have chased him except Delilah stepped in his way. He braced himself for a reprimand.

"You okay?" she asked, sliding her hand over his arm. Romulus' nod wasn't enough to fool her. "Let's go somewhere to talk," she suggested. When it mattered, Delilah could be understanding and patient. He let her lead him away, his eyes lingering on Remus' back. Something told him it would be a long time before they saw each other again.

Chapter 15

Athena counted off the seconds in her head. By her estimation, it was 2:53. For the nineteenth time, she checked to make sure preparations were ready. She took a deep breath, bit a fingernail, and took another deep breath. It should be about 2:54 now.

She jumped at the loud knocking at the door. *Calm down!* she scolded herself. She couldn't give in to panic. Not now. Not when she was so close.

"Ma'am, this is Scott Williams. Do I have permission to enter?"

Normally, she would have the guards solve a riddle before allowing entry, but she didn't want to risk making Scott angry and having him call for backup. "Every person has the power to make others happy. Some do it simply by entering a room," she answered.

A man who looked like he spent his whole life on steroids entered. His hair was bleached blond, and a Grim Reaper tattoo sat on his left upper arm. "Ma'am, it's time to go," Scott said, his voice a shade higher than what one would expect from a man of his physique.

One guard like the plan called for. Selene really was an extraordinary Resident. Now all that needed to be done was to get this singular guard to warm up to her. Concentrating, she tapped Scott's mind.

Why is she staring at me like that?

"You're all by yourself?" Athena inquired.

"They found me qualified enough to deal with you on my own." *Supervisor sent me here by myself. He's hoping she will attack me, that prick!*

"You're not scared of me, are you?" she asked sweetly.

Scott appeared unmoved, though Athena heard his heartbeat speed up. "Ma'am, I was sent here to get you, and I was told you wouldn't give me any trouble. Am I going to have to call for backup?"

She knew each guard and employee was given a panic button. If an employee ever felt he or she was in trouble, all they needed to do was press the button and security would come running to their location. The button did make escaping difficult, but it wasn't unbeatable. After all, he could hardly press it if he was dead.

"Of course not, Scott. I wouldn't dare make trouble for my newest friend. Might I inquire as to what time it is?"

Smart ass bitch! "Its three-o-two."

Athena smiled. "I'll tell you what, Scott. If you wait eight minutes with me, I can promise you won't have to deal with the supervisor again."

Can she do that? "Why should I believe you?"

"Because I'm tired of Macbeth...the supervisor. He really is an annoying pest. And, to be honest, I'm scared to go back on Ambrosia. It does stuff to your mind." She shuddered convincingly. "Plus the tests they're going to perform. Prodding and poking me. Making me do things I don't want to do."

As expected, pornographic images came into his mind. His eyes traveled down her figure and she had to fight to remain still. "I can see why you would want to avoid that, ma'am. However, my task was simply to be an escort, and I was told you made a promise to be on your best behavior."

"You're repeating yourself, Scott. Yes, I agreed to play docile Resident for the afternoon. I just need a moment to get my head on straight. What time is it now?"

"Three-o-four."

"Wait six minutes with me, please, Scott. I bet I could make it worth your while."

I bet you could! "And how's that, ma'am?"

What a deplorable human. Athena suspected he was chosen for this task for that reason.

"Well, for starters, I could tell you stuff that no one else knows. Like, for example, do you know what a shuriken is?"

Where is this leading? "No, ma'am, I don't."

Athena sat straight up in her bed and began playing with a strand of hair. "The shuriken, loosely translated, means hidden blade. Small weapons designed to be thrown at your opponent. Undoubtedly, you've heard of ninja stars?"

The bitch is pulling my leg! "Yes, ma'am, I have."

"Well, that's the western term for shuriken. It's a shame, because, in truth, ninja stars really don't do the shuriken justice. Only a handful of shuriken are star-shaped. My favorite shuriken is the bo shuriken. What time is it?"

"Three-o-seven. Where is this going, ma'am?"

"I'm getting there." Scott was getting impatient, so Athena stuck out her chest as best she could to keep him interested. "Now, the bo shuriken are basically thin needles. Some are almost invisible to the naked eye. I've been told there are some so thin that a handful can fit inside a pen."

"Ma'am, this is interesting, but why would I care about it?"

"What's the time?"

"Three-o-nine."

"Excellent. Now where was I?"

"The bo shuriken."

"That's right! Thanks! Now, the bo shuriken was never meant to be a killing weapon. It served more as a distraction. To give time for an escape or attack. The needles are too small to do much damage, but then I started thinking, what type of potential would a bo shuriken have in the hands of a Resident like me?"

Enough of this! "Ma'am, how does this affect me in any way?"

A loud explosion shook the room, followed by two more resounding booms, the last one making the lights temporarily flicker.

Scott turned around, temporarily distracted. "What was that?"

As soon as he turned, Athena leaned left and aimed, throwing two bo shuriken in rapid succession. The first hit him in the left side of his throat, the second right beside that. Gasping in pain as the blood began to spurt, Scott fell to his knees, clutching his throat. If he had reached for his panic button right away, perhaps he would have made it in time. Athena had a contingency plan in case he did, but it would have lowered her chances of escaping. It was thus fortunate that Scott was initially, and understandably, focused on trying to stop the surge of precious blood escaping the wound, so much so that he thought of the escape button belatedly.

"Uh-uh." Athena strolled over and snatched the button from his hand. She then pulled both needles out of his throat, quickly backing up as the blood really began to squirt out. "You don't want to mess up our good time, do you? Don't bother speaking," she advised, tossing the button in a corner and ambling towards a stack of books. "I tried to put both needles in the jugular vein. You do know what that is, right?" Athena reached for his mind. "It appears that you don't. Well, let me explain."

Another explosion rattled the room. With one casual backhand, Athena knocked the stack of books to the ground. Reaching down, she pulled a bag from the rubble.

"A common misconception is that the jugular vein can be hit by attacking any point on the throat. Simply not true. Rather, the jugular vein is actually four veins in the throat, two internal and two external. A cut in the internal veins, if done correctly, will result in a significant loss of blood." She frowned at all the blood spluttering about. "Though, to be honest, I didn't think it would be this bloody," she admitted, wrinkling her nose. It would be difficult to hide all the blood from prying eyes, which meant her plan for Pandora's Box to be unaware of her escape until hours later was probably a bust. She was annoyed, but shrugged, as there was nothing that could be done. A slow smile brightened her features. "Now, as a gentleman," she said to Scott, "I expect you to close your eyes."

She slipped off her jeans and t-shirt, leaving only her bare essentials. Reaching into the bag, she pulled out a guard uniform and quickly changed. She slipped the remaining three shuriken into her back pocket for a later party.

"Are you still alive?" she asked, listening for the shallow sound of breath. "Excellent! I would hate for you to die without finishing our conversation." She completed the outfit with a matching cap.

Scott tried to say something, but only a gurgling sound escaped.

Athena leaned down in front of him. "I said don't try to speak," she scolded. "I'll tell you what. I'll let you in on a secret that only one other non-Resident knows." She leaned in closer and whispered, "I can read minds."

This bitch is crazy!

Athena frowned. "I'm not crazy," she reproached. "Please

remember, Scott, words can be hurtful." Athena grabbed his leg and dragged him to the bed, leaving a bloody smear wherever his body went. In the distance, another explosion was heard. With inhuman strength, she lifted him up and slammed him onto the bed. "Of course I understand," she conceded. "I'd be a little irate too if I knew I was dying."

I don't want to die!

"But you're going to." Athena fished in Scott's pockets and pulled out his ID card. "I'm babbling, aren't I? Sorry, I'm just so excited. Today is a big day for me." Scott didn't respond, still trying to stem the flow of blood from his throat. Athena felt a momentary pang of pity. "They say blood loss is one of the worst ways to go. If you want, I can end your suffering now."

No!

"I completely understand," she said empathetically. "Better to go out fighting. Unfortunately, I'm on a time table, so I really must be leaving. Farewell, Scott!"

She grabbed the covers and pulled them over him. He was too big. All it would take would be one good look to tell that Athena was not the one under the covers. However, with a little luck, this deception would buy her the time she needed.

She unlocked the door using her newly acquired keycard, and stepped out into the hallways of Pandora's Box.

Chapter 16

It was hard to imagine never seeing Romulus again. For all the fights they had, for all the distance between them, they were still brothers and Romulus was the best friend he'd ever had. This morning, his new life had seemed full of possibilities. Now it just looked impossibly lonely.

After speaking to Romulus, Remus immediately drove home. If he was right, Maris would soon learn of his plans and would lash out to stop him. He would go home, pack up his meager belongings, and be gone within twenty minutes. He didn't care how cowardly it would seem. Slinking away in the middle of the day was better than facing an enraged Maris.

He parked in the driveway. On the way to the door, he looked around, but didn't see or feel invisible eyes watching him. He opened the door. "I'm home!" he said loudly. He held his breath, but when no answer came, he quickly got to work. He only had two suitcases, which was fine, as he really only needed one. He had just packed his prized collection of Pokémon cards from fifth grade when he heard the sound of conversation. He ran to the window and saw four guys heading towards the front door. They had come in what looked like a moving truck, and that truck was currently blocking his car in the driveway. It had been stupid of him to park in the driveway; it had been stupid to come home at all instead of jumping on the nearest highway and bolting. The door opened, meaning they had a key, and the group of men entered.

Remus should have hidden, but instead, he just stood stupidly in the center of the hallway as they came in.

The leader, a tall bald-headed man with a thin mustache, blinked when he saw Remus and then waved at him.

Remus didn't return the wave. "Who are you?" he demanded with much more authority than people usually expected from him.

It must not have been impressive, as the bald-headed man ignored Remus and spoke some instructions to the people behind him, who then all scrambled in different directions. He turned to Remus. "Name is Clive Johnson. We were hired for a job."

"By who?"

He looked at Remus as if he was stupid. "Maris Sylvia. The owner of the house."

Of course it had to be Maris. But these were not men his father usually employed, and none of them were making any moves against him. Was it possible their job had nothing to do with him and this was all a coincidence? In that case, Remus should take his bag and leave. Clive was looking at him with bemusement, and Remus realized he had been staring for a few minutes.

"What's the job?"

The man shrugged. "We were told to take everything in the house. At least that's half of the job. Are you Remus Sylvia?"

"Yep." A strange job, but Remus was just starting to believe he could escape. "What's the other half of the job?"

Clive smiled and withdrew a gun. "You are."

Dr. Pluck was in his office shuffling through papers when the first explosion hit. He'd been having a tremendously bad day before that. Only half the staff bothered to show up and Dr. Pluck had spent the whole morning making frantic calls, except everyone's phone seemed to be turned off. He managed to call Caleb in, but had no idea where the cocky redneck had run off to.

"What was that?" Dr. Pluck asked nervously. Before his bodyguard, James, could answer, two more explosions sounded out. "Find out where they're coming from!"

James, a ginger-haired man who wore a face loaded with freckles, took out a radio. "Captain Froce, I need a report. What's going on?"

"Don't know," a voice crackled back. "They seem to be coming from different parts of the facility."

"Any damage?"

"Minimum as far as I can tell. I would have men checking if I had men to send."

"Go to red alert and secure the gates," James instructed. "No one enters or leaves the compound unless I or Dr. Pluck says so. Check all the Residents' rooms and make sure all of them are accounted for. Also send backup down here. This could be a disgruntled Resident looking for revenge."

An image of Athena flashed in Dr. Pluck's mind, and he suppressed a shiver.

Froce argued, "Sir, we don't have the manpower to get all this accomplished!"

"Get it done!" James ordered. Turning to Dr. Pluck, he said, "Sir, we should stay here until we know what's going on."

Dr. Pluck swallowed as another explosion echoed down the halls. *Like I would risk leaving this room.* "Agreed," he said, his throat dry with anxiety and fear. "What's happening, James?"

James scratched his head. "If I had to guess, I'd say you're seeing a response for allowing Athena to leave yesterday."

"Do you think she knew this would happen?" He knew the answer, but wanted confirmation.

"She's crazy, sir, but she's not stupid. The question isn't if she knew, but rather if she cared."

"I told Titanos this was a terrible idea!"

They both jumped at the knock on the door.

"Who is it?" Dr. Pluck snapped, trying to calm down his nerves.

"Sir, this is Juliet Dickenson. Captain Froce sent me to assist you."

Dr. Pluck glanced at James, who shook his freckled head. Neither of them had heard of Juliet Dickenson. It wasn't strange not to know all the names of the employees, and it wasn't uncommon for a female to be working at Pandora's Box. However, put those two facts together along with the circumstances...

"Athena?" James mouthed to Dr. Pluck.

Dr. Pluck shook his head. Athena's voice was more melodious, and Juliet's voice had a southern twang to it. Still, there were other unhappy female Residents to think of.

"Give us a second, Dickenson," James called out. "By the way, is it chilly out there?"

They both waited with baited breath for the correct response to the security question. "The hot chocolate warmed me up," she responded impatiently. "Sir, we have a crisis and there are other things I could be doing besides answering security questions."

"Sorry, but you can't be too careful, Dickenson," James said, smiling slightly as he swiped his keycard. The door started to slide open. "You'll never know when the enemy will—"

Two tranquilizer darts hit James squarely in the chest as Athena stepped into the room. James staggered back and reached for his own tranquilizer gun, but Athena kicked him in the leg, causing him to fall to his knees. Another kick to the head sent him flying to the ground where he laid motionlessly.

"Well howdy, y'all!" she shrieked cheerfully, sticking with the southern accent. "Dr. Pluck, will you be ever so kind as to take your hand off that there button?"

Dr. Pluck removed his sweaty thumb from the panic button.

"Thank you kindly. Now, I reckon you should take a seat so we can have ourselves a little conversation."

"Cut it out!" Dr. Pluck snapped, trying to sound unconcerned.

Athena blinked, and for the first time since Dr. Pluck met her, looked apologetic. It would have been a terrific victory if she hadn't been holding a gun at him. "Overdid it, didn't I?" she continued in a normal tone. "It's just as well. We only have a minute to talk before we have to get going. First thing, the panic button. Excuse me for saying so, but you're seriously understaffed. The few men that you do have are spread across Pandora's Box. You might press that button before I can get to you. Of course, I'll have ten minutes to kill you in a number of painful and creative ways."

Dr. Pluck nodded stiffly. "Are you the cause of whatever the hell is going on out there?"

"Don't have time for stupid questions." She tapped James with her foot. "It should have become abundantly clear that I created the diversions. Now, the second thing..."

Dr. Pluck flinched as Athena shot herself in the arm with the same tranquilizer gun she used to shoot James.

Dr. Pluck felt a surge of hope. Athena really had lost her mind. All he had to do was keep her pacified until the tranquilizers took effect.

"I'm really tired of people thinking I've lost my mind," Athena sighed. "And tranquilizers haven't affected me since I was fourteen." She waved her arm around, the darts still embedded in her skin. It's vital that you understand I'm drug resistant."

"What do you mean drug resistant?" Another thought occurred to him. "And how did you know what I was thinking?"

"Lastly," she continued, as if he'd never spoken, "and this is imperative, so please listen up. You really need to know that I hate you. Your existence is a continuous source of rage for me. Every breath you take incites a new wave of fury. It would give me no greater joy than to kill you right now."

Dr. Pluck felt his hands start to tremble. She might as well have been discussing the weather. "You don't want to kill me, Athena!"

Athena gave a frustrated sigh, as if he was a particularly dense student who just didn't get it. "Are you paying attention, doc? I just said I did."

"If you surrender, we'll forget this whole thing ever happened! You don't have to take the Ambrosia shots...and I'll make sure you go to the mall once a day."

"That's very reasonable of you," she said kindly. "But I'm afraid I must decline."

"Be reasonable, Athena. You can't escape."

Athena grinned playfully. "Of course I can, silly. Because you're going to lead me out."

Dr. Pluck stared, flabbergasted. "You can't be serious! No one would ever believe it."

Athena grimaced as she took the tranquilizer dart out of her arm, and then glared hatefully at the gun as if it was to blame. "No one would believe it, you say? Who wouldn't believe that the great Dr. Pluck, so consumed with saving his own life, abandoned Pandora's Box in its time of need?"

"And your presence?"

Athena studied her nails before biting at one of them. "Of course, the courageous Dr. Pluck, fearing for his own safety, brought a security guard with him to protect his wellbeing." For the first time, he noticed she was wearing a guard's uniform.

"Pandora's Box is in lockdown mode. There's no way to escape—"

"Without the security code, which you happen to have," Athena said, sounding fed up. "I told you we don't have time for games. Of course you could try to give away my presence once out in the halls. I'm sure we'll pass many guards on the way to the gate. Keep in mind the only weapons your people have are dart guns, which, as you now know, have zero effect on me. There's also the fact that I hate you. So if I am found out, you can be well assured I'll use the last moments of my freedom to kill you as unpleasantly as my very creative mind can come up with, and please forgive my lack of modesty. Of course, you could make this whole argument moot point by refusing to take me at all. In that case, I'll kill you now. I'm sure Mr. Titanos would appreciate your sacrifice."

Dr. Pluck wiped sweat from his brow. Screw it. He would not die for a job he could barely stand, and she still had the tracker in her arm. They could always hunt her down later.

"When do we leave?"

Athena pulled out an old crossword puzzle, crumpled it, and tossed it dramatically into the waste basket. "Now."

Chapter 17

The universe hated Remus. Remus already knew this, but it had really outdone itself these last couple of days. Now, he sat in his own kitchen, tied to a chair, while burglars robbed his house. They actually took the time and effort to tie him to a chair, using rope they had brought with them. And they double knotted it! Guarding him was a short, stocky man with a minor case of acne.

"You have a name?" Remus asked.

The man grunted in reply.

"Well, of course you *have* a name," he continued. "What I mean to say is, will you tell me your name?"

Another grunt.

"Quite the chatterbox, aren't you? The reason I ask is I find it best to know your captor. Makes the time go by faster."

"How many times have you been held hostage?" The thug's voice was surprisingly shrill, and Remus, being in a dangerously reckless mood, was already thinking of cracks he could make about it.

"Actually none," Remus admitted. "But I did almost get kidnapped the other day, and he was polite enough to give me his name. Of course, he didn't stop by Wal-Mart to spend the fifteen dollars on rope and, frankly, I'm honored you think so much of my physical prowess to justify the cost."

"Tell him your name already," Clive yelled from the other room. "It's not like it matters anyway." The implication of the statement was not lost.

The minion grunted. "It's Bruno."

"Bruno?" Remus repeated, snorting. "Your mom seriously

named you Bruno? She watched *The Godfather* one too many times?"

"Don't mess with me, kid."

"It's okay, it really is. I know how you feel. Actually, I never had a dumb mom, but I basically get it."

Bruno slammed his fist into Remus' face. "Stupid kid!"

Remus tasted blood in his mouth and tried not to moan too badly. Bruno raised his fist to hit him again.

"Easy, Bruno," Clive said, quickly reappearing to come to his rescue. "I'll take it from here. Help Grant with the TV."

Bruno stomped off, still muttering to himself. Clive waited until he left the room before raising a bushy eyebrow in Remus' direction. "Do you have a death wish, kid?"

Remus checked with his tongue for broken teeth before answering. "Figured I was going to die anyway."

"That's true," Clive agreed casually. Remus knew it, but Clive's reaffirmation chilled him. "However, there are different ways to die. Quick and painless, or slow and not so painless."

"I see."

"You don't look too choked up about it," Clive observed. "About now is where people usually plead and beg for mercy."

"Will that help?"

"Not really."

"Then why try?"

Clive shrugged. "I just told you you're about to die. I expected some emotion."

"It's been an emotional couple of days. I pretty much used up my reserve of fear, and all I have left is cynical sarcasm."

"Yes, I heard about what you did to Mr. Bob the other day," Clive said, grinning.

"So, is this you taking revenge?"

Clive snorted and Remus heard the echo of one of the men laughing from the other room. "Are you kidding? Revenge for that asshole? I laughed myself to tears when I heard what happened. Naw, it's like I said before. This is just a job."

"So my dad hired you to kill me and rob the place?"

"Your dad hired us to kill you and make it look like a robbery. And what better way to do that than to actually commit a robbery?"

"Eloquent," Remus complimented, his heart pounding. He had known they were here to kill him, but it still didn't make sense. His father would want to torture him...teach him a lesson, but killing him over twenty thousand was too extreme, even for Maris. There had to be more at play. Maybe something about where the money was supposed to be going?

"I thought so. Again, you don't seem surprised. Did you know about this?"

"What? That my dad was capable of ordering a hit on his son?"

Clive chuckled. "I like you, I really do. Your dad also asked me to pass on a message."

"The anticipation is killing me."

"He wanted me to tell you that you were way too young to challenge him, and that he would find the blond and her people and put an end to them."

The blond and her people? Remus didn't know what the heck his father thought was going on or what he thought Remus had done. Whatever it was, it was enough justification to kill him.

"You okay, kid?"

"I'm actually sick to my stomach."

Clive nodded sagely. "That's a common occurrence. You wouldn't believe how many people throw up. If it makes you feel any better, you're doing better than most."

"Why the robbery?"

"Your dad's a politician, isn't he?" Not quite, but it would do no good to correct him. "Imagine him weeping over your lifeless body and vowing revenge on all criminal elements. I hear he wants to run for office again, and this is the type of stuff the media eats up."

It was sick. Too sick to bear. "No," Remus whispered. "You can't do this."

Clive beamed. "There's the fear! I was starting to think you weren't human."

"He's going to kill me, then use me to boost up his ratings?"

"Kind of ingenious, I think. A man who uses every opportunity to his advantage is just the type of man we need in Washington." Clive checked his watch. "I'm going to help move the stuff out. We should be finished shortly and then we'll deal with you. I'm sure Bruno wants to whack you now, but you wouldn't believe how distracting it is to work with a dead body in the other room." Clive grimaced at the memory before walking off.

"Take your time," Remus yelled. He struggled with the rope to no avail. He was going to die in this house to further his father's ambition. The universe was a disgusting piece of crap.

Chapter 18

Mycheal Lawyer had been assigned to the gate ever since he'd seen Athena two days ago. They told him he wasn't safe as long as she had a grudge against him, but Nick Hensley, the other guard that was with him, had become her new favorite pet. For the hundredth time he wondered what aspect of himself had set her off.

"Stop thinking about her," Payton scolded. "I need you here."

Mycheal snapped out of it. "Yes, ma'am. Sorry. Anything new?"

Payton checked the monitors. She was a bubbly strawberry blond woman whose enthusiasm surpassed any ordinary cars salesman. As soon as they met, she started telling him how lucky he was to be partnered with her and how many guys would kill for the opportunity. At one point, Mycheal was ready to kill to get rid of the opportunity. "Still quiet. What do you think it is?"

Around 3:00, a series of explosions had rocked Pandora's Box. There was the first initial panic, but when no obvious attacks came afterwards, Pandora's Box calmed down.

"I figure it's like what they've been saying. Some Residents disgruntled over Athena's trip decided to take action."

"But it doesn't make sense," Payton argued. "The bombs were located in different sections of the building. How would they pull that off?"

"Maybe it was a joint effort."

Payton shook her head. Despite her constant chattering, Mycheal could stand Payton for the most part, although she did like to argue over the stupidest of topics.

"Let's say I bought that," she said. "How were they able to make the bombs?"

"From what Captain Froce said, they were all household bombs."

"Where would a Resident get household items?"

"Fine," Mycheal said, his temper flaring. "What do you think happened?"

Payton shrugged. "How should I know? I think I might try calling Froce again. Maybe he can—"

"Shut up! There's a car coming."

Payton glowered at him for telling her to shut up, but she turned her attention to the approaching car. "Interesting," she murmured before pressing a button on the intercom. "Attention, passengers of the black sedan. We are in lockdown mode, which means no one's allowed to pass this point. Identify yourself or we'll be forced to shoot."

The one good thing about the gate was, being the last defense, they were given real guns. Mike had already picked up his rifle in preparation. Some might have called such a powerful gun an extreme measure, but after hearing what the Residents were capable of, Mycheal was glad to have it. "Who do you think it is?"

"It's Dr. Pluck's sedan, but I can't see the driver," Payton answered, tension cracking her voice. She spoke into the intercom. "I repeat, you are not allowed past the gates. Stop and identify yourself immediately. This is your last warning."

No response. Mike raised his gun when...

"This is Dr. Ahab Pluck. I repeat, this is Dr. Pluck. Do not shoot. Do not shoot."

Payton glanced at Mike, who only shrugged in reply. "I'm going to need your identification code, sir." There were two codes. One legitimate, the other to be used if under duress.

"2761548. Open the gates!"

"Sir, we're in lockdown mode."

"Do you think me a fool? I know we're in lockdown mode. I'm the one who initiated it!"

"I'm not allowed to let anyone in or out of the compound!"

"It's against regulations to disobey your superiors. I have the access code, which means I can leave whenever I damn well please."

"But sir..."

Mycheal grabbed her arm and shook his head. "He's running away." Mike felt a hatred boiling up inside of him. The reason he had been kicked out of the Army was for failing to obey the orders of a coward. Payton looked equally angry, which automatically made her more endearing in Mike's eyes.

"Yes, sir."

The gates were opened and the sedan crept through. "Coward!" Payton yelled as the vehicle passed.

Mike chuckled. "I'm surprised you did that."

Payton smiled back. "I'm surprised you didn't."

Mycheal was about to suggest they call Froce and tell him of the new developments when he saw a flash of blond hair in the back of the seat. He opened his mouth to yell.

"Yet another mistake made by Athena. It's nothing to be concerned about."

"You okay?" Payton asked, noticing his expression.

"It's nothing to be concerned about," he assured her.

"That was completely awesome!" Athena gushed, sitting up and climbing into the front seat. "The way you commanded them to open the gates and the way that woman called you a spineless turd." She sighed. "This is a lot more fun than I had imagined." Glancing at Dr. Pluck, she smiled. "I forgot your first name was Ahab."

"I don't know how you would have known in the first place." The women's words still echoed in his mind. Was he a coward?

"Don't let it bother you too much," she advised. "You're going to need to pull over right about now."

"Okay." Dr. Pluck stopped the car and pulled over. *Look at me! Following her every order, bowing to her every whim.* She was peering out the window, her complete dismissal rankling the good doctor. She wasn't paying attention to him. One swift blow and he could—

"Did you know Ahab was the name of the captain in *Moby Dick*?" she interrupted his thoughts. Her eyes were bright with admiration. "Now there was a man who wasn't afraid of anything. He traveled the sea chasing after this whale, which was so much stronger and more powerful than him. In the end, the whale killed him." She gave a small sigh and a half-glance in his direction to see if he got her meaning.. "Interesting story, don't you think?"

She knew his thoughts. He didn't know how she knew, but he was certain of it. "You're a monster," he murmured, his words meant more as a fearful observation than an insult. "You're not human."

With unnatural grace, she snatched the keys from the ignition. "If I'm not human, it's only because you made me that way. Stay here. If you leave, you die."

She left the car without waiting for a response, clearly confident her threat was enough to keep him in line, and traveled to a tree off the road. *If I was a braver man, I'd take my chances and run.* However, he knew from experience how hateful Athena was. There was no doubt she would chase him down and kill him.

Athena dug around in the dirt for a few minutes before she returned with a look of triumph. "Look what I found," she exclaimed upon entering the car. In her hand she held a dagger.

"Don't kill me!" Dr. Pluck screamed, sliding away from her. "Please don't kill me!"

Athena giggled. "Stupid Dr. Pluck. I don't need a dagger to kill you. If I wanted you dead, you would be dead."

"Then what's it for?" He was still highly suspicious. It wouldn't be the first time Athena had lied to him.

Athena stared. "Do me a favor. Try not to think where the tracker is located."

It took Dr. Pluck a beat longer than it should have, but once his confusion lifted, he realized she had to have been talking about the tracker in her left arm. The one on top of her Radius head.

"That's all I needed." She plunged the knife into her own arm, splashing his seats with blood.

Dr. Pluck screamed again. "What are you doing? Jesus Christ!"

"Shut up!" she snarled, her words coming out as a pained hissed. She continued to whimper as she used the dagger and pried a small object out from underneath her skin.

Maybe he could escape now, while she was wounded!

"Don't be stupid, doc. I don't need both hands to kill you.

Give me something for my arm!"

"I don't have anything!" he wailed.

"Crap! What type of doctor are you? In that case, pull out and take a left at the end of this road. We're behind schedule." Dr. Pluck moved to obey. "What are you doing?" she yelled.

"What?" he screamed back, frightened.

"Don't ignore safety rules," she chided sternly. "You can't hit the road without first hooking your seatbelt." She pointed to her own seatbelt, which was securely fastened across her chest.

Dr. Pluck bit his tongue. The monster was playing a childish game with him, yet there was nothing he could do, so under her expectant gaze, he hooked his seatbelt, put the car in gear, and took the left.

"Where are we going?" he dared to ask.

"How close are we to the mall I was at yesterday?"

Blood was still oozing out of the gash in her arm and Dr. Pluck couldn't help but look at it. "About twenty minutes."

"Good." She rolled down the window and tossed the bug out. "Get there in under fifteen and you get to live."

The car skyrocketed in speed, Athena squealing in delight. There was no way he could let her escape now that the only means of tracking her was gone. Fighting her was one option. Despite what she claimed, she was disadvantaged with the use of one hand. Maybe he could trick her? Unless she really could read minds, in which case it was useless. He had to find out for sure.

Concentrating with all his might, he thought, *"What do you think is happening at Pandora's Box?"*

"I imagine they found out I was missing," the Resident responded at ease. "But they haven't yet deduced I'm with you. Coward that you are, they probably figured you were running away. It is your nature, and you don't have to think so hard. I was following your thoughts the whole time."

"Damn it!"

"Can I scold you for thinking of bad words?" she wondered.

"Why are you doing this? Just let me go!"

"No," she said coldly before succumbing to a high-pitched giggle. She switched moods so effortlessly. "I haven't forgotten what you did to us. Despite your beliefs, being a lab rat isn't enjoyable. In fact, I would venture to say the lab rat has the better deal." She straightened, suddenly indignant. "At least they get cheese for their trouble!"

"I was only trying to help you!"

"Your thoughts betray you. We were nothing but a meal ticket to you. To be honest, Dr. Pluck, I doubt you'll live much longer."

"You said you would let me live!"

"Did I?" the sadistic creature asked in puzzlement. A smile of recognition crossed her lips. "That's right, I did. Drive."

A stiff silence filled the car, Athena choosing to play with a strand of her hair while Dr. Pluck clutched the steering wheel with trembling hands. They entered a main road and Dr. Pluck was relieved to see there was almost no traffic to impede him. He glanced at Athena and found her staring at him. "What I want to know is how a doctor wouldn't carry any bandages?"

"I'm not that type of doctor. Are you feeling okay?"

Her eyes flashed as she must have read his thoughts. "Don't. I'm not injured enough for you to attack me. If you look closely, you'll find my wound is doing much better."

It was true. Her wound seemed to be healing almost in front of him. The bleeding had slowed to a reluctant stop and, as he watched, the first layers of new pink skin were appearing.

He was astonished. Of course he knew Residents, on average, healed faster than humans, but Athena's healing was nothing short of miraculous. "Incredible! Do you know what this means? If I can run some more tests—"

"Forget it, doc. I bled on your seat. You can try to take a sample of that if you live through this ordeal. By the way, we're here."

Dr. Pluck looked up, surprised. He had been so fixated on Athena he didn't even realize they had arrived.

"Managed to get here in under eight minutes. Superb job, doc. Park on the other side of the street. There we can part ways." The statement was deliberately ominous.

He parked per her instructions. "So, we're here."

Athena nodded. "Yep." A shadow crossed her face as if she had a troubling thought. "Doc, there's not another tracker your boys managed to hide in me, is there?"

"What? Of course not!"

Athena stared at him.

"There's not!" he protested, and it was the truth. Why waste money on a second tracker when there should have been no chance of her finding the first one?"

Athena relaxed. "Okay, doc. I believe you."

"So I guess you can let me go now," he croaked, knowing the answer even as he dared to hope.

Athena giggled. "Silly man, you're the only one who knows where I am!"

She shot him twice in the chest.

"We're about done here, kid," Clive informed as he walked up to Remus. "We're packing up now."

"Are you *sure* you're done? You don't want to take the light bulbs or the paint from the wall?"

"Witty," Clive commented. "I haven't seen witty in a long time. Hits are usually too scared to crack a joke, and you've seen the crowd I run with. You've really made my day."

"I'm sure you want to repay the kindness?" Remus suggested.

Clive smiled, but there was no humor in it. He wanted to get the job over with. "Close your eyes," he kindly advised, pulling out a gun. "It's never good to see it coming."

Remus fidgeted in his chair.

"Squirm all you want, it won't do a lick of good."

"Can't help it. Someone's aiming a gun at me." He fidgeted again.

"Suit yourself." Clive aimed carefully for Remus' chest and Remus took a deep breath, as if that would help, and closed his eyes. There was a loud boom...

"What was that?" Clive yelled.

Remus opened his eyes and discovered he was not dead. Clive had never fired his gun. Was this salvation or another trick of the universe?

Then he heard her voice. "Trying to define yourself is like trying to bite your own teeth."

Chapter 19

Athena was tired by the time she got to her location. She stopped near a tree to catch her breath and rest. The run from the mall to Remus' house had taken no more than fifteen minutes, but had left her terribly exhausted. Unlike other Residents, Athena didn't possess an unlimited amount of stamina, so short breaks after strenuous activity were required to avoid collapsing.

She looked up at Remus Sylvia's house; it was enormous with marble columns and archways. Even Athena, who had never lived in a house, could tell that it was too excessive. As she watched, a man left the front door, carrying two boxes on top of each other.

"That's interesting," she remarked. Long bouts of solitude had taught her it was okay to talk to herself.

She extended her mind. *I'm so hungry. I can't wait till Clive whacks the kid so we can go home. Maybe I'll get a pizza. How far is that pizza joint? What's that Chinese place called again?*

She noticed a decent-sized rock lying beside her. A moment later, the rock soared through the air and hit the man perfectly on the head. He went down cold.

"Crap! Crap! Crap!" she screamed, momentarily forgetting her rule of never panicking. An essential element of her plan was about to be "whacked." It was actually funny. In all the years she had taken dissecting her plan, all she had guessed could go wrong, it never crossed her mind that her chosen human would be assassinated the next day.

Another man appeared from behind the moving van parked in the driveway. "What the fuck?" he yelled, spotting his fallen comrade on the floor. Then he saw Athena. "Did you do this?"

"I did!" Athena said, forcing tears to her eyes. "I was aiming for the window, but he got in my way!" She didn't have Selene's mental manipulation and so had learned the incredibly useful art of blatant lying.

"Get out of here!"

"I can't," she cried, running to the door. "Not until I give that cheating bastard a piece of my mind!"

The thug got to the door first and blocked her way. "Lady, you don't want to go in there. It would be a big mistake."

Athena did a mind check. There were four presences inside the house. Two by the front door and two in the kitchen. Not as bad as she had previously thought. None of them were well trained, and Remus was one of presences in the kitchen. He seemed unharmed...except the other presence was planning on killing him!

Athena jerked out her dagger and, with a quick slash, slit the thug's throat. "*She cut me!*" the doomed man thought stupidly. Using her full strength, she kicked him and sent him crashing through the front door.

"Holy shit! He's bleeding!"

"Grant! Can you hear me, Grant?"

Finally, one of them noticed her. "Who the heck are you?"

"Trying to define yourself is like trying to bite your own teeth," she yelled as a cheap trick to buy time.

The one on the right reacted first. Dropping the box he was carrying, he reached for his gun. With a flick of her wrist, Athena sent the dagger sailing into his guts. He stared dumbfounded at the hilt of the dagger before slinking to the ground.

The other guy was a shade quicker. The bullet tore through her leg and she collapsed on the blood-soaked floor.

Crap! She had known she was in no condition to fight, and felt a moment of deep self-loathing. Not only had she broken her number one rule of not panicking, she had allowed this no-one to take her down. Selene would be so disappointed—if she still felt that emotion. Thor would be kinder, but even he would be shocked that she had been defeated so easily. Pandora's Box would catch up to her if she didn't improve her game.

The gun was now pointed directly at her head. "Who the

hell are you?" he demanded. "What are you doing here?"

Her mind kicked into overdrive. "Don't kill me! Please!" She forced a tremble to her body and held up a hand. I'm just here to do a job."

Clive never said anything about another job. "What job?"

Sensing an opportunity, she said, "Clive hired me to kill you; to kill you all."

The thug blinked. "Why?"

"He said he was tired of splitting the money with you idiots," Athena said, improvising. She discreetly wriggled her leg. The bullet had taken a chunk of skin, but beyond that there was very little muscle damage. "I was paid thirty-five thousand in cash."

It's a trick! "Not sure I believe you, lady."

"Hold on." With great care to use slow and deliberate movements, Athena took an envelope from her pocket and tossed it. "There's twenty thousand in that envelope. If you let me go, I'll get you the other fifteen."

I'll just kill you and take it anyway! "Okay, so where's the rest?"

"In my car, but I parked a couple of blocks away. What about Clive?"

That bastard! "What about him?"

"You plan to let a bastard like that go when he just tried to kill you?" A guy with average intelligence should have been able to spot the ruse instantly, but you did not become a hitman because you possessed an Einstein IQ.

"Stay here," he ordered after a brief moment of thought, which was probably the longest he thought about anything. He was clearly not a thinker. If he was, he would have wondered why Clive would hire a girl to carry out the hit or why he would choose the location of a job to initiate it. "I'll be back and then we can get that money."

He left and Athena sighed. This was not going as planned. Action had to be taken to prevent the loss of Remus' life. Wincing from the effort, she crawled to the box the first thug had dropped and searched for a suitable weapon.

Chapter 20

"Athena?" Remus wondered out loud.

Clive swiveled the gun in his direction, his face hard. "Who is Athena?"

"I don't know!"

"You knew her name."

Good point. "I only met her once, I swear it."

"It's the girl," Clive breathed. "Kid, I thought Maris was going crazy. I didn't believe you had it in you, but..."

Athena's voice interrupted as it echoed down the halls. "Don't kill me! Please! I'm just here to do a job."

"Leave her alone!" Remus shouted, his stomach sick with dread.

"For someone who only met her once, you sure care a great deal if something was to happen to the lady," Clive observed.

"She has nothing to do with this."

"Why is she here?"

"I don't know!"

"What job is she talking about?"

"I don't know!"

"Don't lie to me. You're no longer dealing with fun Clive. You're dealing with angry Clive now."

"Just to be sure, wasn't fun Clive the one about to kill me?" The remark probably would have earned him a bullet if Clive's focus hadn't been elsewhere.

"You son of a bitch!" Bruno screamed, entering the kitchen, gun held high. "You thought you could kill me?"

Clive took a step back, staring at the gun now focused on his head. "What's going on?"

"Drop it."

"What?"

"Drop your gun, or I swear I'll kill your ass!"

Remus couldn't decide if this was a good development. He had gone from about to die, to standing in the middle of a duel. What was even more worrisome was that one of the duelers was the type of guy to say things like "kill your ass." The other suffered from split personality, one fun and the other angry.

Clive dropped his gun and held his hands up. "You better have a good reason for this," he growled.

"They're all dead. Grant, Ajay, Bill. They're all dead because of you!"

"I didn't do anything!"

"The girl already confessed, you idiot! You sent a little girl to kill us?"

"Calm down," Clive soothed, hands held out in a complacent manner. He took a step towards him. "Listen to what you're saying. I didn't hire no girl to kill you. That's crazy."

The gun wavered. "She told me you did. She had the envelope full of money you gave her."

"She was lying." Clive took another step towards Bruno. "You and I are friends, remember? We've been through thick and thin; ain't no way we're going to allow these two kids to mess that up."

Remus' mind was racing. An envelope full of money? Boy did that sound familiar.

Bruno dropped his arm. "She knew your name," he said, still sounding a tad suspicious

"Then what Maris said must be true." Clive looked at Remus then back at Bruno. "Is she still alive?"

There was definitely a misconception circling around, but Remus didn't know what it was and doubted anyone would believe him if he tried to clear it up.

"Yeah, I left her in the hallway. Busted up her leg pretty bad."

"Then let's go talk to her. We'll make her pay for what she did."

Unacceptable. Remus was prepared to accept his own death. However, he could not comprehend the death of Athena, no matter how much trouble the conniving woman brought into his life.

"He's lying!" Remus cried out. "He told me he paid a chick twenty thousand to do you all in. He was practically boasting about it!"

"You bastard!" Bruno screamed.

"He's lying, Bruno! Don't believe—"

The bullet went through Clive's head and splattered Remus with blood and what appeared to be parts of his brain. Remus wasn't sure if he screamed or not, but he did know he threw up.

"Disgusting," Bruno sneered. "Thanks for the heads up, but it's your turn now."

Remus vigorously shook his head, still unable to speak.

"What's the matter, you think I'm going to spare you simply because you saved my life?"

"No," Remus croaked. "I'm pretty sure it's your turn."

Bruno had a second to think he was crazy before Athena tackled him from behind, sending them both to the ground. "Get off me, you bitch!"

Athena gripped the hammer she had with both hands, raised it up high, and with resounding force, smashed the back of Bruno's head in. Bruno's body flopped almost comically before becoming still. This time, Remus knew he screamed.

Athena stood up and limped towards Remus.

"What are you doing?"

A laugh escaped her lips, and the sound was terrifying. "Trying to save your life, which is way more effort than I thought possible. Now hold still." Grabbing a kitchen knife, Athena cut away the rope. "Stay," she ordered, as if he was in the state of mind to move. She disappeared behind him. Remus heard her turn on the water faucet, and wondered what she was up to. He kept his eyes closed because looking at the two bodies sprawled across the ceramic tiles of the kitchen floor would be enough to shred his sanity.

He felt Athena's presence in front of him and carefully cracked an eye open to look at her. A second later, she stuffed a wet washcloth in his face and started to scrub vigorously.

"Cut it out," she said icily when he tried to move his head out the way. "I need to get as much blood off you as possible." Remus wondered why, and he must have asked the question out loud, because she answered. "Because you will stand out significantly with blood splattered all over your face."

"Sticky," he mumbled, still unable to make coherent sentences. Once again, she seemed to know what he meant.

"The sticky substance is cerebrospinal fluid. It acts like a cushion, providing basic protection to the brain." She finished scrubbing and stuck her face near his to scrutinize her work. Even in his addled state, he couldn't help but observe her beauty. "You're good. Still got a little in your hair, but it's not too noticeable. Okay, it's time to go." When he didn't move, she grew impatient. "Come on!"

Remus sat frozen in the chair. This couldn't be happening. Not even the universe was this evil. One man had his head cracked open, and he was wearing the other man's brains in his hair.

"I said come on!"

"I can't, I need to stay here."

The life he wanted no longer seemed fun and adventurous. He wanted to go back to normal and safe. He would ask Maris for another chance. Maris did just try to kill him, but maybe if he begged...

Athena slapped him. Hard. "Stop being an idiot! Maris sent men to kill you. He won't give up simply because you beg him. And even if he did, do you really want to go back to that sociopath? If you're going to waste your life, then I might as well kill you and collect the reward myself. Get up!"

"I have to go to the police," he mumbled, suppressing the urge to throw up again. "I have to rescue my brother."

"The police can't do anything, and rescue your brother from what?" she asked bluntly. "He's safe, you're the one Maris wants to kill."

He closed his eyes again, this time trying to block out her words. She was right of course. Whatever the reason, Maris wanted him dead, and a feeble apology wouldn't change a thing. "Who are you, and how come every time you show up, life goes to hell?"

"I can explain all that later, but we're in danger right now. We can't be caught here. Please, Remus," her voice was pleading. "Get up and come with me."

Through their one encounter, Remus knew Athena wasn't one to beg, and something about her pleading cut through the fog in his brain. He stood up on unsteady legs.

Chapter 21

Matthew Titanos stormed in, livid. "I want answers!"

Caleb raised an eyebrow. "It'd be mighty helpful if you asked a question."

Mr. Titanos slammed his fist into a desk. An action that did nothing to impress the Texan, but it did make the two guards behind him jump. Everyone was on high alert, waiting for the next Resident jailbreak. "You're making jokes?"

"No, I'm making a point. You ain't gonna get nowhere barging in angry, looking for someone to blame. And I don't appreciate being hauled in like a criminal by your boys here."

Matthew took a seat and rubbed his temples. Two hours ago, he received a call from Captain Froce, declaring Pandora's Box had gone into lockdown mode. The day had gone downhill from there. A half hour later, Froce called and informed Matthew of Dr. Pluck's cowardly departure. Another 15 minutes flew by before Froce called with the devastating news that Athena was not in her room, nor did she seem to be on the grounds. The little brat had escaped!

"So, what do we know?" It looked like Matthew was asking the entire room, but really he was only talking to one person.

That person coughed and all eyes fell on Eris Yang, Mr. Titano's personal secretary, and the one woman he could not live without. Eris Yang did it all. She spoke more than nine different languages, had two degrees in business, and could persuade any man to give up vital information through a variety of means. It had taken her only an hour to get all the facts of the attack and organize it into a neat little packet.

"Athena was scheduled for a round of Ambrosia at three

o'clock," Eris began, her tone clipped and concise. "A guard was dispatched around two-fifty-three to collect her. At precisely three-ten, the first bomb went off in the men's bathroom. Fifteen seconds later, two more bombs were set off, the first in the kitchen; the second in a storage closest. Twenty-one seconds later, three more bombs were set off. The first of these—"

"Is she really going to name every bomb location?" Caleb interrupted, a dark scowl plaguing his features.

Eris looked up and adjusted her glasses. A slim woman of Eastern descent, Eris was the ideal secretary. She never asked any questions beyond what her job dictated, and was seven times more capable than her boss.

"I was under the impression that you wanted *all* the facts."

Matthew cleared his throat. "Thank you, Ms. Yang. We're pressed on time, so if you don't mind..."

"Certainly, Mr. Titanos." She glanced back at her notes. "A total of twelve bombs were detonated in the course of five minutes. All of them strategically placed."

Captain Froce, the man in charge when Caleb was gone, spoke up. "The bombs caused no fatalities, and very little damage was reported. My best guess is they were nothing but a diversion."

"At three-twenty-nine, the gates were opened under the direct order of Dr. Pluck. He left the premises a minute later. At four-fifty-one, Athena was discovered missing. In her bed was the corpse of Scott Williams."

"Why did it take so damn long to find out she was missing?" Caleb growled.

"We didn't have the manpower," Froce answered. "You have to remember we were only working with half our force."

"That's way too coincidental," Matthew observed. "The day she planned on escaping, no one showed up?"

Caleb nodded. "I agree, but how the hell did she pull it off?"

Mrs. Yang shuffled some papers. "I noted that none of the personnel from her trip the previous day clocked in."

The statement was greeted with silence. "Who was in charge of that operation?" Matthew demanded.

"Chris Burlington. He's been with us for six years."

"Find him and bring him here."

"Yes, sir." Ms. Yang took out her phone.

Mr. Titanos took a deep breath. He could do this. He was groomed and prepped to take over his father's business, and we wouldn't let one little girl get in his way. "Can't we locate her using the tracker?"

"We could if it was still on her."

Matthew had not expected this and he stared at Ms. Yang until he heard Caleb huff his impatience. "What do you mean?"

"Apparently, somewhere down the road, she removed the bug from her skin."

Matthew felt his confidence melting away. "How did she manage that?"

Froce shrugged. "With her, anything is possible. She might have chewed it out for all we know. The only good news is she has to be injured after a wound like that."

Matthew suppressed a shudder. How badly did she want to escape if she was willing to cut herself open? "How did she even know about the tracker?"

Caleb snorted. "Are you stupid?"

"Caleb..." Matthew warned. For once, his tone was imposing enough to make the other man pause.

"She knew the same way she managed to set off all those bombs. Or the way she made this place a ghost town the day of her escape." He looked around. "Someone from the inside was helping her."

"I came to the same conclusion," Froce said darkly. "And I'll give you three guesses to figure who it is."

"Dr. Pluck," Matthew guessed, not really knowing, but just thinking of the guy he most wanted to go down for this.

"Exactly."

Caleb frowned. "Now hold on a sec. I thought them two hated each other?"

Froce waved a dismissive hand, and Matthew noticed how Caleb glowered at him. Just great...the two highest-ranking personnel in Pandora's Box didn't get along. "Obviously, they were faking the grudge to prevent suspicion."

"I'm not convinced. Ain't no way hostility like that can be faked."

"We got proof," Froce said smugly.

"I'd love to see it."

The intercom buzzed. Matthew edged towards a guard

and glanced nervously at the door. "Who's there?"

"Sir, we have a man here to see you. A pause. "Sir, it's Dr. Pluck."

"What the hell did you do?" Maris roared.

"Nothing!" Romulus yelled back. "I did nothing."

After the mall, Romulus had further decimated his credit card by taking Delilah out to dinner where she kept up a constant flow of babble in an attempt to distract him from the beating happening at his house. It had almost worked when Maris' men stormed in and kidnapped them both. They were taken to a small hotel room where Maris was waiting, eager to jump down Romulus' throat.

"Did you go back to the house?"

"No!"

"You're a lying piece of crap!"

"Sir?" Delilah said timidly. She flinched when Maris glared at her, Romulus resolving then and there to never forgive his father for dragging Delilah into this. "Romulus was with me the whole time...ever since school."

Maris glowered. "Fine, I believe it. But did you tell Remus that—"

"That you planned to have Remus beaten? No, I didn't, but he's smart enough to figure it out." Romulus braced himself for the answer. "Did something happen to Remus?" Maris stared at him, and Romulus tried again. "Is Remus still alive?"

"As far as I can tell, yes."

Romulus didn't know if Maris thought that was good news or not, so he took great pains to hide his happiness. "Where is he now?"

"I don't know!" Maris yelled, getting up and pacing. Romulus realized that his father was actually worried. No, it was more than that. His father was scared. What had happened? "I don't know what type of attack this is."

"Attack?"

"Four guys were sent to the house to speak with your brother. Rough him up a bit...put the fear of God in him. Three of them are dead. The last one isn't expected to make it through the night."

Romulus stared, mouth open. "You think Remus killed them all?"

"Don't be a fool!" Maris snapped. "Of course your brother couldn't pull this off. No, he had professional help."

"Who do you think it is?"

Maris' eyes flickered, indicating he was about to lie. "Not a clue. But until I do, you are not to leave this room without my permission."

"You can't do that!"

"I am doing it. I'll have someone escort the young lady home."

The thought of one of Maris' goons driving Delilah home sickened him. Delilah knew him well enough to know what was going through his head.

"Don't worry about me." She pecked him lightly on the cheek. "I'll be okay."

Romulus watched with regret as Delilah was led away. She had become a pillar of strength. The only person he could rely on or trust. "I won't forgive you if anything happens to her," Romulus growled.

He expected his father to snap at him, but instead Maris chuckled. "Both my sons are becoming men," he said with something very much like approval. "It's just a shame..." Maris stopped, shaking his head. "It's a shame," he muttered to himself.

Delilah gave him one last reassuring look before she was escorted away.

Chapter 22

Athena opened her eyes and found herself in the car. Alone. The coward had run away! To be fair, she probably could have handled the situation better. It hadn't worked in her favor to take the time to pull her dagger from the one man's intestines, causing another puke reaction from Remus. Honestly, the boy was sensitive and she might have a need for the dagger. He probably also had qualms about her stomping the guy she had beaned with a rock when he had begun to stir, but that just made sense. She couldn't have any reports of Remus floating around this early in the game, and chances were the man would survive his injuries.

A glimpse in Remus' mind showed he was in shock, his thoughts too jumbled to interpret. With a little coaching, she managed to get him into the driver's seat. With a lot of coaching, she got him to drive. Once on the highway, exhaustion hit. Overextension of telepathy, healing, and physical skills all came with a price, so it couldn't be helped when she fell asleep.

To add insult to injury, the brainless jerk had snatched the $20,000 as well. Athena tried to move, and winced from the effort. No way could she catch up with him. He had left her. Panic was beginning to bubble up when the door opened and the brainless jerk sat down.

"Brainless jerk, where have you been?" she demanded.

Remus raised an eyebrow. *What's her problem?* "I went to get supplies."

"Supplies?" she asked, her annoyance already turning to curiosity. "Like what?"

Remus handed her a bag. His mind seemed to be a lot

clearer. "You need to change. You can't go around in that stupid uniform all day long." She noticed he had also switched outfits. She looked in the bag, displeased to find a bright yellow skirt instead of a suitable pair of jeans. What was worse, the shirt was a pale magenta. Apparently, his definition of going unseen was to wear clothes so bright that the enemy would be forced to look away.

"What's the deodorant for?"

You stink. "I just thought you might appreciate some."

Athena sighed, not offended. "I sprinted seven miles just to get to your house, not to mention the fight when I got there. Pine-fresh sweat is not among my talents."

She ran to my house? "From where?"

"The mall."

Why? And how did she know where I lived?

"By the way," Athena took out Remus' wallet and grinned cheekily. "You might want this back."

Remus snatched his wallet, his expression anything but grateful. "You thief!"

"Without it, I would never have been able to find you."

"So you stole it! You're a thief!"

"Thieves respect property. They merely wish the property to become their property that they may more perfectly respect it," she quoted.

A twitch that might have been a smile passed across Remus' lips. "Bullshit."

Athena laughed, then winced as her throbbing leg reminded her how stupid she had been. "You're ungrateful. I, a girl weighing no more than a hundred and twenty pounds, valiantly risked my life to come to your aid." She hissed silently as her leg throbbed again. "Honestly, when I woke up and found you missing, I jumped to the obvious conclusion."

"Don't make anything out of it," he warned. "I'm only here for answers." *I couldn't leave her alone injured! What type of person would I be?*

She was sincerely touched, although puzzled by his thoughts. "Well," she said. "I guess I'd better change." With one fluid movement, she removed the top of her security outfit and started working on the pants.

Remus quickly looked away. *What is she doing?* "What are you doing?"

"I'm changing," Athena said, faking her puzzlement

"You're supposed to change inside the store! In a dressing room."

"And allow everyone to see my bloodied clothes?" Athena asked, pulling off her pants. "Think, Remus, think!"

"But..."

"If it bothers you that much, look the other way."

"I am!"

"Then don't peek."

Don't look, don't look, don't look, don't look, don't look, don't look, don't look, don't look, don't look.

Athena suppressed a giggle, her mood significantly brightening.

"Are you done?"

"Why, Remus, I had no idea you were so shy."

"Come on, Athena."

"Why don't you look and find out?"

Remus risked a glance and found her fully clothed. "Good. Now give me your leg."

"Being a little forward, aren't we?"

Remus reached in a bag and took out some bandages. "Do you want me to wrap it or not?" he asked irritably.

Why was she pushing him? Because it was in her nature to peck, but she had to do better if she wished this to last. Athena raised her leg and placed it in Remus' lap.

"That's a nice looking leg."

Athena sighed. At their core, all men were the same. Remus glanced up at her face. "I still need my questions answered."

"You haven't asked me anything," she reminded, and watched as he bandaged her leg with care.

"Why did you trick me at the mall? Why did you take the money and my wallet? Was it all just a game to you?"

"Yes." Feelings of guilt were not in her nature, but she felt a twinge of it as Remus' shoulders jerked back.

So she never cared about me.

He lapsed into silence, so Athena spoke up. "You asked for the truth and I'm trying to give it to you. At the time, you were nothing but an unexpected source of entertainment, and I never dreamed my actions would jeopardize your well-being.."

"So you thought I could lose 20k and everyone would be peachy about it?" He tightened the bandage. "What did you think was going to happen?"

"Didn't you hear me? I wasn't thinking about you." Athena reconsidered. "Actually, that's not completely true. I was thinking about you all day yesterday...it's complicated. "You about done with my leg?"

"Yeah. Who told you about the envelope and about Maris?"

Athena withdrew her leg to examine the bandages while considering Remus' mental state. At first glance, he seemed too sensitive for a complete explanation of what she was and what she could do. However, a closer assessment revealed a remarkable resilience hiding inside her newest friend. Only hours after seeing his old life burned away and witnessing his first murder, Remus was already thinking rationally and seeking information to help his survival odds. Truly impressive for a man who'd had no dealings with her world in the past. Still, her secrets weren't the type you just blurted out.

"I have ways of getting information."

Remus stared coldly at her. *She's still playing games.* "I thought you were going to be completely honest with me?"

"I'm trying. I can't tell you, not without opening Pandora's Box."

Of course, the pun was lost on him. "You must be working for one of my father's rivals."

Athena shrugged, letting him believe that might be the truth.

"Why were you at my house earlier? To save me? To recruit me?"

"How would I have known those thugs were going to be at your house?" she asked reasonably. "I came by to return your belongings and to express my sincerest of apologies for taking them in the first place."

Does she really think I'm that stupid? Athena knew this wouldn't be easy, but she was still discouraged about how poorly this conversation was going.

"It's also possible that I dropped by to ask for a favor."

"What was the favor?"

"Does it matter?"

Yes! "It does to me!"

"I wanted you to drive me somewhere."

Remus' abrupt laugh was a cross between disbelief and surprise. So you brutally murdered three guys for what? A taxi?"

His righteous tone was starting to grate. "I killed three guys because they would have murdered you. I risked my life to save yours. That alone should warrant me some trust."

"Trust needs to be earned," he retorted angrily. "And you've done nothing to earn it; in fact, just the opposite." Remus, who Athena began to think was a bit of a whiner, held out his hand and started to tally up her offenses. "You lied to me, conned me out of twenty thousand dollars, stole my wallet, stalked me to my house, and committed triple homicide. I don't want to go anywhere with you, Athena. You're talking about trust? Trust me when I say I'm thinking about leaving you here."

Athena gritted her teeth. These were not empty words. He was seriously considering leaving her here, and his cantankerous attitude was beginning to irk. Like most humans, Remus would respond to threats from a Resident, but wouldn't appreciate it, and it would severely impact their relationship in the long run. Perhaps a subtle reminder of her abilities would be enough to deter him from any rash and unforgivable actions. "I killed four men today."

"You only killed three. Bruno shot Clive."

"True," Athena agreed. "But before that, I killed someone else."

Remus held an impressive poker face, although his thoughts exposed his shock. "Why?"

"Because he was in the way of my survival. Just like you are now."

"Is that a threat?" Remus demanded.

"No, it's the truth. If you leave me out here, then I will be dead the following morning. I'm not sure if I could allow that to happen."

"So, what would you do if I made you leave?"

This wouldn't work. Another glimpse in his mind showed that a threat, no matter how indirect, would shut him down completely, so she deftly switched tracks. "I would die."

Remus blinked, the words taking some of the energy out of his anger. She felt his turmoil. Listening to his internal conflict gave her new insight into Remus' mind.

A couple of minutes passed. Then...

"Buckle up," he ordered, starting the engine.

"Did Romulus contact Remus in any way?"

Delilah shrugged. "Like I said, I never left his side after school. It's possible he texted him without me knowing, but it's doubtful."

Maris gave Delilah his best intimidating glare. Usually, he would believe her, but Remus' initiative had him rattled and Delilah's loyalty was strictly based on money. If she thought Remus could succeed in dethroning him, than she would switch sides without a backwards thought. Delilah stared back wide-eyed, her gaze screaming naïve innocence. Maris wasn't fooled; too many men had fallen by the hands of a scheming woman. He snorted to let her know her testimony was in dispute before asking, "What's going through his head?"

"Romulus? He thinks you're a heartless bastard. He wants to help his brother, but doesn't want to go against you. A man with a virtuous personality and a cowardly heart. I've got to tell you, your offspring doesn't have much love for you at the moment."

Maris grunted. "He'll get over it."

"So did you do it?" Delilah inquired, leaning forward eagerly. "Did you kill your own son?"

"Tried to."

Delilah looked surprised, but surprise could be faked. "I thought you had him killed and was just telling Romulus he ran away."

It was actually the exact plan Maris would have used if Remus hadn't legitimately escaped.

"So it's true," Delilah breathed. "No way he escaped on his own. Remus got himself some muscle. But how?"

"You're becoming awfully inquisitive," Maris growled.

Delilah glanced to see how serious the subtle threat was before lapsing back to deep pondering. It was a painful fact to admit, but this whore was one of the most intelligent person on his payroll and she seemed to genuinely hate Remus. If she could come up with insight, Maris would swallow his pride and listen. When she didn't speak, Maris prompted her. "Obviously he used my money to buy some men." When Remus had given the money to the blond, Delilah had followed her while Romulus dealt with Mr. Bob. She had pictures of the blond girl entering a van with a squad of men...all of them sporting concealed weapons. Delilah had taken pictures to show to Maris and Maris had reached the obvious conclusion—his son was trying to take over his empire.

"Is twenty thousand enough?" Delilah asked.

"Not for anyone professional. No one who can take out Clive's team." Maris realized he was treating the whore like an equal. "But that's not your concern, is it?" he snapped.

Delilah shrugged and held out her hand, the meaning clear. If he wanted a strictly professional relationship then she needed to be paid. He handed her an envelope. She carefully opened it up and counted the money meticulously while he waited. He had done this ritual numerous times in the past, and knew she wouldn't respond to anything until all her money was accounted for.

"I want you to stay close to Romulus," he said when she was done. "At some point, Remus will try to contact him. Bring him over to his side. When he does, give me a call."

"How am I supposed to stay close to him? You have him locked up in a hotel room."

"For as much money as I'm paying you, I'm sure you'll find a way."

Delilah looked at the money and smiled. "You're right, I will. Now, if you'll excuse me, I'm going home for a bit. I spent the whole day convincing your arrogant son that he is the center of my universe and I now need a long, hot bath." She went to leave. "And for what is worth," she called over her shoulder, "I think you're a heartless bastard, too."

Chapter 23

Remus glanced at the gauge. "We need gas."

Athena didn't respond. She had maintained the air of a somber mourner since their last talk, spending the majority of the ride looking out the window. The idea that, after kidnapping and threatening his life, *she* was the offended one still rankled.

"We also need to figure out a destination. We can't keep on going nowhere."

"You ever look at the night sky?"

Remus was beginning to realize Athena was a bit flighty. "Pardon?"

"The night sky," she repeated dreamily, not bothering to look at him. "It's mesmerizing. I read about it, but never dreamed it was so...big. And all the stars glittering and winking at me. It's breathtaking!" Then she quoted, "Surely the stars are images of love."

If this was another game, it was a strange one. "You act like you've never seen the night sky before."

"Would you believe me if I told you I never have?" she asked with earnest. "Just to see the night sky makes it worth all the effort."

She was obviously in her own world now. Unlike Remus, who couldn't stop thinking about Clive's brain exploding.

"Stop dwelling on it," she said, sounding annoyed. "They would have killed you without hesitation."

"Doesn't mean they deserved death." In the back of his mind, he recognized he had gotten used to the fact she always seemed to know what he was thinking.

"That's exactly what it means!" The sheer amount of exasperation in her voice was almost funny. "After they killed you, what would they have done? They would go kill someone else. You weren't the first, and you wouldn't have been the last."

"What gives you the right to be judge, jury, and executioner?"

"People like you who are too caught up in their pointless morals to make the necessary choices. Now hush, you're ruining my magical moment."

Grumbling to himself, Remus turned into a gas station. "What happened to all life is sacred?"

"Death is a punishment to some, to some a gift, and to many a favor."

Answering a question with a ridiculous quote. God, she was frustrating! He entered the parking lot of the gas station and parked beside one of the pumps. He was about to add something when he suddenly broke into a cold sweat. Something was wrong; his instincts were screaming that a threat was racing towards them and that there would be no place to run. He swiveled his head to look at her and paled when he saw her expression.

Athena had her head cocked, as if she was listening to some invisible voice. Her usual beautiful face was contorted with a look of such intense bitterness mixed with rage that Remus was tempted to close his eyes. The look reminded him that, even though she was pleasant, in both features and attitude, she was still a confessed killer and he was still her hostage. Strangely enough, the look wasn't directed at him. Instead, her stare shot past him. He followed her gaze and saw a black Jeep pulling up to the pump beside them. When he looked back, Athena had returned to normal, making him briefly wonder if he'd imagined the whole thing.

When she didn't speak, he said rather nervously, "I'm going to put gas in the car."

Athena turned to face him, her grey eyes shining. "Can I do it?"

"Do what?"

"Put the gas in the car?"

Remus stared. He could never tell if she was serious. "You're serious?""

"Incredibly so."

"Knock yourself out then."

Athena squealed with delight and leapt out of the car.

A sudden thought occurred to him. "You have done this before, right?"

She had removed one of the gas nozzles. "Nope."

"Do you at least know how?"

"Not a clue," Athena said cheerfully. She pointed the nozzle at her eye. "Gas comes from here, right?"

Remus took the nozzle away and gave Athena a quick tutorial. "So remember, gas goes *in* the car. Not in the eye or mouth. Got it?"

"Keep on talking to me like that," she said sweetly, "and I'll find an ideal place for this nozzle to go."

Ignoring what he hoped to be a joke, he said, "I'm going to pay for the gas and get us some snacks. I'll be back in a second. Don't blow anything up." He left her happily pumping gas, and walked into the store.

The opportunity of escape did not go unnoticed. With Athena figuring out the gas pump, he could easily duck through the back exit. Or better yet, use the station's phone—he'd forgotten to bring his with him when Athena was killing everyone—to call the police. Athena wasn't a fool. She must have been aware of the possibility he would try to run, and must be counting on his ignorance to keep him timid. She knew the situation, he didn't.

He entered the store, the door making a welcoming jingle, and walked over to the cashier. "Excuse me."

The cashier looked to be in her early 40s and had so much makeup on her face Remus was surprised she didn't suffocate. She glanced up from her magazine, clearly irritated that someone had the gumption to interrupt her. "May I help you?" she asked in a nasally voice that suggested she grew up in a helium factory.

The door jingled again, and three more guys entered the store. They wore oversized coats that people only wore if they were concealing a weapon or if they suffered from some thyroid disorder. One of them glanced disinterestedly at Remus.

"Two things. I need to pay for a full tank of gas, and also..." He lowered his voice. "I'll pay you fifty bucks if you let me borrow your cell phone."

Romulus' cell phone rang. "Hello?"

A brief moment of silence. "Romulus, is that you?"

Delilah must have sensed his shock. She had miraculously managed to sneak in without Maris' men knowing, and Romulus was initially angry that she would take such a risk, but touched that she would do so for his sake. "Remus?" she mouthed.

Romulus nodded and pressed the speakerphone button. She had a right to know what was going on. "Remus! Where are you?"

"I'm around," was the cryptic response. "Is Maris there?"

"No. God, I've been so worried about you."

Remus laughed dryly. "I bet." It sounded like Remus didn't believe him, but his next words were said with warmth. "You're okay?"

"Still kicking." There were so many questions Romulus didn't know where to start.

Delilah tugged on his sleeve and mouthed, "Where is he?" Eventually, he would ask that question, but to do so immediately might make Remus suspicious enough to hang up.

"What happened?" he asked instead. "What happened at the house, Remus? Three men dead and the fourth knocking on death's door?"

"Did you know Maris sent those men to kill me?"

Romulus' breath caught in his throat. By not directly answering the question, Remus was giving the impression that he'd killed them or he'd had them killed. Also, his statement was ridiculous. "Maris sent those men to scare you. He's a bastard, but he wouldn't kill us, Remus."

"No, he definitely tried to kill me." Remus' conviction was clear.

Delilah leaned in to Romulus, her breath soft against his cheek. "We can't help him unless we know where he is," she whispered.

Romulus nodded. "Where are you at?"

"Why?" Remus asked sharply.

"So that we can help you."

Delilah looked horrified, and Romulus didn't understand why until Remus responded in a voice so low that it could barely be heard. "We? Who's we?"

He had made a mistake and the only way out was to come clean. "Delilah is with me."

"Of course she is," Remus said scornfully. Remus had never used scorn in the past.

"Yes, she is." He didn't like the disrespect to Delilah. "What's your problem?"

"Remus, I only want to help!" Delilah said tearfully.

The silence over the phone was almost disdainful. "Look, I have to go. I'll talk to you... What the... Get off me!"

There were sounds of a struggle over the phone. "Remus!" Romulus yelled.

The sound of Remus yelling, a large clatter, and then nothing but heavy breathing came over the phone. "Who is this?" a deep, rumbling voice asked. Romulus remained silent. "I said, who is this?"

Romulus disconnected and threw the phone on the bed. Delilah was trembling. "Who was that?"

"No clue."

Clark checked and saw the Resident humming happily as she pumped gas. He was at the pump, directly across from her, and his task was simply to observe her until further notice. He grabbed the nearest nozzle, not bothering to see what type of gas it was, and stuck it in the tank. He checked again. Still there.

A squad of seven had been dispatched to track down and monitor the wayward Resident. They had followed the animal and the boy for over an hour now. When the duo stopped for gas, options were discussed and a plan was formed. Four would stay near the van and keep a close watch on the Resident while the other three would have a long chat with the boy.

Ethan rolled down the window. "What's she doing now?"

Clark spared a glance. "She seems to be done. Now she's just staring at the pump."

Ethan tapped his hand on the driver's wheel impatiently. Clark knew the explosion was coming and patiently waited for it. "What I don't get is why we can't hit her with a couple of tranqs and be done with it?" Ethan blurted out. "I mean, we could have been home by now and this level one crisis could be over."

"You know why," Clark said for the fifth time. "There's been a report that tranquilizers are ineffective against Athena." Secretly, Clark was thrilled at the report because it meant they were allowed real guns along with the tranq guns.

"And so we just followed her as she got farther and farther away!" Ethan spat. "It's bullshit!"

"I don't know why you're yelling at me. If I had it my way, I would put a bullet in her brain." He let out a slow breath and ached for a beer.

Ethan grumbled, "Bureaucratic bullshit."

"Excuse me," a voice said shyly.

Clark whirled around and saw the animal standing timidly behind him. *How did I let her get so close?*

"Excuse me," she repeated. "But can you help me?"

They had been spotted, but their cover remained intact. Maybe this could provide an opportunity. "Certainly, ma'am. What can I do for you?" he asked, giving her his warmest smile. They were supposed to keep tabs on her until backup arrived. But if Clark got the chance to end it early, he would.

She peered up at him with solemn grey eyes. Clark kept his smile plastered on his face, although he could feel beads of sweat appear above his eyebrow. Why was she staring at him like that? Why did she approach them. Maybe their cover was blown. In that case...

A smile broke across the Resident's face. One so full of warmth that Clark found himself smiling back without realizing what he was doing. *She's good,* Clark grudgingly admitted to himself. *Best to keep on my toes.*

The Resident pointed at the boy's car. "I'm finished pumping gas and I'm not sure what to do next," she said plaintively. "My friend left to go inside and it's asking for money."

What a dumb animal, Clark thought to himself, amused. T "You never pumped gas before?"

"I lived in an Amish community my whole life. This is my first trip to the city."

"Really?" Clark asked, entertained by the Resident's lie. "And what brings you to the city?"

"Me and my boyfriend are getting married," she responded instantly. "My family doesn't approve, so we're running away."

"Is that so?" The story was farfetched, but it wasn't the worst cover story ever created. It would help explain all the things she wouldn't be used to, and why the two were worried about people coming after them. "Well, let me take a look at it."

"I'm sure your boyfriend will be back soon," Ethan interrupted. "We're kind of busy." It was a clear message. Their job was to simply observe and not to interact with the Resident in any way.

"Don't be silly. We can't just leave the young lady, especially so close to her wedding day. It will only take me a sec. I'll be right back, and then we can go home." Ethan didn't look convinced.

"Thank you!" The Resident beamed at him. "I don't want my fiancé thinking I'm a total idiot."

"No problem. Just lead the way." She led him back to the boy's car, humming a strange but familiar tune. Once at the pumps, Clark pretended to look at the gas pump while thinking on how to take the animal down. He could use the tranq gun on his right hip, but if they were ineffective, then it would give the animal a chance to escape. He could use the pistol on his left, but then the bosses would be mad for killing such a valuable creature. Decisions, decisions.

"So what's your fiancé like?" Clark asked, stalling for time.

He heard her sigh behind him. "Oh dear, this is an embarrassment. I'm afraid I lied to you," the animal said regretfully. "He's not my fiancé."

"Is that so?" Warning bells were beginning to ring. "Who is he?"

"He's a boy I kind of kidnapped," she answered. "He doesn't know it yet, but I just recently escaped from a secret organization, and I'll bet dollars to donuts this organization is doing everything in its power to recapture me. "It's going to be a mess explaining the whole thing to him."

Clark laughed uneasily. "That sounds a little crazy, ma'am." Either the animal was stupid or his cover had been compromised. Either way, he would end this soon. His hand drifted to his left. The next time she spoke, he would act. "So, ma'am, why is this organization after you?"

"Because they think of me as little more than an animal," the animal said from behind, her voice inches away from his ear. She had covered the distance between them in a mere second. "They think I'm their property, that I belong to them. There are even those who think I'd be better off dead." Her voice was right next to his ear. "Isn't that right, Clark?"

His arm snapped to his gun, but the Resident was too fast. The animal grabbed the back of his neck and slammed his head brutally on the sharp edge of the gas pump twice. He was dead before he hit the ground.

"Poor Clark," Athena breathed as she kneeled. She reached for his holster and withdrew the dead man's pistol. "Poor stupid, insignificant Clark."

She straightened as she heard the thoughts of the people who foolishly chased her with only seven men in a Jeep that was anything but bulletproof. *"Clark! That monster!"*

The passenger door began to swivel open.

Athena fired, the first shot startling her. Thanks to telepathy, she knew how to fire a gun, but since she'd never personally experienced it, she wasn't ready for the kickback. The second shot went wild as well, but the third bullet shattered the passenger's window and continued forward to break the driver's window as well. Both passenger and driver had been ducking low, which was the only reason they survived.

"Seven people?" she asked loudly. "You thought to contain me with seven men and a pitiful Jeep?" She fired a fourth shot.

As a telepath, she knew the person in the back of the Jeep thought he was hidden because of the tinted window and planned to shoot out the window to surprise her with a hail of bullets. She was ready, but before he could try his doomed plan, the driver stopped him.

"Idiot! If you hit the fuel pump, you will explode the gas station!"

Athena frowned. What were they talking about? She dug deeper and found that a lifetime of action movies and games had passed down the lesson that a fuel tank would explode if you shot it.

"Ridiculous!" she laughed as she fired another shot, the bullet sailing through the back window and ripping through the face of the man who thought to surprise her. His mind went dark. "Exploding a gas station? How absurd!" she continued, more to herself, as the only people close enough to listen were too busy cowering.

Using her hind legs and her Resident strength, Athena jumped straight up in the air. The way the passenger had ducked down low, it would have been unlikely she could have shot and killed him without shooting through the metal door, but now in the air, she could angle the gun down and shoot at him. She fired two bullets, the first one going through his upper back, but the second one missed him entirely. Oh well, she never claimed to be a master marksmen. By the time she landed on her feet, the Jeep had squealed forward. She might have given chase, but her injured leg was throbbing in pain. It had almost completely healed, but her reckless jump had not helped. She stretched her mind and, with surprised pleasure, realized the driver had been hit with a lucky ricochet. He was bleeding out and only with luck would he make it to a hospital in time.

Athena let the Jeep drive away and turned towards the convenience store. Remus had not yet returned and even without telepathy, she could have surmised the three men who had entered the store were keeping him hostage. What to do? She could charge in, guns blazing. Or...

"Exploding gas station," she said to herself, the beginning of a smile forming on her lips.

Chapter 24

Remus' face hit the floor and though he struggled to get up, it did him little good. Out of the corner of his eye, he saw one of the men grab the cell phone.

"Who is this?" the man demanded.

Remus prayed that Romulus was smart enough not to answer. "I said, who is this?" There was a click as Romulus disconnected, and the man threw the cell phone down. He turned to where Remus was helplessly pinned. "Who was that?"

"The sex hotline," Remus panted. It was a stupid thing to say, but he was too tired and terrified to be clever. "I already paid for the full half hour. You owe me fifteen bucks.

"Get him up," the man ordered, and Remus was yanked painfully to his feet. "Remus Sylvia?"

"And what if I am?"

"Cut the crap, Remus," the lead man said, obviously unimpressed. "This isn't a movie."

Unfortunate, as Remus was running through movies in his mind as a guide . "Who are you?"

"You don't need to know my name. Not if you want to return to your normal life."

Remus swallowed. These people were nothing like Clive's group. "What do you want with me?"

Remus felt the grip of the man holding him grow loose. Not enough to break free of, but enough to convey they didn't think him an enemy. "We just want your help apprehending a dangerous criminal. A menace to our society."

"Athena?"

"Correct."

"Why? What has she done?"

The ringleader's face leaned in close. He had a long scar traveling from his chin to his hairline. His eyes were wild. The eyes of a fanatic who desperately believed in his cause. "You were there when it killed those four guys earlier, correct? You can see that, and ask what it's done?"

A vivid recall assaulted Remus. Dead bodies and unseeing eyes. So much blood. "They were going to kill me," he argued. "Athena saved my life."

The squad leader grinned at the absurdity of the statement. "And she managed to swoop down in the nick of time to save your life? That's convenient."

He had no response. The coincidence of her coming at just the right time had not escaped him.

"You've been played for a fool," the ringleader told him. "Nothing happens that Athena doesn't want to happen. It is a twisted malevolent spirit!"

"It?" You act as if she isn't human."

"That's because it isn't!" The ringleader almost screamed. "*It* is an evil creature you have crossed paths with. The death toll she's stacked up is staggering, and once it is through with you, you'll just become another of its victims."

His fear and urgency seemed so convincing. "What do you mean by creature?"

The ringleader let out a frustrated sigh. "You're not stupid, kid. You must have seen signs of it. A coldness. Perhaps its sadistic nature and lust for death. Her kind feeds on pain and misery, and if you don't believe she's a monster, you must, at the very least, believe she's a sick human being who desperately needs help."

The universe had hooked him up with a psychopath! "What do you want me to do?" Remus asked, still not convinced but seeing no other way.

"That's the spirit, kid!" the ringleader yelled, slapping him hard on the back. "With your help, there's no reason we can't apprehend her without casual—"

Three gunshots rang out from the gas pumps, followed by a short scream. Everyone in the store froze and Remus could hear the clerk attendant whimpering and praying. After a moment, there was another barrage of gunfire followed by wheels squealing on the pavement.

"What's happening?" Remus demanded.

Instead of answering, the ringleader took out a radio and

yelled, "Status report! What's going on out there?" No answer. "Respond!" The radio remained silent. "Can anyone hear me?" No answer until...

"George Hacker?" Athena asked over the radio, a note of pleasant recognition ringing in her voice. "Bless my stars, is that you?"

Chapter 25

"*I need help!*" Athena thought, as she sprayed gas all over the car, the smell becoming unbearable. There was no answer and, for a second, she was afraid her message wasn't being received.

"*I have already helped you,*" Selene thought back. "*On multiple occasions, and as of now, you have yet to repay my help to you.*"

Athena breathed a sigh of relief. Her range of telepathy was a mile, and Selene's range was a bit shorter than that. However, the one time they had moved Athena, the two telepaths realized they could reach each other from any distance. This had been tested only once, though. She continued to spray gas on the car, whistling as she did so. "*You know the favor you ask of me won't be possible until months down the road. Added to that, I'm the only one stupid enough to take on the favor, so you need me alive!*" Selene did not like being coerced and predictably lapsed into silence.

"*Last time!*" Athena promised. "*I swear!*"

"*How will I be able to aid you? You are well outside my range.*"

"*Don't worry about that!*" Athena thought grandly, stepping back and admiring her work. Gas covered the car and the immediate surrounding area. Now all she needed was a catalyst. "*For I, Athena, have a plan!*"

A very, very long mental sigh. Then, "*What do you wish of me?*"

Athena grinned in evil triumph.

George felt the old terror. He thought he had gotten over his fear of her, but it was still there, bright and burning. The scrawny redheaded kid looked fearfully at him. At least he was thinking straight. Maybe he could be used to trap it.

"Athena," he spoke over the radio. "It's been a long time. I'm surprised you remember me." He walked warily over to the entrance door, prepared to dive for cover in case Athena tried to take a couple of shots at him. The way the store and the gas pumps were situated, George didn't have a clear view of Athena or the car Remus used to drive them. He took a couple of steps back lest he make himself too much of a tempting target.

"I would never forget you, George," she exclaimed, as if they were lifelong friends. "What's it been, five years? I must confess I never thought I'd talk to you again. Not after that nasty incident with the mirror's edge."

George touched his scar. "It's a constant reminder of you, Athena."

"I'm touched."

"What happened to my men?"

"Well, three of them are dead," she said matter-of-factly. "I killed one. Took his gun and shot two more. The other one drove your van off before I could get to him. I was disappointed actually. They barely offered any type of resistance! Not very well trained, were they?"

George ignored the jibe. "Athena, it's time to come home."

"Really? That was your incredibly persuasive argument to convince me to surrender?"

"We've got the boy here," George said, glancing at Remus. "It'd be a shame if anything happened to him."

There was a moment of silence in which Remus looked horrified.

Then a giggle came floating from the radio. Athena's laughter was the stuff of nightmares; the sound was used to strike fear into enemies, and was more effective than any words would ever be. "Back to your old tricks, I see. No wonder I tried to carve up your face!"

"You're going to let this boy die for you?"

"Remus is nothing to me," Athena responded, her voice

chillingly cold. "I needed a driver and I needed to keep myself entertained. He provided both. However, I don't understand why you think me so stupid that I would surrender my newfound freedom for the sake of him."

George watched Remus' face fall. "He doesn't look too happy about it," he noted. "Athena, we will kill him."

"Of course you will. I wouldn't' expect anything else from you, George." Then Athena let out a yelp of pain.

George exchange glances with Patrick, the man holding Remus. Was Athena injured? They had found a heap of her blood at the boy's house, but was it enough to give them an advantage?

"Kid," George called out to Remus. "Is she hurt in any way?"

"Healthy as a horse," Remus said coolly. "In fact, we were thinking of running a marathon."

"This is you're last warning, no more wisecracks!"

The kid looked like he wanted to retort but thought better of it.

"Good. Now does—"

"You're not really going to kill me, right?" he blurted out with a nervous smile, as if he thought this whole setup was an elaborate prank.

"Of course not," George lied, ignoring Patrick's pained grimace. "I threatened you to try and get her to surrender peacefully. We're the good guys here."

The boy stared at him and George stared back, trying to project the aura of gruff sincerity. Over the years since Athena carved up his face, he had been part of over a dozen shadow ops and had become an expert in lying to civilians, a particularly easy task. The meek and innocent didn't want to believe there were monstrosities in the world, and thus would readily accept any lie, no matter how implausible, just so they could cling to their naïve beliefs that evil did not exist.

Remus let out a deep breath and muttered something under his breath about the universe before saying in a rather frank tone, "You're lying. You're going to kill me."

George's first reaction was to deny, but he decided against it. The boy seemed too positive. "Orders from above to kill all witnesses. Sorry, kid, nothing personal."

"You know you're the second guy today to tell me it wasn't personal before he tried to kill me," Remus mused.

"And honestly, it really doesn't make me feel any better that it's not personal. So, tell me, what is my motivation to help?"

"Beyond ensuring the capture of a mass murderer?" The reports on Remus' background had been extensive and George knew he had leverage. "What about your brother?" Remus' eyes flickered. "It'd be a real shame if unspeakable evils were to visit him."

"She was shot in the leg," Remus said woodenly. "And I think she has a cut on her left arm. That's all I know."

"Hello?" Athena's voice called over the radio. "Anyone there?"

"Just having a chat with your boyfriend. He tells me you were shot in the leg. I hope it's not too bad?"

Silence greeted the statement. "Just for that, Remus Sylvia, I shall commit the one travesty you asked me not to commit. There will be no survivors."

George barked out a laugh. "That's the Athena I know! I've missed the quotes, I really have." He grinned at an upset Remus. "She doesn't sound too happy, does she? I'm guessing she can't move around too much with that busted leg. Perhaps she's still in the car?" He laughed gleefully "We got her. You hear that, Athena? We got you!"

"You did," she said, resignation clear in her voice. "It's true, I can barely move. Certainly not enough to escape your backup, which will be here any minute." A sigh. "Then I'll be whisked away to Pandora's Box to plot my next escape."

George heard a humming in his ear. "Your next escape?"

"Of course, silly. You don't think I'm going to stop, do you? I'll go back, apologize up and down for a month or two and become the company's golden girl again. Wait a couple of years and try the escape attempt all over again."

The humming was growing louder. "You're not serious!"

"Oh, absolutely," she said cheerfully. "I fully expect that my next escape attempt will be even more spectacular, and I do hope you will be there to try and capture me. Only next time, bring more masculine men. I swear one of them screamed like a little girl when I shot him. One of them was begging, going on about his wife and children. Really, it's embarrassing!"

The humming was growing intolerable. "Damn you, Athena," he growled.

"It's like they say: a good retreat is better than a bad

stand."

George threw the radio against the wall. Everything the monster said would come to pass. She would apologize tearfully to that fool, Matthew. Matthew would be harsh at first, but then would ultimately dismiss it as an adolescent mistake. Two years later, he would be in the exact same position, hunting her down. This had to end. *He* had to end it!

"Someone looks grumpy," the boy mocked, though the tremor in his voice betrayed him.

"If I were you, I wouldn't remind anyone I was still alive," Addressing his men, he said, "We're heading out. We take the boy with us; he could be useful as a shield. Our mission is to find the target and eliminate it."

"What? That was never part of the mission," Patrick argued. "We were supposed to track and observe her movements until backup arrived."

George Hacker looked down at the smaller man. "And then what? Have her locked up again? Have her escape again? Be back doing this same dance again? She killed our people, and she will do it again! She's an animal who needs to be put down."

Rodger was nodding his agreement, but Patrick looked dubious. "Sir, think it out for a moment. She's supposed to be so injured that she can't even limp away, yet she took out three of our guys?"

George Hacker was not used to looking at thing from different angles, but what Patrick said made sense. Athena could be setting a trap for them. He looked over at the kid. "What was she talking about? The one act you asked her not to do?"

Remus shook his head. "I don't know. Really!" he protested when Patrick scoffed. "I don't know what she's talking about."

He seemed sincere, but something felt wrong. Maybe Patrick was right...

"He's overreacting, she's not that bright."

"Athena's not that bright," George sneered. "You're overreacting, Patrick, and I'm through talking about it."

"Sir, she's obviously trying to get you riled up. I can't condone this decision."

"You don't need to condone it. You don't even have to understand it. You do, however, have to follow my orders.

We're leaving and I'm giving you orders to kill her on sight. I want her dead."

Remus stumbled outside, and was immediately assaulted by the toxic smell of gas. George shoved him again, his two goons following close behind. Remus looked around, and while his car was visible, Athena was not.

"Split up," George instructed. "Patrick, you cover the back and, Rodger, you get the side. If she tries to escape, shoot her. Patrick, take the whelp with you, and if he tries to escape, shoot him as well."

Slowly, and with dedicated efficiency, they separated and circled the car, Remus being held captive with Patrick. He waited until they were out of earshot of the other two. "So, you don't seem too happy with this plan," Remus observed in a hush tone. "Killing girls just doesn't do it for you like it used to?"

"I see she's taught you well," Patrick commented. It wasn't a compliment. "I have no qualms over killing her. However, this is a stupid move. We're playing straight into her hands and my commander is too much of a fool to see it."

"You were supposed to wait until backup came. Take her in alive."

"You're scared for her safety." There was an odd note of pity in his voice that Remus didn't understand. "This means you truly have no idea what manner of creature you've allied yourself with. By the end of the night, I expect you will come to understand. Assuming you live that long."

He was garbling nonsense now. "Why would she stay in the car?" Remus asked. "She's probably long gone by now."

"If that's true than you have nothing to worry about."

"Except, of course, for my own life."

"That's not my decision."

Remus fell silent as they edged near the car. He'd been cursed by the universe with a delicate nose, and the stench of gas was enough to make him gag.

Finally, they were close enough for Patrick to peak in. "Nothing, sir."

George kicked the car in anger. "Search it. We have to

find her!"

The man named Rodger tore the door open and stuck his head in.

"What about you, kid?" George asked. "Did she say anything to you?"

"Said she was heading for Mexico."

"Don't mess with me, kid. I'm warning you."

"You hear that Remus? That's my warning to you."

The right neurons connected in Remus' brain. The smell of gas was too strong. Remus checked the ground. It was covered in gasoline, and if his super nose was correct, someone had doused the car with gas as well. Athena couldn't possibly have done all this by accident, even if it was her first time pumping gas. *"I will commit the one travesty you asked me not to do."* He had asked her not to blow up the car.

"Crap!" Remus yelled, and dove for cover just as the world burst into flames.

"I'm scared, Romulus," Delilah whimpered. She sat on the bed, hugging a pillow. "What has your brother gotten into?"

"I don't know." Romulus was angry and scared for his brother at the same time.

"Call Maris," Delilah suggested. "Maybe he'll know what to do."

Romulus hesitated. "Remus thinks Maris is trying to kill him."

"Do you?" Delilah asked, the slightest trace of disbelief in her voice.

As much as Romulus hated his father, there was no way he could imagine Maris killing his own son.

"What other options do we have?" Delilah continued reasonably. "Remus has gotten himself in a mess he can't handle and personally, I blame his low intelligence. Maris and his connections are the best chance we have of saving him. Afterwards, you and I can figure out a way to keep Remus safe."

Romulus felt his feelings for Delilah grow. Once again, she was the voice of logic and reason. "You're amazing, you know that?"

Delilah smiled, but before she could answer, the door exploded open. She screamed as three men in identical black suits came pouring in. Romulus was on his feet in a second. "Who are you?" he yelled. They weren't his father's men...too well dressed and not ugly enough.

"Romulus Sylvia?" one of them asked.

"I know who I am!" Romulus snapped. "Do you work for my father? Get your hands off her!" Romulus shouted, as one of them grabbed a terrified Delilah. He ran, determined to protect her, but was shot twice before he could get near her. Delilah screamed and was shot once.

Chapter 26

Remus felt the heat of the explosion wash over him, followed by a deafening roar that reverberated loudly and painfully within his skull. For the first few seconds, he lay on the ground unable to see. He worried the universe had taken away his eyesight, but slowly it returned; the world a foggy image sharpening into focus like a picture being developed. The first things he saw were bright orange lights, oddly mesmerizing but fearfully close. As the ringing from the explosion died down, he heard the crackling of flames and was finally able to see the charred remains of what used to be his car. "She blew up my car," he murmured, his now cracked lips causing him aggravation as he spoke. He thought he heard the sound of bullets followed by a high-pitch giggle, but he might have imagined it. Moments later, he felt hands dragging him away from the wreckage. "Let go, Athena!" he yelled, struggling vainly, only to have the grip tighten. "Leave me alone!"

"This isn't Athena," Patrick growled. A second later, he was hoisted up and slammed against the store's walls. Patrick's face hovered inches from his, blood gushing from a wound over his left eyebrow. "She's gone. Left you behind." He waited a second for Remus to digest this. "Did you know that was going to happen?"

"No!"

"Why would you dive out the way if you didn't know it was coming? You must have known!"

"No...I mean, yes...I figured it out just before it happened," Remus stammered. He struggled, but Patrick's grip was ironclad. "We have to leave before the pump explodes!"

"You didn't bother to warn anyone?" Patrick shouted, his voice cracking. "My people died in that explosion. Roasted to death just so you could save that animal! You are as bad as she is!"

"I didn't know, I didn't think!" Remus rambled. "I'm not a trained solder like you are. I just reacted. I didn't want anyone to die. I didn't want to be in this mess in the first place. Please let me go!"

Patrick hesitated, his face looking drawn and haggard. "You can't be allowed to tell anyone what happened here."

"Who would I tell?" Remus countered. "Who would believe me? Just let me go, and I swear I won't tell anyone. Please just let me go back to my life!"

Patrick's grip loosened, and Remus saw the beginning of doubt in his eyes when Athena grabbed Patrick's head from behind and snapped his neck like a twig. The whole thing took less than a second.

"Well, that was eventful," Athena remarked as Patrick slumped to the ground, an expression of horrified surprise forever etched on his face. "We should probably go. Won't take long for people to notice the fire."

Remus was too shocked by the brutality of the murder to utter a sentence. She had killed a man without a morsel of regret or remorse. *"You truly have no idea what manner of creature you allied yourself with. By the end of the night, I expect you will come to understand."* Remus now knew what Patrick meant, and he understood the depth of senseless violence Athena was capable of.

"You look a little pale," she observed worriedly. "You feeling okay?" When Remus didn't answer, she shrugged. "You're probably feeling a bit overwhelmed. Just need to sit down for a while." She turned and walked towards the road. "It's a shame what happened to your car," she called over her shoulder. "I was able to save the money and a few choice items, however. We need some new transportation and I had an idea."

Remus' fear changed into anger. She had ruined his life, and still expected him to follow her every move. She was the reason his dad wanted to kill him. She was the reason he'd ended up with pieces of brain on his shirt. She was the reason Patrick was dead. Athena was the reason his life was a mess!

"Athena!" he screamed, finding his voice and dashing towards her. She turned around, surprised, just as Remus plowed into her, knocking them both into the ground, her head bouncing on the pavement.

"This is the second time," Athena commented. If she was hurt by the fall, she didn't show it. "We're not making a habit out of this, are we?" She struggled, but Remus was securely on top of her, pinning her to the ground. "We really don't have time for this."

"Tell me why!" he demanded. "Why you killed him!"

"Because he was going to kill you," Athena stated.

"No, he was going to let me go!"

"Maybe," she allowed. "Maybe not. He was struggling with the decision, but I couldn't risk him making the wrong one and killing you before I had a chance to intercede."

"So you killed him?"

"Correct."

"How can you be so callous about it?" Remus snarled. "You took human life."

"Would it make you feel better if I cried?" she asked reasonably. "If I broke down and pleaded for forgiveness?"

"It would show me that you're at least human!"

He had crossed a boundary. Her eyes narrowed and her body tensed. "Never get tired of that one," she said softly. "You can wrestle with your conscience later. Right now we need to leave."

"No!"

She smiled thinly. "Do you really think you can keep me here against my will?"

Remus had wondered why she was being so docile. If what Patrick suggested was true, then she could easily escape from him.

There was a twinkle in her eye, and before Remus could interpret it, a heavy blow from behind sent him flying off her. "Get off her!" a voice yelled. "Where's your respect? Perverts like you make me sick!"

A stunned Remus looked up at his assailant, a heavyset Indian man who obviously thought he was doing the right thing, and of course he couldn't be blamed. He'd seen a fire at a gas station and stopped to see if he could render assistance. Then he'd spotted a female being held against her will by an angry man with specks of blood on his shirt.

"You're okay, ma'am?"

"Thank you," Athena said tearfully as she stood up on wobbly legs. "He just went crazy!"

"What happened here?" the man asked, looking at the fire with awe.

"I don't know. We saw the fire and came to check it out when he just tackled me! I was so confused! I didn't know what he was doing!"

Athena's whole demeanor had changed to play the part of the terrified victim. Her voice was higher and shook when talking. She kept on glancing around nervously, and her arms were wrapped around herself. If Remus hadn't known any better, he would've believed Athena's ploy.

"She's lying!" he croaked, trying to clear his head.

"Don't you move!"

"Listen to me. She's not who she says she is. She's—"

"Is that a Thunderbird?" Athena interrupted, determinedly staring at his car. "1986, if I'm not mistaken?"

Remus felt a chill and had to wonder if Athena would kill a man for his car. Stupid question; he knew the answer.

The man whistled, keeping a close eye on Remus as he did. "I see you know your cars. It is indeed a 1986 Thunderbird. Do you need a ride?"

"Get out of here," Remus yelled, getting up on unsteady legs. "You're going to die!"

The man turned his back on Athena to glower at Remus. "Listen, you young punk, I don't take lightly to being threatened by a—"

Whatever names he was about to say would forever remain a mystery because at that moment he fell silent. The reason was the wicked looking dagger that Athena now held to his neck.

"Just to clear things up, he was actually warning you about me. Not threatening you himself," Athena informed, dropping the helpless victim act. "Now, I'm going to need two things from you. First, your email address."

"Why do you need my email address?" he asked, bewildered. A question Remus echoed in his mind.

"You're really questioning the girl with a knife?"

"Don't kill him!" Remus ordered. "If you do, I won't drive you anywhere."

"Shut up, Remus," she ordered calmly. "Sir, you're email

address, please?" He babbled off a name and a row of numbers. "I'll remember it. Now if you will be so kind as to pass
your keys to my friend here."

"You don't want to do this," the man reasoned, obviously
under the impression that Athena would respond to reason.
"You have your whole life ahead you."

"Thank you, I appreciate the advice," she said, a slight
edge in her voice. "Now throw the keys."

The man fished in his pocket and threw the keys at Remus, who managed to catch them despite his natural klutzi-
ness. For a second, Remus thought of throwing the keys as
far as possible.

"That will make me very unhappy," Athena warned.
Something in her voice spoke of violence. "Unlock the door
and start the engine."

"No," Remus said, feeling like he was signing his own
death warrant. "I won't accompany a murderer."

"Damn it, Remus!" she hissed, more exasperated than
angry. It was the first time he'd ever heard her curse. The
first time he'd ever heard her sound frustrated rather than
mocking or angry. "Are you that blind to the reality you find
yourself in?"

"I have a problem with murder. Go figure."

"You're so quick to judge even though you don't know
what the hell you're talking about!" Athena said, fired up.
She let go of her hostage and gave him a push. "Go," she
instructed.

Without another word, the man ran towards the street as
Remus stared nonplussed. "Why did you do that?"

"Because I'm not the person you think I am. I'm not a
senseless killer. Every action I did was required. Justified!" It
almost seem like Athena was trying to convince herself. "Are
you willing to die for a misconception?"

"You're threatening me?"

"No, idiot!" Athena snapped, and Remus realized how ag-
itated she really was. "The police are coming. I can hear the
sirens."

"I don't hear anything."

"You're going to have to trust me on this one. We have
less than three minutes to escape before we get arrested."

"And if we do?"

"I will be captured and you will be killed," Athena said

flatly. "And that's if you're lucky. If you're unlucky, if they stop to think about it, you'll be tortured first to see if you're holding back any information."

Remus had no reason to doubt her claim. From what he'd seen, these people were vicious, and Patrick had already said he knew too much to be allowed to live. Only, he didn't know anything, and the only way to get the information was through the blond girl with the crazy grey eyes standing before him.

"There are two rules," he told her. "Rule number one: If I say it's over, we're done. We leave and go our separate ways."

Athena nodded eagerly. "Done."

"Rule number two: You tell me everything. Complete honesty. I want to know what you are and who's chasing you."

"Fine!" Athena cried desperately, and even Remus could hear the faint sound of sirens. "Can we go?"

They left thirty seconds before the police showed up.

Chapter 27

Dr. Pluck was tired, his plush body unaccustomed to physical strain and abuse. After the tranquilizer Athena had shot in him wore off, he had groggily but dutifully returned to Pandora's Box, where he had been placed in handcuffs on sight and dragged down the hallways as if he was one of the Residents. In a room too small for one inhabitant, three of Pandora's interrogators assaulted him with impossible questions for the better part of an hour. Words like "traitor" and "murderer" were tossed around with unnerving frequency, and there were a few offshoot suggestions of allowing the Residents to have their way with him. They even went so far as to suggest a relationship between him and Athena, and by the end, Dr. Pluck was quite nervous about his future. They left the room, taking the chairs with them so that Dr. Pluck was forced to crouch in a corner, and that's where he remained, gloomily wishing he had lobotomized Athena when he'd had the chance. After what seemed like hours, the door swung open and Tyrone Froce walked in.

Froce was the second-in-command, right under Caleb, and Dr. Pluck had been trying for years to get the man promoted. In the Marines for nine years, Froce didn't have the aura of a military man, but of a thinking one. Soft spoken by nature, Froce always wore a thoughtful expression on his face, as if working out some puzzle he could only see. Far more likeable than Caleb, Froce held the respect of most of the employees at Pandora's Box and Dr. Pluck thought he would do a better job of running operations. It also helped that Froce and Caleb had a deep-seated animosity towards each other, though no one seemed to know how and when it originated.

"Tyrone, thank goodness," Dr. Pluck said, relieved. "You've got to get me out of here!"

"Stand up," Froce commanded, his rumbling voice echoing within the small confinement, and sounding strangely hollow.

Dr. Pluck blinked before slowly getting to his feet, his knees creaking loudly in the process. "Tyrone, what's going on? They have been absolutely horrible to me; insubordination doesn't even begin to cover it! When this is all done, there will be a great deal of terminations going around, I tell you that much."

"I've been ordered to take you to the head administrator's office," Froce explained, ignoring the majority of his rant.

"You mean my office?"

"Your former office," Froce corrected. "Please extend both of your arms." Froce produced handcuffs.

"Is that necessary?" Dr. Pluck asked, rubbing his wrists. "I chafe easily."

"This is your one and only warning. If you resist again, I have permission to use force."

Dr. Pluck stared, shocked. He and Froce had always gotten along splendidly, bonded by a mutual hatred of Caleb. "I wasn't resisting! I was simply asking a question!"

"Sir..."

"Okay, okay. I suppose we all must follow orders."

Dr. Pluck offered up his hands. Froce cuffed him, and while Dr. Pluck was deeply resentful of how he was being treated, he did notice Froce didn't tighten the handcuffs too much, allowing for plenty of movement without unnecessary discomfort. It was a small peace offering, but one that Dr. Pluck eagerly accepted. Froce led him out the room and into the hallway where two more guards were waiting. Dr. Pluck paused to look back at the dinky interrogation room, too small to put janitorial supplies in, and promised to have it boarded up if he survived this ordeal.

Tyrone cleared his voice. "Sir..."

"Yes, yes, I'm quite eager to get going myself." With Tyrone in front and the other two guards behind him as if they actually thought he would make an escape attempt, they walked Dr. Pluck down the hallway, past the rooms of over a dozen Residents. He could feel their cold, maniacal eyes following his process.

"Thank goodness you got me out of there, Tyrone." He tried again to make conversation. "I didn't think I would last the whole night."

"There are a lot of people who thought you should stay in that room for a couple more days," Froce retorted, his voice not disrespectful but definitely not friendly. "It was Mr. Titanos who gave the order to release you, because the situation has become dire and he believes you have the answers we need."

"I've already told you, I don't have any answers and what do you mean the situation has become dire?" Dr. Pluck asked, confused.

Tyrone paused, probably wondering how much he should tell him. "A scout team was dispatched to keep tabs on Athena and her movements. Fifteen minutes ago, the team was obliterated. Only two men survived and one of them isn't expected to make it to sunrise."

"That's horrible!" Dr. Pluck exclaimed, trying to show the right amount of emotion. In truth, he cared little if some stupid flunky was careless enough to get himself killed. However, men like Froce took losses like this personally and Dr. Pluck wanted to appear sympathetic.

"Added to the man Athena killed in her room, that makes six. Six men's deaths on Athena's and her helper's shoulders."

"Her helper?" Dr. Pluck repeated.

Tyrone remained silent, but shot him a look full of implicated meanings.

"Surely, I'm not a suspect?"

"No, sir," a guard behind him snickered. "You're not a suspect. You're the prime suspect. I heard that after the head honchos see you, they're sending you straight to Lamia's room for her evening meal."

"That's enough, Delmon!" Tyrone said sharply. The guard instantly quieted down, but the damage was already done. Just imagining Lamia's teeth ripping into his skin was enough to vacate Dr. Pluck's brain of all rational thought.

"But I had nothing to do with this!" Dr. Pluck sputtered, close to tears. "Tyrone, surely you must know this is some elaborate plot to frame me. If there's a traitor here, I bet it's Caleb!"

"Sir, I believe all your thoughts on the subject should be discussed with Mr. Titanos, not with us."

Dr. Pluck fell silent. Tyrone was right; he would accomplish nothing from talking to well-paid lackeys. He had to talk to Matthew Titanos and force the playboy to listen to reason.

They arrived, and Dr. Pluck was pushed inside by Delmon, who instantly went to the top of his list for termination. He stumbled, catching himself just before he would have fallen, and found the room already occupied. Mr. Titanos sat at his former desk, which made him despise the man even more. Beside him was a gorgeous woman who was busily typing on a laptop. Off to the side sat Caleb, lost in his own thoughts, and Mr. Burlington wasn't far away, looking deeply confused. Tyrone Froce closed the door behind him, making him the final occupant in the room, and Dr. Pluck was surprised he was allowed to attend this meeting.

"Good evening, Dr. Pluck," Matthew Titanos greeted with a rather grim smile. "I trust Mr. Froce here has already informed you of our current situation?"

"Yes, he has. And let me say, I deeply regret the loss of those men."

Caleb snorted derisively from the side.

"I believe you're sorry," Mr. Titanos said, shooting Caleb a warning glance. "I believe you regret your actions; you wouldn't be the first one she's tricked." He lowered his head in what was supposed to be a gesture of humility before glancing up at Dr. Pluck. "What I need you to do now is tell us where she's heading and what she plans to do."

"I told you, I don't know!" Dr. Pluck cried. As he was yelling, he fully digested Matthew's barely disguised implication and grew even angrier. "You think I willingly helped her? I was her hostage, you idiot!"

"Dr. Pluck, calm down," Mr. Titanos ordered, both Caleb and Tyrone shifting closer to him.

"I went over all this already!"

"Yes, you have," Mr. Titanos said, a ghost of his old arrogant smile on his lips. "Ms. Yang, will you please repeat Dr. Pluck's story?"

The women straightened up and adjusted her black-rimmed glasses. "At around three-twenty, Athena infiltrated this office and, under the guise of a guard, shot Dr. Ahab Pluck's bodyguard, a Mr. James Anderson, three times with a tranquilizer gun she had acquired. So far, this story can be collaborated with James Anderson. Shortly after that, she forced Dr. Pluck, under pain of death, to walk her out of Pandora's Box. It should be noted that several employees saw Dr. Pluck leave with a blond guard who never seemed to look up. It should also be noted that all witnesses swear Dr. Pluck never made any attempts to warn or signify in any way that he was in danger."

"Because she was going to kill me!" Dr. Pluck interrupted.

"In that case, you should have died like a man!" Froce interrupted, making his position clear that he was no friend of his. "Now, because of you, five good men are dead."

"That's enough!" Mr. Titanos snapped. "Ms. Yang, if you will continue."

Ms. Yang acted as if she hadn't been interrupted. "Around the time of three-thirty, Dr. Pluck used the verification code to access the gates. This can be verified by a Mycheal Lawyer and a Payton McKay. Again, no sign or hint of distress. According to Dr. Pluck, he was then forced to drive two miles down the road where she exited the vehicle and collected a knife."

"It was a dagger," Dr. Pluck interrupted.

"A dagger," Ms. Yang amended, though her voice carried traces of resentment at being corrected. "Athena then proceeded to remove the tracker chip in her arm."

"How did she know where the chip was?" Caleb asked.

Ms. Yang checked her notes. "According to Dr. Pluck, Athena used some form of telepathy to rip the answers away from his mind," she said with a straight face.

Not a smile could be seen, though Caleb looked to be struggling. Ms. Yang glanced up once, and then continued. "Blood splatter analysis of Dr. Pluck's car concludes that Athena did, in fact, cut herself. After the incident, Dr. Pluck was compelled to drive Athena to the mall. Upon arrival, Athena shot Dr. Pluck twice with the same tranquilizer gun she used on Mr. Anderson. Puncture wounds on his chest corroborate his statement. He awoke several hours later and instantly made his way here," Ms. Yang concluded.

Everyone was silent for a moment as her words sank in, Dr. Pluck being the first to speak. "You have to believe me, everything I said was true."

"Bullshit!" Froce exploded, finally abandoning his neutral

demeanor. Dr. Pluck lost a bit of respect for Froce. Just because a few of his colleagues died did not give him the right to act out, as death was one of the hazards of the job, and Pandora's Box made sure all of their employees knew this. "You're saying she's been telepathic this whole time and no one noticed?"

"If he's a liar, he's not a bright one," Caleb pointed out. "Why come up with something so unbelievable?"

Froce deftly switched targets, focusing his energy on Caleb. "So you're saying you believe she's psychic?"

"I'm saying Athena is a smart lass and she loves to pretend. She might have made him believe she was psychic."

"Why are you defending him?" It was a good question. "You can't stand the doctor."

"No, I can't, but I'm pretty sure she couldn't either. It makes no sense that they were plotting together." Then, fixing Froce in a scrutinizing glare, he said, "Why are you so quick to condemn him?"

Froce fell silent and Matthew spoke up. "If Dr. Pluck didn't help Athena, then who did? Someone had to have set the bombs up and, if we can believe what Dr. Pluck said, someone left that dagger for her."

"Don't forget someone gave her the location of the tracker, and only a few people knew about that," Froce piped up, glancing at Dr. Pluck. It was clear he hadn't given up on the subject. "Unless you're buying that she's psychic."

"Psychic," Matthew repeated with a troubled frown. "When I was talking to her, it seemed like she would frequently answer my thoughts. But I just..." His voice trailed off. "I mean she's perceptive. It might not have been anything."

Dr. Pluck would not let this lifeline slip through his fingers. "Is it really that implausible?" he asked, taking it as a good sign that no one told him to shut up. "She was always operating one step ahead of us, and come to think of it... Caleb, did you tell her about Mr. Titanos?"

A dangerous move, relying on a much-hated adversary. Caleb scratched his beard. "She and I don't chat unless I'm asking real nicely for her to behave."

"Then how did she even know about you?" Dr. Pluck addressed Matthew.

"She knew because you told her," Froce interrupted.

Ms. Yang coughed. It was clearly a practiced cough, showing just the right amount of respect without being too submissive. "There are recorded accounts of Residents displaying the gift of telepathy. It's a rare ability, but not an impossible one."

Dr. Pluck wondered how this secretary came by this information, but protecting his life was first priority and he nodded vigorously. "You see? It's true!"

"And she hid it all this time?" Froce snorted. He looked around incredulously, as if baffled everyone was accepting this theory. "Even if she is psychic, it still wouldn't explain the explosions or the note she left behind." Caleb grunted in what could have been reluctant agreement and Mr. Titanos nodded sagely as if Tyrone had just made a profound statement.

"What note?" Dr. Pluck asked, realizing events had taken a turn for the worst but not knowing why.

"The note Athena left you just before her escape," Froce answered, his deep baritone resonating with triumph.

"She never left me a note!"

"It was on the back of a crossword puzzle we found in your trashcan," Matthew intervened. "It thanked you for all you did and said to make sure your escape route was still viable."

In a flashback, Dr. Pluck recalled Athena wadding up a piece of paper and tossing it in his waste basket. "That bitch," he whispered.

Chapter 28

Athena couldn't take her eyes off the night sky. It was so beautiful, so illuminating, the stars twinkling and winking at her as if they held some enigmatic secret and were daring her to try and seek it out. Surely it wasn't this beautiful every night. If so, how could the human race ever get anything accomplished? People would work all day, stare at the sky all night, and never have any time for sleep. No matter how her venture ended, she would not, could not, regret escaping, for it was worth it just to look up at the night sky, even if it was just this once. But yet...there were pressing worrisome matters that must be addressed.

Remus coughed, trying to get her attention, but Athena ignored him. She had given up trying to read his thoughts, as he was constantly at war with himself, always questioning and analyzing everything he and others did. It made him an interesting person to talk to, but also made her weary trying to read his mind. He was hesitating, not yet having gathered the courage to address her, and she took the time to think.

They had found her. They had located her position and had been following them for the last two hours. She had allowed it because she had hoped to find out how they were tracking her...all she knew was that a Ms. Yang had given them instructions over the phone, but she did not know how Ms. Yang had discovered her. She would have waited another hour, but the car needing gas had foiled her strategy. Now she was back to square one, not knowing how they had located her. Another bug? No, she had asked Dr. Pluck and his logic made sense. Why waste two trackers on an unimportant Resident? Maybe it wasn't on her end. Maybe they'd

tracked Remus through his car. Or perhaps they had a Resident who had the ability to locate people. There was another possibility of—

"So, who were those men chasing you?" Remus finally asked, an unwelcome interruption to her musing.

"I don't know."

The car squealed to a stop, sending a surprised Athena crashing into the dashboard.

"Ouch!"

"Seatbelt," Remus advised.

"That wasn't funny!" Truth be told, Athena would have found it hilarious if it wasn't for the new bump on her noggin. She'd pulled a variation of the same trick earlier with Dr. Pluck.

"Wasn't meant to be. You told me you would answer all my questions honestly." Remus had found his courage. It was unfortunate timing. "They definitely knew you and you even reminisced with one."

He was talking about Hacker. "George was just a regular guard when I met him. What he is now is beyond me."

"You said he was a guard. What did he guard?"

Cars were honking behind them and she raised an eyebrow. "You might want to go."

"You might want to answer my question," he countered, and Athena had to admire his spirit. No one ever questioned her except for the other Residents, and a good chunk of them wanted to kill her. It was refreshing to find a capable soul that wasn't too afraid to speak his mind.

"They guarded Pandora's Box," she answered. Remus moved the car forward and the honking behind them subsided.

"What's Pandora's Box?"

"In Greek mythology, it was a box Pandora was given to guard."

The car lurched to a stop once again, and was followed by the expected noise of cars beeping their displeasure.

"Cut that out!"

"Then answer my question!"

"Pandora's Box is a facility designed to keep people like me away from society."

The car started back up again and she went back to watching the night sky.

"So it was designed to protect regular people."

"I never said that," Athena said crossly. "Of course, that's what Pandora's Box would have you believe. In reality, it protected the founders and workers of Pandora's Box. If the public knew what types of experiments were being performed, they wouldn't stand for it. At least that's what Mr. Burlington says."

"Mr. Burlington?"

"One of the guards of Pandora's Box. I quite liked him."

"So the people at this facility do experiments on you? And that's how...that's why you are what you are?"

"And what do you think I am?" she said, extending her mind so she could hear the truth he was too tactful to say.

A killer.

She laughed bitterly. "Again, it's easy to throw stones from your high moral ground."

"I didn't say anything!" A short silence then, "You do that a lot. Seem to read my mind."

"It's a gift," she said, staring at the moon. "It's so bright."

"What's so bright?"

"The moon. It's so bright!"

A pause. Remus was scheming something, but Athena was too distracted and too tired to care. "How long has Pandora's Box been around?"

"A long time. They have Residents who've been there for forty years or more."

"Residents?"

"The proper term for people like us," she explained with more patience than she felt. She'd never had a conversation with someone who didn't already know the basics. For that matter, she hadn't really had a normal conversation for a while, preferring to speak in quotes or talking with Selene telepathically. It would take a while to develop proper social skills. "Don't ask me where the name came from; even I don't know."

"What can Residents like you do?"

"All kinds of things," she said vaguely, bracing herself in case he decided to stop the car again.

"Like completely healing from gunshot wounds they got only hours earlier?" he asked snidely, staring hard for her reaction.

He was observant and Athena made a note of it. "How long have you known?"

"Ever since the gas station. You were active enough to scare off a vanload of maniacal gunmen, pour a ton of gasoline on my poor car, may she rest in peace, and ignite the gas for a big fiery explosion, despite a big chunk of your leg being shot off." He paused as a question occurred to him, one Athena hoped he wouldn't ask. "How did you ignite the gas?"

"A little knowledge is a dangerous thing. So is a lot," Athena quoted.

"You promised…"

"I promised to be upfront with you about everything, and I will," she interrupted. "However, some knowledge you can't come back from. Ask me again and I will tell you, but you won't like the answer, nor will you be better off with the information."

Remus was silent, the raging war within his head so loud and irritating Athena was forced to tune him out and return to her own questions that needed to be answered. How did Pandora's Box find her? She'd destroyed their implanted tracer and had secretly stolen and discarded Remus' phone when he wasn't looking.

She dived into his mind, ignoring the background noise of his big moral dilemma, and discovered the only contact he had made was with his brother after Hacker's team had already caught up with them. Furthermore, she was positive George Hacker had been fired years ago, and she didn't recognize any of the other people on his team. Perhaps…

"Why did you lie about not knowing the guards?"

"I didn't," she responded, spotting a plane flying above them. She had never seen a plane before. Just looking at something that big fly was breathtaking. "The only one I knew was George Hacker. One would initially assume that the other guards were from Pandora's Box, but that makes no sense. The people back there were too afraid of me."

"What do you mean?"

"Most Residents at Pandora's Box refuse to reveal any but a small amount of their skills," Athena explained. Unlike before, when she found his probing questions annoying, she now wanted to answer them, for it was helpful to bounce ideas and theories off a perceptive mind. "As a result, Pandora's Box's expectations are much lower than they should be. If we're able to wrestle a grown man to the ground, they're happy. They don't realize that some of us can take on a dozen grown men all hyped up on steroids."

"Can you?"

"Not important," she said, neatly evading the question. "The point is, those men knew the full extent of what I might be capable of. They knew tranquilizers wouldn't work on me, and the fact that they wanted to kill me was troubling to say the least."

"That's not enough evidence. Perhaps Pandora's Box simply knows more than you think."

"Maybe," she allowed. "But add the fact that I didn't recognize any of them...and I make it a point to know everyone who walks through Pandora's Box. Plus, I'm positive George Hacker was fired a long time ago."

"So who do you think it is?"

Athena thought about it a moment. "There's a rumor," she began, ready to give voice to a theory she had long since held, "that if a Resident does ever show any...unique...abilities, then they are taken to another facility. A facility equipped to handle their special talents."

"So you think these guards came from this facility?"

"I think if it did exist, they would be more than capable of dealing with my..."

"Ability to read minds?"

Athena snapped out of her daze and turned to stare at Remus. For the first time, she realized the last half of their conversation he hadn't actually been speaking. Remus had been sending her his thoughts in an effort to prove or disprove her telepathy. She had been so focused on the night sky and her own musings that she failed to recognize what he was doing. He had tricked her. Despite her brilliance and her ability to read minds, he had pulled one over on her. She had been tired and preoccupied, but still...

"Oh Remus, you're going to be so much fun," she commented happily.

Chapter 29

Tyrone Froce was probably the second most respected person at Pandora's Box, the first being Caleb. He'd grown up in a poor neighborhood and had vowed to leave as soon as possible. Joining the army at 18, he quickly rose through the ranks as one of the most skilled shooters and combatants the military had ever seen. He was destined for great things until one mistake ruined his career.

"Mr. Froce?"

He snapped out of his daze at Mr. Titanos' mention of his name. "Sir?"

"Caleb asked if that was all the evidence you had against Dr. Pluck."

"Isn't it enough?"

"Not nearly," Caleb growled. "Frankly, I'm surprised. By the way you talked, I reckoned you had something better than a piece of scrap with some writing on it."

Froce geared up for a fight. It seemed like they butted heads on every single issue, and Froce harbored deep suspicions that Caleb was secretly a bigot. "A piece of scrap confirming that Athena and Dr. Pluck made contact. What more do you want?"

"Some actual proof! You don't think a gal as smart as Athena could forge a note to make it look like the doc was guilty?"

"And why would she do that?"

"To throw off suspicion, probably so the real culprit could get off free," Caleb said, staring hard at Froce.

"It does make a certain amount of sense," Mr. Titanos mused. He glanced almost nervously at Froce. "You did say you found the note inside his waste basket? Seems like an odd place to put incriminating evidence."

Froce realized his persistence was actually putting him under scrutiny. He struggled to think of a counterargument. "So you're convinced of Dr. Pluck's innocence solely on Athena's hatred for him?"

"She would never work with this scoundrel," Caleb confirmed. Dr. Pluck looked like he wanted to argue, but realized Caleb, a man he personally despised, was the only one advocating for him. "Athena had too much pride, and besides, she wanted the man dead."

"Then why didn't she kill him? She had a prime opportunity in his car, but instead, shot him with tranquilizers. Not the actions of a girl obsessed with his death."

For the first time in history, Froce saw Caleb at a loss of words. "That is a good point," Caleb grudgingly admitted, and Froce felt a brief sense of victory.

"We move on and return to this issue later," Mr. Titanos interrupted, killing the argument. "I'm curious to know how she managed to prevent most of the staff from showing up."

Out the corner of his eye, Froce saw Chris fidget. Chris Burlington had been with Pandora's Box for three years and there were no red flags in his work history...except for his friendliness with Athena.

"Something you would like to share?" Froce asked.

Chris glanced up with puzzlement, but his confusion wasn't aimed at Froce. "I don't..." He trailed off. "I don't remember."

"Don't remember what?" Caleb snapped.

"If I knew that, then I would remember," Chris snipped, very close to insubordination. He tapped his head as if he could somehow jar the memory loose. "I think something happened on the way back from the mall, but..."

"But?" Caleb prompted impatiently.

"But...I don't remember."

Caleb looked ready to explode, but Froce held up a hand and was pleasantly surprised when Caleb fell silent, even though he still glared at Chris with unbridled suspicion. Froce had a theory; an impossible silly theory, but one that would explain most of the miracles around Athena's escape.

"Has anyone checked with those who didn't come in?" he asked.

"I did," Ms. Yang announced, her eyes glued to her laptop. It must have been a riveting game of solitaire.

"How many?"

Ms. Yang stopped typing, her gaze lifting up to meet Froce. "All of them," she announced, as if the answer was obvious.

Froce blinked. It had been well over a hundred people who hadn't shown up. When did she have the time to contact them all?

"A few claimed they forgot it was their day to work," Ms. Yang continued. "However, the vast majority of the employees claimed Edward Gantz called them and told them there was a scheduling mishap and that they wouldn't be needed."

"Has anyone seen Edward since?" Froce asked.

"I haven't been able to locate him." By Ms. Yang's remorseful tone, it was clear she saw this as a personal failure. "I tried his home, cell, and emergency contacts. No one has seen him since yesterday."

"So, Edward is the traitor," Dr. Pluck concluded, clearly trying to deflect suspicion.

Caleb snorted at the obvious attempt. "I'll rustle up some men to check out Edward's home."

Froce nodded, but wasn't quite finished, though he hesitated to say his theory out loud. "*If,*" he began, emphasizing the word. "If we believe she can read thoughts, then is it possible she can send thoughts as well. Control people?" The room grew silent, though not with the air of disbelief Froce had been expecting. "It would explain how she managed to get the bombs in without anyone knowing. And how so many people didn't feel like showing up today along with Chris' memory problems."

"Yes!" Dr. Pluck piped up. "And how she made me leave Pandora's Box with her."

Dr. Pluck's flimsy justification immediately had Froce wanting to take back his theory.

Mr. Titanos was looking expectantly at his secretary, who continued to look at her screen. "Ms. Yang?" he finally asked.

"Yes, it's entirely possible," she answered even as she continued to type. "There have been many documented cases of Residents having mind control abilities. Some can manipulate feelings and emotions, and others can literally control one's actions."

Another brief silence and Caleb narrowed his eyes. "I don't appreciate being kept in the dark like this. I ain't never heard anything about no mind control!" He glanced at Froce who quickly nodded his agreement. It was strange to think that only a crisis could make the two get along.

"Because you weren't cleared to know," she said the same way one would say, *"Because I said so."*

"Like hell we're not cleared! If we're risking our lives, we deserve to know the whole picture."

"Six men died trying to recapture her!" Froce said, picking up from Caleb. "Did they know what they were getting into?"

Caleb frowned. "Come to think of it, who the hell ordered the attack?" He glanced at Froce, who shook his head.

Dr. Yang's expression didn't change, though her typing did become louder as she began to slam each key with unnecessary force. "The attack was ordered by Mr. Titanos, the senior."

"My father," Mr. Titanos, the junior, translated wearily.

Caleb still looked disgruntled. "How the hell did you find her? I thought she removed the bug in her arm."

"That information is classified."

"Classified!" Caleb repeated incredulously.

Ms. Yang, with a suffering sigh, closed her laptop to give Caleb her full attention.

"This ain't the time for jokes. You have means of tracking down Athena and you don't feel like sharing? Why the hell not?"

"It's classified," Ms. Yang repeated, much like how a teacher would repeat to a particularly slow student. "Which means I am not allowed to go into any details."

Froce took a step forward. "Are you people so worried about keeping your secrets that you're willing to let innocent lives be destroyed? Athena is smart and she's adapting fast. If we don't work together, she'll disappear forever. Do you want one of your precious secrets running amok, doing god-knows-what?"

"Thank you, Mr. Froce," Ms. Yang interrupted politely. "Your complaint has been noted. Rest assured, we will do everything in our power to capture Athena and see that justice is done for the people she's murdered. In the meantime, please continue with *your* duties instead of worrying about ours. Let's not forget, if you were doing your job to begin with, we wouldn't currently be in this situation."

"Passive aggressive," Caleb muttered. He had reached a wall, but like any good tactician, he decided to take an easier path to victory. He stared hard at Mr. Titanos. "And what about you, sir?" The "sir" was said with a slight sneer. "Is this your decision as well?"

Mr. Titanos sighed heavily, and for a split second, Froce sympathized with the man. Out of the five other people in the room, two were becoming more belligerent by the second. Another two were under heavy suspicion of being a traitor, and the last one was calling the shots.

"Is there any way my fath...Mr. Titanos...can be persuaded to be a tad more cooperative?"

Ms. Yang opened her laptop and studied the screen. "Mr. Titanos found your theory on Athena's mind control to be a valid concern. He's sending a specialist in to investigate. You will be kept in the loop."

"Specialist?" Caleb growled, still very much discontented.

"It will do," Mr. Titanos said grandly, as if satisfied with the way things were going. "Moving on." It was clear he was desperately trying to regain control. "What about the boy accompanying her?"

"His name is Remus Sylvia, age seventeen," Ms. Yang stated. "Lives with his dad and twin brother."

"The mother?"

"Unknown. Currently trying to find her now."

Mr. Titanos frowned. "With all our resources, we can't pinpoint the whereabouts of an ordinary woman?"

"I will dedicate more resources into finding her," Ms. Yang promised. "We do have the brother and his girlfriend in lockdown. The father has managed to elude us."

Mr. Titanos nodded. "I guess we better talk to them."

Chapter 30

Romulus felt his heart quicken as she neared him, her footsteps echoing unnaturally loud. Sweat began to pour down his face as he started to shake uncontrollably.

"Oh, dear Romulus, I thought you would be braver than that," she mocked.

"You killed my brother!" he screamed. He tried to scramble back, but found he could not move.

"I did," the blond agreed affably, her head cocked to one side. "His death was an exquisite one!" She looked at him, her grey eyes alive with great anticipation. "I hope your death is just as enjoyable." She reached out and started to shake him.

"Get off me!" he yelled, terrified. "Get off me!"

"Wake up!"

Romulus awoke, still screaming, and found himself in a small room decorated only with a bed and toilet. Still panting heavily, he struggled to sit up. He wiped the sweat from his brow and studied his bearings.

"You okay?" Delilah asked. "You were screaming for five minutes."

Romulus wiped the remaining sweat off his face. "Where are we?"

"Do you remember anything that happened?"

Romulus struggled to access his memory, but his head was still foggy. "Some men broke in," he remembered. "And...and they shot us!"

"With tranquilizers. They obviously didn't want us dead."

"Why?"

A shrug. "I woke up fifteen minutes ago. Banged on the

door, screamed until my voice grew hoarse. No answer."

"My father must be behind this!"

"Doubt it. If it was you're father, we would know by now. He's very egotistical like that."

Delilah was different. Instead of pouting and whining in her usual manner, she was acting practical, even efficient. Wasting not a breath on useless words or emotions.

"Can you stand?" she asked, standing back to give him room to try. Romulus got to his feet and fought off a wave of dizziness. "You're okay?"

"Yeah." It was a minor lie. Romulus sat back down, shaking his head to fight off the drowsiness.

"They kidnapped us in broad daylight," Delilah murmured, and Romulus wasn't sure if she was talking to herself or him. "A bold move, and they're obviously not scared of Maris. This must have something to do with your brother and that girl."

"Think she's some type of escaped convict?"

"No, Romulus, I do not," she said, acting like he was an idiot. "They do not shoot people with tranquilizers simply because their brother ran off with an escaped convict. If I had to guess, I'd say we stumbled upon something bigger."

"Like what?"

"Like your brother's plan to take over Maris' organization."

Before Romulus could object, their attention was diverted as the door creaked open and a man dressed as a cowboy, followed by a tall black man, walked in. Romulus instantly had thought of attacking.

"Wouldn't recommend it, boy," the cowboy advised, his Texan accent matching his wardrobe. "I reckon the tranqs haven't fully worn off, and you don't want to go upsetting my partner here."

"Who are you?" Romulus demanded.

"Name's Caleb, and the man standing beside me is Tyrone Froce. People just call him Froce."

"Why'd you kidnap us?" Romulus asked, studying the two. The cowboy looked like he had once been in shape, but had since given in to the temptation of food. A tad on the beefy side, he supported a ridiculous bushy mustache that Romulus half-suspected was fake, a cowboy hat that would have looked silly in an old western movie, and a pair of dark sunglasses that had Romulus wondering how he could possibly see in the dimly lit room.

"Calm down and lower your voices. It's about one-thirty in the morning. People are trying to sleep."

"There are other prisoners here?"

"You answer our questions, not the other way around," Froce said. Tall and athletic, he wore an intelligent expression that Romulus had seen many times, usually on the faces of his father's thugs when they were pretending to be clever and sophisticated.

"And why should I?"

Caleb took out some pictures from his back pocket. "I reckon you'd want to look at these."

Romulus glared suspiciously, but stepped forward. Caleb made no move as Romulus snatched the pictures. He took one glance and felt like throwing up. The first picture showed a man with half his face blown off. He shuffled pictures, hoping for a better sight, but was severely disappointed. The second one showed a man on the floor with his skull caved in. The third man had his throat slit.

"Those are pictures of your house," Delilah said from behind, standing on tiptoes so she could see.

"My house," Romulus said, sickened. "This is my house?"

"Yes, sir," Caleb answered. "And I reckon you know who the killer is."

"The blond?"

"Her name is Athena," Froce said, perfectly in tune with his partner. "Say, Caleb, what do you imagine she'll do once she gets tired of Remus?"

Caleb scratched his stubby beard, deep in thought. "I reckon she'll kill him. And not a regular death. She's known to get bored easily, so I reckon it's going to be a truly horrible, torturous death. Something to keep her entertained."

"Who," Delilah began, but then corrected herself. "What is she?"

"Something that never should have been allowed to live." Caleb answered. "And we need your help to track her down before she kills again."

"I don't know anything," Romulus protested. "I only saw her once."

"You know your brother. Any answers you might have will be extremely beneficial."

Romulus weighed his choices. "And who exactly are you people?"

"Son, you ought to know better than to ask questions like that."

"Once we answer your questions..."

"You're free to go," Caleb promised. "I'll personally guarantee it."

"Fine, but Delilah doesn't leave my sight."

"A man protecting his girl," Caleb said knowingly. "I can respect that." He cracked his knuckles. "Shall we begin?"

Chapter 31

Remus woke up startled as Athena pounded at the door. He rolled down the window. "Did you get the room?"

She grinned widely and held up a key. After fifteen minutes of trying to hide his thoughts from her, Athena had suggested they get a room for tonight. That brought another wave of unwanted thoughts, all of which he was sure Athena had caught. Did she have to have telepathy? Why was the universe so cruel?

"Don't bring up the universe crap again," Athena scolded firmly. She had made no pretense to try and hide her ability ever since he'd figured it out. The opposite, she took every opportunity to tease him for any random thought he might have. Partial payback for tricking her.

"I don't tease you that much."

"For the last time, stay out of my head!"

She laughed gently, and Remus was struck with how beautiful she was.

"That's sweet of you. Now hurry up."

Together they walked into the grungy-looking motel, past two hookers who were openly rubbing against one guy. "You two should join the party," the guy called out to them and Athena paused, looking thoughtful, but Remus quickly dragged her away.

"I wasn't going to accept," she protested in the elevator, her face turning a pretty shade of pink.

"Of course not," Remus said complacently.

"I wasn't!"

"I believe you."

Their room was a one-bedroom suite that consisted of

only the bare necessities—a kitchen, a TV, and one lamp in the corner. Overall, not the worst place he'd ever stayed in.

"This is heaven to me," she said, spinning around gleefully. "I've never had so much room to frolic around in!"

"Frolic? People don't frolic anymore."

"So, what do people do?"

"They hang out. They watch movies, play games. People haven't frolicked in years."

"Sounds like fun. I haven't watched a movie since I was eight." With a squeal, she jumped on the bed. "This bed is so bouncy! Isn't this bed bouncy?"

"The absolute bounciest," he agreed. She had opened the door to her childhood and Remus had every intention of stepping through. "Your last movie was when you were eight?"

"It is difficult to speak to the belly, because it has no ears," she said, stretching lazily on the bed.

She was speaking in quotes again. "What?"

Athena raised her head. "They that die by famine, die by inches."

"Come again?"

"Hunger is sharper than the sword," she clarified with exasperation.

Comprehension dawned on Remus. "You're hungry?"

Now that she mentioned it, Remus realized he was as well. He had skipped breakfast, in a hurry to leave before Maris woke up, and he'd spent lunch arguing with Romulus. What time was it anyway?

"It's about one-thirty in the morning. You haven't had anything to eat this whole day?"

"I really wish you'd stay out of my thoughts. It makes conversation a bit one-sided."

"Doesn't have to be. There are ways to hide your thoughts. Protect them from invasion."

This was a very appealing idea, but Athena mentioned it too nonchalantly for there not to be a catch. "How?" he asked with folded arms

With a sigh, she rolled over so she was lying on her stomach. "I'm not completely sure of the process."

In the back of Remus' mind, he realized she was trying to be as honest as possible.

"I don't know if your mind innately gets the ability as a form of adaption or if you physically...or I should say mentally...train yourself on how to produce a mental barrier." Remus was confused and Athena hurried to explain. "A human who I consider to be my friend and who knows of my telepathy eventually gained the ability to block me out."

"How many times have you tested this out?"

"Only once," Athena said with enough reluctance for Remus to know she didn't want to admit the answer. "But I know of other humans who have the same mental blockade and can only assume they went through the same process of staying near a telepath until the mental blockade forms."

He mulled it over. Talking to Athena was like trying to figure out several riddles at once, and he tried to solve them one at a time. What did he know? Athena had promised she would be completely honest with him and he believed she would keep her word, so all the information she had stated was true. She had brought up the mental barrier on her own, which meant she wanted to talk about it. She had given him a ridiculous amount of information on the topic, and that meant...she was nervous? Or perhaps she had hidden something in her answers? Either way, it pointed to something she wanted to talk about but was hesitant to approach.

Athena laughed, and Remus realized with chagrin that he had been silent for the last three minutes and that Athena had been listening to his mental musings. Instead of ridiculing him, she cocked her head to the side, an action she was fond of doing, and simply said, "You're extraordinary."

"I..." Remus felt his face flush and, in the moment of his embarrassment, an answer came to him. "How much time would it take with a telepath for this mental barrier to form?"

Athena didn't blink when she answered, giving no indication as to whether he was right or wrong. "It took my friend a little over two years. Of course, without more data, I can't say if it will take you more or less time to produce the same effect."

There it was. She was asking about his long-term plans. Did this mean...? Remus felt a moment of panic. Was she asking him to stay with her? For a long-term period of time?

"It was just a suggestion," she snapped at him as she read his reaction. "Do you always have to overthink everything?"

"When are you going to answer the rest of my questions?" he asked bluntly, ignoring her barbed insults. There was no way to trick a telepath into revealing information.

She laughed. "Of course! Remus with his ever thirsting lust for knowledge has to know more about the experiment! Has to analyze every aspect of it. Has to see what makes it tick."

"What's your problem?" She was quickly growing nasty.

"I am not!" she said petulantly. Then, apparently realizing how childish she sounded, she took a deep breath and smiled. "Sorry. Hunger might be making me grumpy."

"I doubt there will be anything open this late. We could look for a McDonalds...Athena?"

She didn't answer. Her eyes were closed and she seemed caught in a trancelike state.

Remus waved a hand over her face and poked her gently—no reaction. He did the only thing he could do...he sat down and waited.

Delilah hated playing the part of helpless damsel. She had struggled too hard to make herself strong. Sacrificed everything for the idea of power, and, as a result, she had a permanent scar that only a few people could see.

Romulus had spent twenty minutes recounting the events of the past day, with Caleb and Froce interrupting to ask about every single insignificant detail. It was so painstakingly slow that at times she wanted to scream. She managed to keep her mask on, however, and answered every question that came her way with a vague answer or a confused look. Finally, the ordeal was over.

"Thank you for your time," Caleb said getting up. "We'll be back."

"You said you would let us go," Romulus protested, sounding like the naïve dork he was.

"And we will, son. We're just going to go have a chat with our superiors and we'll be back to take you both home."

Caleb nodded at Froce and they both left. Delilah heard the distinct click as the door locked.

"We'll be okay," Romulus promised her, though he was really trying to reassure himself.

Delilah fought her first instinct to tell him to stop being an idiot. "Really?" she asked, wide-eyed. "Are you sure?"

"I am. Once they confirm we know nothing, they'll take us back. It's the way these things work."

"Well, that's a relief!" Delilah exclaimed, giving a convincing shudder. "Those men were scaring me."

"We'll be okay." The idiot was starting to repeat himself. "I just hope they find my brother before it's too late."

"Why?" she asked, and Romulus gave her a sharp look.

"He's my brother, my flesh and blood. I don't want that psycho to kill him."

She'd had enough. Standing up, she walked over to Romulus, placing her hands on both sides of his head. "Romulus," she said as gently as she was capable of. "Your brother left you to die."

Romulus jerked away from her. "Remus would never..."

"Never what?" Delilah asked. "Never plot against your father? Never watch while this girl killed four men?"

"He's obviously a prisoner of hers."

"Funny how he didn't ask for help when he called," she shot back. "Funny how he just so happened to give twenty thousand to this girl...on accident."

Romulus scratched his head. "Did I tell you how much was in the envelope?"

Oops! Delilah kept her calm and injected a note of impatience into her voice. "You had to or else how would I have known?" She waited until he nodded, the light of suspicion fading from his eyes. "It's quite a coincidence. Your brother giving her the money." It was so dreadfully obvious. Romulus couldn't be that dense, yet he looked confused. "I'm saying he paid off that lunatic to attack your house!" she all but screamed.

"I know what you're saying," Romulus responded. Delilah knew she had overstepped by the way he looked at her, and she felt a tingle of nervousness run up her spine. "But I'm still confused because I thought you knew Remus. He wouldn't leave people dead in his wake and he wouldn't team up with a killer."

Time to backtrack. "I'm sorry, you're right," she whispered, working up some tears. "I'm just so afraid for you. What happens if they think you're involved?"

Romulus' face relaxed. He stood up and embraced her. "I'll be fine and so will you. We'll be back home in no time, and I'll take you to the most expensive restaurant in town."

Delilah sniffed and tried not to cringe at his touch. "I believe you. And I hope Remus is okay." Remus, the only person who had ever seen past her mask. The only person who saw her for the ugliness that she was. She hoped Remus died a very slow and painful death.

Chapter 32

Athena awoke with a cough, startling Remus, who had dozed off in a chair. "How long was I out?" she asked, her voice hoarse.

Remus didn't have a watch, and so he had to take a guess. "Maybe ten minutes."

She nodded.

"If I ask what you were doing, will you tell me or will you dance around the issue?"

A playful smile. She was back to her default mischievousness. "Only way to know for sure is to ask."

"Athena, what were you doing?"

She teased him by remaining silent as she scooted to the edge of the bed so that her feet were touching the ground. "If I concentrate, I can extend my telepathy to about a mile. Of course, the downside is my physical body is defenseless." She looked up, blood dripping from her nose. "You could have escaped or even killed me, and I would have been helpless to stop it."

Remus did his best to keep his mind blank. "Your nose is dripping."

"You're learning," she noted with a grin. She used her sleeve to wipe the blood. "There's a grocery store still open about a block away. Manager's kind of a dick, but you shouldn't have any problems."

It took Remus a second to get it. "You did all that just to get a bite to eat?" For some reason, the notion was funny.

Athena looked affronted. "I told you I was hungry!"

"And you couldn't find a Burger King?"

"A Burger what?"

He thought about explaining, but dropped it as it wasn't worth the effort. "Okay, there's a grocery store. What about it?"

Athena tossed an envelope to him. "Twenty thousand minus the cost of the room. Take the Thunderbird."

The envelope suddenly became extremely heavy in Remus' hands, the air of ease they had briefly shared vanishing instantly. Athena was giving him the money and the keys to the car. An oversight? No, more likely a test or another mind game.

"You're overthinking again," Athena scolded.

"What am I supposed to think? You willingly give me the means to escape and I'm not supposed to think trap? What do you expect me to do, Athena?"

She stretched back on the bed. "The way I see it, you have two choices. The first choice is you can take the money and run for it. The second choice is you can go, bring back something to eat, and we can talk things over."

"So what am I going to do?" Remus asked. "You're psychic; you should already know the answer."

"I'm telepathic, not psychic," Athena corrected. She closed her eyes. "I read minds, not the future, and I have no clue what you're going to do because you don't even know. I can see the conflict. The agonizing choices as you weigh the pros and cons. Escape will get you away from me and all the evils I might inflict on you. On the other hand, leaving means no answers. You have no grasp of your situation and that's eating at you. Not only because you would never quench your insatiable curiosity, but also because not knowing can get you killed. Those men could come after you. Your brother could be in danger even as we speak."

"Shut up!" he snapped, shaken to the core. He felt naked, almost exposed. In the duration of two minutes, she'd managed to make him feel small and insignificant...just like his father.

Athena opened her eyes and sat up with a jerk. "Remus... I'm so sorry." And she did look remorseful. "I didn't mean to dive that deep."

Remus couldn't trust himself to speak. He took a deep breath, and another one. Athena waited patiently, legs crossed. Finally, he found his voice. "Once we eat, no, *during* the meal, I want to know everything. No more half-truth, no more mind games. I have to know. I have a right to know."

"You do," she agreed quickly. She was trying to make up for her intrusion. "You have every right to know exactly what type of game I've put you in."

"You think this is a game?"

Athena smiled, but her eyes were looking elsewhere. "Get some food. I'll be here waiting."

"Let them go," Caleb growled. The day had been shit since the moment he'd woken up, and now he was about to be made a liar. "I promised them they'd be released once they answered our questions."

"And that should teach you not to make promises you can't keep," Eris Yang answered. She had been gradually taking control over the situation ever since the beginning, and now it seemed she was abandoning all pretenses. "They stay exactly where they are until this situation is resolved. Mr. Titanos' orders."

Caleb glanced at Mr. Titanos, the junior, hoping the man would grow a pair. "I'm assuming she means your father and not you?"

Mr. Titanos shrugged his helplessness. "What do you want me to do, Caleb? Do you think I like this situation any more than you?"

When Caleb had first met Mr. Titanos, he had been confident and cocky. Now he looked like a sulky kid who'd just gotten his favorite toy confiscated.

"What my dad says goes."

"It's funny how your secretary has more contact with your dad then you do." Caleb glanced at Froce to make sure he was still with him. They'd never gotten along before, but a common goal had united them as temporary allies.

"Best leave him alone," Froce advised snidely. "He has to listen to what his *daddy* says."

Caleb nodded approvingly. When in doubt, one should always revert back to fifth-grade tactics.

Mr. Titanos looked like he was about to snap, but restrained himself. He turned to Ms. Yang. "When do you expect this situation to be resolved?"

"According to the timetable...three hours."

"And how the hell you know where she is?" Caleb demanded.

"You are not permitted to know that," Ms. Yang answered, almost before he had finished his question.

He snorted. "With you people, it's all about preserving your precious secrets. You don't care a damn about the perils your precious projects and experiments put people in. I refuse to take one more order from a mamma's boy and a cold-hearted bitch!"

Caleb's temper was legendary. It was said that even the Residents quaked with fear when Caleb lost it, but Ms. Yang didn't bat an eye. "For a man quick to make accusations, you're awfully slow to point the finger in your direction."

"And what the hell does that mean?"

"You accuse almost everyone of being in cahoots with Athena, yet you ignore the fact that you knew her the longest, and she even considered you to be her friend."

Caleb shut his mouth, stunned. He hadn't expected this move. Mr. Titanos was casting suspicious looks his way. Froce, to his credit, wasn't about to condemn his new ally, but Caleb knew he had to be considering Ms. Yang's words.

"I'll assume your temporary lapse of control was due to the stress caused by Athena's escape. In the future, please refrain from raising your voice."

"You talked about a specialist," Froce said, for once throwing Caleb a lifeline. "Are we permitted to know that?"

Ms. Yang looked at her notes. "Brandon Badger. He's the leader of a squad that specializes in recuperation of assets. Over a dozen operations without any casualties, civilian or otherwise."

"Brandon Badger," Caleb repeated, deciding he didn't like the name. Seemed like the type of fake name a child would come up with to sound dangerous. "What's his record like?"

Ms. Yang sighed. "Despite evidence to the contrary, I'm choosing to believe you're not a stupid man. You should know that information is not permitted to you."

"You said over a dozen operations," Froce intervened, before Caleb and Ms. Yang could get into it again. "Recuperation of assets, which I assume means recapturing Residents...but I never heard of other Residents escaping."

"Mr. Titanos, the senior, has his interests diversified to

ensure protection." It was a nice way of saying the boss didn't trust them not to spill the beans to the media. Caleb growled, but kept his silence, as it was clear Froce was having a better rapport with Ms. Yang than he was.

"Is there a plan to capture Athena alive?" Froce fired off. "How are they going ensure no one else gets caught in the crossfire, and that the media won't get wind of this?"

Ms. Yang gave a tolerant sigh. "You're being melodramatic. This will not be a superhero battle with guns blazing and grenades exploding. The group will find Athena, collect her, and return her to our other facility with none the wiser."

"Awfully confident," Caleb couldn't resist saying. "She managed to outsmart us."

"That doesn't necessarily speak to Athena's intelligence." She didn't say it spoke to their competence, but then again, she didn't need to. "Mr. Titanos looked at all the variables before dispatching Brandon's squad. They will succeed."

"And we won't see Athena again?"

"No. But I will tell you once she is captured." It was the only concession they would get. Ms. Yang's cell phone rang, the melody of an old disco song, *"Burn Baby Burn."* It seemed uncharacteristic of the stiff woman, and Caleb and Froce exchanged looks. "I really can't miss this call," she said, glancing at the screen. "And I doubt we have anything more to talk about. Please continue your investigation into her escape, so we can make sure another unpleasant incident like this never arises."

"Bitch," Caleb muttered as Ms. Yang walked away.

Chapter 33

Athena did another mind sweep. No suspicious markers and no indication that they had been found. It did nothing to put her at ease. Her enemies had found her once and it would be foolish to think they wouldn't find her again. She should have a few hours before the next attack, so she chose the time to test Remus, as there might not be another opportunity.

She reached out and found his mind. He was in the grocery store, still struggling with indecision. She wasn't lying when she told him she didn't know what he would do, and the chance that he might not return was making her anxious. She had handled the whole thing wrong. She should have been more considerate and less snappish, but had been pissed off by his immediately incredulous reaction to the thought of him staying with her. Given how things had ended, maybe she should have waited before sending him out alone.

"No," Athena commented, reverting back to the old habit of talking to herself. "I can't watch him twenty-four hours, and even if I could, an involuntary partner is more useless than not having anyone at all. Events are escalating quicker than I imagined, and I need to gain a sense of how likely he is to abandon me. But maybe I could have..."

"You are being foolish."

Athena winced as Selene's voice vibrated in her head. *"Keep it down! Sheesh!"*

"You stop to rest as if you are safe. You take unnecessary risks without thought of consequences. At the pace you are setting, you will soon die and thus be unable to fulfill your

promise to me."

Athena was touched. Selene was actually worried about her. *"First off, thank you for the assist with old George back there."*

"You are aware that my natural range extends only a little bit farther than yours. Even with the use of your energy, and depleting most of my strength, I was only able to implant a subconscious thought. Nothing more."

"Of course. You do sound a bit ill. How badly did the process drain you?"

"Why are you wasting precious time with these pointless questions?" Selene thought.

Athena's smile became a thoughtful frown. Something had gone wrong. Even if Selene was worried about her, she would never act upon it unless...

"What's going on at Pandora's Box?"

"That is an appropriate question," Selene approved. *"Events have played out as you predicted. They are too busy trying to figure out who your mole is, and because of that, their search for you is somewhat hindered."*

"Well gosh darn it, Selene, I'm a bit confuddled! That sounds like good news!"

"Ragnarok is involved."

Athena's breath caught in her throat. *"Crap!"*

"You didn't know?"

"I suspected, but none of Hacker's crew was thinking about where their paycheck came from and I didn't think to rummage around in their minds. How did they find me?"

"I don't know, and I'm not willing to put my mind in jeopardy to find out. There's a Resident here masquerading as a human."

Athena was growing impatient. *"Yes, we both already know that! An agent of Avalon!"*

"No. This one belongs to Ragnarok. She is playing the role of a secretary. She's like me, Athena. She knows the uselessness of emotions."

"Swell, start a club. Can you get inside her mind?"

For someone who practiced the art of no emotion, Selene's answer was shockingly ferocious. *"No! I told you, I will not risk myself for you again!"* Selene took a second to calm down. *"I was in her mind and she saw me, Athena. She knew I was there. Because of you, I have felt fear again."* Selene went on to say, "*Interfering with your fight was an error on my part. I do not know why you are clinging to that boy; I do not know why you are resting when you should be running, but I do not care enough about your wellbeing to jeopardize my own. You will receive no more assistance from me.*"

Athena felt Selene sever their connection, the same way one would slam a phone down. She did another mind sweep, still nothing. Though a bit more cantankerous than usual, Selene had, nonetheless, made some decent points. She needed to come up with escape routes if—no, when Ragnarok found her again.

She was just about to work on that very topic when a phenomenon outside cleared all other thoughts from her head.

Remus picked up the tomato sauce and threw it in the cart, for the fifth time asking himself why he was shopping for his kidnapper. Romulus would say he was being stupid. Maris would call him an idiot, and unfortunately, he would have to agree with both.

"*And once it is through with you, you'll just become another one of its victims.*" George's voice rang in his mind. His advice would have had a lot more weight if George hadn't been planning on killing Remus himself. But then, "*Remus is nothing to me,*" Athena had sneered. "*I needed a driver and I needed to keep myself entertained. Remus provided both.*" She would say it was all an act, but damn if she didn't sound convincing.

He picked up a case of orange soda and started looking for the meatballs. He was going to cook spaghetti. He only now realized the fact that he had been subconsciously gathering the ingredients to cook for his kidnapper as well. Not even a strong case of Stockholm syndrome could explain his actions.

In a haze, he picked up the rest of the ingredients and made it to the front of the store. Because it was near the end of closing, only one lane was opened and manned by an elderly lady who had long ago lost the dexterity to scan and bag groceries in a speedy manner. She had on a nametag that said "Sheryll" in big, bold letters with a smiley face on the end. Remus remembered Athena saying the manager was somewhat of a dick, and he had to agree, as the thin, balding man was behind a counter, texting on his phone instead of helping the lady with the quickly growing line.

"Beg your pardon," a voice said politely.

Remus looked around to see a woman vying to get his attention. Standing beside her was a small girl who was playing with two toy snakes. Though it was unlikely an attack would come in this form, recent events had made him paranoid and he surveyed them with a great amount of suspicion.

The woman coughed. "Pardon me, but I happen to be in a bit of a rush and I only have these three items." She held up her hands showing a loaf of bread, a box of sugary cereal, and a pack of cookies. "So I was rather hoping..."

A line cutter. He doubted the woman was really in a rush, but he also couldn't muster up the energy to care and he shrugged his indifference.

"Thanks," the woman gushed, and Remus caught traces of a faint British accent. A few people behind him grumbled their discontent, but they would get over it. Or they would have...

"Oh dear!" the woman exclaimed, emptying the entirety of her purse onto the conveyor belt. "I'm terribly sorry, but I do seem to have left my money in my room. This is dreadfully embarrassing." The discontent behind Remus was growing to mutiny levels and had attracted the manager, who was strolling over with an expression of wintry disapproval.

"I got it," Remus offered, taking out the envelope and selecting a hundred dollar bill. He doubted Athena would have a problem with this, and even if she did, the money wasn't hers to begin with. "I'm paying for mine and hers at the same time," he told the cashier, but had to repeat himself, as she didn't hear him the first time.

"Well, aren't you a polite chap." The British woman beamed.

Remus smiled politely just as the manager reached them. "Is there a problem?" he asked, far too loudly with hands on his hips.

Remus nodded. "Yep," he admitted. "My good friend, Sheryll, is dealing with a long line. Could you help her with the groceries?"

The manager sniffed, turning towards the cashier. "I told you if you can't keep up—"

"She's doing a fine job," Remus intervened. "There are a lot of customers and she just got overwhelmed."

"That's not my job," the man exclaimed, trying to stare him down. Just hours ago, Remus had stared into the eyes of hardened mercenaries wanting to kill him. A pompous manager didn't even rank.

"Okay," Remus said with a shrug. "In that case, move so I can do it." He didn't think his words were particularly inspirational or funny, but as soon as he said it, he heard a guffaw of laughter behind him followed by the clapping of approval, which quickly grew into a thunderous roar. The manager glared at him with gritted teeth. Athena would have a laugh if he was to get thrown out. Then the manager's eyes hit the floor and he sidled up next to the station to help bag groceries. He pointedly didn't look at Remus afterwards, which was fine, as Remus was already uncomfortable with the attention he was getting.

The British woman and her child left, and Remus was right behind them, though by the time he made it out the doors, they were gone and it was raining furiously. The universe was back to its old tricks. He was drenched by the time he got to the car and seriously considered driving in the other direction. Unless Athena had super speed, there was no way she would catch up to him before he escaped her mile radius.

Remus put the car in gear and headed for the hotel. He needed to know the answers...to protect himself and to protect his brother.

He parked the Thunderbird and stared at the sight in front of him. Athena was standing at the front of the hotel. At first Remus thought she was waiting for him, until he realized she was looking straight up at the sky. *This ought to be interesting.*

He approached her, groceries in arms. "Athena?" he called tentatively. "You okay?"

"Isn't it beautiful?" she breathed, not looking in his direction. "The most astounding sight you've ever seen?"

"The rain?" he asked, stopping just out of arm's reach.

"Tiny droplets of water falling from the atmosphere. Why do they fall?" Remus was just about to break out in a lecture about condensation and moisture in the air when Athena cut him off. "I'm not looking for a scientific reason, Remus. Quit ruining my magic."

So far, she had been too enthralled with the raindrops to even look at him. Remus didn't want to temper her mood, but still... "It's just rain, Athena. It's common."

"Their fall is so beautiful, their descent more magical than anything I've ever seen," she said dreamily. "Anyone who says sunshine brings happiness has never danced in the rain."

Remus recognized a quote when he heard one. "Who said that?"

"I did, just a moment ago. I am not without my own creativity."

Remus, feeling like he had accidently insulted her, struggled for something to say, but Athena beat him to the punch.

"You came back," she observed, still not looking at him.

"Did you know I would?"

"Not at all. I hoped you would, prayed you would, but I didn't know. Why did you come back?"

"I want to say it's for my brother..."

"But?" she pried.

The groceries started to slip from his arms and Remus had to readjust them. They really must have looked stupid to bypassers. "I'm...not sure. I don't really know what to think." As he watched, a frown formed on her lips, and he had the feeling he had said the wrong thing once again. "We should really get out of the rain, the food is getting soaked."

"Can you honestly look at the rain and not feel happy?" Athena asked, her tone mournful. "What is wrong with humans that they can ignore such beauty, or worse, consider this phenomenon an inconvenience instead of the magical miracle it is?"

Remus caught the implication that she didn't consider herself human.

"Remus—"

"If you don't want to hear my editorialization then you can stay out of my head," Remus pointed out before she could voice her complaint. She fell silent, and he watched her face, witnessing the wild happiness that showed through, uncaring of whoever saw it. Raindrops bounced off her skin and she looked to be in eternal bliss. Like a little kid on

Christmas, and Remus felt something move within him.

Finally, she looked at him, "Am I really just a mystery to you?"

The blunt question caught him off guard. "No," he answered, the truth surprising him. "You're not."

"Do you think of me as a monster?"

"I don't know what to think of you, Athena. You're so guarded, and it feels like a war trying to get information from you."

Athena nodded, accepting the fact.

Do you think of me as expendable?"

"I said that to save your life," Athena explained, reading his mind and knowing what incident he meant. "George would have killed you just to spite me. Pretending you meant nothing was the only way to protect you."

Her words rang true and Remus had thought as much already. "Come on. I'm hungry."

Chapter 34

"I'm hungry!" Delilah complained, her voice amplifying and echoing in the small room.

"How can you possibly be hungry at a time like this?" Romulus asked, more out of curiosity than judgment, but Delilah saw it as an unforgivable offense and she placed hands on her hips as she glared at him.

"I've been kidnapped and held in a small damp room. I'll be hungry if I want to!"

Really, there was no rational counter argument, and besides, he much preferred a whiney Delilah to the cold-hearted women who had earlier wanted to condemn his brother to death. Since their conversation about Remus, Delilah had reverted back to the sweet, snobby girl he had grown to love.

"We should be getting out any moment now."

"You said that a half hour ago!"

Had it only been a half hour? It felt like so much longer, time moving incredibly slow as they both waited to find out if they would live or die. The door creaked open before he had time to think of something reassuring to say, Caleb blocking out the doorway. Romulus jumped to his feet, positioning himself in front of Delilah.

"It's about time," Delilah whined indignantly from behind him. "We've been waiting for hours!"

Caleb grunted something that might have been an apology, and Romulus noticed how he made no moves to draw closer, but doubted very much he intimidated the older man. "How you two doing?"

Why he thought they would want to exchange pleasantries was beyond Romulus. "When will we be released?" he demanded. Caleb didn't speak, which was answer enough. "You said you would let us go," Romulus hissed, now understanding why Caleb stayed out of arm's reach. If he was closer, Romulus would have slugged him. "You gave me your word!"

Caleb nodded. "Yep, sure did."

"And so...you're admitting you're a liar," Delilah ventured, blinking innocently when Caleb glared at her.

"It ain't gonna be much longer. No more than two hours or so I was told."

Romulus opened his mouth to demand to be released, but a sharp pain in the back of his leg stalled him.

"As long as it's not going to be much longer," Delilah said haughtily, acting as if she believed the deceitful soldier. "But you are going to feed us, right?

Caleb looked lost. "Considering your predicament, I didn't figure you to be starving."

Romulus felt rather than saw Delilah puff up behind him. "I've been kidnapped and held in a damp room! I will be hungry if I damn well please!"

If their lives hadn't been at stake, Romulus might have smiled as she used the exact same argument against him as she was now using on Caleb, and the cowboy wannabe was already holding his hands up in a gesture of complacency and surrender. "Fine, fine. I'll see if I can rustle you up something in the kitchen."

"Least you can do!" Delilah quipped to his retreating back, the door sliding closed with a metallic *click* as Caleb exited.

Delilah waited until Caleb was gone before sliding her arms around Romulus' waist and leaning in as if to give him a kiss.

"It will be o—" Romulus started.

"Shut up," she said harshly, her whisper a tingle on his ear. "And don't give us away. They might be watching." Romulus couldn't possibly give them away as he was too shocked to react. "They're keeping us alive in case we can give them Remus," she continued. "After that, they're going to kill us. We need to come up with a plan before that happens."

Froce watched Caleb stomp towards him looking like an angry grizzly bear. "How'd they take it?"

"How would you take it if you found out you're spending another couple of hours as prisoners?" Caleb retorted. He took a deep breath, which actually seemed to help his disposition. "Can we get them something to eat?"

"They're hungry?" Froce asked, very much surprised. Caleb glared at him. "I'll call the kitchen and see if they can scramble up some sandwiches."

Caleb grunted an acknowledgement as he walked past and Froce had to rush to keep in step with him. "So what do we do now?"

"I reckon we do the same thing we been doing since Athena decided to walk out the front door. Figure out how the hell that girl escaped!"

"Isn't that a moot point if she has mind control power?"

"I reckon it is, but I don't know what else to do!" Caleb cried, frustrated. "I should have gotten out of this business a long time ago. I'm no longer cut out for it, not like you young whippersnappers."

Froce sniggered. "Excuse me, sir, but did you just say the word whippersnapper? Maybe you should think of retiring."

"Shut up," Caleb said, instantly changing his tune. "I'll still be out capturing Residents long after you're in the grave."

Froce made a great presentation of shaking his head in disgust, but was secretly relieved that Caleb had snapped out of his funk. He might not love the guy, but Caleb represented the best chance of capturing Athena with minimal casualties.

"You want to go over the report again?"

Caleb took the report from Froce and quickly flipped through it. "There's something that has been weighing on my mind."

"What is it?"

"Athena had one visitor before she escaped."

"Nick Hensley. We already spoke with him. He claims Athena didn't tell him anything."

"You believe him?"

Froce snorted. "He's a snake, even amongst this crowd. I

checked with some of his colleagues and some of them say Athena was looking out for him...protecting him against other Residents."

"Interesting," Caleb mused. "Either she was being nice, and I've never known Athena to play nice without a reason, or..."

"Or she had a reason for keeping him safe," Froce supplied.

"Where is he now?"

"Close by. The night has been so hectic that I haven't had the chance to question him further. I could get him and..." Froce stopped talking when he realized Caleb was staring at him. "Problem?"

"Look at us, getting along," Caleb huffed. "Almost enough to make me sick."

"Okay." Froce stopped, Caleb stopping with him. "What is your problem with me? You're bigoted?"

"Bigoted!" Caleb said a tad too loudly, attracting attention. "What do you mean?"

"It means you dislike or are prejudiced against—"

"I know what it means!" Caleb interrupted. "And I'll have you know I'm mightily offended. My best man and godfather to my children is black." Caleb paused. "Well, he used to be."

Froce was confused. "Used to be black?"

"No, idiot! Used to be godfather. When my first wife and I got divorced, she told me he was no longer welcome as godfather." Caleb held up a hand. "And furthermore, my second wife of two months was Latino!"

"Only two months? What happened?"

"She became crazy. Hate that one...but not because of her race," he hurried to say. "Because she threw a knife at me." Caleb scratched his beard. "In truth, I thought you hated me."

"I only hated you because I thought you hated me!" Froce objected.

They stared at each other a moment longer. "Damn those mind-controlling Residents," Caleb said solemnly, and Froce laughed before falling into another uncomfortable silence. Finally, Caleb coughed awkwardly. "Put your lazy butt in gear and get Nick in an interrogation room. If you pay attention, you might just learn something."

Chapter 35

"That smells heavenly." For the last 45 minutes, Athena had been on the balcony, observing the rain fall, but the smell of pasta had lured her to the kitchen.

Remus did a quick check on the sauce. "It's about ready, you mind setting the table?"

Athena looked uncertainly at the table. "Yes...set it. Um...so that's when you..."

She wasn't joking. She truly didn't know what setting the table meant. Just like she didn't know what an escalator was or how to pump gas. Remus pictured himself setting the table and wondered if she would pick up on it.

"Got it," Athena said brightly. She started opening up cabinets in her hunt for utensils.

"So you see images in a person's mind as well?"

"No questions until dinner," Athena admonished. "That was our deal."

"And you plan to answer *every* question?"

Athena hesitated, and Remus got the sinking feeling she was trying to think of a way out. "I am not!" she protested. "I just think the deal should be modified...for fairness."

"I cook you dinner, you answer questions."

"But how do I find out about you?" she protested.

"You read minds!"

"Only surface thoughts. I don't know what your favorite colors are or your favorite movie." Her eyes grew big as Remus placed the bowl of steaming spaghetti in the center of the table. "That looks good."

Remus sat down. "What does knowing my favorite color have to do with anything?"

Athena shrugged. "It might not matter, but it would make me more comfortable." Her smile was thin. "You assaulting me with questions while trying to figure out what makes me tick does not sound like a fun night."

It was hard to believe Athena didn't have a hidden agenda, but he couldn't see what harm would come from answering her inquiries. After all, his life had been tragic but relatively uneventful up to this point so it wasn't like he had anything to hide. "Deal. You answer my questions, I'll answer yours."

Athena's smile was considerably brighter. "Awesome, and by the way, when can we eat?"

"Help yourself." With blinding speed, Athena grabbed the pot and started shoveling a very generous helping on to her plate. "Save some for me!" he yelped when it appeared she might take the whole pot. Athena finished and Remus helped himself to a smaller portion. "Do you always eat this much?"

"Is that your first question?" she teased. She took a bite and her eyes grew even bigger, seeming to take up her whole face. "That has got to be the best food I ever tasted! This is exquisite, the use of spices, magnificent. A work of art! A masterpiece!"

Remus felt his cheeks redden. Except for Delilah years ago, when they were on speaking terms, no one had ever complimented his food in such a way. Romulus never seemed interested and Maris would only scoff at it. "Thanks, so now the questions?" Athena was too busy stuffing her mouth to answer, so she waved a hand in compliance. Who'd taught her manners?

"Is that you're first question?"

"No, and thought questions don't count." He took a breath. "The idea of the government performing experiments to make the next super solider is too...cliché. Anyone who read a decent comic book could have thought of that."

She had stopped eating and stared with open curiosity. "Is there a question in there?"

"Right now, just an observation. You purposefully simplified your initial explanation to make it seem like an idea from a comic book."

"Still haven't heard a question."

"What did you leave out?"

Athena chewed on a meatball, deep in thought. "To be

honest, that question is vague, but I'll cut you a break, seeing how this pasta is the epitome of happiness." She leaned back in her chair. "To start, I never told you Pandora's Box was government owned. From what I understand, it goes through great pains to stay hidden from the government."

"Then how—" Remus began.

"You asked a question and I'm answering it," she said with sharp edge. "Shut up until I'm finished."

Remus fell silent, feeling like a scolded puppy.

"Now about Residents... My summary of them was correct. They are human beings with the potential to mutate or evolve, depending on how you look at it. What I left out is that twenty percent of the world's population is at least a Class One Resident."

"Twenty percent? That's insane!" he yelled, standing up. "People would notice."

"No they wouldn't," she said, sounding irked. "Sit down so I can explain."

Remus took a seat, feeling a tad embarrassed for overreacting.

"All Class One means is the potential is there. Sometimes they have minor abilities. Maybe their eyesight is a little better, or they can memorize whole songs just by listening to them once, but nothing above that. Now a Class Two Resident is what I'm classified as. Class Two is the positive verification of abilities. In my case, my strength improves along with my speed and reflexes. Not to mention these." She pointed at her unique shade of grey eyes.

"And your mind reading."

She shook her head. "No, only a handful of Residents and one other human knows about my telepathy. I also hid how strong and fast I really am, so I guess I could be classified as a Class Three Resident, which is basically a stronger Class Two."

Remus' head was spinning from all this new information. He took a bite of his spaghetti and discovered it was, indeed, quite good. Athena was being too forthcoming with the information. There was something there that she didn't want him to ask, so she was bogging him down with other information.

"Overthinking every little thing," Athena sighed, but the way she said it made it seem like a compliment.

"What am I missing?"

Athena shook her head vigorously, causing her blond hair to wave. "Uh-uh. I more than answered your question. My turn."

So that was the game. Keep him occupied so he wouldn't stumble upon the big secret. Fine. He'd play and win. "Go ahead."

She took another bite and sighed blissfully. "Where did you learn to cook like this?"

Remus blinked. Not what he was expecting. "My mom left...died...when we were young and my dad couldn't be bothered with us. For the first six years, we lived off pretzels and doughnuts. I happened to stumble across this cook book and things went from there. I did all the cooking, and it frustrated my dad so much he actually spent money on a maid so I would stop. I still cooked in secret, though. It was my passion, and it relaxed me when things got too tense."

"Is that the reason you cooked tonight?"

Remus thought it over. "Most likely."

Athena looked at her empty plate and reached for the pot. "Your go."

"What's a list of all your powers?" he instantly asked. It would be helpful to know exactly what she was capable of.

She winced as if he said something politically incorrect. "The preferred term is capabilities. Powers makes people think of red capes and fighting evil." She tapped her fork on the plate. "Like I said, augmented strength and speed along with quicker reflexes and telepathy. Slightly better hearing, but my eyesight is slightly worse than the average human being. My memory is better than most, and I have the unique ability to sense other Residents as long as they're in my vicinity." She stopped and Remus got the feeling she was leading up to something. "I can also generate a small charge."

"Generate a small charge?" he asked dubiously. "And what does that mean?"

Without another word, she extended her hand, palm facing towards him. Electricity jumped from her thumb to her pinky and Remus jerked back, banging his knee on the table. "Holy crap!"

"Calm down," Athena scolded with a smile. She held the charge for a couple seconds, probably so he would know he wasn't imagining it, before closing her hand. "You're in no danger of being electrocuted. I can only manage a small jolt, but it does have its uses."

It dawned on him. "The fire at the gas station...that's how you caused it?"

"Yep." Athena had finished her second portion and was eyeing the pot. Remus wasn't finished with his first, but quickly gave himself another helping in an effort to make sure he had enough to eat. So much for saving some for breakfast.

"My turn," Athena declared brightly. "Who's us?"

Remus frowned. "What?"

"You said Maris couldn't be bothered with *us*. Who's us?"

"Us is me and my twin brother, Romulus."

"That's right, you have a brother named Romulus." She giggled. "Just like in mythology?"

Most people wouldn't get the reference, but occasionally someone would know the dark story of Remus and Romulus. "Apparently, that was the only book my father ever read. Despite our names, we were always close. At least we were until..."

"Until what?"

"One question per customer," he reminded her. He decided to change tactics. "You said you lived your whole life in Pandora's Box. So how it is that your vocabulary is better than mine? And how come you don't know things like what an escalator is or how to set a table?"

Athena frowned reproachfully. "That's actually a joint question, but I'll answer. I like to read."

"I'm glad we had this talk."

"I mean it," she insisted. "Tons of books. When I was eleven, I was getting so out of hand that they were actually talking of terminating me from the program."

"Which means you get to go home?"

Athena gave him a look. "As a last ditch effort, someone gave me a copy of *Romeo and Juliet*." A hungry look entered her eyes. "I finished the book in a day and I wanted more. Pretty soon, my room had stacks of books, each one portraying a different aspect of life. A different window to the outside world!" She sighed blissfully. "Those books saved my life and they planted seeds in my mind to escape."

"Is that why you spout off quotes?"

"Nope." She was talking with her mouth full. "Simple boredom. For the last four years, that's how I talked. Using quotes to get my point across."

She didn't get it the first time so Remus tried again, focusing his thoughts. *It sure is rude for people to talk with their mouths full. Oh, if only she knew how bad-mannered it truly is to—*

Athena threw a spoon at him. "Prick!" she shouted, though her eyes glinted playfully. At least it wasn't the knife.

"I was just thinking to myself!" Remus protested. "Not my fault you can't stay out of my head." Athena snorted as Remus slid the spoon back across the table. He could almost convince himself he was having fun. "Next question is yours."

She made a great deal of slowly chewing her mouthful and swallowing before responding. "I have read all of Shakespeare's plays, which feature some of the worst family relations that could possibly be imagined. Yours might not be the worst, but it's definitely in the running."

"Is this a question or an insult?"

Athena blinked. "Are you insulted if I speak against your brother and father?" she asked, sounding baffled. "Are you really? Wait, no, don't answer. That's not my question. I know you wanted to leave them for some time, but you never did. Why?"

Remus believed he understood what she'd meant about feeling like a lab rat as she studied him, head cocked for his verbal or mental answer. "I don't..." He had more questions to ask and couldn't afford to be tripped up here. "I don't know if I can explain being afraid of change. Yes, it was a crappy situation, but the alternative was an unknown, and the unknown is often times terrifying." By her expression, Athena's confusion hadn't changed, and it reminded Remus how different they were. She had spent years trying to get away from her life. The fact that she was heading to the unknown didn't seem to be a deterrent. "Also, there was Romulus. If I'd left him behind, Maris might have taken his anger out on him."

"Take him with you then."

"He wouldn't have gone."

Athena's face became unreadable. It looked like she wanted to say more, but instead opted to take a swig of soda, her eyes lighting up as the liquid touched her tongue.

"Tastes syrupy!" she observed. "Your go."

"So what will you do?" Remus asked, watching as she set the glass down. "After your escape, I mean."

Athena glanced at him with renewed interest and something that might have been respect. "Your words imply that you know my escape is far from over," she noted. "How...perceptive of you." She twirled her fork through her spaghetti. "I don't know," she confessed. "I don't know what I will do, but the point is the choice and the consequences will be mine."

Remus all too clearly understood the desire to make your own choices.

"Aww, that's sweet, you empathizing with me," Athena mocked.

His warm, fuzzy feeling vanished. "Do you understand what intrusive is?"

"Maybe. Ask on your own go, for now it's my turn." She was reaching back for the pot of pasta and scraping the bottom. If Remus wanted another helping, he had to eat quickly. "Why haven't you gotten rid of Delilah?"

Remus almost choked on a meatball and began coughing.

"I mean you know she works for Maris," Athena continued, raising her voice to be heard over his coughing. "You know she's a spy for him, so why do you allow her to remain?"

"You mean kill her?" Remus rasped, finding his voice.

Athena shrugged. "I guess you could. Or you could tell your brother about it. If he knew, then your father would have to remove her. It's simple."

Whether she was trying to or not, Athena was coming off as condescending, and he hated how she was discussing his family as if she had known them for years. "I don't want to talk about it."

Athena's lip twitched. "Fair enough. Your go."

"If you were a prisoner all this time, how did you make it to the mall?"

"I don't want to talk about it," Athena said, her eyes issuing a clear challenge. Remus had expected this and so wasn't surprised. If he didn't answer questions, neither would she. "My go. What's all this nonsense about the universe?"

"The universe has a thing against me," he said, reciting

his usual pitch. "For what reason, I don't know, but it's constantly hounding me with bad luck and impossible situations. In my younger days, I tried to fight the universe, but it always came to no avail. Now I just accept the inevitable."

Athena sighed. "We're going to have to work on that," she muttered.

"Wha—"

"Nothing. It's your go!" she exclaimed with too much exuberance.

Remus wanted to ask what she meant, but decided against it. "What made you into...what you are?" He winced. The question came out poorly.

"It's okay," she said gently. "Do you know what Ambrosia is?"

Remus wracked his brain for the answer. "Isn't it what gods ate?"

"Very good," Athena said, seeming impressed. "It's the food of the gods. It's very rare for a Class One Resident to move up to a Class Two Resident naturally. So, someone created a drug called Ambrosia that helps with the mutation."

"And that turns you from a Class One to a Class Two Resident?"

"Not right away. In fact, it's a very slow process and it depends on the Resident. I've been taking Ambrosia shots since I was born, one every other week, and I'm only a Class Three Resident. Though I know Residents half my age that are more powerful."

"So what's the downside?" It was a different question, but she seemed not to notice.

"Besides being treated like a freak?" she said bitterly. "Ambrosia has an adverse reactions to the psyche. All types of problems arise, which is why some refer to us as monsters. And there are some who've lost all sense of reason and become nothing more than animals. Residents have done some terrible things in the past. There's also the matter of the physical change."

"Physical change?"

"I was lucky. I only received vibrant grey eyes. There are some whose transformation ensures that they will never be accepted by your society. When I was eight, they upped my dosage of Ambrosia. You can't imagine the pain and agony that tore through my body at any given moment. I spent the next four years trying to kill anyone who ventured too close. That was the reason they almost terminated me from the program."

She had just divulged a lot of personal, and probably painful, memories. Remus wondered if he was supposed to reciprocate. It was her turn to ask a question.

"Why did you go to such lengths to protect me?"

The fact that it was said so nonchalantly indicated it was an important question.

"What do you mean?"

Athena glared suspiciously at him. Like she was trying to figure out if he was being coy or not. "Directly after I acquired the money—"

"Stole," Remus corrected.

"Before you knew who I was and thought I was some troublemaker working against your father. You could have given your father an accurate description of me but didn't. Why?"

Athena had given hints that she thought he was intelligent, and it was a shame that Remus was about to dash her expectations, for he truly did not know what she was trying to ask. "You said it yourself," he said slowly, hoping insight would strike him. "I was trying to protect you."

"Why?" Athena insisted aggressively. "Only thing you knew about me is that I betrayed you. Why be a fool and risk yourself to give information that wouldn't have helped him anyway?"

It rankled, Athena calling him a fool. "I didn't know the information wouldn't help him," Remus shot back. "If Maris had found you, he would have done horrible things to you."

"So?" Athena asked, unfazed.

"So?" Remus repeated incredulously. "So I don't think anyone, regardless of the offense, deserves that."

Athena blinked before smiling slyly, her grey eyes hiding her thoughts. "Sorry. It's your go."

It was time to stop dancing around the issue. "If they found you once, they might be able to find you again."

Athena had lifted her fork to take another bite, but at his words, she slowly lowered it. "I know."

"Then why are we here and not running?"

Athena paused for a second. That second became ten seconds. "Damn you, Remus." She said it with a grudging smile, and Remus got the feeling he might have won this game. "We're here because we want them to attack."

"Why?" Remus blurted. "Why not keep driving."

He was afraid Athena would take this as a separate question, but she answered with a quote. "To be prepared is half the victory. If they have a way of tracking us then it's not *if* they will attack, but *when,* and we want that 'when' to be on our timetable. Not after we've both been up for forty-eight hours in the middle of nowhere."

She sure was throwing out the pronoun "we" awfully freely. To give himself time to think, Remus absently jabbed his fork in his spaghetti for another bite, but when his fork scraped plate, he looked down to find it empty. Athena's plate was empty as well. The pot with the last little bit left was directly between of them.

Athena's eyes sparkled with mischief. "Three..." she said. What was she doing? "Two..." she counted down, glancing meaningfully at the pot. *Oh crap.* Remus reached over to grab the pot. "One..." Athena finished, leaning over, her hands snapping out quicker than Remus' eyes could follow. She grabbed the pot's handle and dragged it out of Remus' reach at the last possible second.

"Mine, mine, mine!" she sang, shaking the last portion of spaghetti onto her plate.

"Not fair!" Remus protested. "Of course you would get to it first!"

"I gave you a three second head start!"

"Yeah...but without warning." He was smiling, despite himself. Despite the fact she had just told him in all likeliness they would be attacked again. He should be cowering in a corner, not competing for spaghetti.

"My go," she said, after taking a bite of spaghetti. Remus noticed she was now waiting until after she chewed to speak, which meant his words had gotten through to her. "Don't read too much into it," she warned.

"Don't read my mind." Before today, he'd never had need to utter those words.

The corner around Athena's eyes tightened and Remus wondered if he had annoyed her again. "In all likelihood, there will be another battle." She took a sip of soda. "If you leave now, there's a decent chance of escape. So...what are you going to do?"

She was looking at him anxiously. Why was he so important? Why did she want him to stay so badly? He would use his next question to figure that out. "I won't...I won't leave," he said, his voice coming out as a barely-heard whisper. It was hardly the most encouraging statement, but the way Athena grinned ear from ear, you would think he gave a rousing speech

"Excellent!" she exclaimed, standing straight up so that her chair toppled backwards. "Well, best to get prepared."

"Wait," Remus cried. "I had one last question!"

"Uh-uh. We started with you so the last question is mine." It was a decent point, but Remus knew she was using it to prevent him from asking his last question. "Besides, we have measures we must take..."

"Measures," Remus repeated, trying the word on his tongue and deciding he didn't care for it. "What type of measures?"

Athena was in the other room, though her voice carried. "Measures to stop us from being murdered by a band of meticulous killers with advanced weapons and tactics," she explained, her voice far, far too cheerful.

"Is it too late to change my mind?" Remus asked hopefully.

Athena stuck her head out of the room, grey eyes alight with righteous indignation. "Yes!"

"Thought so," Remus sighed. "How can I help?"

Chapter 36

Nick watched pensively as Caleb and Froce strolled in. "Good evening, Mr. Hensley," Froce said formally. "Or rather good morning."

"You can't do this to me!" Nick cried, all but sure the two men could hear his heart pounding. "I haven't done anything wrong!"

"He's mighty jumpy for a man who hasn't done anything wrong," Caleb observed.

"Give him a break; it has been a long day," Froce argued in Nick's defense.

"I suppose. But he could at least hear the question before he starts denying shit."

"Sorry," Nick interceded quickly. "I'm just worried. If one of them escapes, maybe more can."

"Hmmm, valid concern," Froce allowed. "But with your full cooperation, we hope we can avoid that."

"Sure, but I don't know how I can help you." He knew Athena was trouble! He wished he'd never set foot in Pandora's Box! "I already told you all I know."

"Well, let's go over it again." Froce took a seat and Caleb followed suit. "You said Athena wanted to see you over some minor matter."

"She...she needed help with a crossword question."

"So she called you?" Caleb asked incredulously. As if the notion of Nick helping anyone with anything was unbelievable.

Nick felt his anger grow. "Yes, she called me! Apparently she thinks I'm smart."

"I thought the gal had more brains than that."

"That's enough," Froce said, and Caleb fell silent with an

arrogant smirk. What Nick wouldn't give to have a swing at him! "Like I said, this incident is stressing everyone out, and any information you might provide would be extremely helpful."

"And like I said, I don't know anything!" Nick declared, his confidence returning. If they had anything on him, they would have sprung it already. "All I did was help her with a crossword problem."

Caleb snorted. "Okay, what was the question?"

"What?"

"You helped her with a crossword question. What was the question?"

Nick's throat went dry. "I don't remember."

"You don't remember?" Caleb exclaimed in mock surprise. "But it just happened today!"

"A lot of stuff happened since then. I don't remember!"

"Do you remember what the answer was?"

"No, I don't...because I never knew what the answer was. I wasn't able to help her."

"So you *are* a dumbass," Caleb said in satisfaction. A statement that left Nick fuming.

"Caleb, please shut up," Froce said calmly. "Now, Mr. Hensley, your statement is you entered Athena's room, she asked you about a question that you didn't have an answer to, and then you left?"

"That's what happened."

"And nothing else?"

"Nope. She asked me a question I didn't know the answer to, so I left."

Froce frowned. "That's funny, because the system shows you using your ID to enter the room, but doesn't show you leaving until fifteen minutes later."

There was silence while Nick scrambled to come up with a life-saving answer, but all he managed was, "What?"

"It just seems odd to me that it took you fifteen minutes to tell her you didn't know the answer. Are you sure you didn't talk about anything else?"

"No, nothing else." Nick struggled to keep his voice from shaking.

Froce shrugged. "Oh well. Maybe you two were just enjoying a comfortable silence. Friends are known to do that."

"I'm not her friend," Nick interjected. It was crucial not to appear close to Athena. "In fact, I barely know her."

"Really?" Froce asked, once again sounding surprised. "According to everyone I spoke to, you and Athena are quite close. In fact, she told the other Residents not to harass you." Another silence. "Why do you think she would do that if you weren't friends?"

"Maybe she felt sorry for me?" Nick offered lamely.

"That's probably it," Caleb agreed. "In fact, who wouldn't feel sorry for such a pathetic piece of crap like you?"

"Caleb!"

"He's lying to us," Caleb suddenly exploded, baring his teeth like a rabid dog. "Hold him here, I'll be back!"

Nick watched Caleb leave. "Where's he going?"

"No clue," Froce said with heavy weariness. "If you're holding anything back, now would be the time to tell me."

"So he left and I'm supposed to pour all my secrets out to you," Nick sneered. "Is that the plan?"

"Mr. Hensley, I, for the moment, will assume you're not an idiot, and will attempt to explain your circumstances to you. Two days after you became an employee of Pandora's Box, Athena made her daring escape with the help of an inside man. Now, I could believe this is all a big coincidence, except for the fact you had a long conversation with her and she went out of her way to protect you." Froce paused, probably expecting him to say something, but when Nick didn't, he continued. "Now, I can also believe she's trying to set you up because that's exactly the type of games she likes to play, except you refuse to tell me the truth. So tell me, Mr. Hensley, what am I supposed to believe?"

The door swung open before Nick could form an answer, and Caleb walked in carrying a baseball bat. Upon seeing the bat, Nick immediately stood up and started to back away. "What do you think you're doing?" he cried out, his voice more high-pitched than he wanted it to be.

Caleb walked forward, his eyes locked on Nick and the bat pointed directly towards his chest.

"Caleb?" Froce said, a warning in his voice. "What are you doing?"

Caleb ignored Froce, enjoying Nick's fear for a moment longer before turning the bat around so that the handle was facing Nick. "Take it."

What type of game were they playing? "I don't think I

want to," Nick said, hoping to sound indignant.

"Take it," Caleb insisted.

"No!"

"Take it, or I'll beat you with it...your choice."

Damn! Nick glanced over at Froce for help, but he only shrugged. Hesitating for only a second longer, Nick snatched the bat from Caleb's hands.

"Smart move, son," Caleb said with a smile. "That bat is your protection."

"Protection against what?"

"Me. You see, I'm tired of you treating us like idiots. Athena's on the loose and you're withholding valuable information that might help us capture her. So, this is what we're going to do." Caleb cracked his knuckles. "Every time you lie to me, I want you to hit me with that bat."

"What?" Froce yelled, standing up.

"And why would I do that?" Nick demanded.

"Because if I think you're lying, I'm going to do my best to kill you with my bare hands," Caleb informed. "And that bat is your best chance of stopping me. Don't you reckon it's best to get your licks in before I attack? Now..." He raised his voice to drown out Force's protests. "Have you told us everything about your encounter with Athena?"

Nick's grip tightened around the bat. "I don't think I want to answer that." He flinched as Caleb took another step towards him.

"Don't blame you, son. I wouldn't want to answer either if I were in your shoes. However, I don't have time to waste on the Fifth Amendment. It's the one that gives you the right to remain silent," he added, seeing Nick's puzzled look. "So I'll ask you again, and if you decide you ain't going to answer my question, I'll still kick your ass."

"I think you should calm down," Froce suggested nervously. "Do you know the repercussions this could have?"

"Do you, Nick Hensley," Caleb started, completely ignoring Froce, "have any information that might explain how Athena escaped?"

Nick took a deep breath and felt a wave of anger twisting within. It was always the same, no matter where he went! Back in high school, he was picked on relentlessly. Stuffed in lockers and trashcans. He was the butt of every joke and thought the Army would change that. Hold sanctuary for him, but instead, he entered a bigger hell. Still being picked on, only this time he was also dodging bullets. The one time he wanted to have a little fun, they kicked him out. And now he found out Pandora's Box was no different. Caleb was the bully and he was stuck cowering below him.

"So what's it going to be?" Caleb asked menacingly. "Are you going to answer or do I have—" Caleb's sentence was cut short as Nick swung the bat with all his strength. The bat sliced across the air on a collision course with Caleb's skull, and for a second, Nick felt a burst of excitement at the prospect of actually taking the man's head off.

Caleb's arm snapped up and the bat made a sickening crunch as the two collided. "Screw you!" Caleb struck with his other hand, aiming for Nick's jaw. Then he wrenched the bat away as Nick staggered back, mouth full of blood. "You actually tried to hit me!" Caleb swung the bat, hitting Nick squarely in the solar plexus, causing him to bend over, almost like he was bowing to him. The next blow was to the back of the head, sending Nick facedown to the ground.

"So what do we do now?" Froce asked.

Nick looked up with watery eyes to see Caleb shrug. "Don't know and don't care. I reckon he really doesn't know anything about Athena. He's simply a dumbass."

"Well if he lives, he's probably going to fill out a complaint," Froce mused. "And that's going to slow us down. Best to just kill him and have someone else deal with the body."

"What? You can't do that!" Nick cried desperately.

"He has a point," Caleb acknowledged. "What are we going to tell the higher-ups?"

"He did attack you first," Froce pointed out. "Just claim self-defense. And if that's not enough, we can always claim he helped Athena escape. He *was* the last person to see her alive."

Caleb scratched his head. "That ain't a bad idea." Then he lifted the bat above his head. "Alright, son. I'm going to try my best to make this as painless as I can, but I can't do that if you're squirming around. So stay still."

"Wait!" Nick yelled, trying not to choke on his own blood. "We did talk!"

"About what?" Froce asked sharply.

"She said if I'd be her friend, then she would help me

with the job...you know, tell me helpful hints on how to stay alive and what the Residents like and dislike. Stuff like that."

"And what does being a friend mean?" Caleb asked suspiciously, bat still above his head.

Nick hesitated. "She didn't...she never specified, but I think she wanted to...I mean."

"Pervert," Caleb said, disgusted. "Bashing your brains in is starting to sound real tempting."

"Anything else?" Froce asked.

"She made fun of Macbeth."

Caleb growled. "You're making stuff up now, boy?"

"No! I swear it!" Nick made a halfhearted attempt to stand up, but the pain was too much.

"I don't know anyone named Macbeth." Froce nodded to Caleb, who lifted the bat higher in preparation of an attack.

"The supervisor, my supervisor!"

"You mean Edward Gantz?" Froce asked. "Why are you calling him Macbeth?"

"I don't know. That's what Athena calls him."

"Why?"

"I don't know!"

Caleb and Froce shared a look. "Is there anything else?"

"No...wait! I gave her a pen."

They acted as if he had done something truly terrible. "What's wrong with you?" Froce demanded angrily. "What would make you do something so stupid?"

"She asked for one for her crossword puzzle, so I gave her a pen. I didn't think..."

"No, you didn't think," Caleb interrupted wearily. He took a step back, allowing Nick to get up on unsteady legs. "Do you remember where you got the pen from?"

Nick searched his brain. "No. It just happened to be in my pocket."

"Was the pen unusually big?"

Nick wondered how Caleb could possibly know this. "Yes, it was. Looked like one of those Rubik's Cube pens."

"Swell, now listen carefully, son, because this is especially important." Caleb leaned in. "Starting from this morning, has anyone bumped into you, or slid against you?"

"What?"

"Could anyone have slipped this pen in your pocket without your knowledge?" Caleb asked impatiently.

Froce looked increasingly confused and a tad affronted about not being involved in the conversation. Nick searched his memory. "I'll guess there were a couple of men who could have done it."

"Was your supervisor one of them?"

Nick finally saw his chance to point the finger to someone else and he immediately jumped on it. "Yes, Macbeth...Edward...whoever you want to call him. He could have definitely done it."

"Thank you, Mr. Hensley," Caleb said, more formally than Nick was used to hearing from him. "You have been a tremendous help." He turned to leave and Froce hastily stood up with a scowl on his face.

"And what about me?" Nick demanded.

"I reckon you stay here until we can get you your walking papers."

"I'm being fired? Why?"

Caleb turned to face him, and Nick flinched from the disdain in his eyes. "Because you're a shit for brains officer who was so concentrated on getting laid that he didn't realize he was being played."

They left, and Nick was stuck by himself. He felt a hot wave of tears starting to form and he quickly blinked them away. He mustn't cry. He wouldn't cry. Another place had rejected him, but he would make them pay. Instead of sadness, Nick now felt a smoldering hatred for all of them. Caleb, Froce, Mr. Titanos, Athena. He would make them all pay.

Chapter 37

Fides was a man named after a female god. He never allowed this dour fact to get him down, though. In fact, from all reports, Fides was very easygoing, an almost impossible trait to find in a Resident. A man in his mid-forties, Fides was slightly chubby. He sported a neatly kept beard with specks of gray beginning to show, and his eyes had that twinkle that one might see in Santa Clause's gaze. Overall, Fides looked like a favorite uncle or a fun school counselor.

The only noticeable thing that set him apart as a Resident was his right arm. The hand was larger than it was supposed to be, and his whole arm seemed stiff as a board with long black and blue bruises running from the length of his hand to his elbow.

"The pain is unbearable," Fides informed one of the officers who was staring at his arm, entranced.

The man across from Fides snapped to attention, embarrassed that his gawking was so easily noticed. "Sorry, sir. I didn't mean any disrespect."

"Oh my, so formal!" Fides exclaimed with a boisterous laugh that had everyone in the van flinching. "Please just call me Fides. And what might your name be?"

After a brief moment of hesitation. "Anthony Badger."

"You don't say." Fides cocked his head and looked to his left at the squad leader who was sitting at the very end of the van.

"Anthony Badger?" Fides mused, stroking his graying beard. "He wouldn't happen to be related to you by any chance?"

Brandon Badger thought about not answering for a split

second, but figured it was best not to antagonize the Resident this early in the mission. Like most Residents, Fides suffered mental instability and his easy-going nature could be replaced with a homicidal rage within seconds. "He's my younger brother and a damn fine officer. Let him be."

"Oh, I meant no disrespect," Fides said assuredly, showing off all his teeth in a giant smile. "He seems like a fine man. A real chip off the old block, if you know what I mean."

Brandon narrowed his eyes, but refused to let Fides know he was getting to him. They had left over two hours ago and according to their most recent information, Athena, Resident of Pandora's Box, was staying at a hotel two cities over. Ragnarok had dispatched 50 men, a total of seven vans, to capture her and eliminate the boy. As squad leader, he was expected to ride with the Resident, despite his personal dislike for the monster smiling charmingly at him.

The vans Ragnarok used for retrieval operations were similar to the vehicles SWAT used. Armor plating for the Residents who knew how to shoot a gun, tinted windows that made it next to impossible for anyone outside to see what was happening within, and in Ragnarok's case, logos of a fake extermination company to fool everyday humans. Like the SWAT design, the back of the van was hollowed out except for the leather seats that lined the interior walls—the better to fit in more men and to make room for all the weapons end equipment they would need to take on one of the monstrosities of human interference with God's territory.

"You want to ask me about my arm?" Fides asked, diverting his attention back at Anthony, who was having a problem not looking at it.

Anthony looked up, once again taken aback. "No, sir, I didn't..."

"No, no, no," Fides scolded. "You mustn't lie. Lying is the deepest and most dreadful sin there is. Lies cloud the world so we can't see it for what it is. And if we can't see the world as it is, how can we progress and make it better? I can't stand anyone who lies. It makes me angry."

Brandon's brother was smart enough to interpret the veiled threat. "Yes, sir. I was wondering about your arm, sir."

Fides smiled. "That's better. Doesn't that feel good? Just remember in the future to call me Fides and not sir. Now you wanted to know about my arm?" Fides cleared his throat like he was about to tell his favorite nephew a bedtime story. Brandon had heard this story many times in the past, and would usually tune the Resident out, but his brother's involvement made him listen to the conversation carefully with his hand resting on the butt of his gun. "My arm is my quid pro quo. My payment for the powers I have."

"Powers?" Anthony asked, almost dubiously.

"Oh yes," Fides said grandly. "Ragnarok would have me call them 'abilities,' but I must speak the truth, and the truth is...I was granted powers to aid your kind."

Anthony frowned at the statement. Ever since he'd first opened his eyes, Anthony had always been a hardheaded kid, doing the exact opposite of what Brandon wanted him to do. Growing up as the youngest of the Badger brothers, he had felt a need to prove something. He'd been granted a full college scholarship, but threw it away to chase his oldest brother into the Marines. After leaving the Marines, Brandon made the mistake of lying to his parents and telling them he was now head of a special terrorist unit dedicated to protecting the country. A year later, Anthony dropped the Marines to try and join the same organization. What was maddening was that he'd succeeded. Anthony Badger had joined Pandora's Box six months ago and one of the higher-ups, figuring he had the same combat prowess as Brandon, had recently promoted him to Ragnarok.

"And what is your ability?" Anthony finally asked. Brandon had forgotten, so new Anthony was to Ragnarok, that he had never seen a true Resident's ability. Sure, he had seen the small miracles the Residents at Pandora's Box could perform, but he had never seen a Resident freeze the blood in a human's body, or watch a man explode simply because a Resident willed it.

"My ability?" Fides asked, sounding puzzled. "I assumed your brother would have told you." In truth, Brandon had been relatively sure he could bench his brother from the mission and had seen no need to confide the abilities of any of the Residents. "My ability, dear boy, is that I can see the truth. Oh, I know the look," Fides said, spotting Anthony's surprised expression at his statement. "No need to be embarrassed, that's your honest reaction and I wish for nothing else. I see the truth and I can give other people strength so that they can also see the truth. That's one of the reasons your brother hates me. He finds my particular abilities distasteful."

"And that ability is to see the truth," Anthony repeated slowly, taking a quick peek at Brandon. He had probably realized he was missing a big vital piece of information that would explain the noticeable nervousness of everyone around, especially those sitting right next to Fides. He glanced again at Brandon, who met his eyes before discreetly shaking his head. It was the wrong move to make.

The stubborn lines on Anthony's face that only appeared when his brother told him not to do something emerged, and in a defiant tone, he asked Fides, "To see the truth. How is that helpful?" Some of the other officers shifted in their seats and Brandon gritted his teeth, wondering if he could get away with pummeling his brother.

Fides smiled serenely at Anthony. "Maybe one day, if you want it, I can give you strength. It feels magnificent. Perhaps..." Fides cut his sentence short as Brandon thrust a gun under Fides' chin.

"Here's some truth for you," Brandon said, making sure his voice was normal, though inside, he was furious that both Fides and Anthony had pushed him to this point. "If you try anything, you die, Resident."

If the squad members in the car weren't nervous before, they had to be now. Brandon could not be allowed to kill the Resident, but none of them wanted to be the first to confront his bull-like temper. Anthony was looking increasingly chagrined at the incident he had caused and Brandon wanted to scream *"This is all your fault!"*

Fides sighed. "So you want him to be as blind as you? Very well."

Fides' shallow words did nothing to ease Brandon's mind. He'd been upset when Anthony joined Pandora's Box. He'd gotten angry when Anthony got promoted to Ragnarok. He'd almost had a stroke of rage when he realized Anthony would be accompanying him in the capture of Athena. He'd tried his best to kick Anthony off the team, but Ms. Yang insisted on it, stating this was the perfect mission to introduce Anthony to the world of advanced Residents. She thought it would be an easy mission, but Anthony knew from experience that any mission involving Residents had the potential to be catastrophic. The best he could do was hope for an uneventful night and a quick return.

"Mr. Badger, would you mind lowering your gun?" Fides asked politely. "I find this position uncomfortable."

Brandon holstered his gun.

"Thank you, Mr. Badger," Fides said, rubbing his chin. "And if it makes you feel better, I find you insufferable as well."

His earpiece crackled before Brandon could respond. "Sir, we're in the vicinity."

"Have teams one and three circle the premises and block off all exits," Brandon instructed, annoyed that he had allowed himself to be so distracted that he hadn't realized how close they were to the destination. "I don't want any chance of her escaping. Teams two and four will enter the premises and stay on the lobby floor. I don't want anyone leaving or entering without being thoroughly checked out. Teams five and six will collect Athena and deal with the boy while team seven hangs back in case things go south. I have high hopes that all this preparation will prove to be overkill and we can collect Athena without any incident. However, if it proves impossible to capture Athena, you have shoot to kill orders. I repeat," Brandon said, looking directly into Fides' eyes. "You have orders to kill any Resident who offers resistance."

Chapter 38

Anthony watched as Fides stretched in the parking lot. This was the first Resident he'd seen outside the walls of Ragnarok and Pandora's Box, and he felt a thrill of excitement at finally getting to see some action.

"Teams one and three, are you in position?" Brandon shouted over the coms. Anthony's brothers had always been protective, but Brandon was the worst. Brandon had their dad's rugged, harsh features; the type you would expect from an action hero. His arms were ripped with bulging muscles, and he wore a cocky expression that said, *"I will beat you, so why bother?"* Anthony had their mom's delicate features, with a face that looked like he'd never completed puberty, and thin, limp noodle arms. True, he had more flexibility than his brother, but no one ever really stated that fact when comparing the two unless as consolation for Anthony's obvious inadequacies. As a result, Brandon was always looking to protect him, which royally pissed Anthony off. It was his own skills that had gotten him into the Marines, into Pandora's Box, and finally into Ragnarok. He was starting to grow tired of trying to prove himself to someone who would always see him as the baby brother.

"We have the perimeter closed down. I repeat. We have the perimeter closed down."

"Don't allow anyone in or out until further orders," Brandon ordered.

"I suppose we should get going," Fides said briskly.

"You're not in charge!" Brandon reminded him, his voice harsh. "You don't give the orders."

Fides bowed slightly in mock apology.

"Move out," Brandon ordered after glowering at Fides for another second. They moved as a perfect unit, and Anthony felt a sense of pride for his big brother, although he could never admit it. From what Anthony had learned, Brandon's squad was the most infamous team at Ragnarok. They always called Brandon for the impossible jobs and he always succeeded.

"Your brother's quite the man, isn't he?" Fides commented, falling in step with Anthony. Anthony did not fail to notice that the other team members gave Fides plenty of room. "He really inspires me every time I see him."

Anthony blinked. "I can't tell if you're serious or if you're being sarcastic."

"Sarcasm is just another form of lying," Fides answered. "And I never lie." His right arm swung stiffly as he walked.

"How long have you known my brother?"

"It's going on seven years now. I first met him when tracking down Magni. He was amazing even back then."

"Was Magni another escaped Resident?" Anthony asked with a frown. "I thought escapes never happen at Pandora's Box."

Fides chuckled. "They don't. In fact, this is the first time I've heard of anyone escaping from the Box. However, attempted escapes do occur at Ragnarok."

"Why?"

"Because, dear boy, we're not all trapped in a cage like the Residents of Pandora's Box," Fides said with a smile. "The majority of us are free to come and go as we please, and a couple of Residents even live outside the compound. However," he continued with a sigh, "there are a few who abuse this trust, some of them quite powerful. That's when your brother is called upon to clean up the mess."

Anthony's eyes were drawn to Fides' arm. "And do they always have a Resident on the team?"

"It's procedure. Ragnarok chooses the best Resident for the job to tag along."

"And why are you the best this time around?"

"You're a curious boy, aren't you?" Fides remarked. "No need to look so abashed. I like a healthy sense of curiosity. Shows that you're trying to seek out the truth. They chose me for two reasons. One is how she left Pandora's Box. Her escape is puzzling a great deal of people and Ragnarok wants me to get to the bottom of it."

"Okay, what's the second reason?"

"Apparently the girl uses treachery and deceit as her primary methods of fighting. I personally find this type of person particularly distasteful, but I'm definitely the best person to fight her. Her treachery won't work on me."

Anthony was just about to take the leap and ask exactly what his ability was when Brandon, up ahead, motioned for silence. They had reached the entrance. With a quick glance behind to check on the team's position, he barged inside the lobby.

"Excuse me, sir," Brandon said to the clerk, sitting behind the desk reading a magazine.

"Just a second," the pimply teen said, looking up with a yawn and then freezing as he noticed the impressive men with the even more impressive guns. "What the hell?" he yelled, reaching for the phone.

Brandon pointed his M4 at him. "Please let go of the phone, sir."

The teen dropped the phone and raised his hands. "Take whatever you want. The money is kept in a safe in the back."

"We're not after money. Calm down and lower your voice. We're looking for an extremely dangerous fugitive." Brandon took out a photo. "Have you seen this woman?"

"*That's* your dangerous fugitive?" the clerk asked skeptically, glancing at the photo of the young blond.

"Have you seen her?"

"Are you police?" the clerk asked, growing bolder by the second. "Can I see some badges?"

"We don't need them," Brandon pointed out. "We have guns."

"They're actually M4A1 assault rifles," Fides piped up. "Very powerful, and they do absolutely horrid things to your insides."

"I'm handling this!" Brandon snarled at Fides, who only smiled in response. "Have you seen this girl? She would most likely use the alias Athena, and it's possible she's traveling with a male companion."

"Haven't seen her," the clerk answered. "But I'll keep my eye out."

"He's lying," Fides said, his smile vanishing instantly. "He knows exactly who she is."

"No I don't," the teen insisted.

The change was instantaneous. Moving quickly, Fides stepped forward, reached across the desk with his bloated hand and grabbed the teen by his shirt. With surprising strength, he pulled the clerk until their faces were only inches away. "Are you calling me a liar?" Fides hissed.

The teen struggled against Fides' ironclad grip. "Let go of me!"

Anthony was the first one at the scene trying to break them apart. In fact, he was the only one. For some curious reason, no one else would approach Fides. Even Brandon was keeping his distance.

"Let him go, Fides," Brandon ordered.

"He's calling me a liar!" Fides shrieked. No longer did he look the part of the kindly uncle. Instead, he looked like a demented madman. "He's calling me a liar!"

"Release him," Brandon commanded, a note of panic in his voice. He glanced around for witnesses, but blessedly, the lobby was completely empty. "Anthony, back off now!"

Anthony, quite nervous that no one else was trying to stop Fides, let go but didn't back away.

"So what if I am?" the teen asked, staring in horror at Fides' bloated arm, but still trying to sound tough.

"Kid, stay quiet!" Brandon snapped, raising his gun. "Fides, if you don't release him, I will shoot! Anthony, back off!"

"So you're calling me a liar?" Fides snarled, completely ignoring Brandon.

Anthony grabbed Fides' arm before his brain could tell him that was a bad idea. "Just let go. We can talk..." The effects of Fides' ability slammed into Anthony. He fell to his knees. What was the point of living? It was meaningless. He would never get the same recognition as his brothers. Out of the three brothers, he was the weakest, the dumbest. His parents didn't even like him; they both wished he had never been born. He wished he was never born! That way he wouldn't have to live in such a godawful world!

Anthony felt strong hands pulling him away from Fides. "Let me die," he groaned. "Please let me die." Then...he was free of Fides' hold.

"Snap out of it!" Brandon snapped, letting go of him.

Anthony, drenched in sweat, started to tremble on the

floor. He started to say something then stopped. Started to say something else, than stopped again. "I'm sorry," he was finally able to grumble. He'd managed to screw up his first mission with his brother.

Usually, Brandon would scold him, but instead, he was silent. If Anthony had to hazard a guess, he would say Brandon was afraid of compounding Fides' depression effects with harsh words. A scream diverted Anthony's attention to the clerk who Fides still held.

"Sir?" one of the officers asked nervously.

Brandon dismissed him with a wave of a shaky hand, and Anthony realized his brother took a large dose of Fides' depressing abilities to save him. "It's too late now and we need the information. Let him be."

"Tell the truth!" Fides hissed.

"She checked into a room about an hour and a half ago," the clerk whimpered, his face turning a chalky white. "Her room is on the seventh floor, room 712."

"And why didn't you tell me this before?" Fides asked, his eyes still transfixed on the teen. "Why did you call me a liar?"

The clerk groaned. "Make it stop!"

"I will as soon as you answer my questions."

"She showed up an hour ago and gave me two thousand dollars to deny their existence to anyone who showed up. She promised me another two grand in the morning if they were still alive."

Anthony was close enough to hear Brandon groan under his breath and he knew why. The mission had just become twice as difficult. It was much easier to capture an unaware enemy than it was to capture an enemy who knew you were coming.

Fides' arm seemed to vibrate with energy. "Anything else?"

"She asked to see our lost and found and told me to give a message to anyone who wouldn't take no for an answer."

"What is it?"

"At the time, I thought she was crazy or playing some type of game."

"Tell me the truth!"

The teen swallowed. "She told me to tell you she's already gone."

Silence greeted the statement.

"Shit," someone said. "She's toying with us, Captain. She's not even here."

Brandon stood up tall, all traces of Fides' ability seemingly gone, while it was all Anthony could do to stop shaking and to avoid crying. Not a good debut for his first mission. "We check it out anyway. Teams five and six will check out the room. Everyone else needs to stay here and stop anyone from leaving or entering." He glanced around. "We've been lucky that no one has heard the commotion thus far. Alex," Brandon said, referring to the man to his left by his first name. No longer part of the military, it was each squad leader's discretion whether to use first or last names. Most stuck with the military tradition, but Brandon preferred first names as a way to bolster comradeship. "You're in charge down here."

"Yes, sir."

Brandon switched over to the coms. "Daniel, there's a chance Athena might not be here. I want you to call Ms. Yang and get an exact fix on her location."

"Will do, sir."

Brandon looked at Fides with a disdainful look, usually only reserved for their middle brother, Tyler. "Fides, am I lying when I say I will pump you full of holes if you don't release that boy?"

"No, I don't believe you are," Fides said calmly. He released the clerk who somehow managed to stay on his feet, though he struggled to find his next breath.

"Fides will come with us. Anthony, you are to stay down here."

Anthony's face burned with embarrassment at having been singled out. He stood up on unsteady legs and nodded stiffly at his brother. "Yes, sir. Understood, sir."

"Move out," Brandon ordered, and the squad went to obey his order.

As Brandon's team moved away, someone tapped Anthony on the shoulder and he turned around with a sharp retort ready for anyone who wished to ridicule or mock him. He instead found Peter Chapman, a smaller-than-average man with dusty brown hair and a nervous smile. Anthony had only met him that night, but had already heard his mom ran the Ragnarok facility.

"First time I felt Fides' ability, I cried like a baby," Peter informed without any prompting or lead up. "Threw up too."

Anthony blinked, not sure if Peter was poking at him, but the man's face stayed sincere the entire time and he said it softly enough so that the Ragnarok operatives walking past would have to strain to hear them.

"Thanks," Anthony said after a moment, surprised to find out he actually meant it. "Peter, right? You're not usually part of Brandon's squad, are you?"

"Nope, on loan tonight," Peter answered, looking around a bit anxiously. Two men exchanging heart-to-hearts in the middle of a combat operation was bound to produce a negative reaction from the others, so Anthony could understand Peter's apprehension, and appreciated the scorn he was risking by talking to him. He was about to do something extremely cheesy and tell Peter good luck when it happened.

"Do you plan to call the police?" Fides asked the clerk in a deceptively calm voice.

The clerk, smart enough to understand the implication, shook his head vigorously. "No...I promise."

Fides sighed. "There you go lying again. I can't stand liars."

"Leave him alone," Brandon ordered.

"He's the only one who knows we're here, commander, and I have strict orders from Ms. Yang to eliminate anyone who's seen a Resident showcase an ability."

Brandon's hand twitched. "Fides, I believe you planned to kill him from the beginning."

"Ms. Yang's orders, Mr. Badger," Fides repeated, his pleasant tone at odds with his challenging gaze. "Do you have any objections?"

Anthony was sure that would set his brother off, for no one, with the exception of their mother, could get away with riling up the oldest Badger brother and not receive, at the very least, a black eye for their trouble. Brandon locked eyes with Fides, and Anthony felt an excited shiver of anticipation at the thought of the Resident finally being made accountable for his actions. But then Brandon's eyes dropped to the ground and he gave a barely perceptible nod.

Fides smiled and turned to face the clerk who had watched the scene unfold with wide, hoping eyes.

"Don't kill me," the teen pleaded.

"Of course not," Fides said soothingly. The Resident reached over the counter and rested his bloated arm on the clerk's shoulder, who whimpered at the contact. "Why, I'm not a killer; I would never kill anyone...instead, I'm going to give you the strength to see the truth."

Anthony could have sworn he saw it. A slight distortion in the air before the clerk screamed a sorrowful note of anguish and despair so potent it had Anthony automatically moving forward to help and only Peter's warning grip stopped him from getting nearer.

"It's too late," Peter stated when Anthony looked at him questioningly.

Before Anthony could ask what he meant, the teen grabbed the sharpest thing, a pair of scissors on the desk, and with one last lingering wail, he stabbed himself twice in the neck.

Chapter 39

Athena's face went pale. "Oh, that's not good."

"What is it?" Remus asked, struggling to tie his shoes. Anything that had Athena rattled could not bode well for his future plans.

"Absolutely nothing!" she responded with false cheer. A brief hesitation, and her eyes got the now familiar faraway look. "You might want to hurry up before absolutely nothing comes barging through the door."

It had taken fifteen minutes for Athena to make all her so-called "necessary preparations." Hopeful that things might look better in the daytime, Remus fell asleep on the couch, only to have Athena shake him awake a mere hour later. Remus had to grudgingly give the universe its props for putting him in such a terrible situation without any sleep.

"You're *still* obsessed with your universe theory?"

"You're *still* reading my mind when there are people downstairs planning on killing us?" Remus countered. "What's happening now?"

"Nothing. Best as I can tell, the leader is arguing with the Resident."

"Best you can tell?"

"You have to remember, I can't see what's happening. I can only read the thoughts and reactions of people."

"And?"

She paused. "The Resident killed someone. The guy manning the desk downstairs."

"The clerk?" Remus felt a wave of sadness. He had seen the clerk twice, once when he walked in, and the second time when Athena stopped to have a chat with him. He had to wonder if Athena had known this was going to happen.

"No, I didn't know, and now is not the time for your doubts. This was outside my expectations." She bit her lower lip. "The leader, a Mr. Brandon Badger, is arguing with the Resident over that now, and that's buying us a couple of seconds."

"Okay." Remus headed for the door. They had discussed a plan in case something went wrong; speed was the key, but when he looked back, Athena was rooted to the same spot. "Athena?"

She was still biting her lower lip and Remus, even though he had just met her, found it strange to see her struck with indecision. "Leave now. Get to the floor below and hide out. I'll distract them, and when you get a chance, run to the car and drive as fast as you can."

"That wasn't the plan we discussed," he objected.

"Their numbers are far greater than I predicted, they have a Resident with them, and though it's now verified they're tracking me, I'm still in the dark on how." She was looking in his direction, but her gaze wasn't focused on him. "The board is stacked heavily against us. The plan won't work."

"So what now?"

She didn't respond. She was taking too long to come up with a plan, to look at all the angles, and it was wasting time they simply did not have.

"Let's call the police."

"No," Athena dismissed off-hand.

At another time, Remus would have dropped it, as any suggestion he made was bound to be wrong, but for this case, he persisted. "You said Pandora's Box wasn't government owned, and I doubt they want their business getting out. If we call the police or create a big enough public fiasco…"

"Then Pandora's Box might back off," she finished, her eyes lighting up as a plan begin to form. "Yes…maybe. It could buy time at the very least. Okay, I'll try your plan."

Instead of relief, Remus felt unsettled. She was relying on a plan that he'd come up with on a whim. The last person who'd relied on him still loathed and cursed him to this day.

"Get to the floor below and wait," Athena instructed. Once I create a diversion, get to the car. I will be right behind you, but if I'm not there in five minutes, go ahead and leave. I'll catch up." Remus briefly thought she was going to sacrifice herself for his benefit. "Oh Remus, you think too much of me," she said with a ghost of her old smile. "I don't believe in sacrifice, especially my own."

"But—"

"Leave. Your window is quickly closing."

With a lingering look, he dashed out the door and immediately tripped and hit the wall. *Damn universe!* Despite the seriousness of the situation, he could have sworn he heard Athena giggling from behind him just before the door slammed shut. After recovering, he ran down the halls at what he hoped was a casual pace. His heart was pounding painfully against his chest and sweat was already running down his face. He really needed to get in better shape if he planned to follow her around. The thought of staying with Athena surprised him.

He rounded the corner and entered the staircase. Praying the universe would show a shred of compassion, he took the stairs down two at a time. Could he stay with Athena? Up till now, he thought he wanted to find the information to keep his brother safe and go home. However, in all honesty, there was nothing waiting for him back home. His dad had tried to kill him, and his brother knew about it and did nothing.

"How much you want to bet that boy is enjoying some sweet Resident loving?" a voice echoed in the stairwell. What were the odds they meant a resident of the hotel?

The voice was close, and the entrance to the sixth floor was still a flight of stairs away. Just like the escalator, he started to leap, taking the stairs four at a time.

"Are you joking?" another voice carried on. "I'd be too scared. She might vaporize your head in the heat of the moment."

"Have you seen her? It's definitely worth it, my man. Definitely worth it."

Remus crashed through the door just as he glimpsed two men turning the corner to the stairs. Did he make too much noise? Had they recognized him and were now galloping up the stairs, intent on putting a bullet between his eyes? At this moment, he would have given anything to have Athena's telepathic abilities.

He started walking down the hall, expecting at any moment to be shot in the back. If he died, who would care? The only person who might show up for his funeral, out of affection and not out of obligation, was the grey-eyed killer who'd gotten him into this mess in the first place. It was beyond sad.

After a minute, he dared to look back and found the hallway empty. Remus breathed a sigh of relief and noticed a manual fire alarm by the door to the stairs. Most hotels had updated to an automatic system, fearing a manual one would lead to frequent pranks but it wasn't uncommon to find a manual system in an older building.

He stared at the alarm and could practically hear the universe whispering in his ear. Daring him to do it.

Chapter 40

The alarm was deafening. Athena had to cover her sensitive ears until they could adjust, but couldn't contain a smile. Remus was more resourceful than he gave himself credit for, and in doing this, he had committed both himself and her to this plan. She stretched her mind, and sure enough, there were hordes of grumpy people waking up. Some would cover their heads with a pillow and hope the noise would eventually stop. Most, however, concerned for their safety, would peek their heads out of the doorways, and a couple of them would see men lurking in the hallways with guns.

The first scream could barely be heard. The second was more of a screech, but the third did justice to all horror movie fanatics.

"Calm down! There's a dangerous fugitive in this hotel!" Brandon, the leader of her executioner squad, yelled. That did nothing to suppress the riot; if anything, it added fuel. *Damn you, Athena!*

She had people she'd never even met cursing her name. "Impressive," she said to herself, picking back up the habit of conversing with herself. She made her way to the balcony, and had just gotten out of sight when the door was kicked in.

"Search the place," a voice filled with frustration instructed. "I doubt she's here, but best to be thorough. I want everything checked. Look for maps, clothes, money, anything. I want everyone else on crowd control. Athena's a slippery one, and she plans to use the chaos to escape."

"He's good," Athena said to herself. She checked to make sure the envelope was still in her pocket.

The first person to approach the balcony was a foul-thinking man. Athena kept track of him with her telepathy. He was a brute who had very definite ideas of what he would do to her if he could capture her alone. She wouldn't regret his death.

As soon as he cleared the screen door, she grabbed him and, in a single motion, threw him over the side of the balcony.

His scream echoed across the night, but before he even landed, Athena had already jumped across to the balcony of the adjacent room. A three-foot gap separated her balcony from the previous one. A regular person could have jumped it with relative ease. For a Resident, the task was almost laughable.

She opened the screen door and was safely in the next room, out of sight, when some of her would-be capturers came running out on the first balcony.

"Jesus Christ! Did he fall?"

"Ain't no way he fell! How many people you know accidentally fall out of a hotel?"

"Then was he pushed?"

"By who? There's no one here. We would have seen it if anyone left."

"Then what happened?"

A different voice. "What happened here?"

"We don't know, sir. We heard Marcus screaming and when we came to investigate..."

"And you saw no one leave?"

"No, sir, do you think he jumped?"

"We were warned that our Resident might have mind control abilities."

They thought she could control minds? Athena smiled at the notion.

A soft thump behind her alerted Athena to the room's inhabitant. She whirled around to find a knife pointed at her throat.

"Stay back!" He was a middle-aged man with a wife and two daughters. Poor guy was obviously unnerved by her entrance.

"Sorry about ruining your vacation," Athena apologized politely, taking a step forward. She made it a policy to never forgive anyone who threatened her life, but decided, given the circumstances, to be lenient. A father trying to protect his children should not be judged with the same measure one would judge a Ragnarok operative.

"Don't move," he ordered, glancing toward the other room where his wife and children hid. "What were you doing outside my room?"

"I was hiding." She took another step forward. "I was in room 712."

"So how'd you get outside?"

"I jumped," she answered easily. "Don't look so shocked, the gap was nothing. You could probably do it given enough incentive. People barged in and I was scared...so I jumped." She took another step forward and ended up directly in front of him. "Are you going to stab me?"

She's just a kid. Just like my Arial. "You can stay here for the time being," he said, lowering his weapon. "Do you have any idea why—"

Athena struck him twice and wrenched the knife from him as he clutched his broken nose. "They're after me. Apparently they think I'm some type of mass murderer. They think I'm a soulless monster who's a danger to society." She smiled sweetly at him. "Silly, right?"

Oh God, I made a mistake. I killed my family!

His thoughts put a storm cloud over her humor. "Listen carefully. Go in the room where your wife and children are hiding and get me a pair of Arial's pajamas." She thought for a moment. "And a hat if you have one."

She could feel the man's bewilderment. "How do you know my daughter's name?"

"Doesn't matter. Now go and be quick or I'll come in, kill you all, and take what I want."

He left quickly, and Athena took the time to do a mind sweep. Thirteen men on her floor alone, fifteen in the lobby, and twenty-one guarding the entrances. They were serious about not letting her slip through their hands. The man she'd thrown off the balcony was already causing a commotion. The police had been called a dozen times already and she expected to make a bigger splash before the night was over.

Remus was safe on the floor below, still looking for a way out and still conflicted about her. *Uh-oh.* Someone had glimpsed him entering the sixth floor, and Brandon was now sending men to find him.

"Damn!" she cursed, startling the poor man who had

come back without her knowing. She almost never cursed. There was nothing wrong with it, but there were better ways to express emotions. She glared at the man, mad at herself for not hearing his return, and he swallowed.

"I have the pajamas you wanted...and a cap. But why do—"

"None of your business!" she snapped. Then, taking a deep breath, she said, "Put the clothes on the table and go tend to your family. Don't leave the room, you won't get far. If anyone asks, you tell them exactly what happened. I forced you at knife point. Do *not* give them any reason to think you voluntarily helped me."

She didn't bother to watch him leave. She stripped off her clothes and put on the girl's pajamas, an action that took less than thirty seconds. She finished her outfit with the cap and casually strolled out the door, the man's knife securely held in her left hand.

The hallways were a circus. Men and women screaming demanding to be released. Men in black uniforms guarding the hall on both sides, refusing to let anyone by. And in the middle of it all was Brandon Badger, talking down the crowd. Beside him was Fides...the Resident. Athena managed to pick his name from Brandon's mind. A quick glance in Brandon's head told her that the two hated each other. Another useful fact that could be exploited.

"Please calm down," Brandon was yelling into an unresponsive crowd. "We are here to apprehend an extremely dangerous individual, and we appreciate your cooperation. If anyone has seen a young girl around the age of sixteen with blond hair and grey contacts, please inform us immediately. We believe her to be the hostage of a sociopath. Most likely, his next victim."

Athena had to admire the man's creativity. He knew no one would believe that a young girl could be dangerous enough to warrant men with high powered guns. But if the girl was a hostage, held by a killer, then instead of hunters, they became rescuers. She had to hurry before a do-well citizen pointed her out to them.

Walking quickly, she blended in with the crowd, shoving aside everyone who was in her way. One guy grabbed her in an effort to stop her from getting in front of him. A second later, he was hopping on one leg, showing all the symptoms

of a man with a broken foot. Athena stopped in the middle of
the crowd and took a deep breath. "BOMB!" she screamed.
"THERE'S A BOMB SET TO GO OFF!"

Nothing helped form a panicky mob more than the threat
of a bomb exploding them into millions of little pieces. People
found new energy and shoved against their oppressors.

"Oh God!"

"Do your job and let us go!"

"Who said that?" Brandon demanded. "There's no bomb,
who said that?" He really was a clever man, but it was already too late.

Athena had made it to the front of the mob when she
"accidentally" tripped and fell into one of the men guarding
the halls. No one saw when she plunged the knife into the
man's chest, perforating the lung and hemothorax. A fatal
wound. Their eyes clashed, and for a moment, Athena felt
regret. This one was twenty-eight, and upon the knife entering his lung, he mentally called out for his mom. She closed
her mind. Nothing was worse than hearing a dying man's last
thoughts.

Athena screamed convincingly as he slumped to the floor.
That was all it took. The crowd was now a mind-numb panicked animal. Its only thoughts were of escaping and saving
itself.

It raged and slammed into Brandon's men, pushing them
aside with ease. It growled and snarled and was so damn
scary that most of Brandon's men didn't have the guts to
stand against it. Athena had slinked back to the middle of the
crowd, careful to keep herself hidden.

"Is that you, Athena?" The crowd had almost reached the
stairwell when Athena heard the thoughts echo inside her
head. She stopped, allowing people to breeze past her, and
looked around for the source.

She soon found it. The Resident, her enemy, was looking
directly at her.

"So you can read minds. That's an interesting trick."

She smiled, unconcerned. There were too many people
between them. Depending on his abilities, it was possible he
could get her before she entered the safety of the stairwell.
However, it was unlikely he could do so without mowing
down all the people between them, a factor Brandon would
find unacceptable.

"*Hiding behind so many people? How dishonorable. Tell me, Athena, have you read my mind? I'm sending my thoughts to you, but have you read my mind?*"

She shook her head. Some Residents knew when they were being read. Others could trap you inside their minds, and still others could destroy the mind if given an opportunity.

"*Smart girl,*" he thought approvingly. Athena felt his mood change. "*You lied. There is no bomb.*"

She raised an eyebrow in response. Throughout their exchange, Fides had not once informed Brandon that he knew where Athena was. The contempt between the two vibrated the air, and she was already thinking of creative ways to use it for her benefit.

"*It seems you're full of lies, Athena. I can't stand people who lie. I will teach you truth, I promise you.*"

To be taught truth. What an interesting concept. Athena had the information she needed, and an update to Remus' plan begun to build inside her head. But first, she needed to tend to his safety. She entered the stairwell.

Chapter 41

"Shit!" Caleb yelped, cradling his arm.

Froce was unsympathetic. "It's your own fault. Why the hell would you let him hit you with a bat?"

"I was being resourceful," Caleb growled. "All you younglings want to do is beat the shit out of a guy."

"Yeah, well, your creativity cost you an arm."

"That's another thing with your generation." Caleb grimaced in pain. "Y'all are too delicate. Can't handle a paper cut without crying for mommy and asking for anesthetics. Give me ten minutes and a cold beer and I'll be back on my feet."

"Sounds good, but you have to wait until we find Edward." Froce glanced at Caleb, briefly wondering why he kept a bat at Pandora's Box but deciding not to ask. "Do you think he helped Athena escape?"

"Don't know, but I do think Athena wants us to *think* he helped her escape."

Tyrone thought it over, but surrendered after a few minutes. "I'll give. How'd you come up with that theory?"

"Athena never used the name Macbeth when talking about Mr. Gantz. That's something new."

"She called him by a different name. So what?"

"And that's yet another thing I can't stand about you young people."

"How did I ever think you were anything more than a cantankerous old man?" Froce wondered.

"You don't know nothing," Caleb continued, acting as if he didn't hear him. "Can you even tell me who Macbeth is?"

Froce scratched his head. "Some dude in some play, right?"

"Some dude in some play?" Caleb repeated while shaking his head sorrowfully. "If I was a crying man, I'd weep for you. It was a Shakespearian play in which the main character, Macbeth, betrayed and killed his king. An action that almost destroyed the kingdom."

Froce finally caught the point. "You think Athena was pointing us to Edward Gantz? Why would she out her accomplice like that?"

"First off, you automatically assume Edward is her accomplice. A fact Athena might be depending on. She's tricky, and I wouldn't put it past her to steer us down the wrong path."

"Just like her note to Dr. Pluck."

The alarms began shrieking their dire warning, and Froce immediately tensed up as guards ran past him to deal with the disturbance. The Resident, Kali, while being escorted back to her cell, must have had a disagreement with the guards, and now two men lay gasping for air at her feet.

"The Residents are particularly rambunctious tonight," Froce observed. "Should we assist?"

"They'll handle it." Caleb pulled out a cigar. "The Residents are just itching for a little attention. Because of our girl, they're now only second priority."

Froce watched Caleb light his cigar. "Sir, you do know you're not supposed to smoke on the grounds?"

"Yes, son, I do." Caleb took a long puff. "Back to what you were saying, I'm not ready to say our man didn't help Athena escape. But if she planted one false trail, it makes sense for her to do it again. Keep us chasing our tails."

"And if Edward did do it?" Froce asked. "What's the reason for telling us?"

"She didn't tell us," Caleb corrected. "She hinted at it. Athena is a fickle girl and sometimes she sees life as a game with rules and a winner. She might think it unfair for her to leave us without some chance of winning." Caleb took another puff. "And another thing. Edward Gantz is one of the guys in charge of making the schedule."

Froce got where he was going. "Do you think he messed up the schedule? It would go a long way in explaining why no one showed up."

Caleb looked uncertain. "I'm just putting it out there. Like I said, he's only one of the three guys who work on the schedule. It would take quite a lot of doing to sneak it past the other two. Plus, there's the timing. Assuming Athena needed to go to the mall first, for whatever reason, she had to be pretty sure Matthew Titanos would agree to that demand before today."

"It's still something to look into," Froce objected. "Even if it is just a ploy."

One of the guards ran toward them a tad too fast for Froce's liking. If Athena could impersonate a guard, so could another Resident. The guard stopped and gave them both a swift salute, one Caleb and Froce returned with amusement. They were all basically just hired thugs and no one bothered to follow the protocol.

"Sir, I couldn't find Edward Gantz," the guard said briskly. "It appears he clocked out an hour before Athena broke out. Several calls were made to his house, all of them unanswered."

"That's suspicious," Froce remarked.

Caleb studied the man. "You're Mycheal Lawyer, one of the new recruits. I thought you were let go."

"No, sir," Mycheal said stiffly. "I was assigned to the gate."

"Is this the same gate that let Athena escape?"

"No, sir, it was the gate that followed orders. Is this the same Athena that I suggested didn't have enough discipline?"

"Sharp tongue on this one," Caleb growled.

"You do know you're not supposed to smoke on grounds?" Mycheal struck Froce as a guy who would stay up all night reading the rule book.

"Yes he does," Froce interceded. "Tell me, do you know where Ms. Yang is?"

"She left a couple of minutes ago."

"Fine, I want you and two others to go by Edward's house and bring him in."

Mycheal snapped another salute before whirling around and walking off.

Froce sighed. "You don't make friends easily, do you?"

"Not my fault," Caleb huffed. "We should probably check out the other two people who worked on the schedule. I also want those two kids we have checked on."

Froce gave a slight nod. "Okay, but first....hand me one of those cigars."

Chapter 42

Remus tried to steady his breathing, but it was difficult. He did not know if pulling the fire alarm had been the right choice or if it was a hindrance to Athena. Perhaps she wanted to keep things discreet. Adding to that, the decision to help her was still under scrutiny. Still, he had made his decision, and the only thing he could do was hope for the best. The universe snorted at this notion.

At first, there was no response and Remus thought for a stupid moment that the hotel would collectively ignore the alarm, but as he watched, people began sticking their heads out of their rooms to confront the commotion.

"What's going on?" someone demanded, a loud, booming voice built to carry. "I have a meeting at seven tomorrow. I don't need this!"

"Probably some damn kid who got bored," a woman said.

"Someone should check with the management, just in case."

A man finally noticed Remus, standing in the middle of the hallway, looking as suspicious as if he was wearing a t-shirt with the word "GUILTY" etched on it. "Did you do this?"

Remus hesitated a moment too long, confirming his guilt.

"You think this is funny?" the man asked, taking a menacing step towards him, muscles already flexing in anticipation for the beating he was about to give.

As was its nature, the universe made sure he was a big guy who could snap Remus' neck without breaking a sweat. At this moment, Remus wished he had thought out his plan a little better, or, at the very least, thought to hide after pulling the alarm instead of standing dumbly in the middle of the corridor, waiting to get caught.

"I asked you a question. Do you think it's funny messing with grown men's business?" the man demanded, flexing his muscles once again. Definitely a bodybuilder or personal trainer. "Answer me!"

"No, sir." He thought quickly. "There are terrorists on the floor above, planning on taking over this hotel..." He lost his train of thought, but it didn't matter. He could tell by their faces they didn't believe him.

"Are you high?" a wizardly old man asked suspiciously.

"Maybe he's mentally challenged," a woman with an English accent said sympathetically. It was the woman from the convenience store and she was pretending not to recognize him, which made sense as she didn't want to be associated with a prankster. Still, it was an amazing coincidence, and Remus' newfound paranoia told him to be suspicious.

"He ain't challenged," the ridiculously muscular man protested, and Remus directed his attention to him, just now noticing he had an arm tattoo that said "DEATH." Well, that certainly wasn't a good indicator. "He's making it up for giggles. Oh, I know the type."

"If you all will stop and listen," Remus tried again, but was sadly interrupted when the guy Remus mentally nicknamed as Muscleman took a step forward and shoved him, forcing Remus to stagger back.

Before Muscleman could follow up, the English woman's voice cut through the ruckus like steel. "Stop rough-handling that poor lad at once! He's obviously suffering through some type of mental trauma and needs support!" She might have been trying to help. It didn't feel like it.

A scream, followed by the rumble of feet, stopped Remus from making a counter-argument, which was a blessing, because at this point, he feared he would only make things worse.

"It's coming from the stairs," a worried man said. "Maybe there are terrorists. Someone should go check."

"Don't be ridiculous," Muscleman snarled, but with a tinge of doubt. "It's a hoax."

The rumble of feet became louder, and then a short man with freckles and blond curly hair popped out of the stairwell. "Men with guns," he gasped. "On the floor above. They planted a bomb. You need to get the hell out of here!" The man with the impeccably good timing vanished before questions could be directed to him.

"There really are terrorists." Muscleman was dumbfounded.

"Are you sure?" Remus mocked. He'd never found the joy in taunting, but couldn't resist rubbing it in. Of course, the terrorist story was fake, but to automatically dismiss it without checking, and to go so far as to suggest he was mentally challenged, royally pissed him off. "Maybe this is really all a hoax. Maybe the crowds of frightened and panicky people you hear galloping down the stairs are all part of an elaborate prank to scare everyone on this floor. This could be a reality TV show and, at any moment, a guy is going to pop out and say, gotcha!"

Muscleman hesitated, and actually looked around. "Is he?"

"No, he's not!" Remus snapped, but then realized he was being unfair. These people didn't expect to be pulled into a nightmare. If you continue to stand around and debate, there's a good chance you'll end up dead."

Muscleman threw up his arms. "Okay, so what do we do now?"

That stopped Remus. "Excuse me?"

"Tell us what to do now!"

In the last couple of days, Remus had seen a man fall down an escalator, a father try to kill his son, a telepathic girl smash a man's head in with a hammer, a gas station explode, and the same girl shoot lightning from her hand. But the most unbelievable, the most incredulous thing he'd seen was someone asking him what to do in a crisis. No one ever asked him for his help or his input, not even his brother, and for a brief moment, he wondered if he had imagined Muscleman's words.

"Get downstairs to the lobby," he instructed. "If anyone has a cell phone, call the police. Do not try to pack anything or take anything with you," he said, eyeing the British woman inching towards her room. "It's not worth your life. Leave now."

The crowd shoved past him, eager to follow his instruction, and Remus felt a thrill of elation. They were actually listening to him!

He frowned at the British woman. "Didn't you hear me, lady?" he yelled, following her inside her room. "I said don't bother taking anything with—" He stopped talking once he saw the pistol in her hand. Even more troubling, the pistol was pointed at him, which quickly and mercilessly killed all feelings of elation. She was one of them.

"Did they come for me," she whispered. "Are you with him?"

"What?" Remus asked, trying to think with a gun aimed at his chest. She wasn't acting like one of the guys after Athena. With super-powered humans and trained assassins on his tail, it would be terribly embarrassing to be killed by a terrified woman.

"My husband," she screamed, waving her gun, and only then did Remus see her small child wrapped around her leg.

"Hey," Remus waved awkwardly at the kid, who waved back as if this was all normal. "Ma'am," Remus directed at the woman, "if you could do me the tremendous favor of not shooting me..."

"Did he send you to kill me?"

"Your husband?" Remus asked, trying to get a grasp on this situation. "No one hired me to kill anyone."

"He's the chief of police," the woman confided with suspicion.

"Good for him!" Her finger twitched, informing Remus that flippancy was not the wisest course. "I mean...why would he want you dead?" The child tugged at her sleeves, all the while watching Remus with solemn eyes. "You're running away from him," he decided.

Her eyes flickered, but the gun remained steady. Remus hadn't taken the time to study her at the grocery store, but he took the time now. She was of average height with mocha skin and short black hair that covered her ears. She could easily be described as attractive; however, her face was distorted in an expression of fear that tarnished her good looks.

Remus licked his lips, deciding on what to say. "Ma'am, I'm not here to kill you, and I can guarantee the people outside are not here for you. Keep the gun on me if you wish, but you need to leave."

"I can't keep her safe," she said more to herself than him. "It's only been two days and I can't keep my own child safe."

"Talk about this later, leave now!"

She seemed oblivious to Remus, and he wondered if he

could sneak back out. They were after him and Athena, and so should leave her alone as long as she didn't try to point a gun at them. That was assuming she wouldn't try to point a gun at them.

"Maybe if I go back," she mused. "He'll understand and—"

"No!" Remus snapped, surprising her as well as himself. Her hand tightened around the trigger, and he winced, but no bullet ever came. "No," he said in a lower tone. "Going back would be the worst mistake you ever made. He might forgive you, but not before breaking a couple bones. Eventually, he will kill you or just get bored. That's when he will move on to your daughter."

"How do you know?" She put a hand around her daughter, who was still clinging on to her leg. This meant she was only holding the gun with one hand, and Remus didn't believe she had much practice with it.

"Because my father's the same way. Our mother left him when we were young, and he spent my entire childhood punishing me and my brother for it. In fact, today he tried to kill me."

She squinted, probably a tad suspicious he was making it up, but not ready to make an accusation. "So, the people here..."

"Are not his, but they are after a friend of mine," he answered. "And I won't...can't...allow that." Something was off about this woman. Remus didn't know where this abrupt and sudden insight came from, but it was overpoweringly certain. He didn't know if she was a threat or even if she was involved in today's craziness, but she was lying. "Please," he begged. "Take your daughter and go."

The woman took a deep breath, seemed to find some inner strength, and nodded. "Okay."

"Follow me." He had no sooner turned to leave the room when he ran smack into three men who, by their attire, Remus knew to be part of the people pursuing Athena.

"Well, look at what we have here," one of them commented with a wide, toothy grin.

Brandon Badger was not having a good night. It had

started with his brother being forcefully added to his team. Things had gone progressively downhill with Fides targeting and killing the teen who had been manning the lobby area. The fact that Athena had been expecting them had been a blow to morale, but Brandon still thought the mission could go smoothly. That was until the fire alarm was pulled just as they arrived at the room Athena was supposedly staying in.

"What the hell?" Marcus yelled, struggling to be heard over the ruckus.

"Someone pulled the fire alarm!"

"Oh shit," Brandon whispered as he spotted Athena's plan. "We got caught with our pants down."

"Sir?"

"What do you think is going to happen when people come out wanting to know what happened and find us dressed in bulletproof armor waving guns around?"

Sure enough, people popped their heads out of their rooms to check on the commotion, and soon a lot of yelling ensued.

"This is inconvenient," Fides observed as if he'd merely gotten mud on his new shoes. Brandon had left Anthony downstairs with the team covering the lobby door while taking Fides with him. He didn't want Fides anywhere near his brother.

"I want you to take half our men and check out the room," Brandon said to Cory. "I doubt she's there, but she might have left something behind."

Marcus nodded and moved to obey his orders. Brandon raised his hands as the halls quickly filled up. "People, I understand your concerns, but please bear with me." He hesitated. He needed to tell them something, but not the truth. A scream from the room interrupted his thoughts.

"What happened?" he asked sharply, but Fides merely shrugged.

People were starting to notice Fides' arm, and some were pointing at it with visible looks of disgust.

"How rude," Fides huffed.

"Don't do anything," he warned. Then, in a louder tone, "I want this floor completely blocked off, and someone tell me what's happening!"

"It's Marcus, sir," Allen said, coming out the room, his face ashen white. "He jumped off the balcony!"

"Jumped or was pushed?" Brandon demanded, his head spinning from this information. His squad didn't lose men; there had been close calls in the past, but he always managed to get everyone home.

"He must have jumped. There was no one else out there except him! Did she make him jump?"

"I don't know." They were defenseless against mind control. There were stories of those who could protect their minds using mental exercises, but Brandon and his troop had never learned them. And if they made it back alive, it would be the first thing he would correct about his squad.

"If your man jumped, then it was of his own free will," Fides said, his tone slightly wishful. "I would have felt it if she or anyone else had forced him to jump."

"He didn't jump," Brandon said forcefully.

Fides looked at him as if he was being inconsiderate. "Brandon, if your man jumped, then we should rejoice for him. He realized the truth and was able to act on it. Of course, he could have picked a better time, but still..."

"My men don't jump!" Brandon thought it over. "What about telekinesis?"

"I wouldn't be able to tell you," Fides admitted. "I can't detect abilities of that caliber."

"Perfect!" Brandon scrambled to find a plan and remembered hearing the door on the previous floor slam shut as they were trouncing up the stairs. "Durkhiem!" he yelled, and the man looked up. Durkhiem was a small odious man, and Brandon wouldn't have included him if it wasn't for the man's ability to shoot and hit anything that moved. "I want you to take two men and check out the sixth floor. You're looking for Athena or the boy."

"Sir?"

"It's just a hunch."

Durkhiem nodded and left.

"Allen, help the others and make sure no one leaves this floor."

"You think she might still be up here.?"

"I don't believe for a second that Cory jumped, and Fides ruled out mind control, so that only leaves us with a few options. If she is a telekinetic, then she has to be close. All the telekinetics I know have limited range."

"Yes, sir," Allen said, leaving.

"I must admit, I'm impressed by the way you're handling things," Fides complimented.

"You won't be for long," Brandon promised. Then, in a loud, commanding tone, he began to speak to the crowd. "Please calm down. We are here to apprehend an extremely dangerous individual, and we appreciate your cooperation." The crowd grew quiet, Brandon's voice reaching them. "If anyone has seen a young girl around the age of sixteen with blond hair and grey contacts, please inform us immediately. We believe her to be a hostage of a sociopath. Most likely, his next victim."

Brandon knew the lie would grate on Fides' nerves, and the Resident didn't disappoint. When Brandon glanced back at him, he could see a vein throbbing in the Resident's neck.

"Was that necessary?"

"Yes, it was."

"Please explain."

As distasteful as he found Fides, he couldn't afford the Resident making waves, so Brandon launched into explanation. "Unless I missed my guess, Athena is on this floor. If she is, she must be starting to panic. There's no way to escape this level. Now instead of this crowd being a liability, I actually made them an advantage. Every one of them is now looking for her, eager to save her. Another way to look at it is, I'm forcing her to make a move. If she's still on this floor, we will know soon enough."

Before Fides could respond, a loud female voice carried across the hallway. "BOMB! THERE'S A BOMB SET TO GO OFF!"

"I believe Athena has made her move," Fides said dryly, watching the crowd react and despair over the newest news. "I doubt anyone is looking for her now. These poor lambs are too busy trying not to get blown up, although that would be an interesting way to go."

Brandon ignored Fides and yelled out to the crowd. "Who said that? There is no bomb, who said that?"

Then the mob surged forward, somehow getting past Allen.

"Stay where you are!" Brandon screamed, but the crowd was past listening to him.

"There's a bomb!"

"Someone help me!"

"One of the cops got stabbed!"

The last statement caught Brandon's ear. Cops? Were they talking about them? He turned to Fides, who seemed to be looking far off in the distance.

"Fides, has anyone lied recently?"

"Not since the bomb fiasco," Fides answered, never taking his eyes off the unseen thing in the distance.

"Damn it!" Brandon pushed and elbowed his way through the crowd. It took him a couple of minutes, but he eventually stumbled across Allen's remains. He knelt down beside the poor man and struggled to contain his anger. Allen had suffered a fatal injury to the chest. He hadn't died right away, so he must have felt it when the crowd trampled over his body.

Rage boiled up inside him, but he pushed it back down. Now was not the time to act rashly. He would need all his wits to capture Athena.

"Sir," a voice called out over his earpiece. "Durkhiem wants you to know that they captured the boy. He was leaving a room with another women and her daughter. He's relatively sure that Athena is still in there."

Brandon processed the information. A woman with her daughter? "Where are they now?"

"The woman's with me. We're heading for the lobby now. Durkhiem is still with the boy."

"I doubt Athena is in that room. She was just up here..." Brandon froze as a thought occurred to him. "I think Athena might be heading down to the boy...Remus." He had grown tired of calling him "the boy." It made it seem like he was an innocent bystander in all this, which Brandon knew he was not.

"You think she would go back for him?"

"I'm sure of it. She won't leave without him."

The crowd had thinned immensely and Brandon turned around, looking for Fides, only to discover the Resident missing.

Remus stared at the man who had spoken. He was a small guy with a thin mustache and balding hair. The other two were thin and weedy and could have passed as twins. If Doublemint Gum ever had a commercial for rednecks, these two would be the perfect candidates.

The woman stood behind him, her child in her arms.

The short man whistled. "First that girl, Athena, and now this lass behind you. You do get around."

"She has nothing to do with this," Remus said, shocked at how steady his voice was.

"Probably true," the short man agreed. "But she's with you, so I guess that means she's involved." He gestured to Twin B. "Take her to the lobby and keep a close eye on her. Tell Badger we have the boy."

Then, speaking directly to the women, he said, "Ma'am, we're here for your own safety. This person is a dangerous terrorist."

She stared at Remus mutely.

"If you go with my friend, he will quickly debrief you and lead you to safety."

After a lingering glance at Remus, she followed Twin B in silence. Remus watched her leave with a pang of regret. He didn't think he could live with himself if anything happened to her because of him.

"And you," Shortman—his new nickname—said, directing his gun at him. "Come out in the hall where I can see you."

Remus obliged. There was nothing else he could have done.

"That's good. Now tell me, are there any surprises in this room? Like an angry Resident, for example?"

"Not sure," Remus said noncommittally.

"This will go a lot faster if you cooperate."

"Once this is over, you're going to kill me, so I find my-self lacking incentive to help."

"You're bargaining for your life?"

Shortman and Twin A were so sure Athena was in the room he'd just left that they didn't bother to check around them. Neither of them was facing the stairway, so they didn't see the door open on the other side of the hall and Athena step out wearing striped pajamas and a cap. She surveyed the situation for a moment, and then started running stealthily towards them.

"What if I told you I could guarantee your freedom if you help us?" Shortman enticed.

Remus carefully kept his gaze away from the quickly approaching Athena. "I'd say you're full of it. There's no way you can promise something like that."

"Maybe, but I don't see anyone else making an offer to spare you."

Remus watched as Athena gathered up speed, sprinting faster and faster until she was nothing more than a blur.

He shrugged. "I've had a gun pointed at me so many times today I think I've become desensitized."

Shortman scowled, but before he could reply, Athena slammed into him at breakneck speed. The full force of the blow was enough to send the small figure shooting forward, and Remus actually had to duck out of the way as Shortman went flying by with an agonizing squeal. He hit the floor and didn't move. Twin A reached for the gun, but Athena gave him a straight-fingered jab under the sternum. Twin A's face went very pale and he doubled over in pain. Athena clasped her hands together, raised them, and gave him a brutal blow to the top of his head. He went down without a murmur.

Shortman groaned, looking like he wanted to get up, and before Remus knew what he was doing, he had run over and kicked the man. With an "oof!" Shortman fell back to the ground and stayed that way.

"Nice job," Athena complimented breezily. "You might want to work on your kick. The way you were doing it, you could have broken a toe."

"I'll keep it in mind." He wasn't going to admit his toe was throbbing in pain, but by her sly grin, she already knew. "Nice pajamas by the way." He was glad to see Athena unhurt.

She smiled. "You're too sweet. I'm glad you're unhurt, too."

He felt his face flush, and it might have been a nice moment if he hadn't remembered the small army searching for them a few floors below. "What do we do now?"

"We wait until the police show up, and then sneak out during the confusion," she said easily.

He nodded, glad to see she was in better spirits than when he'd left her. He was about to ask if she'd spotted the woman and her child on the stairway when a voice rang out from behind them.

"Lies!"

Remus looked and saw a middle-aged man, slightly overweight with graying hair. The most unusual aspect was his right arm. It was larger than his left and hung stiffly at his side. Black and blue bruises covered it from finger to shoulder.

Athena immediately stepped in front of Remus as if to shield him, which gave Remus all the information he needed.

"That's right, Remus, this is the Resident they sent after me," Athena started in a conversational tone. "From what I gather, his name is Fides, which is really sad, because Fides is a goddess' name. Why would you name a man after a goddess?"

She wasn't exactly speaking to the other man, but he answered anyway. "I have already dealt with that injustice a long time ago," Fides said, slowly walking towards them with the air of a man who held all the cards. "I'm quite used to all the juvenile jokes. I find that being teased is a far better fate than being known as a liar."

Athena raised an eyebrow. "And when did I lie? You don't like my plan of sneaking out while you tussle with the cops?"

Fides shook his head. "Not what I'm referring to. You see, you lied when you said there was a bomb. Your friend lied when he pulled the fire alarm. There was no fire."

"Oh yeah?" Athena shot back as if this was a fight between siblings, and Remus realized with dread that she might be enjoying herself. "Brandon lied when he claimed I was kidnapped by some terrorist." In the back of Remus' terrified mind, he recognized how odd it was for Athena to call the man in charge of her enemies, and a guy she'd never personally met, by his first name. Formalities must be a limit only to the non-telepathic.

"He did, and I might show him truth later. But we're here to talk about your crimes, not his."

"Hmm, that sounds boring," Athena complained. "And it really doesn't seem like you need the both of us. You mind if my friend leaves?"

Fides had been slowly ambling forward, but at the question, he paused to think. "Besides your thinly veiled lie to hide your concern for him, I have no other objections."

"You'll let him pass without killing him?"

Fides shook his head. "I'm not a killer, Athena."

She scoffed, still placing herself between him and Fides.

Behind them, one of the twins groaned and Remus shot him a glance. He was beginning to feel powerless, his life nothing but a bargaining tool between the two.

"You killed that poor kid downstairs. Made him stab himself with a pair of scissors and then stuffed him in the back room."

"I showed him truth," Fides stressed earnestly, as if he really cared that they believed him. "I'm not a killer."

"Fine. In that case, can my friend pass without you showing him truth?"

"As of now, I have no orders on him," he said with a shrug. "It's possible I might be sent to deal with him later, but right now he can pass without fear."

Athena nodded and spoke directly to Remus. "He can't lie. Get out of here...walk past him and don't look back."

On an intellectual level, Remus knew he would be of no help, yet he did not move...did not want to leave Athena to fight this monster alone.

Athena tore her gaze from Fides to stare at Remus with twinkling eyes. "Really?" she said in an almost childlike voice. "That's sweet of you, but I'll be okay." She gave a smile meant for no one's benefit but his. "I won't lose."

"Telling more lies again?" Fides taunted.

She kept her eyes on Remus, though she raised her voice to answer. "Even if I lose, it would be a mistake, not a lie." She leaned in to Remus. "The whole plan involves a quick escape. If you're not ready with the getaway car, then there's no point."

Remus felt like a coward as he briefly touched Athena's shoulder before sprinting for the exit.

Chapter 43

Athena watched Remus run past Fides and exit through the door.

"What an exceptional young man you found," Fides commented.

"He is," Athena agreed.

Fides sighed theatrically. "It's a shame he had to get involved in this mess. You do know being involved with a Resident greatly decreases his life expectancy?"

"We're not involved." She was annoyed when she felt her face flushing. "Not the way you're thinking."

"I doubt it matters in the long run. The fact that there is a connection is enough for a death sentence." He looked at her thoughtfully. "You're a smart girl, you should know that. Why involve him if you care so deeply about his welfare?"

"Remus will be okay," Athena said, ignoring the bulk of his question. "I'll make sure of it."

Fides smiled. "A noble sentiment, but it's really not up to you, is it?"

The smart move would be to eliminate Fides as soon as possible, but if what she suspected of Fides was true, then he could be useful to her in more ways than one. "From what you've told me, you can't lie." She paused, working out the correct phrasing in her mind. "So if I ask you if you could destroy my mind if I attempt to read yours..."

"I would be forced to tell you, I could not," he answered happily, delighted by this new game. "Not only can I not lie, but I can also tell when people are lying to me. So if I asked you if you can control minds..."

"Then you can tell I speak truth when I say I cannot," she finished. "I'm limited to only reading minds. Now if I ask you how you found me..."

"I would tell you that we're tracking your movement using a small device we inserted in your body when you were just a baby, but I would decline to tell you exactly where it is...just to be on the safe side."

So it was another bug in her body. One that Dr. Pluck and the others knew nothing about. She had expected as much, but now that it was confirmed, she could plan out her next moves. But before that, she had to kill Fides, who was waiting in hopeful anticipation of her next question. She took a peek into Fides' mind...

A wave of depression slammed into her and she yelled in shock. Fides' thoughts screamed for death. His agony threatened to overcome her and before she knew it, she was down on her knees, struggling for her next breath. She severed the connection before Fides' mind could do her more harm.

"You are unharmed?" Fides asked with what seemed to be sincere concern.

"You're a very depressed man," she gasped, getting back on her feet while trying to steady her nerves. His mind was almost as bad as Lamia's.

Fides wrung his hands in an anxious manner. "I do apologize. I didn't know my state of mind would be such a burden to you."

"So when you told me you couldn't destroy my mind..."

"It was a mistake, not a lie," he snapped, clear warning in his voice. The slightest implication of him being a liar would drive Fides over the edge. "At the time, I didn't know you perceived emotions as well as thoughts."

"I see." She finally got her heart rate under control and steadied her trembling body. "I was mistaken about your abilities. You're an empath. You can't cause people to feel depression; rather, you project your own emotions into their minds." She took a deep breath. "How do you live like that? I barely stood a second in your mind."

"And now we come to my deepest flaw!" he announced importantly, seemingly delighted. "My inability to see the final truth. The truth that can only be seen on death's door. I have tried numerous times to cross that threshold, but sadly, I fail every time." He raised his right hand to his face. "This arm pains me so much and yet I do nothing about it." Looking at Athena, he said, "That is why it is my duty to teach others the ultimate truth."

"And what is the ultimate truth?" Athena asked, but only because she felt required to. One of the men she had taken out had dropped his gun, and it now lay two feet from her foot. However, by herself, she had no clue how to operate an assault rifle. She was buying time, trying to find an appropriate mind to pluck the information from.

"The ultimate truth?" Fides repeated, wagging his finger at her. "The ultimate truth is that life is pain and despair. There is no point living such a meaningless existence. Why would anyone subject himself to such a continuance? Sadly, people do not realize this truth, so it's my job to reveal it to them, so that they might find a greater truth."

"There's a greater truth?" Athena asked. She had found a mind. A man named Anthony Badger, who, coincidentally, was the brother of Brandon Badger, the man leading the siege. In order to get the information she required, she would have to dive deeper into his mind, which would mean leaving her physical body defenseless.

"Yes, the greater truth," Fides responded, acting like a professor teaching an eager pupil. "The truth that men have sought since biblical time—what is after death? Now, my dear Athena," Fides said, clapping his hands. "We've spent a lot of time with our chat, and I enjoyed every minute of it, but I fear our time is up and, in truth, I feel like I no longer have your full attention. So, I guess it's on to the main event."

Athena quickly shut down her telepathy. She hadn't expected the conversation to end so abruptly. She knew Fides was about to activate his ability and knew she had to stop him at all costs.

She darted forward and slammed her fist into his face. Her fist sank into his skin almost like his body was made of dough. She pulled her fist out and ducked as Fides swung his deformed arm at her. She hit him with a follow up combo, aiming for the chest and face, but each blow was absorbed by his elastic skin, and she barely had time to jump back as his arm came crashing down on the spot where she had just been. The floor shattered where Fides' arm hit, and Athena stared at the spot. She knew she had to avoid his right arm.

"You're quick," he complimented with a grin. "I must confess, I haven't had a good brawl in years."

"What's your skin made of?" she demanded.

"A while ago, my body began to replace bones and skin

with some type of cartilage material." He sighed. "Now the only thing I have left is my hideous right arm."

Athena redefined her fighting style. She would not survive a direct hit with his right arm. The best bet would be to go for the eyes. If she could blind him, that should give her enough time to—

He lunged! Using the same darting move she had surprised him with, Fides covered the distance between them and grabbed her by the throat using his right arm. Athena tried to tear free, but his grip was ironclad.

"Quicker than you thought?" Fides asked knowingly, casually lifting her into the air. "Don't worry, you're not the first to make that mistake and I doubt you will be the last." He watched her try to claw away his hands. "It's no use. My grip is unbreakable. You really should have relied on your instincts instead of trying to think out every move." He studied her face. "Looks like you are trying to say something," he observed. "Very well, speak your peace.."

His grip lessened slightly. Just enough to give her a couple of vital breaths, but not much else. "You forgot to ask if I have any other abilities," she rasped with a grin.

Athena could tell Fides found her grin to be disconcerting. "And can you do anything else that you neglected to mention?"

"You bet! I shoot lightning!" She extended an arm and directed a spark of electricity into Fides' face. The charge was minimal, and Fides was more surprised than hurt, but he did lessen his hold on her, which was all she needed to pull herself free. She jumped back and grabbed the assault rifle lying on the floor. She looked up and saw Fides directly on top of her. He was too quick!

"Lies!" he hissed. "You told lies!"

He swung his arm, and there was nothing Athena could do to avoid it except to try to brace for the blow. The arm slammed into her ribcage and she heard bones cracking as she was sent crashing through a door and into another room. Using the momentum, she rolled, gun still in hand, and quickly got back on her feet, narrowly avoiding another of Fides' swings. The man moved so quickly it was almost like he was teleporting.

She checked her surroundings. They were now in one of the rooms. She definitely had some cracked ribs, but she could stand the pain if need be. If she was right, this room had a balcony. If she could lure Fides to the balcony, she could throw him off. She doubted even he could survive such a fall. Now she had to...

Depression washed over her, and she fell to her knees as unwanted thoughts and miserable memories from her past attacked her.

"There you go, thinking too hard again," he scolded, watching her sink to the ground with unsympathetic eyes. "I guess I shouldn't expect too much from a filthy liar."

"I didn't lie!" Athena tried to struggle to her feet, but found she couldn't move. "I told you I shot lightning and I did!"

"You made it seem like I was going to be electrocuted. Your move was a bluff!"

"Then it was your interpretation that was a lie, not my words. Like you said, if I was to lie, you would have caught it." She groaned as the depression worsened. "All things are subject to interpretation. Whichever interpretation prevails at a given time is a function of power and not truth."

"One of Athena's famous quotes," he mocked. "I was hoping to hear one. It's very profound."

She lost track of what he was saying, caught up in her own depression. Life was unfair. Why was she cursed to spend her entire life in the confines of a prison? What did she ever do? "I know the world isn't fair, but why isn't it ever unfair in my favor?"

"Saw that one in a comic strip before," Fides acknowledged.

Athena realized she was now on the bed. Fides must have picked her up and placed her there without her knowing. A thought crossed her mind, bringing with it another wave of fear and misery.

Fides chuckled. "Calm yourself, girl. I simply assumed you would be more comfortable on the bed. Now excuse me for a moment. I have to make a call."

Fides was a monster, but so was she. How many people had she killed? How many had suffered because of her existence? "Murderers are not monsters, they're men. And that's the most frightening thing about them," she cried out.

No response from Fides. Athena hadn't planned to kill anyone once she escaped Pandora's Box, she really hadn't. Instead, she wanted to do something different with her life, but look at her now. A dozen people had died by her hands, and Remus' life was forever ruined.

Remus. If she didn't escape, then he would die. That thought gave her motivation and made the depression slightly more bearable, allowing her to draw out of her weakened state. Tilting her head, she saw Fides on a cell phone. For some reason, the thought of Residents owning their own phone was absurdly funny and she had to stop herself from laughing.

"I have Athena," he said.

She was sitting in his chair in his office, talking on her cell phone!

"What the fuck?" Maris growled.

She actually had the gall to hold up a finger to silence him. Maris opened his mouth to scream at her, but stopped when a thought occurred to him. How on earth did she get past his guards? Where *were* his guards? Something wasn't right. The one thing Maris could do was smell when something was rotten, so instead of yelling, he settled down and studied her.

"Excellent," the woman said smoothly into the phone. "And what has she told you?" A pause. "So no mind control abilities?"

Mind control? Must be code for something else. She was slim with oriental features and long, silky dark hair. Looked like one of those high-class prostitutes.

"That's interesting. So she had to have help. Find out who it is." Then, rather testily, "What do you mean it's having no effect now?" The woman drummed her fingers on the desk. "Fine, if you can get nothing else out of her, then kill her and be done with it."

Maris raised an eyebrow. She was talking about killing people in his office. Who was this woman?

"Fine! Show her truth!" Another pause. "That's not working either?" She gave a long sigh and smiled at Maris. She put one hand over her phone. "I'm sorry for the delay," she said, as if he was expecting this visit. "I'll be with you in a moment. You can have a seat if you wish."

By acting as if this was her office, she was setting the tone for the next conversation. Maris grudgingly admired the balls on this one even as he thought of ways to kill her. These must be the people his son had gotten into bed with. The ones he hoped to use to overthrow Maris and take over. The ones who had killed the hit men he had hired and kidnapped Romulus to use as leverage. That they sent a woman was a clear sign of disrespect.

"Fine, go after the boy then. Strip him of any information, then kill him." She snapped the phone shut and gave Maris another smile, although it looked a little strained this time. "Your son, Remus, is quite a nuisance."

"Oh?" It was no surprise that this new group would back-stab and kill Remus. What was surprising was that they didn't wait to swallow up Maris' organization before committing the act.

"Mr. Sylvia," the woman greeted, standing up and thrusting out a hand. "I'm Eris Yang, and we have much to discuss."

It was clear she thought this would go down a certain way, but Maris absolutely hated playing by someone else's script. Instead of shaking her hand, he took out his pistol and moved to the side so he could cover her and the door at the same time.

To his disappointment, the woman failed to look scared or even surprised. "I'm already behind schedule, so I have very little time for games," she surmised.

"You have till the count of three to tell me where my sons are." He knew how this was supposed to go down, for he would have planned it the same way. Maris was supposed to sit down, his back facing the entrance. The woman would distract him so that Maris wouldn't hear the hit man come from behind until it was too late.

"Really, Mr. Sylvia."

"One," Maris counted. There was a good chance Romulus was dead, but Maris held out hope. If both sons were dead, then his legacy would die with them.

"Please, let us sit and discuss the matter like..."

"Two."

"...rational people. I guarantee you have the wrong misconception of us."

"Three." Maris' hand tightened around the trigger.

"Romulus is alive," the woman hurried to say.

"Where are my sons?" Maris repeated. "The next words out of your mouth better be a location."

"Foul little man."

Maris instantly switched his gun towards the door where a man was now standing. It was a surprise that this man had managed to sneak up on him, especially since Maris knew this would be their plan. It was even more surprising because this man was a giant, who had to duck his head to get through the doorway. Maris should have seen and heard him coming. What really suspended belief was that two ravens rested on both sides of the giant's shoulders. As Maris gawked, the birds' beady eyes seemed to glare back at him. The giant had intricate tattoos covering his face and neck, and he loomed over Maris, staring down at him with clear disdain.

"I asked you to wait," the woman scolded.

"I didn't want to," the new man rumbled, as if that was excuse enough.

The woman sighed and removed her glasses to rub the bridge of her nose as if fending off a migraine. "Mr. Sylvia, this is my associate, Horus. He is—"

"Your hit man," Maris sneered.

"Hit man?" The giant bellowed out a laugh as if Maris had said something truly funny, and the windows seemed to shake with his guffaw. The ravens cawed as if echoing his laugh. "We don't use hit men. We use assassins. Though one isn't needed for one like you."

"Please wait in the hall," Ms. Yang instructed.

"He has a gun," Horus pointed out. "And you are not invulnerable."

That's right, Maris did have a gun. The sheer bizarreness of the man had been enough to temporarily make him forget, but he snapped out of his terror. Looking at Horus, he saw no weapons. Giant or not, he would still die from a bullet to the head.

"This is what's going to happen," Maris yelled, reestablishing control by pointing the gun at the giant's head. "You will tell me where my sons are or—" Maris screamed as the gun suddenly grew so hot that he was forced to drop it. He looked at his hand to see that the flesh was still sizzling, and the skin was bright red and already blistering.

"I will assume you are satisfied," Ms. Yang said to the giant.

The giant rumbled back a reply. He walked towards Maris, who was sure he was about to die. This giant could easily crush his head using his hands alone. However, instead of grabbing him by the throat, he reached down and grabbed the gun. Despite it being scalding hot a moment ago, it didn't seem to hurt the giant at all. "I will wait fifteen—" The raven squawked and the giant nodded. "You're right. I will only wait ten minutes." He looked at Maris one more time before shaking his head. "Hit man," he mused as he ducked out the door.

Maris strained to hear the sound of him retreating, but either the giant was surprisingly light on his feet or he was standing just out of sight.

"Mr. Sylvia, I fear we got off to a most egregious start," Ms. Yang said, sounding wearied.

"You're damn well right we did!" Maris snapped.

"However, you did pull a gun on me," the woman continued.

Maris was still clutching his injured hand. "How did you do that?" he demanded.

Ms. Yang adjusted her glasses. "Mr. Sylvia, when you are ready, I will tell you a story. One you won't believe right away, but is nevertheless true. Afterwards, depending on your answer, and my gut feeling, we might reach a deal."

"What type of deal?" Maris asked, his business sense kicking in.

"Unlimited financial security along with aid in obtaining any political position you desire."

It was a lie. It had to be a lie because it sounded too good to be true. "And my sons?"

"One of them has shown promise and we hope to utilize him in the future." Ms. Yang's eyes zeroed in on Maris, her gaze smoldering. "But one of them must die." She might have been crazy, but she was crazy with a giant monster waiting in the hallway.

"I'm going to need a drink." Maris pointed to the good vintage on his desk.

The woman shook her head. "Apologies, but I prefer both parties to be sober in making a deal." Of course she did.

Maris took a seat. "Then hurry with your story."

Ms. Yang began. She was right; he didn't believe a word of it.

Chapter 44

Athena wriggled her arms, testing her capabilities. Her energy had been sapped. She could barely move, and at this moment, it would have been highly hazardous to her health if she managed to get hold of a knife. But with each passing second, the pain lessened. Her mind, which had proven to be durable in the past, was steadily becoming used to Fides' psychological torture.

Fides was still on the phone. "No. No mind control ability. Which leads to the question on how did she escape in the first place?"

So they hadn't figured everything out yet. Athena smiled. The advantage still belonged to her.

"Fine, I'll ask." Fides looked at her. "Athena, who helped you escape?"

"Bite me," she snapped.

Fides blinked owlishly. "Excuse me?"

"I said bite me!"

Fides hesitated for a second and got back on the phone. "This is a trite embarrassing. It seems I'm no longer having an effect on her." A pause. "She's resisting me." Another pause, then in an annoyed tone. "You know I can't kill anyone. It's not in my nature. I merely show people the truth."

Athena's heart skipped a beat.

"It will be as you wish." Fides placed the phone on the table. "Athena, I'm pleased to tell you that I have the honor of showing you truth." He walked into the kitchen and disappeared from view.

Athena struggled to get her body working. She had resisted Fides' emotions so far, but she had no idea what a full power blast would do to her. Her legs moved feebly, refusing to obey her commands.

Fides came back, wielding a knife, and Athena laughed sardonically. "You plan to stab me? I thought you never killed anyone?"

"You've regained enough of your senses to recognize humor," Fides noticed. "That's admirable. And this knife isn't for me, my dear, sweet, Athena. It's for your benefit." He tossed the knife on the bed, near her hand. "One person I showed truth to didn't have a handy weapon nearby. He actually clawed his eyes out, trying to reach his brain. I find this way is more humane."

Athena knew what would happen next, and took a deep breath as the depression rolled over her. Horrors! Life full of pain and destruction. Remus was right. The universe was an insane asylum where evil ruled with an iron fist! Evil wanted you to live so it could suck the life out of you. The only way to thwart evil and escape its grasp was with death.

Before she knew it, the knife was in her hand, pointed at her throat.

"That's it, Athena," Fides crooned. "Recognize the truth and act on it!"

She should be proud. Very few people had the strength and drive necessary to embark on this course of action. She would join a club of elitists!

Athena held the knife steady. Her intent was to cut the major artery in her throat. It would only take minutes for her to bleed to death, and then she could move on from this cursed world and pursue greater truth!

Fides' voice was like a drill in her mind. "You tried your best, but in the end, you can't escape the truth. Life isn't worth living."

"No one ever finds life worth living," Athena started.

"That's right, they don't," Fides agreed in triumph. "You get it!"

But then she continued, "One has to make it worth living." She looked up at Fides, whose face was hovering inches above hers. "No one ever finds life worth living; one has to make it worth living. That's my quote."

"But I don't understand," Fides stammered. "What about the truth?"

"I deny your truth," Athena spat venomously. "Your truth

is the way of cowards and fools, refusing to live life because you deem it too hard. A coward gets scared and quits. A hero gets scared, but still goes on." For a moment, Athena felt her depression grow as Fides redoubled his efforts, but a second later, it slid off her and she was in control. "To put it simply, I think you're a miserable excuse for a man or Resident, and there's not a place in this universe in which your mind can beat mine!"

Fides stood up straight, staring coldly at her. "I see I was mistaken about you. You poor delusional bitch. Did you really just call yourself a hero?"

Athena flinched at the cruelty of his words before reminding herself she didn't care what he thought.

Fides watched a minute longer, perhaps hopeful she would change her mind before picking up the cell phone. "It appears she's too delusional to see the truth, however, she won't be going anywhere for a while."

Athena still had the knife in her hand, but lacked the energy to use it. Her weakness frustrated her.

"Fine, I'll go after the boy and tell Brandon exactly where he can find Athena. She's so weak, I doubt he will have much of a problem with her."

"You're not touching Remus," Athena stated.

"I'm afraid I am," Fides said, snapping his phone shut. "I wonder if you will still cling to your worthless life once he's dead."

"Probably not," Athena admitted, then with a sly smile, she said, "But I do have a gift for you." She paused as Fides looked at her expectantly. "I'll promise you your death before the night is over."

Fides cleared his throat. "Athena, I think it's clear you are not in any position to issue such threats."

Athena struggled to a sitting position. "It's not a threat, but rather a promise. It's what you want most, isn't it? You can tell when people are lying, can't you?"

Fides hesitated, and Athena saw a flash of what might have been hope in his eyes. "I don't see how, but if you could grant me truth, then I will be forever grateful. I would be sure to repay you in the next life."

"I will hold you to that promise."

Fides almost smiled before turning around. For a moment, his back was completely exposed and Athena struggled to throw the knife, but her body simply would not respond.

"Goodbye, Athena, and may you find happiness in whatever truth finds you tonight." Fides left to kill Remus while Athena struggled to fight off unconsciousness.

Remus tried to push aside the feelings of guilt. Athena was more than capable of protecting herself. Chances were she would make short work of Fides. That's what he told himself, but it still felt an awful lot like abandoning her to die. At the door to the stairway, he glanced backwards to find the two Residents talking amicably like lifelong friends. Hesitating for only a second more, Remus entered the stairway and galloped noisily down the stairs. With only a flight left to go, he rounded the corner and immediately stopped as the barrel of a gun was shoved quite rudely in his face.

"Don't kill me!" he cried out, at the same time squeezing his eyes shut in expectance of the bullet.

"You're Remus?" If the voice had been more authoritative, Remus might not have had the strength to answer, but since the voice was as timid and hesitant as he imagined his own to be, he cracked his eyes open and found a slightly built Ragnarok operative with big ears and a youthful face littered with freckles that made him seem even younger. "Remus?" he repeated impatiently.

Remus took a step away from the gun, for all the good it did him. There was no way he could move faster than the soldier's trigger finger and they both knew it. "Before I answer...I would like to know if any kill orders have been placed on this Remus fellow."

To his surprise, the gunman smiled, which would have been disarming if Remus didn't remember how affable Clive, the cold-blooded killer, had been. "It depends on the next person who finds you. If Fides happens upon your trail, you're a goner." He noticed Remus' grimace. "You already met Fides," he noted. "And you're alive, which means Athena must have been there to run interference."

The way he said Athena's name made Remus protective of her. "She saved me," he said coldly, belatedly realizing the barrel of the gun hadn't moved an inch from his face.

The gunman shook his head, a movement that seemed one more of pity than disagreement. "If you only knew...and I don't have the time to explain it to you." He lowered his gun and gestured down the stairs. "You might be able to sneak out unnoticed. Go, hide in the crowd and hope my brother can stop your Athena. If he's successful, he might decide to forget about Remus Sylvia."

Remus paused for a moment before rushing past him. He tensed, waiting for a bullet to slam into him from behind, but when he heard the gunman moving up the stairs, his feeling of dread evaporated, only to be replaced with an unexpected emotion—resentment. All of them, Fides, that gunman, even Athena, had given him orders to run away because they thought him useless in a fight. It made him want to prove them wrong, and that was a dangerous attitude to have when he was the only one of them who didn't have a gun or supernatural abilities. He crashed into the lobby and found himself amidst hundreds of people, all squished inside.

"If you will just be patient," a voice yelled out, "we will have you on your way."

"There's a bomb, let us out!"

"There is no bomb," the voice said. "Those are just rumors used to spread panic."

Remus pushed and elbowed his way to where the speaker was. He was a young man with brown hair and a killer smile. He flashed the smile more than once, trying to calm down the crowd.

"Why can't we leave?"

"Because there's a very dangerous individual in the hotel, and we think he started the rumor of a bomb to create a diversion."

Remus noted the pronoun "he." So, they didn't want anyone to know this so-called terrorist was a girl.

Remus saw the man lean in toward another gunman and whisper something, though the only word Remus was able to make out was "police."

The first man gestured for him to lower his voice, and Remus had to edge nearer and hope the mass of people would shield him.

"Any word on the target?"

"We have the boy, and we're hoping he can fill us in on

her whereabouts. There's another person that might be involved." He gestured, and Twin B came forward with the woman and her child right behind him.

Remus froze as his and the woman's eyes locked, and for a moment, he felt sure he was about to be outted. But she said nothing, so he retreated back into the multitude of people before she could change her mind, or before Twin B recognized him.

He made it to the exit, finding that the crowd became denser the closer he got. Where was Athena? She should have dealt with Fides by now. He started to move towards the stairway, and froze as he saw Fides walking purposely toward the two men he'd eavesdropped on earlier.

Remus' heart plummeted. The universe had played the cruelest trick it could think of. If Fides was down here, walking around, then that meant Athena was either captured, or worse...dead.

Chapter 45

Brandon's earpiece crackled. "Sir, this is team one. The police just showed up."

"Stall them," Brandon instructed. "We should have enough fake credentials to keep them busy for a while."

"Yes, sir."

Before Brandon could even take a breath, it came to life again. "Sir, I can't get a response from Durkhiem."

Brandon closed his eyes and briefly considered tearing the earpiece off and flinging it at the nearest wall. "Hold on. Anthony, are you there?"

"In the lobby. It's beginning to look like a circus in here. We managed to contain the crowd, but it won't take much to set them off again."

"Keep them under control. Have you seen Fides or Durkhiem?"

"Nope...I mean no, sir."

"Put a man by the stairs and elevator. They should be looking for Fides, Durkhiem, and obviously Athena. Also have men sweep the crowd." He paused and considered his next move. "Double the guards at the door and have them check each person. If he or she isn't one of the people I just mentioned, then let them go."

There was silence. "Are you sure? Opening the doors could give Athena the potential chance to escape."

"I know, but at this point, we don't have a choice. Time is against us. The police are going to realize we're not who we say we are and, if that happens, they'll arrest us all."

"You don't need to worry about Athena," Fides' voice hummed over the radio. "I have Athena under control."

"Where are you?" Brandon demanded.

"I'm in the stairwell. There's no need to worry about your men. They're on the sixth floor, unconscious but alive."

"You left without permission!"

"And it's a good thing I did," Fides shot back. "I captured Athena. You can come down and kill her."

"Kill?" Brandon asked, confused.

"We have new orders. Apparently, Mr. Titanos has found Athena to be more trouble than she's worth."

Brandon breathed a sigh of relief. With the police hovering nearby, there would be no way they could sneak Athena out. Fides' story didn't add up, however, and Brandon was determined to confront it.

"Why didn't you kill her?"

"It would appear that Athena is too weak to recognize truth."

Translation: He had no effect on her.

"Fine. Stay there and I'll be right down."

"I'm afraid I cannot. I must show the boy truth. I'm already in the lobby looking for him."

"I didn't give you that order!" Brandon snapped.

"My order came from over your head. I do apologize, but I must obey them. Do not fret, Mr. Badger; Athena is harmless now. I left her weak and shaken on the bed of room 608. I should mention that her most noticeable ability is to read minds. Be careful about that, for she's wily enough to try and get inside your head."

"Damn it," he cursed. The hallway was now completely void of all life except his men. "We're going to the sixth floor," he informed them, noting their concerned looks and sympathizing with them. They had never been this exposed before, and the natural reaction was to retreat and regroup. However, if Athena was weakened by Fides, then they had to take the opportunity to end her. "Athena is in room 608. Fides tells me she's helpless, but we all know not to trust Residents."

Despite their obvious reluctance, his men immediately formed up behind him, and he felt a sense of pride in his team. When he'd first taken over eight years ago, his squad consisted of nothing but military deserters and looters, but through years of careful training and weeding, his team was now an elite group, on par with any of the military's highest and most prized professionals. He led his men down the stairs, their footsteps echoing hollowly within the staircase.

At the sixth floor's entrance, he hesitated, painfully aware that Athena, twice now, had caught him by surprise. Motioning for his men to back up and take cover, Brandon kicked the door open and hurried through, gun raised and finger a hair's width away from squeezing the trigger. No one immediately in sight; he checked behind the door before relaxing. As his men began to trickle in, he did another sweep, his heart stopping when he spotted two bodies wearing Ragnarok's uniforms slumped against the wall on the other side of the hallway. He fought the urge to run over, knowing full well that might be Athena's plan. A gasp from behind; Peter Chapman tried to rush past him, and Brandon was forced to shoot out an arm to intercept him. "Idiot!" Brandon hissed. "You trying to get killed?"

Peter stared at him numbly and Brandon feared he was in shock until he nodded his head slowly. Once more taking the lead, Brandon crept forward, checking every window and crevice. In reality, the trek towards the two motionless figures took only minutes, but for Brandon it seemed like forever until he was standing above his fallen comrades.

Both men had suffered stab wounds to the face. Durkhiem had been stabbed multiple times and Brandon found it difficult to look at him without retching.

"The girl is a monster," someone said, and Brandon had to agree. Anyone, be they Resident or human, who could commit such heinous acts deserved to die.

"Keep it together." Brandon swallowed, finding his own bearing before continuing. "She wants us to lose it so we won't."

He saw one or two nods of agreement, but most of his men's faces were set in grim, hard looks. The door to room 608 was slightly ajar. An invitation to enter? Athena's psychological profile stated that she enjoyed playing games.

Brandon steeled himself and motioned for everyone to take cover before taking a step back and kicking the door. What Brandon saw behind the door surprised him so much that, for a moment, he was utterly speechless.

"What the hell?" Peter murmured, and Brandon agreed.

Anthony stood in the middle of the room, looking as casual as if he was staying there for vacation. Upon hearing the door swing open, he looked up guiltily at his brother.

"What the hell are you doing here?" Brandon demanded, quickly getting past his moment of speechlessness. "Where's Athena?"

"Not here," Anthony responded, having the nerve to actually sound defiant and reproachful at Brandon's tone.

So enraged was he, Brandon almost forgot he was leading a tactical operation to capture a Resident who had already killed four of his men. "Spread out," Brandon ordered. "Search everything." His men obeyed, a couple casting incensed looks at Anthony, and Brandon couldn't blame them. If any one of them had tried such a stunt, he would have thrown them in a deep, dark cell for weeks.

"You didn't answer my question," Brandon said coldly. "What are you doing here when I gave very clear orders for you to remain downstairs?"

Anthony looked at the floor, finally showing a morsel of guilt, but far too late for Brandon's liking. "I was worried."

"Worried or not, you follow orders!" Brandon snapped, giving in to the temptation to tear his brother a new one. "Damn it, Anthony, you endanger all our lives when you pull these stupid stunts. I'll make sure you never work at Ragnarok again. Once we—"

The last of Brandon's words got stuck in his throat, never to be voiced, because at that moment, a bullet ripped Anthony's head apart, ending his brother's life.

Chapter 46

Remus watched with a mixture of dread and hopelessness as Fides walked across the room. Could Athena be dead? No, not Athena. He shook that notion out of his head. Athena had probably escaped and Fides was down here looking for her. Regardless if that was the truth or some delusional lie he was telling himself, Fides' presence still meant trouble for him.

Remus hid behind two women chattering indignantly on how much they were going to sue the hotel, and watched Fides as he crossed the room talking calmly into a radio. Not the actions of a man who was looking frantically for his charge. Remus shifted uncomfortably. Athena could not be dead. She'd taken a bullet to the leg and had been ready to run marathons a mere couple of hours earlier. No way would someone like that be killed so easily.

Using all his ninja skills that he'd acquired by lodging over a hundred hours on Ninja Heroes 3, Remus slunk closer to Fides. The Resident stopped when he got to one of the guards walking around to try to keep the crowd calm. The guard physically tensed as Fides drew nearer. Whatever Fides' abilities were, it was enough to scare this trained soldier, which meant it was more than enough to terrify Remus.

Remus dared not get closer, and he was only able to pick up a couple of words of their conversation.

"Where's Anthony?" Fides asked serenely.

Remus didn't hear what the guard said, but whatever it was amused Fides greatly.

"...Brandon won't like that," Fides said joyfully. "Especially since..." The rest of what he said was impossible to hear. The guard asked something else and Fides responded. "No, not dead yet. But soon..."

The universe, fearing it had given Remus too long of a break, caused a rather large woman to bump into him, and Remus was sent stumbling forward. At the same time, the woman screeched as if he had been the one to cause offense. The guard Fides had been talking to raised his eyes at the commotion and frowned in puzzlement as he spotted Remus, but before he could say anything, Remus scooted back into the crowd, his heart pulsing with fear and another almost unrecognizable emotion—relief. Athena was alive, but the way Fides made it sound, she wouldn't be for long. He had to find a way to save her.

He concentrated on the task, but surrendered to hopelessness only a few minutes later. There was no way to escape! Even if Athena did get down here, what could they do? Plus, he had to rescue the crowd, for it was his and Athena's fault that they were in this mess, and Remus wouldn't be able to live with himself if anything happened to them. Remus spotted Muscleman a couple of feet away, and a ridiculously ludicrous idea that could only possibly work in the cheesiest of movies began to form in his head.

He slipped up to Muscleman as casually as he knew how. "Don't be surprised and don't scream."

Muscleman looked at him, speechless, which unfortunately didn't last long. "What are you doing here? What's happening? What's going on?"

Remus held up his hand, cutting Muscleman off, and he was immediately struck with silence. "Listen to me closely. I'm sure you noticed all those men with guns guarding all the exits?" He raised his voice, and, as he'd hoped, it caught the attention of the surrounding guests.

"Do you know what's going on?" someone pressed him.

"I do," Remus said, with what he hoped was confidence. "These men are not part of the U.S government. These are very evil men who are part of a terrorist ring."

A collective gasp went up immediately followed by a couple of snorts of disbelief. "How do you know?" one of the guests demanded. "You're nothing but a kid yourself."

"I thank you for the compliment. In reality, I'm twenty-four. My boyish looks help me with infiltration." A day ago, Remus would never have tried to pull off such a ridiculous scam. He'd always known he never had the confident bearing of a man with authority.

"And you want us to believe you're some type of FBI agent," a guest wearing a bulky black coat scoffed.

"No, I don't," Remus admitted, knowing that the next lie would be the most important. "I expect you to believe I'm Homeland Security."

"You're full of it!"

"He was the person who pulled the fire alarm," an elderly woman interjected. "If it wasn't for him, we might have never known these people were slinking around."

"*You* pulled the fire alarm?"

Remus nodded impatiently. "Yes, and I don't have time to go over the same material again. If you're going to listen to me, then listen and don't interrupt. If not, then be on your way."

It was a gamble, and Remus half expected the entire group to collectively leave at once, but no one budged. In fact, he was attracting more attention.

"Good. Now listen carefully. Whatever they've been saying is pure crap. *They* are the terrorists. Has anyone seen a big man with bruises running down his right arm?" A couple of people nodded. "That is your lead terrorist. A man who goes by the name of Fides."

"Fides?"

"The goddess of truth, and no, I don't know why he picked a goddess' name."

"Is there anyone else with you who can help us?"

Remus shook his head regretfully. "I have support, but they're a couple of miles away. You have to understand, we had no idea they would pick this dismal place as a target. I was sent in to keep tabs on them, but by the time we realized what he was up to, it was already too late and I was cut off from my team."

The sound of gunfire made everyone instinctively duck. Remus paused to listen, and, in the back of his mind, he realized that gunshots no longer had the same effect on him that they used to. The shots were faint and promised a narrow hope. Athena must be alive or else they wouldn't be shooting. Unless that one shot was the finisher?

More shots followed, answering Remus' question. Sometimes the universe had a shred of mercy.

"What are they doing?" Muscleman asked fearfully.

Remus thought quickly. "They're killing anyone they can find, and they probably intend to hold us as hostages. After which, they'll kill us anyway. If you want to avoid that, you have to do exactly what I say."

The crowd nodded eagerly. Never before had Remus had people willing to obey his every order. It felt intoxicating and exhilarating at the same time. Is this what his dad felt like? Was this why he acted the way he did? Remus took a second to calm down and told them his plan.

There were mixed expressions of skepticism and he couldn't blame them. His plan lacked finesse or subtlety. If Athena had been here, she could have probably come up with the perfect elaborate strategy, but since she wasn't, his would have to do.

He waited for the others to get into position. More shots could be heard from above, and Remus hoped Athena was giving them hell. He thought about his plan some more. And the more he thought of it, the more he realized how incredibly stupid it was. If he didn't act quickly, he would eventually lose his nerve.

"Here we go," he muttered. Then, at the top of his lungs, he yelled. "HEY FIDES!"

The lobby was already deathly quiet, the people listening for the sound of any more gunshots, so his voice could clearly be heard. The crowd moved away from him so that Remus stood in a small circle all to himself. The whole thing was almost too theatrical. Like every kid, he used to have dreams of facing down armies of evil aliens, mad scientists plotting to take over the world, and killer robots. In all his daydreams, he never realized how frightened he would be.

His heart banged painfully within his chest as Fides turned and gave him a welcoming smile. "I believe your name is Remus? I must say I'm quite surprised to see you call me out. Is it possible you want to be educated on truth?"

As soon as he had yelled Fides' name, guards began to make their way to Remus. With the density of the crowd, it would take them a couple of minutes to get over to him.

"Is it true that the poor clerk is dead because of you?" Remus asked, recalling Athena's words. "*You killed that poor kid downstairs. Made him stab himself with a pair of scissors and then stuffed him in the back room.*" He also remembered that Fides stated he wasn't a killer, so he hoped the way he presented his information was acceptable to him.

"It's true," Fides responded serenely, confirming what Athena had said. He couldn't lie and had to speak the truth. "I showed the boy truth, and as a result, he died." The way Fides talked, Remus realized it would have been better if he had said Fides and his team were part of a religious cult instead of a terrorist group.

The crowd was getting fearful. Up to now, they had clearly been hoping they were under the wings of the good guys, but this newest evidence suggested otherwise. However, Remus wasn't done.

"Is it true that you wish for everyone here to be dead?" Remus asked, keeping a watchful eye on a particularly determined guard. He would reach Remus in a matter of moments.

"That is also true," Fides agreed. "I would like nothing more than to see everyone here enter the sweet release of death."

"Fides, shut up," someone said harshly, but the damage was already done.

The crowd squirmed with fear. All they needed was a little extra push.

"There's no need to panic," one of the guards said quickly, but his words were overshadowed by another voice.

"There's a bomb set to go off in five minutes!" A voice could clearly be heard from near the entrance. "Five minutes!"

Remus almost smiled at Muscleman's performance. It had taken some talking to convince him that faking a bomb scare was in the best interest for everyone. As he expected, the masses went up in panic. Remus had just proven that Fides and his gang were the terrorists, so now he had no problem convincing them a bomb was set to go off.

The crowd surged forward just as the one determined guard reached out to grab him. Either Muscleman and his group of cohorts had been able to subdue the soldiers guarding the front entrance, or the crowd's fear of the bomb outweighed their fear of a couple of men with guns. Either way, the river of people was flowing out the doors and into the parking lot and Remus was determined to get swept up in the currents.

The guard's hand missed Remus by inches, forcing him to duck back into the crowd for cover. Bending down, he quickly scooped up the bulky black coat one of the guests had left for him.

He looked back and almost cried out in fear. The look on Fides' face was a mask of homicidal rage and anger.

"Leave the boy alone!" a frustrated voice yelled as more shots rang out. "The commander needs immediate backup!"

Another stroke of good luck. Remus had learned to be cautious of these moments, because this was when the universe struck the hardest. He followed the flow of the crowd until he breezed past the double door, stomping on the now ridiculously ironic "WELCOME" floor mat situated below, and filling his lungs with a huge helping of the night air as he stumbled outside.

He blinked a couple of times, stunned that his ridiculous plan had gotten him this far, before making a mad dash for the Thunderbird. All around him, cries of help rang into the night air as people tried to outrun the upcoming explosion, and Remus felt a pang of regret for his deception.

He reached the Thunderbird and looked around, half expecting Athena to come running up. Instead, he saw the woman with the little daughter, running down the parking lot. They had escaped after all. Their eyes met and she gave him a short smile, and Remus, for the first time in years, felt a sense of accomplishment. He should have known better. Her eyes widened in fear a split second before a hand grabbed him and spun him around to come face to face with an angry Fides.

"You lied!" Fides hissed.

Chapter 47

"Please explain to me again why I'm here." Payton's voice was deceptively sweet.

Mycheal never took his eyes off the old rundown excuse for a house. "Because Froce told me to bring a couple of men with me to find Edward Gantz."

Payton looked back as if expecting to see someone else accompanying them. "So you thought a couple men meant just little old me?"

"Athena's escape has stretched Pandora's resources beyond the breaking point. Plus the fact that the other Residents still need to be pampered and taken care of to avoid any more riots, we couldn't deprive Pandora's Box of any more men."

Payton nodded, absentmindedly playing with one of the curls in her hair. "That's the worst bullshit I ever heard."

Mycheal was regretting his decision to bring her, but still argued his position. "We're here to investigate Gantz's disappearance, and if possible, bring him in. And I chose you because...you really are the only one I know there."

"That's sad," she remarked, exiting the car. She waited for Mycheal to do the same before adding casually, "You know, you wouldn't be the first man to try to flirt with me under guise of a mission."

"Are you really that—" Mycheal stopped before he said something she wouldn't forgive. Payton was looking up at the house, seemingly paying him no mind. A gust of wind slammed the shutters closed, the noise echoing eerily.

"Creepy," she said with a shudder. "Best to get this over with before I lose my nerve. Stay behind me, gun ready in case Gantz comes out swinging."

She strolled forward before Mycheal could respond, and a second later, he followed, feeling resentment she had wrestled control from him so easily, though he should have expected it, she being the superior officer. The house loomed in front of them, looking every bit as creepy as Payton claimed it to be. She knocked loudly on the door then moved to the side to avoid incoming bullets.

"Edward Gantz," she yelled. "It's Payton Trist. We're here to discuss an incident that happened at your place of employment earlier." She paused for a response. No movement could be heard from within and Payton sighed before fishing in a pocket and taking out an odd coin that glittered peculiarly in the moonlight. "Edward Gantz, you have ten seconds before we break down your door," she yelled, glancing down at the coin with a frown. "I repeat, we're in a crisis situation, and it's imperative we speak to you at once." No answer, so she tried the doorknob.

The door offered no resistance, creaking hollowly as it swung open.

"Sheesh, how much more haunted can you get?" she asked, but without any real humor. She glanced back at Mycheal. "It's troubling that this door was unlocked." Mycheal agreed with a slight nod. She looked around. "We cover more ground if we split up, but I've seen too many horror movies to try such a cliché maneuver. Why the hell would Edward stay in such a place?"

"Apparently, he inherited it from his grandma," Mycheal said. The house was dimly lit and strangely bare. Not a picture or table to be seen.

"Inherited from dead relatives," Payton observed, nodding sagely. "Classic haunted house history."

As he watched, she flipped her coin in the air and caught it on the back of her hand. Mycheal had seen her play with the coin before, but thought it inappropriate to do so in the middle of an operation. He was learning that the majority of Pandora's Box operatives found protocol to be nothing more than loose guidelines.

"Classic sweep, bottom to top," she issued, taking the lead.

Mycheal would have protested, but Payton had a stubborn streak that rivaled his own bullheaded personality, and because she had seen more time at Pandora's Box, he figured it appropriate she took the lead, although a couple of minutes of investigating with her quickly changed his mind. She moved from room to room with a casual air that Mycheal found reckless. She never checked corners or slowed down when entering a new room, and her hands were never near her gun. Any half-decent thug would have been able to surprise and subdue her before she could even mount a defense, and what was worse was that damn coin she insisted on playing with. Every few seconds it would fly into the air and land on the back of her hand, her shoulder blade, and one time on the tip of her index finger. The situation became unbearable when Mycheal was checking a closet and she flipped the coin so that it landed on his head.

"Cut that out!" he snarled. He threw the coin back and she easily caught it. "Residents are running wild and you're playing around."

"I understand the situation far better than you," she said mildly. "I have had more experience with Residents."

"Then why—"

"There's no one here, Mycheal. Whatever happened already happened, and there's no sense getting so worked up over it."

"You don't know that," he retorted. "And we owe it to everyone who has lost their lives today to treat this mission with the respect it deserves."

"You're right," she relented, and Mycheal blinked uncertainly. She'd given in with surprising ease. "This is the last room down here," she continued, putting her coin back in her side pocket, a move Mycheal accepted as a peace offering. "Let's move upstairs." She left the room in such a hurry he had to struggle to catch up. "Edward Gantz must have been an extremely lonely man," she mused loudly, her curly hair bouncing as she walked up the stairs.

"Why would you say that?" He spoke in a low whisper, hoping Payton would take the hint.

"I haven't seen a picture or photo of a loved one yet. There are only minimum signs that this place has been lived in at all. If it wasn't for the dirty dishes in the sink and the suit we found on the sofa, I might be thinking this was all a trick to lead me here on a romantic rendezvous."

Mycheal's left eye twitched. "We should keep the chatter

to a minimum. Never know who might be waiting behind the next corner."

Payton sounded slightly surly. "I know protocol; I was a military brat for the majority of my life." She nodded, more to herself than to Mycheal. "Yep. I was daddy's little military girl. When I turned eighteen, it made sense to join up. I was in the Marines for six years before being discharged for refusing to do a mission. My daddy was so ashamed that he quit talking to me, and I haven't seen or heard from him since." She fell silent and Mycheal did not respond.

They checked a couple more rooms, all without incident. Mycheal was extremely thorough when he searched, pulling out drawers and checking air vents, while Payton merely flitted around a little before declaring the room "unhaunted." Her cavalier attitude was fun at times, but annoying when actual work had to be done.

They were heading for the bathroom when Payton started up again. "So what's your story?" she asked with a grin.

Mycheal was saved from answering because of her sudden mood change. Her muscles tensed, and her face looked unrecognizable without her constant smile attached to it. "Get ready," she said quietly, becoming completely serious for the first time since Mycheal had met her.

"What is it?" he whispered back, sweeping the area with his eyes. He saw nothing that would have set her off.

"There's..." She hesitated briefly. "You can't smell that?"

Before he could ask any follow-up questions, she darted forward and rounded the corner. A second later, he heard a sharp intake of breath and Mycheal, fearing the worst, chased after her. As soon as he turned the corner, he saw her hovering at a bathroom door.

"Don't rush off!" he exclaimed, but then fell silent. The stench was the first thing to hit him, and through watery eyes, he spotted the missing and very-much-dead Edward Gantz. Gantz's final resting place was the inside of a large porcelain bathtub where he laid fully clothed with his head slumped down and his mouth opened at an awkward angle. An ordinary person might have mistaken him for sleeping, but Mycheal had seen enough horrors to recognize the unnatural stillness that only a corpse could make. Mycheal had met Edward twice, and had not enjoyed his company either time, but still...

Gantz's eyes were still open, staring blankly at the unseen, and there were no marks on him that gave any clue as to how he died, although a spilled bottle of pills on the bathroom counter was a strong hint.

"Suicide?" Mycheal suggested, staying professional. Emotions could be felt later, but now they had a job to do. "Maybe the guilt over what he did became too much for him?"

"Possibly" Payton said, sounding like she believed it as much as Mycheal did. "Though why choose a bathtub? And the way the body is stinking up the place, he's been dead for at least two days. It would mean that after he set the bombs, he went directly home and killed himself."

"So what are you thinking?" He had already drawn a conclusion, but wanted to see if he and Payton were on the same page.

"I'd say someone went through a lot of trouble to pin this on Gantz and then killed him so he wouldn't be able to object," Payton answered. "We gotta keep this under wraps. Call Pandora's Box and tell them what we found. We probably shouldn't touch anything else until someone arrives."

He reached for his radio.

"Mycheal," Payton whispered.

Her tone was fearful, and Mycheal was on instant alert, looking for the threat. At first, he saw nothing, but then he followed Payton's gaze to the window. Six ravens were resting on a tree branch, six coal-black eyes staring silently at them. One at a time, starting from the far left, each raven flew off. The last one stared right at Mycheal before letting out a mournful cry and flying off.

"Definitely haunted," Payton confirmed.

Chapter 48

When she was thirteen, Athena had once read a biography of a solider on the front lines of World War II. The book detailed the soldier's first kill and how taking a life distressed him so greatly he thought about ending his own. As the gun recoiled and the bullet tore through the wall, hitting the intended target and killing him almost instantly, Athena liked to think if she had been born outside Pandora's Box, she would have felt the same gut-wrenching guilt that tormented the soldier. At the most, she felt only a twinge of regret that grew when she heard Brandon Badger's cry of anguish over the death of his brother.

After Fides left, she laid on the bed for several minutes, struggling against the other Resident's staggering effects before finally gaining the energy to move. Fides, obviously thinking she was no longer a threat, hadn't bothered to remove the gun and knife. Or, maybe he intentionally left them, hoping she might utilize these tools to fulfill her rather rash promise to him.

"What do you intend to do?"

Athena blinked in surprise as Selene spoke to her, not only because Selene had sworn off contact and the other Resident rarely changed her mind, but because the question was so silly, it almost didn't dignify an answer.

"I intend to win," Athena thought, picking up the knife and walking out into the hallway where the two gunmen who had attacked Remus still laid unconscious. *"What other option is there?"*

"How?" One of the gunmen groaned and opened his eyes. Before he could cry out, Athena swooped down and

stabbed him twice in the stomach. There were other ways to end his life more quickly and less painfully, but she wasn't feeling particularly charitable to the men who had planned on killing Remus. As he was bleeding out, she turned to the other man and did the same; the only difference was he was fortunate enough not to wake up.

Dropping the knife after she was done, she realized she had yet to answer Selene's question. *"You'll see,"* she thought, walking back in the doorway, across the room and onto the balcony, stopping only once to pick up the gun. *"Now stop pestering me. I need to concentrate."*

Once on the balcony, she practiced her newly learned trick, and leapt from the room's balcony to the next with the gun in her hand. She had barely enough time to get in position as she felt a mind approaching.

Anthony, worried about his brother, entered the room she had previously left, expecting to find her. She might have felt remorse if Anthony's plan hadn't been to kill her as soon he spotted her. Rather than acting immediately, she waited for Brandon to show up. It was imperative.

While waiting, she took the opportunity to check up on Remus, and had to bite down painfully on her lip to stop herself from yelling obscenities at the foolhardy plan he had concocted. Idiot! If she didn't act soon, he would be dead, and all because of a stupid adrenaline rush and the subconscious need to prove himself. Men and their testosterone.

She was so deep in her own pondering she almost missed Brandon's mind when it entered the room beside her, along with twelve other minds. She waited for them to spread out before taking a deep breath and firing off a single shot. The high powered bullet easily punctured the wall as if it was no more than paper, and when it struck Anthony's head, his mind instantly went dark, like a candle being snuffed out.

Athena felt Brandon's shock, his immediate denial, and then his fury.

"Did I hit anyone?" she yelled, cackling madly. She fired off another burst of bullets, killing another poor soul.

She dove out the way as Brandon's response, a barrage of bullets, went zipping by her head. "YOU BITCH!" he screamed, firing another burst.

With her telepathy, Athena had an advantage over her

enemies, but she was still drained from the fight with Fides, and her cracked rib was throbbing painfully.

She spun out the way, barely dodging a bullet that would have torn through her arm. "What's with all the anger?" she yelled gleefully, then jumped out of the way, knowing bullets would follow her voice. "I was only following orders."

She squeezed off two shots, careful to come close, but not actually hit anyone. Athena knew their exact positions while they could only guess hers. She held her breath and hoped Brandon wasn't too overcome by his grief to take the bait.

"What do you mean orders?" A part of him wanted her to speak so he could ascertain her position; another part was genuinely curious about what she had to say. Still another part was trying to distract her while three of his men ran around, intending to burst through the door and corner her.

She waited until they were at the door before shooting two of them down. "I was given a task," she called out. "If I could prove myself competent enough, I would be considered for a position in Ragnarok."

No bullets greeted this statement.

"You're saying this is a test?" The words were calm, but Athena could feel the rage emanating from his mind. So much so that she was tempted to shut down her telepathy just so it wouldn't reach her.

"I considered it more a rite of initiation." She tensed up for another round. When none ever came, she continued. "I was supposed to avoid capture for seventy-two hours before returning to Pandora's Box to get my reward. I'm sad to say I haven't even made it twenty-four hours. I thought it was hopeless, the title of Ragnarok operative forever out of reach, but that was before Fides came down and offered me a new deal."

"What deal?" Brandon demanded. "Tell me!"

She did a quick scan. The operative she had spared at the doorway was trying to drag one of his comrades she had shot and thought dead to safety. He still clung to life, but wouldn't last much longer. There were a couple of minds in the other room she needed to keep track of, but most of them were too stunned to do anything except follow orders. That was the problem with becoming unaccustomed to friends dying. When it did happen, you had little mental defense to help you deal with it. She stopped at Brandon's mind, and shivered briefly at the graphic images on how he would kill her playing through his head.

"He told me if I could kill fifteen of Ragnarok's stellar employees, then I'd pass the test," she said cheerfully. Another quick check on Remus. He was making his move now, that hopeless idiot. Athena couldn't help but feel a slight admiration for his bravado.

"Fifteen men?"

"Yep, and by my count, I'm up to six." She crossed her fingers once again, hoping Brandon was astute enough to pick up on what she'd said.

"You killed eight."

"No, I didn't," Athena said, trying to sound confused. "I pushed one off the balcony, I stabbed that one guy on the seventh floor, and I shot four guys just now."

"You're forgetting about the two you stabbed in the hallway."

"What? They're dead?" Athena said, putting the right amount of surprise and anger in her voice. "After I knocked them out? They were supposed to be my kills!"

"You saying you didn't do it?" Brandon asked sharply.

"No. Those two I can't take credit for."

Fides, Brandon thought angrily.

Athena smiled. He'd arrived at the conclusion she wanted. What a reliable puppet he was turning out to be. She'd even taken the time to stab one of them over and over again, and had been careful to place the knife under the body. If Brandon found it, he would think his two men had been subjected to Fides' truth and brutally killed themselves.

"I've been told you have telepathy."

"Limited," she lied. "I can't read your mind because you're out of my range. If I could, I would have shot you first instead of that other schmuck."

Brandon's rage bellowed in Athena's mind, blinding her for a second, and she almost didn't duck fast enough to avoid the oncoming bullets.

"Sheesh! And we were having such a polite conversation too. Must have been close to the guy whose head I ripped apart."

"And how do we know you're not lying?" he screamed.

She laughed as manically as she knew how. "I don't care if you think I'm lying or telling the truth. Why does it matter?

You're not going to leave this place alive. I only told you the story to buy time. It's been a pleasant chat, but now you must die!"

She started pumping bullets into the wall, laughing as she did. The vibration of the gun felt good as it went off in her hand, and she had to watch herself to make sure she didn't lose control. As she intended, none of the bullets came close to touching Brandon.

Brandon and his men fired in response, and Athena flung herself across the room. Other Residents assumed because she had telepathy she could easily dodge bullets, but the reality was far different. No one could completely predict where a random bullet would go, especially in this situation when they were firing blindly. Since they didn't know, she couldn't pluck the answers from their heads. The best way to avoid bodily harm in this situation was to be in a completely different area from where they thought she was, letting them concentrate their bullets while she stayed relatively hidden.

Sweep the room.

As soon as Brandon had this thought, Athena realized she had made a costly mistake. Thinking his grief would overcome him, she'd unwisely bet Brandon would be too traumatized to try and outthink her. He had understood she might have dodged his first onslaught, and planned to riddle the whole room with bullets in an effort to either lure her out or kill her. Abandoning the gun, she scrambled to her feet and made a mad sprint to the balcony as bullets pounded through the walls, zipping past her head in near misses. On the balcony, instead of jumping to the next room, she hoisted herself over the railing, her ribs screaming in protest. She held on for a second before releasing her grip. For a moment, she was in freefall before she grabbed on to the railing on the floor below. Instead of the sixth floor, she was now on the fifth, and, if memory proved correct, the Thunderbird should be directly below her.

Her broken ribs were now roaring obscenities at her, and she just barely managed to clamber off the railing and on to the balcony. Collapsing in a chair, she struggled for a moment to catch her breath. Of everything she wished to enjoy outside Pandora's Box, this type of intense pain was not one of them. Her escape was not supposed to be easy, but neither should it have been this endless cycle of battle and death. With a slight whimper, she heaved herself off the chair, and realized her borrowed pajamas were drenched in blood—her blood. A bullet must have hit her, and until she knew the extent of the damage, she shouldn't make another move.

She was checking for the wound when a desperate cry brought her to her knees. *"Athena!"* Despite only knowing each other for a short period of time, she instantly recognized Remus' mind. Reaching out, she found him near the Thunderbird and...Fides was torturing him!

She limped over to the railing for confirmation. Fides was standing over Remus, watching as his body convulsed in agony. Athena quickly went through all her options in her head. There was no way her cracked ribs would allow her to scale down the building quickly enough, and even if she could, she would be no match against Fides.

She cursed herself for not bringing the gun, and hot tears began to form in her eyes. If she didn't do something soon, Remus would die.

Maris tried to wrap his mind around Ms. Yang's detailed but short lesson on Pandora's Box history while the woman waited patiently for him to speak. He had scoffed at her ridiculous story...until she had given a demonstration. Now, he could barely breathe without coughing, as his room was filled with smoke. It was still hard to believe, but Maris had to consider it might all be true.

He looked at Ms. Yang. Seeing her in his office and wearing professional attire made him ache to call one of his girls in for a little role-playing, but he refused to be sidetracked by his healthy libido in the middle of what could possibly be the most important decision of his life.

"So," he said, forming his thoughts. "You're saying this drug can transform people into...what? Superheroes?"

Ms. Yang's smile was indulgent. "In the extreme, yes. Although, it would take more time to see those results, and the term 'superhero' is one we try to avoid as much as possible."

"How long would it take?" Maris asked greedily.

Ms. Yang shrugged. Oddly enough, the woman seemed pleased with Maris' enthusiasm. "There's no way to tell with this new version of the drug. Before this, it would have taken years."

"What type of stuff will my sons be able to do?"

She shrugged again, this time less patiently. "I already told you, there's no way to calculate. Some of the possibilities are pyrokinesis, telekinesis, telepathy, or maybe just an overall improvement of physical performances."

For the hundredth time, Maris wondered if this was some type of prank. Romulus and Remus with telekinesis was almost incomprehensible...and yet it would be an extraordinary legacy. The image of his sons flinging his opponents through the air with their minds made Maris almost too giddy to speak. Any novice negotiator or politician would tell you it never benefited to appear too excited over a deal, so Maris strived to rein in his emotions. "You will help my political career and, in return, you want to try some super drug on my son?" He tried to sound disapproving at the thought of his son being experimented on, but wasn't sure if he had succeeded.

"Plus yours and your son's discretion over past events," Ms. Yang added.

Maris pondered it over. "And if I say no?"

"You won't," Ms. Yang responded with a deliberate smile that didn't quite reach her eyes. "Mr. Sylvia, I'm an excellent judge of character, and my first impression of you is that you're too smart to let an opportunity like this go by. Plus, you know that it's not wise to have too many powerful enemies." The sound of ravens crying balefully out in the hallway emphasized the threat.

Maris had long recognized that he had no choice, but it didn't pay to act like it. Forcing a laugh, he said, "You sure know how to bargain. Fine, I'll agree with your little experiment...as long as it's safe."

"Sure," Ms. Yang said, with too much indifference for Maris to believe her. "One contingency that I feel I must address." She leaned forward, putting her hand on his desk. "You are aware that we are considering only Romulus for this project? Remus is not eligible...indeed he is most likely dead at this point."

Maris knew he should have said yes. It was the only conceivable answer, yet he hesitated. "Why Romulus?" he asked.

Ms. Yang had already explained this, and from her expression, she hated repeating herself. "We took a blood sample from Romulus. Standard procedure with all of our guests." Maris snorted when she said "guest," and the woman tilted her head forward in wry acknowledgement that the term was absurd. "The results were nothing less than extraordinary. Your son's genetic makeup is extremely compatible with Ambrosia."

"But doesn't that mean Remus might also be compatible to Am...bresa?"

"It's Ambrosia, and yes." Ms. Yang paused. "I did wonder if that had anything to do with why he was...but it matters not. Remus' first meeting with our organization was as our enemy, and as a rule, we can't allow that." The temperature in the room was rising quickly. Maris wiped a sheen of sweat from his forehead. "You already tried to kill him...surely you don't mind if we finish the job," Ms. Yang said reasonably. "Right?"

Maris waved a tired hand. "Do what you want."

"Excellent." The heat in the room died down. "Now—" Ms. Yang was cut off by her phone going off to an old disco song. Pulling out a bundle of papers, she looked at Maris. "If you will just sign these, we'll get your son to sign a separate copy." She reached for her phone. "Please excuse me. I'm afraid this call is rather urgent."

Maris studied the large stack of papers, and had to wonder why a shadow organization, who felt licensed to kill and kidnap whenever they wanted to, would even bother with something as mundane as a contract. Flipping through the pages, he grudgingly admired their handiwork and attention to detail, for it was well written and it was obvious that real effort had been placed in writing it. He flipped through more pages and realized the scam. The wording in the contract made it seem like he was signing Romulus into a rehab facility. Clever, for if Maris ever tried to go to the police, they would wave this document around. Perhaps blame him for his son's drug problems. If Romulus ever told tales of being experimented on, they would blame it on delusions from the onset of drug abuse. Maris smiled sardonically. He had been outmaneuvered, but not for long. No, he would figure out their weakness and exploit it.

"What?" Ms. Yang said in a hushed tone. "That's impossible!" Perhaps he would figure it out sooner than he thought.

Maris tore his eyes off the contract to study Ms. Yang. Whatever news she had received was clearly unexpected, and to see such a stunned expression on the otherwise smug woman was both gratifying and worrisome. Maris found himself hoping Remus was giving them hell.

Ms. Yang placed the phone down and didn't speak for a moment. "Your son is more resourceful then we gave him credit for." Her tone, perhaps supposed to be light, came across as very bitter.

Maris laughed harshly and tightened his hold around the contract. "Resourceful is never a word I would use to describe Remus."

"You really hate your son."

It was more of a statement than question. It wasn't hate that he felt for his son, but it would take too long to explain, and a woman wasn't capable of getting it anyway. "He's not worth a pot to piss in!" Maris growled, playing the character she assumed him to be. Let her think he was shallow. She would eventually regret underestimating him. "Useless, weak, and not a set of balls on him," he continued. "I halfway think he ain't mine!"

Ms. Yang's expression was unreadable. "I see."

Maris was almost afraid to ask the next question. "What happened?"

"Why do you care?" It was becoming increasingly clear she did not approve of Maris, which was nothing new. Very few people liked Maris upon getting to know him, and yet he still commanded power and respect. Just went to show how little popularity meant in the grand scheme of things. "It's nothing for you to be concerned over. However..." She stood up. "It does mean I have to go and fix the mistakes of those I thought reliable. One of our people will explain the circumstances to Romulus, and if he agrees to the terms, he will be returned to you sometime in the morning."

She left, her speed indicating the gravity of the situation.

Maris leaned back in his chair, secretly glancing at her ass as she walked away and feeling extremely satisfied. He had a new enemy to take down. One that thought themselves above him...it would be a pleasure.

Chapter 49

Remus' body convulsed in agony as guilt, remorse, sorrow, and other emotions he couldn't even name assaulted his body, forcing him to relive every embarrassing and awful moment of his life all at once, and there were so many awful moments. A sound halfway between a cry and whimper escaped his lips. Through bleary eyes, when they weren't squeezed shut, he could just barely make out Fides' form as the Resident hovered above him. No longer looking like a kind uncle, the monster now appeared as a demented madman with crazed eyes and a gentle smile that poorly hid his malicious intent.

"What was that, dear boy? I didn't quite catch what you said," Fides said, looking down on him. "Perhaps you could repeat it?"

Another jolt of depression shot through him, forcing words out his mouth. "Stop! Please!"

"Such manners," Fides approved. "But I'm afraid I cannot. Only you can make this stop, but not before answering a couple of questions honestly. Now," he continued, watching Remus' body squirm on the ground. "How long have you and Athena been planning this caper?"

Remus didn't understand the question, so he didn't answer. What was the point? The universe had won. He was a pathetic excuse for a man with nothing to live for, only to be used and forsaken by manipulative and ruthless monsters. Forsaken by his own brother, despised by his own father, forever without friends or family. The only person he might have cared for was the reason he was suffering now.

"Remus, you must answer me," a voice said, cutting

through the depression that fogged his mind. "When did you first contact Athena?"

"Two days ago at the mall," Remus answered, hoping the truth would damper the oppressive depression. "First time I ever saw her was at the mall!"

"And you planned an escape in that period of time?" Fides whistled. "Impressive is an understatement for that feat. Now, Remus," Fides said, raising his voice to be heard over Remus' wail of despair, "how did Athena escape and what part did you play in this endeavor?"

"I didn't help Athena escape...at least not Pandora's Box. I don't know how she did it."

The pain lessened to slightly manageable levels. Just enough for Remus to crack an eyelid and look up at his torturer.

Fides seemed to weigh his words then let out a sigh. "It seems I have reached another dead end. How frustrating. Very well, Athena's method of escaping still remains a mystery. Let's move on. If Athena only met you two days ago, then, pray tell, why did she drag you along on this grand adventure of hers?"

"She can't drive so she dragged me along to drive the car. That's it."

Misery and pain slammed into Remus and he cried out, his voice a weak and feeble plea for help. Bile filled his mouth and he convulsed on the ground, his head slapping against the Thunderbird's tire. Death right now would be a welcome reprieve. *Athena!* In his pain and haze, seconds away from the release of life, her name was the only one he could think of, her face and mocking smile the only image in his mind. If he was to die, he wished he could see her face just one more time.

"Why do you lie to me, Remus?" Fides said, sounding like a disappointed father who just caught his son sneaking out at night. "I thought our relationship had moved past that point."

"I'm not lying! She told me she needed me to drive the car and that I might provide entertainment!" The pain lessened again as Fides chewed on his words and Remus took a deep breath.

"That might be what she said, but that's not what she meant. What was the real reason she chose you as her companion?"

One of the grievances Maris had with Remus was that he thought too much, and he guessed it was true because, even in his current state, through the depression threatening to send him over the edge, a lightbulb clicked on in Remus' head. "That's the question."

"Excuse me?" Fides said politely.

It was the question he should have asked during their truth game. So obvious, yet she'd kept him enthralled with stories of Residents, and off-balance with her own personal probing. She had singled him out and chosen to disrupt his life, yet the question on "why him" hadn't crossed his mind.

Fides had grown impatient waiting for an answer. "So I must assume you do not know?"

"I don't know," he confirmed. Vomit was starting to spill out of his mouth, and he was fairly sure he had pissed on himself. This wasn't how he wanted to die.

"So why did you decide to go with Athena? Did she force you?"

"No, she gave me a choice."

Fides shook his head regretfully. "I'm afraid you have been most unhelpful, but do not fret; I will not hold that against you. It's not your fault Athena fed you controlled information."

Remus must have passed out for a couple of seconds, for the next thing he knew, Fides was gently calling out his name. "You have regained consciousness," the Resident said, sounding delighted. "A marvelous feat, but I'm afraid you approach the end of your strength. I'm not a needlessly cruel man so, in the interest of mercy, I shall let you borrow enough of my own strength to commit truth." He looked around with a slight frown. "Do you happen to have a knife or gun on you? This goes a lot smoother if there's a weapon nearby."

Many horrible and impossible things had occurred that night, but the only thing Remus would remember in graphic detail from his stay at the hotel, besides the spaghetti dinner with Athena, was the gory and bloody end to Fides. Before Remus could answer his question, a 32-inch bulky TV crash-landed on Fides' head. Remus blinked a couple times, sure he had imagined the whole thing, but the imagery didn't change. A TV seemed to have fallen from the sky, its impact zone being the top of the Resident's skull. Remus' thoughts flashed to one of those old cartoons in which an anvil was dropped on the character's head. But instead of bouncing up and down like an accordion before righting himself back up, Fides fell awkwardly to the ground and disappeared from view behind the Thunderbird.

Remus felt a weight lift from his chest as Fides' powers dissipated with his death, but he still felt drained. Seconds stretched to minutes, and all he could do was lie on the ground, his own vomit and excrement surrounding him.

"Remus!" A sharp musical tone too beautiful to carry his name sliced through the air, and Remus craned his neck, looking for the source. In his delusional state, he thought her to be an angel, but as lucidity returned to him, Remus made out Athena's figure peering down from over a balcony's railing. She was alive! It was then that he realized, perhaps more slowly than he should have, that the dropped TV hadn't been divine intervention, but Athena's interference. As he watched, she seemed to be mouthing something over and over again.

He had no idea what she was saying and Athena looked frustrated as she seemed to realize this. She placed her hands over her face and crouched down so Remus couldn't see her. Then she sprung up and uncovered her face. Was she imitating a jack in the box? His thoughts must have reached her for Athena looked like she was ready to throw something down on top of him. She repeated the action twice more before Remus got it.

"*Hide,*" he thought. "*You want me to hide.*"

Athena nodded.

"*I don't have the energy to move, let alone hide.*"

Athena pointed to the Thunderbird.

"*You want me to hide in the Thunderbird?*"

Athena nodded again.

"*I can do that. What about you?*"

She held up seven fingers before disappearing, leaving Remus wondering how he was going to get in the Thunderbird when he couldn't even move his legs, and feeling resentful that Athena didn't recognize this problem. In the end, he rolled under the car and hoped it was a good enough compromise. Of course, he hadn't counted on Fides still being alive.

"Oh Remus, my dear boy. It appears I have failed to

show you the truth you so unknowingly seek."

Remus looked over and would have screamed if he'd had the energy. Fides was lying on his side behind the Thunderbird, his neck bent at an impossible angle. He should have been dead. Was the universe really ready to defy physics just to torture him a little bit longer?

"You're probably wondering how I'm still alive," Fides said with a crooked smile to match his crooked neck. "Well, like I told Athena, I'm made up of a special cartilage material..." Fides noticed Remus' expression. "Ah, but you're not interested in such technical babble. I am alive and, in the end, I suppose that's all you care about."

Curiously enough, Remus was no longer afraid of the Resident. Whether it was because he was too drained to feel fear, or because he was in a state of such overwhelming shock that it prevented him from feeling any emotions, he didn't know, and didn't particularly care. "Am I about to die?" His voice, while hoarse, was remarkably steady considering the circumstances.

"Probably," Fides answered easily. "Oh, but not by my hand, I'm afraid. I can't seem to draw out my powers, and I have been trying quite earnestly for a couple of minutes." Fides sighed blissfully. "Athena, clever girl that she is, knew exactly what she was doing."

"You're not..." Remus hesitated, and Fides looked at him with honest puzzlement. Remus wasn't an expert in biology, receiving a B+ in the class, but it seemed any normal person would be in intense agony if they had the misfortune to live through a broken neck. "You're not upset about what happened?" he finished.

"Why would I be?" Fides asked warmly. "I will survive this night only if extremely unlucky. I no longer feel the depression and agony that has gripped me these many years." Fides paused. "Come to think of it, I can't feel much of anything. No more pain..." Fides let out a sudden laugh. "What a glorious gift Athena has given me. I am eternally grateful to her."

Remus, not knowing what to say, remained silent and hoped Athena would arrive soon. The very faint sounds of sirens could be heard in the distance, bringing with it mixed emotions. Assuming these were real police, the people hunting Athena would have to back off, but the cops could also become a hindrance to his and Athena's escape.

"Already thinking about more pressing matters," Fides observed, giving him an appraising look. "No need to look so abashed. My time is all but done and I have no regrets save one." Fides closed his eyes and Remus thought him dead until he spoke again. "You."

"What about me?"

"If Athena had only waited a few more seconds, I am quite sure you would have acted upon the truth and been free of this miserable life. Does that not bother you?"

"No," Remus answered, surprised of his own certainty. "I am not at all bothered she interrupted you murdering me."

Fides looked disappointed. "I'm sorry to hear that. I thought you had grown up and realized the truth, but it seems you are still a child."

He was all set on ignoring Fides, but found himself yelling at the Resident instead. Something about being called a child by a condescending maniac really irked him, and the offense far outweighed the maniac trying to murder him in the first place. "Just because I didn't want to die with drool on my face, wriggling on the ground like some damn fish does not make me any less of a man."

"It's not the *way* you would have died that's important," Fides said with far too much enthusiasm for a man on death's door. "The fact that you recognized truth and acted upon it...that's the important aspect."

"Your truth maybe. What gives you the right to force your truth down my throat?"

"My truth," Fides repeated, puzzlement transforming into scornfulness. "Absolutely ridiculous, you poor fool. My truth is your truth. By its very nature, truth is irrevocable, never changing, and absolute."

"Are all Residents like you and Athena?" Remus shot back. "One-dimensional and easily defined by one philosophy or ideal? Athena with her quotes and games and you with your sick obsession to force a universal truth onto every situation?"

"Really!" Fides huffed, having the nerve to be offended.

"Four years ago, if asked, I would have claimed my brother as my closest friend and confidant," Remus continued. "Now, if you ask me the question again, I would say... I would give you a different answer." The argument was a very simplistic one, and was based more on opinions than truths, but it seemed to have momentarily stumped Fides. It was also possible the Resident's cognitive functions were operating at slightly less than 100% thanks to a TV landing on his head. "If I had met you three days ago, I might have been a perfect candidate for your 'truth.' Now I wish to live...you don't get to take away my ability to choose."

"Three days ago, you say?" Fides words were beginning to slur and his eyelids continued to droop lower and lower. He was dying and it was just Remus' luck that he would be there to witness his final moments. "That would be right before you met the young Athena, would it not?"

"You know the answer." A suspicion began to haunt his thoughts, one that had been chasing him for a while now. "She has telepathy, but does she have anything else?"

Fides started to chuckle, but the action was ruined when he spat up a wad of blood that landed inches away from Remus' nose. "For all your talk of knowing your own mind, you fear it lies to you. You wish to know if she possesses mind controlling capabilities. Rest assured, she does not. Your thoughts are your own, although I suspect they're heavily influenced by cleavage and a pretty smile, which brings me back to my original point."

"And what point is that?" Athena still had yet to arrive. There was a joke in there about women being late, but Remus was too tired to think of it.

"You only think that's truth," Fides said smugly. "The truth didn't change; just your ability to see it clearly."

Remus changed tactics. "And how do you know your truth is the real truth?"

Fides was silent. Every time he paused, Remus feared he might have died. "What type of question is that?" he asked finally. "I just know the truth."

"You just know?" Remus repeated incredulously. "You're supposed to be a connoisseur of truth and that's the best you can come up with? You just know?"

"The truth is the truth," Fides said between a fit of painful coughs. "Why do you try to confuse me?"

"Did you ever try looking for different truths?" Remus probed, starting to feel like a sadist for disabusing a dying man of his beliefs. "Or did you just stick with the truth most convenient for you?"

"It is the truth!" Fides screamed, and the effort sent him

coughing again.

Remus heard footsteps approaching and, for a second, felt relief. Athena had finally arrived. The relief vanished as he realized something was wrong. There were multiple footsteps, and all were too heavy to belong to the nimble Athena. They must have belonged to the mercenaries, which meant he was going to die in the next couple of minutes. Fides watched the multitude of expressions cross his face, his own set in a painful grin.

"Perhaps we will find truth together," Fides whispered, just before a pair of combat boots stopped right in front of him. "Brandon, I am glad you made it out in one piece."

"Is it true?" the person named Brandon said, his tone managing to be both unemotional and full of promised violence all at the same time. If he found it bizarre that the Resident's neck and head now formed an L shape, he hid it.

"I'm afraid you mistake me for Athena," Fides said with a sigh of regret. "I cannot read minds, and thus am unsure of what you are—"

The boot was swift as it rose up beyond Remus' sight and slammed into Fides' abdomen with brutal force. Only Remus' lack of energy kept him from crying out.

"My men dead," Brandon's voice shouted at the gasping Fides, anger making it waver uncontrollably. "My brother dead. All so Athena can pass some initiation rite to join Ragnarok. Is it true?"

"Oh, is that what Athena told you?" Fides rasped. "I must say I'm disappointed in your naivety. Let us move past this moment and talk of other things." Fides' body and neck were angled so that he was always looking underneath the car, right at Remus. Brandon and his men would assume that the nasty little smile Fides gave was for them instead of Remus...that was until the Resident ratted him out.

"Remus, her companion, is..."

Brandon's foot rose once more, and this time, Remus was able to close his eyes before the blow struck, but Fides' cry of agony still painted a vivid image. "Answer my question!" Brandon demanded. "Did Ragnarok know of your plan to test Athena? Was Ruby Chapman aware she was sending us off to compete in this pointless game?"

Remus held his breath while his mind raced frantically. Trapped underneath a car with no line of defense and waiting for a dying man to reveal his location left him with very few options. Ironically enough, Athena was his only real hope, and for all he knew, she could have been captured and killed already.

Speaking for Fides had grown difficult, and as the man struggled for words, another voice, softer and more reasonable spoke up. "Sir, look at him. The man's dying and only Athena could have done this, which means she is not his friend."

"She betrayed him!" Brandon shot back belligerently. He had clearly found a culprit to blame for the disaster and refused to look elsewhere. It reminded Remus slightly of his dad. "That's what she does."

"Oh, but you're wrong," Fides said, with a sound that might have been a chuckle. "And if I could have a moment to speak without being assaulted, I could tell you the truth you so desire."

There was a moment of silence in which Remus was all but sure they would be able to hear his heartbeat. "Speak," Brandon commanded. Remus shut his eyes and silently cursed out the universe for the last time. Here it was, his moment of death. Fides would tell them his location, and then they both would die in a blast of bullets.

"Athena didn't betray me. I asked her to kill me." Remus' eyes flew open to stare in astonishment at Fides. He dared not get his hopes up in case the other man was just toying with him before swinging the axe, but as he watched, the paralyzed Resident's left eye fluttered in what could have been interpreted as a wink. "After I spoke with Athena at length about the new terms Ragnarok offered for her initiation, I asked her, as a kind gesture to an old man, to end my miserable, wretched life. She agreed, but disappeared. I had thought her lying until I came out here looking for the boy, Remus, and a TV landed on me. Quite a sense of humor the young girl has."

The second voice piped up angrily. "Ruby Chapman would never—"

"Oh, but she didn't know, of course," Fides interrupted. There was a new enthusiasm to his voice, as if lying thrilled him to no end. "This goes above even her lofty head."

Remus expected Brandon to explode, but his voice was no more than a whisper and somehow more awful than him screaming. "I will make every one of you burn in hell," he stated levelly, each word carefully spaced so that there were no misunderstanding. "All you Residents, every scientist involved, and your unnatural creation, Ragnarok and Pandora's Box...all of you will die."

"Now you're just being melodramatic."

"Where is the boy?" Brandon spat.

Remus' heart skipped a beat, but before he could get appropriately nervous, Fides had already answered. "Fled, I'm afraid. Athena's killing blow happened just before I could catch him. She really does seem to have a fondness for him." Fides blinked. "I'm curious, Brandon, did you mean all that hogwash about revenge and—"

Time slowed down as Brandon's first bullet ripped into Fides' cheek, and Remus hoped that was the bullet to kill him because Brandon continued to fire, emptying his entire clip into the Resident's head. Remus had never heard an automatic gun go off, and the sound was like mini explosions being set off right beside his ear. When Brandon was finished, Fides' head no longer resembled a human face, but instead looked like a badly cut and rancorous sliced meatloaf; Remus struggled not to throw up again.

"Gentlemen," Brandon said calmly, as if he hadn't just decimated a man's head. "Fides is dead and I am no longer your commander. My last order is to run. As fast as you can. Ragnarok will not look kindly on this, and I suspect they will try to fix the situation by issuing a purge."

"And you?" the second voice asked.

"I'm staying. There's a chance Athena has not yet escaped, and I will have words with her." Remus heard the mummers of voices, but Brandon's enraged words cut them off. "I have given my final order and I expect it to be obeyed!" If Brandon was staying, that meant Remus would be forced to continue hiding. What the hell had the universe done with Athena?

Chapter 50

Once upon a time, Athena had believed in the tales of princes and princesses and adventures of good triumphing over evil. That was before her mind was shattered into pieces, before she learned that ideals of good and evil were notions trumped up by the naïve to explain the chaotic world around them. Athena did not believe in good and evil, but recognized her actions towards Remus were selfish and wrong. She had pulled him into a world he was ill-equipped to handle, knowingly put his life in peril for a game he did not understand, and continued to manipulate him to fit her own needs. Her injuries slowed her down significantly, which meant Brandon would get to Remus before she did.

Brandon had quickly checked the room she had disappeared from, and when he discovered she wasn't there, his rage almost shut down her telepathy. He thought she was making her way to the parking lot to reunite with Remus and was determined to catch her in the attempt. With her injuries, he would succeed. The only path to victory laid in Remus remaining hidden long enough for Brandon and his team to lose interest, or until the police broke through Ragnarok's blockade. That was her plan until she plucked from Remus' mind that Fides still lived. It was an oversight on her part, one that could prove fatal to Remus unless action was taken.

Athena hobbled/sprinted out of her room and made her way towards the steps, Brandon's team already way ahead of her. "Universe, if you can hear me like Remus claims," she muttered. "Stay the hell out of my way!" Crashing through the door to the stairwell, she exerted her telepathy, which was beginning to groan loudly at its misuse, and discovered that Brandon Badger, ever the cautious one, had placed two guards at the bottom of the steps just in case she had been taking her time getting out. Frustration at the other man's aptitude lessened the guilt of killing his brother. Down the stairs she limped, considering her options as she descended. The lobby's elevator was covered by only one guard, but he was both watchful and experienced. Utilizing the elevator would mean fighting her way out of a cramped space against an opponent with an automatic weapon. A plan formed; one that was several steps above recklessness and one she would have never considered if Remus' life didn't hang in the balance.

Rounding the last turn, she spotted one of the guards at the bottom of the steps and launched herself from the top of the stairs. He had been turned sideways, but must have spotted movement out the corner of his eye, for he turned around and gawked for a second, his brain trying to process the image of a girl flying at him, before attempting to raise his gun. Athena slammed into him before he could fire a shot, wrapping her legs and arms around his body and essentially trapping him in a massive bear hug.

"Shoot her!" he screamed to the other guard, the veins on his forehead bulging in fear and rage.

"To aim is not enough, you must hit," she quoted, smiling at her captured victim, but talking to the operative who was taking aim behind her. "You sure you can hit me without killing your partner? Especially with such big and powerful bullets that can rip through me and your comrade at the same time?" Athena didn't know whether this was true, but neither did the operative.

"Release him!" he ordered.

"Only if you can guarantee my safety," she countered. "Get Brandon Badger on the horn and tell him I'm willing to surrender peacefully."

"Release him!"

"Watch him die, kill us both, or contact Brandon," Athena snarled. "Choose!" He hesitated before shifting his gun to the side and reaching up to his earpiece. Athena leaned in to her captive's ear as if about to tell him some secret. "He chose wrong," she whispered before viciously biting down onto the side of his neck and tearing out a chunk of his skin—a painful injury to be sure, but one that he would recover from if he could survive her. She slid down his body, grabbed the gun from his distracted hands as he was screaming in pain, and twirled behind him in one swift move.

The other operative, realizing he had been tricked, had already repositioned his gun to cover her movement, but wasn't quick enough to prevent her from hiding behind the injured man. She raised the gun, making sure the barrel touched the back of her hostage. "Same situation with just a minor alteration. Watch him die or drop your weapon."

"She will kill us both!" the injured man snarled.

"I promise, I will not," Athena assured. As the other man hesitated yet again, she leaned to the right and shot a burst of bullets around her hostage's body and into the other operative's head.

"You filthy liar!" the hostage screamed as his friend fell to the ground. Disregarding his own safety, he turned around to confront her. "You said—"

Athena slammed the butt of the gun into his face with just enough Resident strength to have him counting sheep for at least a couple of minutes. "I said I will not kill you *both*," Athena explained to his unconscious form. "One of you is alive, and so my promise is kept."

Reaching out with her telepathy, she tracked the other guard who had been guarding the elevator. The plan was to wait until he ran over to investigate the gunshots, and when he got close enough, swing the door open and ambush him with the gun. However, an unexpected but pleasant surprise had arisen. Despite the man's experience, watching the whole operation fall into pieces and with the police only minutes away had proven to be too much, and he had fled as soon as he heard the gunshots.

"*Selene?*" Athena thought, wondering if the other Resident was aiding her again, but there was no response and Athena doubted she was involved. Fear had simply gotten the better of him.

She walked into the lobby, which was now completely deserted, and exited the hotel, but had to stop as a wave of dizziness hit her. Even a Resident had limits and she was approaching hers. She stumbled forward, determined to reach the Thunderbird, and was only a mere ten feet away when a loud voice called out to her.

"Athena!"

"Uh-oh," she muttered as Brandon Badger ran forward, all his thoughts dedicated to her demise. How could she have possibly forgotten about him? "Can't we talk about this like civilized—" she began hopefully, but had to duck behind a truck as a barrage of bullets was fired in her direction. "This is really becoming tedious," she called out, her nervousness making her rant. All her energy had been used on Fides and she had nothing left to fight Brandon, but the key was to make sure he didn't figure that out. "You fire bullets, bullets miss me, and I escape unscathed."

"You can barely stand, let alone move," Brandon declared, his voice a flat monotone. He continued to move forward, his pace cautious but unrelenting. She needed a plan, but as she was thinking, her vision began to blur.

"How unfortunate," she sighed, on the verge of hysterical laughter. Most Residents had some version of rapid healing, but in Athena's case, her healing came at the cost of other abilities. Sometimes it was her sanity that took a hit, or her strength and speed would lessen to human standards for a couple of hours. More often than not, her telepathy would become unusable until she had recovered fully, but it wasn't uncommon for her to lose her sight. On top of that, her hands were starting to shake, which meant any plan involving the gun was now a risk. She checked Remus' mind, relieved she could still use her abilities. He was physically okay, but his mind felt ready to snap. Peeking into Brandon's mind, she discovered that it wouldn't take much to send him over the edge. "Why are you after me?" she called out, adopting an annoyed tone. "Don't you have anyone else you can bother?"

"You killed my brother!"

Athena poked her head around the truck and smiled condescendingly. "Poor little Brandon lost his little brother," she said mockingly. "Would a deep and sincere apology make you feel better?"

"You!" The night was filled with gunfire as Brandon unloaded his gun; Athena barely ducked her head in time to avoid the first bullet and, in his rage, Brandon didn't bother to count his shots. His gun clicked empty, and Athena was already moving while he rushed to put a new clip in.

At her peak, she could have easily caught up to him before he reloaded, but with her cracked ribs, bullet wound, and energy running low, it was a toss-up.

She fired as she approached, but her trembling hands made the shots go wild. Brandon ducked behind a minivan where he finished reloading. Her telepathy saved her and she ducked behind the same minivan on the opposite side just as he leaned out and fired a burst. She landed painfully with a gasp, her gun slipping from her, and immediately she had to scramble forward as Brandon dropped to the ground and fired bullets underneath the van in an effort to get to her. Athena leapt up, intending to jump on the top of the van, run over, and ambush Brandon from above, but as she was leaping, a bullet hit the top of her foot and, in her agony, she misjudged the jump. With a yelp of pain, she crashed to the side of the van, rocking it slightly, and had to cling tightly to the top, as Brandon was still firing bullets underneath her. The bullets stopped and Athena scanned Brandon's mind before quickly releasing her grip and ducking as low as possible. Bullets shattered the van's windows directly above her head as Brandon attempted to surprise her. She was going to die if she didn't do something, and that realization gave her a brief adrenaline burst. Getting a good grip on the minivan's undercarriage, her body adamantly telling her it couldn't be done, she lifted and turned the whole minivan over.

Brandon realized what was happening a split second before he would have been crushed. He dove out the way, and Athena, thanks to her telepathy, knew where he would land. He hit the ground and immediately rolled over onto his back, searching for her position. She was still hiding behind the now-overturned van, and she dashed out as if she planned to rush him, but quickly retreated again when Brandon started firing. She waited until the gun clicked empty for the second time before rushing over, this time for real.

I'm not going to reload in time, Athena heard in his thoughts. He also realized he wouldn't be able to get to his feet, so, still on his back, he abandoned the gun in favor of a combat knife in a side sheath. He expected her to get close and try to grapple for the knife, but Athena refused to drag this fight out any longer. She dashed as fast as her injuries allowed, and leapt, aiming both feet for Brandon's abdomen. The leader of the Ragnarok team gasped as the air was forced out of his lungs and he laid there, momentarily helpless.

"That was for all the unnecessary kicking and stomping you forced on Fides," Athena informed, kicking the gun away from him. She studied him thoughtfully, and then delivered a brutal blow to his ribs, feeling the slightest of pleasures as she heard them crack, before bending down and snatching the knife away.

I'm going to kill her, Brandon thought wrathfully. *And that boy too!* Athena, upon hearing his thoughts, walked over to his legs, whistling a tune the Resident, Dionysus, liked to whistle, and plunged the knife into his kneecap, pushing it in until only the hilt remained. His cries of torture were just enough to pacify her anger.

"Why don't you simply kill me?" he yelled, spit flying out of his mouth, his face contorted in rage.

"You're dead anyway," Athena responded, neatly side-stepping the question. "You failed to kill me, you got caught, and you killed the Resident working with you." She did a systematic check to make sure he wasn't carrying anymore surprises before turning her back on him.

"I'm going to kill you!" Brandon yelled, tears of rage and frustration falling from his face. "I swear I will!"

Athena, without bothering to look back, said, "Nothing is more costly, nothing is more sterile, than vengeance." She tried to reach out with her telepathy to check on Remus, but found her ability had finally thrown in the towel. She could no longer access her power, and if it followed normal protocol, she wouldn't be able to access it for at least an hour. "Superb," she sighed.

Limping the final couple of feet towards the Thunderbird, she bent down and looked underneath. "Remus?" she called hesitantly. Her eyesight had worsened, but she should still be able to see his movement.

A hand clasped her shoulder and Athena twirled around, fists flying to neutralize the threat.

"Ouch, knock it off!" Remus cried, cringing in pain and touching the emerging red imprint on his face.

"Sorry!" Athena apologized, covering her mouth in embarrassment. "So sorry! It's just...what are you doing sneaking up on me?"

Remus glared at her indignantly, and Athena fought the urge to snicker. "Sneaking? There was no sneaking! After recovering from the brink of death, I rolled out because I heard gunfire and found you standing over that man!" He made a movement that Athena couldn't quite see, but guessed he was pointing towards Brandon. "You walked over to the car and I followed to see if you were alright. That's when you sucker-punched me!"

"Sorry," Athena repeated bleakly.

Remus stank of piss and puke, but she thought it best not to mention it. His skin was a bit paler than usual, but other than that, her now limited sight could not spot any wounds or life threatening injuries.

The same must not have been true for her, for the next time he spoke, his voice had softened to a more concerned tone. "You look like shit."

Athena giggled. "It's funny because it's true!"

Remus paused, and Athena realized it was possible she wasn't making any sense. As the adrenaline left her body, she felt drained and unfocused. "We need to leave before the police arrive," he said. "Did you find out how they're tracking you?"

Athena blinked, surprised he would still remember that conversation. "Yes, but I need more information. I bought enough time..."

"You're a stupid kid," Brandon called out. The fool was trying to struggle to his feet with the knife still embedded in his knee. Athena imagined, with some degree of satisfaction, that the pain must have been awful. "Do you know what she is? What she's done?"

"Silence is the most powerful scream," Athena retorted, annoyed by the interruption. "Losers of the game should remain quiet; lest the winners realize they're still alive."

"She talks of games while butchering human lives." Brandon sounded bitter, which Athena thought was incredibly unfair. She hadn't asked his team to track and hunt her. "She killed my brother just for the sport of it."

"Your brother," Remus mumbled. "The man in the stairwell."

Without telepathy, Athena could not be sure what he meant. "I killed his brother because he was trying to kill me," she corrected, wishing she had killed Brandon when she'd had the chance. But no, that would have messed up her eloquent plan, and if she killed him now, Remus definitely wouldn't approve. "We need to leave or else be caught by the police."

"How close are they?"

Athena winced. "Um..." she said nervously. "Here's the catch. I can't tell."

"What?" Remus asked, sounding like he was hyperventilating, but at least breaking away from his trance. "You can't tell? How is that possible?"

"I overused my ability trying to save you," she answered

defensively. "I don't know their exact position, but I do know its best we go."

"Overusing an ability," Remus complained mutinously, but at the same time moved towards the driver's seat. "Does Superman ever overuse his flying ability? X-ray eyes? There hasn't been one comic book issue in which Professor Xavier runs out of telepathy points." Athena smiled to herself. Remus used sarcasm and dry wit as a coping mechanism, and though she didn't get half his references, she was glad he was dealing with her world.

"Your brother," Brandon called out. "Do you care about his life?"

Brandon was desperate to stop them, but in his desperation, he had struck gold. Remus stopped in his tracks. "What about my brother?"

"He's being held in one of our facilities."

"Why?" Remus demanded, his voice rising.

"Because of her!"

Athena tried to come up with a counter, but her thoughts were jumbled and it was becoming increasingly difficult to keep track of the conversation.

"Kid, by aligning yourself with her, you have aligned yourself with the enemies of mankind." Athena thought the statement was way too dramatic, but Remus seemed to be hooked and she could think of nothing to break the spell. "If you don't surrender now, your brother..."

"What about my brother?" Remus asked when it was clear Brandon wouldn't say anymore. "What about my brother?" Brandon still didn't respond, and the silence sent a chill traveling down Athena's spine. What she'd thought was simple theatrics could be something more sinister. Remus took a step forward, but she grabbed him and pulled him back. "Let me go!" he demanded, struggling against her grip. It was a mark of how tired she was that he almost succeeded.

"Is he breathing?" Athena asked. He continued to struggle and she squeezed down tightly. "Remus!" Something in her voice caught his attention and he stopped. "Is he still breathing?"

A second passed as Remus studied the fallen man. "His chest is rising, but he's not making any other movements," he answered, his voice subdued as he realized something was off. "He's not even blinking."

"Are we alone in the parking lot?"

"You can't look around and tell?" he shot back. She remained quiet, waiting for his answer. "We're alone...place is practically deserted. No, wait. There's a man about three hundred feet away." Athena heard his heartbeat speed up as fear gripped him. "Athena, he's not moving either."

For a bizarre moment, Athena wanted to sit down and cry. There was another Resident involved in the game; one who, judging by their work, was far more impressive than Fides. A moment of pity, anger, and resentment swelled up inside her. "Remus, get in the car," she ordered softly, straining her ears for any sound of movement that would give away the enemy's position. In chess, this would be considered the final moves of the game. A situation in which the king was in check and the player was only able to make one or two valid moves. The opponent thought she was cornered, but Athena would show them otherwise.

She heard the car door open and close as Remus obeyed her instructions, and the engine started up a moment later. Remus backed the car up, running over the remains of Fides' body, and, for a split second, Athena was sure he was going to leave her. Then the car slowed to a grudging stop beside her. She gave Brandon's frozen figure one last fleeting glance before opening the door and sliding into the passenger's seat. The car rocketed off before she could even close the door, and she was appreciative that Remus understood the urgency of the situation.

"Describe what you see outside," she ordered.

"There are a couple of stragglers, people who abandoned their cars to hoof it," Remus answered, no longer questioning why she couldn't see it herself. "All of them are like Brandon, frozen in mid-action."

"Any cars blocking our path?"

"No, nothing that I can see...wait. There are two police cars blocking the entryway."

If a trap was to be sprung, it would be right before they left the lot. On the street, there were too many variables that might lead to a clean escape. Athena considered telling Remus to turn around and drive away, but that would still mean they were trapped, and she doubted the mysterious Resident wouldn't have the other exits covered. "Is anyone moving?" she said instead.

"No one outside. I can't see any movements within the car, but that doesn't mean there's not."

"Understood. Keep driving."

"But..." Remus hesitated, and she realized he must have reached the same conclusion of a forthcoming trap.

"Remus, if this is an enemy, we're dead," Athena explained, deciding to level with him. "But I'm starting to think this isn't Ragnarok or Pandora's Box, otherwise you would be frozen as well. Keep driving and trust me."

Remus snorted derisively, but the car continued to creep forward. "Athena, there's a message written in red paint...or what I hope to be red paint, on one of the car's hoods."

"What's it say?"

"I can't see. Give me a second." Before Athena could protest, he had exited the car.

"Of all the reckless..." she muttered to herself, seriously incensed at his rash behavior. Anger became worry when he still had not returned a minute later. Another half minute passed and she began to panic. The Resident could have already snatched him up without her knowing. Experimentally, she touched her telepathy and winced as a backlash of pain caused an instant headache. It was barely usable, but if she concentrated, she should be able to tell where Remus had gone and if he was even still alive. Taking a deep breath, she started to focus only to have her concentration broken as the door opened.

"Remus?" she demanded, her eyes able to make out his red hair but not much else.

"You really can't see, can you? How long does your blindness last?"

"Idiot!" she hissed. "Don't ever do something that stupid again. I thought someone had captured you."

"You wanted to know the message," Remus flared back. "And normally it wouldn't be suicidal to leave a car. Only with you!" Time passed as both took a moment to cool down. "The message said 'Avalon is watching. Sincerely, Medusa.'"

"Avalon," Athena breathed. "And Medusa. Interesting. Is there any way to get past them?"

"Not without driving onto the curb and sidewalk."

"Do it," she instructed.

She felt the car jolt as it ran up a curb and then bounce as it dropped down onto the street and soon sped up, leaving the trials of the hotel behind. They had survived and won what should have been an impossible game, but not without a bit of unwanted assistance. Avalon was involved, and her mind reeled from the implications of what that meant. Unfortunately, Remus refused to give her a moment to herself to ponder past events, insisting on peppering her with questions she barely knew the answers to.

"Is this Resident from Pandora's Box or Ragnarok?"

"No one in Pandora's Box has this ability. I would definitely know about it."

"Then it's someone from the sister organization you were talking about. Ragnarok."

"If it was, you would be paused as well. On top of that, they allowed us to escape.

"Perhaps they're following, waiting for reinforcements," Remus argued.

Athena chuckled hollowly. "If they knew my condition, they would know reinforcements are not needed." Remus wisely didn't answer her self-pitying statement. "No, I believe the message they considerately left for our benefit is true. It's a cover-up." Remus didn't get it, so she explained. "I think they're only here to make sure the existence of Residents remains a secret."

"So what happened to them?"

"It's like you said, their minds are paused." She studied a woman in a car as they drove by. "I doubt any harm will come to them and they'll probably wake up none the wiser."

"How can you be so sure?"

"Because the goal is not to attract attention, and nothing attracts attention more than a massacre." Athena's heart began to slow back to normal beat, but she still felt ill at ease. "There are Residents who can perform these miracles," she said sourly. "I feel inadequate."

Remus sped up. "That's what you call it? A miracle?"

"What would you call it?" she asked reasonably, but Remus didn't answer and she didn't have the strength to dwell inside his mind.

A wave of weariness slammed against her. She was dead tired and fighting armed men with zero hours of sleep. She tried to fight it off, but eventually sunk into a deep slumber, just as Remus said, "I can't do this anymore."

Chapter 51

Ms. Yang continuously paced the room, past Caleb, Froce, and Dr. Pluck, who were all lined up and looking like nervous recruits on the first day of boot camp. After returning from her mysterious trip, Ms. Yang, dropping all pretense of being an overworked and overly efficient secretary, immediately called a meeting, its purpose unknown, but the likely reason was to royally chew them out and assign blame. Matthew had been incensed about having control so easily ripped from his hands, but had chosen to keep his peace, lest his secretary decide to give him a reminder of her abilities.

Ms. Yang stopped pacing and abruptly turned around, her eyes narrowing on Caleb's tinted sunglasses. Even inside, the man insisted on them. "Explain," she ordered. "I need to know everything you uncovered about Athena's escape."

"You're right," Caleb said in mock whisper to Froce. "I think the boss only hired her because of her looks."

Matthew laughed dryly, but stopped as Ms. Yang's shoulders tensed. She was on edge and possibly scared, which meant his father was not happy with recent events. It was times like this that he wished for a cold beer on some small island, far away from the problems of Residents.

Ms. Yang let out a deep breath before nervously adjusting her glasses. He was right, she was scared. "Now is not the time for games, Mr. Wentworth. The situation has deteriorated quickly, and I need your complete report in order to right the wrong of Athena's escape."

If Ms. Yang had high hopes of being a motivational speaker, they were cruelly dashed, for there was only one part of her statement they responded to.

"Caleb Wentworth," Froce said, looking at Caleb in complete shock and utter glee. "Why didn't you tell me your last name?"

"If I wanted you to know, I would have told you," Caleb huffed.

"Yes, sir, Mr. Wentworth."

"Someone's itching for an ass-kicking!"

"Gentlemen!" Ms. Yang yelled as she lost all patience. Matthew was the closest one to her, so only he felt it—the intense heat that radiated off her at the height of her anger. Then it was gone, and Ms. Yang was back under control. "Your report, please."

"Athena escaped because of Nick Hensley," Caleb stated, smoothly switching into professional mode, obviously eager to get off the topic of his last name. "An idiot who passed her a pen that hid a ton of small needles, which proved to be fatal to Scott Williams."

"So Nick was her accomplice?"

"No. He says someone stuffed the pen in his pocket without his knowing, so when Athena asked for a pen, he handed her that one, even though he had no idea where it originated from."

"And you believe that?" Ms. Yang asked skeptically.

Caleb's hesitation was brief but noticeable. "Yep. As hard as that is to swallow, it makes sense. Nick Hensley was only here a couple days, and an escape like this would take months, if not years, to implement."

"Plus, Nick isn't the smartest guy in the bunch," Froce added. "It's easier to imagine him as a pawn than as the mastermind."

"Okay, then do you know who the traitor is?" Ms. Yang asked almost pleadingly, while tapping her fingers against her thigh.

"We have an inkling," Caleb admitted, though not sounding too happy about it. "Athena, for whatever reason, left us a few clues that pointed straight to Edward Gantz, one of the logistics supervisors. When we sent a couple of men to check out his house, they found him dead by drug overdose, the apparent victim of suicide."

Ms. Yang studied Caleb's face. "But you don't believe that to be the case."

"I just think it's too neat. The person who helped Athena

all of a sudden feels remorse and decides to kills himself before we're able to question him?"

"It does seem amazingly coincidental," Ms. Yang allowed. "But do you have any proof to the contrary?"

"Not yet."

"In that case, we shall move on until you have another theory to present. Now—"

"Wait a minute," Froce objected. "We tell you there's a traitor undermining us and killing our men, and you dismiss it as unimportant?"

Matthew inwardly sighed. These meetings were starting to become predictable. After Froce made a valid but whiny point, Caleb usually countered with a wisecrack.

"Like she said, we have other things that need to be done," Caleb said placatingly, and Matthew raised an eyebrow, waiting for the punch line. "Like getting Athena's cell ready for her." He turned to Ms. Yang. "Exactly when will Ragnarok's top-notched solders be arriving with Athena in handcuffs?"

Ms. Yang glared daggers, but said nothing.

"What's the matter?" Caleb pressed. "Like you said, Ragnarok's people are much better than our own dinky little crew, so they should have had no problems capturing the gal and bringing her in."

"There are a couple of problems," Ms. Yang admitted.

Matthew wiped his brow as the intense heat emanating from Ms. Yang's skin returned. Caleb and the others might not have noticed yet, but they would soon, and the realization would bring a rush of unwanted and pointed questions. As casually as he could, he started to make his way toward her.

"What type of problems?" Dr. Pluck piped up.

"It seems Athena has escaped from our operatives," Ms. Yang said, almost choking on the words. "Not only that, the ones that Athena didn't kill have been arrested for terrorizing a hotel."

Caleb laughed, but there was no humor in it. "Because of your arrogance, people are now dead. What happened to that fancy specialist you sent with them?"

"Killed," she answered, clearly unhappy with being the one answering questions instead of the one asking them. "And there's more."

Matthew had reached Ms. Yang's position, but had yet to formulate a plan on how to gain her attention. She must have seen him approaching, but continued to ignore him, whereas Caleb had notice his movements and Matthew could tell he was watching closely, despite the sunglasses.

"More than letting Athena escape and having your men arrested?" Froce asked incredulously.

"Another organization has found out about Athena's escape."

"There's another one?" Caleb roared at the admission, diverting his attention away from Matthew. "This is ridiculous!"

Matthew took a step forward so that he was in Ms. Yang's peripheral view and wiped the sweat from his eyebrows with the back of his hand. Ms. Yang's expression didn't change, but the heat immediately vanished as if someone turned off a switch.

"Do you think we have a monopoly on Residents?" she said tartly to Caleb. "Yes, there is another one, but unlike Pandora's Box and Ragnarok, it's run by a rival of Mr. Titanos. Someone who doesn't hold him in the highest regard."

Caleb scowled at Matthew. "If his son is any indication, I can see why."

Matthew was way past caring what Caleb thought of him. He took a step back to Ms. Yang's side and, as he did, his secretary's hand brushed past his. In his four years of working with her, Ms. Yang had not once allowed Matthew to touch her, spurring his advances with threats of bodily harm. The light touch was maybe her way of thanking him...or perhaps her hand had accidentally touched his and he was reading too much into it.

"The point I'm trying to make is that they now know of Athena's escape," Ms. Yang reiterated. "They even interfered to keep the public from catching on."

"So why didn't they capture Athena?" Dr. Pluck said with a frown. "It would have been helpful."

Ms. Yang nodded her head in agreement. "It would have and that's why they didn't do it. They love that we're scrambling to cover our trail."

"Two questions," Caleb growled. "You're using the word 'they' a lot. Is there anything else we can call them?"

After a brief hesitation, she said, "Avalon."

Avalon was one of the many topics that were above Matthew's clearance level, but occasionally, Ms. Yang would let information slip. Both Avalon and Pandora's Box were organizations that dealt with Residents, but that was where the similarities ended. Pandora's Box was a human-based facility that created and controlled Residents, while Avalon was run by Residents and created new ones to bolster their ranks.

"Second question," Caleb began. "Is it possible they had anything to do with Athena's escape?"

Ms. Yang mulled it over for a moment. "Unlikely. I doubt they would make such a bold and public move against us. However, this is a grave concern to Mr. Titanos because Avalon will be watching the situation very closely, looking for a weakness to exploit. Mr. Titanos wants Athena captured immediately."

"Then go send more of Ragnarok's men after her," Dr. Pluck suggested, the first hint of scorn in his voice.

Matthew bristled at the disrespect. Froce and Caleb being asses was barely tolerable, but Dr. Pluck acting insubordinate when he could have prevented Athena escaping by simply calling out during the time she was leading him out of Pandora's Box was beyond unacceptable. Ms. Yang must have heard it too, for she stared at the little toad in silence, her gaze threatening on hostile.

Dr. Pluck shifted uncomfortably, glancing at Froce and Caleb for support but finding none. It was a rare moment of unity, possibly the only one that would ever happen as everyone silently showed their disfavor for the doctor. Eventually, Dr. Pluck's eyes hit the floor and that's when Ms. Yang spoke.

"Unfortunately that's not possible. Athena managed to convince the commander, Brandon Badger, that Ragnarok was responsible for this incident. As a result, Brandon is publicly pinning the whole affair on Ragnarok."

"I'm sure the big man has enough cops and politicians in his pocket to get off," Caleb huffed, his tone perhaps a smidge less confrontational than it had been.

"He does," Ms. Yang acknowledged, following Caleb's lead and adjusting her voice so that it was less condescending. "But it's going to take some time for him to smooth this over. And since this is considered an act of terrorism, Homeland Security is involved. Mr. Titanos and all of his properties are under heavy scrutiny and he can't do anything that looks remotely suspicious."

Caleb frowned. "So how the hell..." He stopped, and opened his mouth in surprise before snapping it shut. When he spoke again, his voice was anything but respectful. "So now you want us country hillbillies to risk our lives and go try to capture Athena."

When Ms. Yang didn't correct him, Froce blinked in confusion. "Wouldn't that fall under the category of 'suspicious?'"

"Legally, Mr. Titanos doesn't own Pandora's Box, his son does. As of now, Pandora's Box is not under investigation as only a handful of people know Matthew is Mr. Titanos' son."

"Really," Caleb said amused. "He was quite the doting father, wasn't he?"

Matthew grinned nastily. "Yep, he was. I see him every week to catch up on life. And what of your children, Caleb? When was the last year you spoke to them?"

Caleb's face darkened, and Froce put a restraining hand on the other man's arm before glancing at Ms. Yang. "Why now? She's already proven she can handle herself. Why not wait until we have enough manpower to ensure a successful mission?"

"Because Mr. Titanos says now. That should be enough."

"It sure as hell ain't!" Caleb said, firing up. "Just because he's desperate does not give him cause to be reckless with our lives. We don't even know what the gal is capable of."

Dr. Pluck coughed. "There is something else to consider. How are you tracking Athena?"

"There's a secondary tracking device in the upper part of her back," Ms. Yang answered. "Why?"

"Have we determined if Athena is a mind reader?"

"She's telepathic. She can read the mind but can't control it."

Dr. Pluck adjusted his glasses, looking like the toad he was. "One last question. Did Brandon or anyone else know about the tracking device?"

There was a moment of silence and the intense heat came back with a vengeance. Ms. Yang look ready to spit fire and if she was the swearing type, she would be cussing up a storm. Instead, she took a deep breath. "That's a very excellent point. Our specialist knew. If Athena can enter the minds of fellow Residents, and if she did a thorough sweep of his mind, she would know the exact location."

"That's a pretty decent-sized problem," Caleb said, quieting down. "If she does know where the bug is, then you can bet her first order of business is removing it."

"We're still tracking her. The strange thing is she seems to be coming back here at high speed."

"I doubt she's turning herself in." Caleb looked at his watch. It was a little after five in the morning. "It's gonna take at least an hour to gather twenty to twenty-five men, and I'm not comfortable with those numbers. Not after Athena took out fifty."

"You *want* to chase Athena?" Froce asked, clearly confused.

"Hell no! But if she removes the bug, then she disappears. I don't want to be looking at TV every time a tragedy happens and be thinking 'that's our gal.'"

"I agree," Dr. Pluck said, clapping his hands together. "We have a responsibility to deal with our mess."

"I don't want to hear another word from the coward who allowed Athena to walk out the front door," Caleb growled. Matthew knew everyone was thinking it, but Caleb just happened to beat everyone to the punch in saying it.

"Enough," Ms. Yang commanded, rubbing her temples, and Matthew felt perverse pleasure in seeing her so aggravated. It wasn't quite as easy as she thought, dealing with these likes. "Caleb, I want you to put together a team. Take whoever you need, but make it quick. You said you could do it in an hour. I'm saying you can do it in a half hour."

"You want us to capture Athena?"

"To follow her, for the time being. We can't allow her to disappear, and if she removes that bug, that's exactly what's going to happen. I'll try to get backup to you as soon as possible, but bear in mind your orders might change if an opportunity arises."

"Fine," Caleb said, sounding civil. "And what about the brother?"

"You mean Romulus Sylvia? I already took care of that. As we speak, I'm having him and his girlfriend released."

Caleb let out a huge sigh of relief and even managed a grudging smile. "Good. One last thing. Some of the boys in the R&D apartments have manufactured some type of high-tech gas. When released, it puts everyone who breathes it in to sleep."

"And you want to use it against Athena?" Ms. Yang shook her head, but then stopped. "No, you want to use it in case she hides behind another crowd of innocent people."

"Yep. Gas is safe and, if used right, it'll take away one of her advantages."

"Clever." It would have been a compliment except for the amount of surprise it was said with. "I have no objections, but only use it a last resort."

Caleb nodded. "I'll assume I'm dismissed," he said loudly, trying to get Matthew's attention.

Asshole, Matthew thought sourly to himself. He was saved from responding by Ms. Yang's interference.

"Half hour, Caleb," Ms. Yang reminded him. She waited a couple of seconds until after Caleb left before speaking to Froce. "You're going with Caleb and I want you to keep a close eye on him."

"You don't trust him?" Froce said angrily.

Dr. Pluck spoke up. "You have to agree, he does make the best suspect," he said. "He has known Athena the longest."

As expected, Froce immediately turned on Dr. Pluck. "He's the one who exonerated you! If it wasn't for him, you'd still be whining on and on about how you didn't do it."

"That's enough!" Ms. Yang said firmly. "Dr. Pluck, shut up. Froce, it's just a precaution. Now, both of you, leave now."

They left, leaving Matthew and Ms. Yang blissfully alone.

"You really think Caleb's the traitor?" Matthew said skeptically.

Ms. Yang shot him an unreadable look and Matthew prepared for a scathing insult. "I'm covering my bases. I plan to corner Caleb and tell him to keep a close watch on Froce as well."

Matthew made a noise. Something between a laugh and a cough. "You really know how to work people."

Ms. Yang shrugged. "Someone has to." Her slight smile took the edge off the insult. "It was fortunate no one found out that I am a Resident. It would have caused severe problems with the staff of Pandora's Box." Matthew figured that was the closest he would get to an apology and nodded in acknowledgement before turning to leave.

Outside the room, he immediately ran into Froce. "Didn't

Ms. Yang give you an order?" he barked, not liking how the solider had been standing beside the door, almost like he was eavesdropping. Tyrone nodded solemnly, his face eerily blank, before walking off, and Matthew had to wonder if perhaps Ms. Yang was correct in having Caleb watch over him.

Chapter 52

Remus was still alive and, for most, their continuing existence was something taken for granted, but he had survived the onslaught of an entire army dedicated to his and Athena's destruction. This wasn't even counting Fides. After facing the universe's deadliest secret, he felt he had a right to take a moment to be relieved. But who was to say Residents were the deadliest secret? Remus pondered this as he switched lanes without using the signal lights. Beside him, Athena mumbled something, and even in her sleep, she sounded mocking and condescending. If Residents existed, what about vampires? Ghosts? Maybe the boogeyman, in reality, was a sadistic escaped Resident who took his jollies from scaring little kids.

So deep in thought, Remus was unaware that he had drifted into another car's lane until the oncoming driver honked his displeasure. Still wound up tightly from his ordeal, he jerked the car's wheel, overcorrecting and sliding onto gravel before regaining control. He checked on Athena, afraid she would wake up cranky and figure out what he was doing, but he found her still fast asleep, the events at the hotel having taken a toll on her and with good reason. She had been bleeding profusely when she'd first entered the car, and it had only taken moments for her seat to be covered with blood. She had paled drastically, her skin now a sickly greenish hue. Supposedly, she would heal rapidly, but as of now, she looked like a guest knocking impatiently at death's door. Remus peered closely, initially trying to see if her wounds had closed, but upon noticing she wasn't moving, he looked for the rise and fall of her chest or a flutter of eyelids...anything that would let him know she was still alive.

"Truck," Athena muttered, without cracking an eyelid, and managing to scare years off what was obviously destined to be a very short life. Remus thought she was mumbling again until he looked back up and had to slam on the brakes, barely managing to avoid the rear end of a truck. It would be a miracle if they didn't die of a tragic car accident by the end of the night.

"More than a miracle," Athena responded with a yawn, confirming she was awake and that her telepathy had recovered. She stretched lazily, but grimaced at the action, a hiss of pain escaping her pale, cracked lips. "Remus, please slow down. You look suspicious going this fast and the police stopping us would be an inconvenience to us both."

"I'm going back," Remus said to her, not bothering to try and hide his intentions from a telepath. He had expected some counterargument and even a physical fight, but what he didn't expect was her silence. When the silence stretched uncomfortably long, he added, "My brother is in danger and I need to protect him." To his own ears, the words sounded cheesy and the idea of him protecting anyone was laughable, but Athena took it all in stride with a simple shrug of her shoulders before she started messing with the radio dial. "You don't have anything to say?"

"What would you like me to say?" she asked reasonably. "Do you want me to convince you not to save your brother?" She played with the radio until it was on something that was loud and upbeat. "They gave me a radio once at Pandora's Box," she recalled, a slight, twisted smile on her lips. "I broke it over some poor guy's head. It was back in my moody teenage years," she added in way of explanation, though Remus had asked for none.

"Athena..." he began, not knowing what he was going to say, but was cut off.

"Do you want me to take the decision from you?" she wondered out loud. "Force you not to go? That way you can claim I was the reason you couldn't embark on a suicidal run to rescue your brother?" Athena appeared to mull it over before shaking her head, and even that action seemed to cause her pain. "No, you're not that much of a coward, are you, Remus?"

"Damn it!" Remus seethed angrily. "Stop being an ass.

You know what I want!"

"I can't know what you want unless you know what you want!" she retorted. "You have too many conflicting thoughts in your head and I'm too tired to sift through them."

"I want..." Remus stopped and took a calming breath. This was Athena's tactic; rile up the enemy so they were more likely to make a costly mistake. She'd done so at the gas station with George Hacker, playing on the man's hatred of her, and again with Brandon Badger, manipulating the soldier's love for his brother against him. Only level heads would triumph. He might have imagined it, but he could have sworn Athena gave a small nod of approval. "I want...need you to help me save my brother," he said carefully.

"I see," Athena mused. "Problem is, why should I care what fate befalls him?"

"Because it's your fault he's in this mess!" Remus retorted, knowing as soon as the words left his mouth he had made a mistake. Athena's cocky smile confirmed it.

"We believe that to err is human. To blame it on someone else is politics," she quoted. "*I* did not kidnap him, nor did I know it was going to happen. Besides, even if I was somewhat culpable, you act as if I should feel remorse.

"Do you ever feel any remorse?" he asked bitterly, knowing he was going further and further away from persuading her to his cause. His comment was meant to insult, but the way she tensed alerted him that he had hit a raw nerve.

"What do you know of me?" she asked sullenly, like a small child being unfairly punished. "All of you so judgmental over the necessary actions needed to survive. I did what I had to!" Athena had gotten loud, practically screeching the last comment at him. Her reference to "all of you" meant there was something and someone else she was speaking of.

Remus shifted in his seat, shooting a fleeting glance at her. She looked so small and sickly, but her presence still vibrated around her. Knowledge of Residents or not, only a fool would dismiss her as a threat. "Ragnarok, Pandora's Box, Residents. It's all so ridiculously unreal; I'm still not completely sure I haven't gone crazy and am imagining the whole thing in my head. In your world, I don't know what would be considered necessary action or not, not sure if there was another way to sneak and avoid these people rather than fight and kill them." He shifted lanes and the car behind him followed his example. Worried it was someone following them, he slowed down and forced the car to go around them, which earned a bemused smile by Athena. "Athena, you enjoy it," he finished, heart pounding in anticipation of how she would take his assessment of her. "All of this. Being on the run, fighting those sent to kill you, even when you're frightened and in pain, I think you're still enjoying it."

"You think I'm a masochist?" Athena asked with no emotion other than curiosity.

"I think you're an adrenaline junkie," he corrected. "I think in the heat of the moment, you don't see those you're killing and hurting as any more than pawns of a game." Athena didn't respond, and as was often the case, the silence drove Remus to pacify. "I mean, I don't know. Maybe..."

"You said what you meant," Athena interrupted irritably. "You will insult more if you try to take it back."

"Okay, but—"

"Put a sock in it!" she said, exasperated, sinking into her seat and turning her head to her window. "Give me a moment."

Remus fell silent, not knowing how badly his words had wounded her, if at all, and wondering what deep thoughts she was pondering. He opened his mouth to speak.

"Uh-uh," Athena warned, not deigning to look at him, and he closed his mouth, feeling like a scolded dog. Another three minutes passed and he briefly wondered if she had fallen asleep when she said, "A trade."

"Trade..." Remus repeated. "What type of trade?"

"Your brother's life for a favor to be named later," she answered, playing with the buttons on the dashboard and accidentally turning on the heat, squealing in surprise as the hot air washed over her. She wasn't moving as stiffly as she had been a mere fifteen minutes ago. "Once your brother is safe, and assuming we're both alive and in one piece, you will owe me one favor."

"What type of favor?"

"Not telling," she taunted. She frowned as she caught the tread of Remus' thoughts. "I would never ask you to kill or maim another human. Nothing that will shatter your well put-together moral compass...just a simple favor that will take no more than a half hour. Forty five minutes at most."

"I need to know what it is."

"No you don't." Athena had managed to turn off the heat and was now messing with the windows, rolling them down and back up. "Don't like it, go save him yourself."

Making a deal with the devil. Remus could not think of a situation in which the metaphor would be more appropriate.

"I need an answer," Athena said, an abrupt mood change overtaking her. No longer annoyed, her expression was apathetically impersonal. She might have taken issue with Remus calling her a devil. If he was to fight Pandora's Box, he would need Athena, but what if he surrendered himself? His life might be forfeited, but perhaps they would spare Romulus.

"Three!" Athena snarled loudly, scaring Remus. A light turned red and Remus slowed the car to a stop with only a slight lurch.

Remus looked at her. "What are you—"

"Two."

"Wait!" Remus cried. "I'm just trying to—"

"One." Athena opened her car door and was out of her seat and onto the street before Remus knew what was happening.

"Wait!" he cried out to her retreating back. He fumbled with his seatbelt, taking a lot longer than a competent adult should before releasing it and stumbling out the door, the cold air knocking against him hard. "Athena, wait!" She was walking down the middle of the street, past the line of cars waiting patiently at the stop light. Her bloodied apparel, pale skin, and slight limp drew a lot of concerned glances. "Woman, I told you to wait!" Remus yelled, intentionally phrasing it in a way he knew would annoy and, sure enough, she spun around as graceful as a ballerina, her eyes already aglow in anticipation of a fight.

"Told me!" Athena repeated acidly, and Remus rushed to intervene before she got hung up on that aspect.

"I agree to your terms. My brother's safety for your favor."

Her expression didn't change. "We would need to do things my way."

"Fine," Remus agreed, although he was growing nervous again. Athena's way was not the way of diplomats and pacifists. She walked towards him, her lips twitching at his thoughts.

"We have a deal, Remus Sylvia. First step in rescuing your silly little brother is to get back in the car and be prepared to drive." The way she said it might have alerted him if it hadn't been for the sudden synchronized honking from three different cars. The light had turned green and Remus' car was blocking the line from progressing and it made for some very irate drivers. "You know," Athena called out merrily as he ran back to the car, cursing the whole way. "I once read that road rage causes over two hundred deaths per year in the United States."

"Hurry up!" someone screamed, taking the time and effort to roll down their window so they could deliver what they must have thought to be a very important message. Remus didn't see when Athena sauntered up to that car and stuck her head in as if speaking with someone. Rushing back, he almost tripped over his own untied shoelaces, but managed to get back to the driver's seat, his face burning with embarrassment.

"That was fun!" Athena exclaimed cheerfully, entering from the passenger's door. "Okay, go ahead and drive."

Remus was preparing to leave when he glanced in the rearview mirror. "There's a man behind us," he informed pensively. "One of the drivers; he's running at us."

"All the more reason for you to drive," Athena said lightly.

Remus shot off, quickly putting distance between them and the driver who stared dumbfounded for a moment before shaking his fists like a classic super villain and running back to his car.

"He didn't seem like one of the mercenaries who are chasing us," Remus observed.

She smiled blandly. "Well, he was after us, but I doubt it was because he knew about Residents. No, more than likely he was after the phone I borrowed from the car."

"You stole his phone?" Remus yelled.

"We need to lose him. Take a left here and then an immediate right." She refused to say anything else until he followed instructions. "Yes, I...acquired his phone and no, I don't feel any guilt at all. The man was cheating on his dying wife with her sister." The excuse felt too much like a soap opera to be true and when he expressed his disbelief, she shrugged, not the slightest bit abashed. "Well whatever his character, we needed the phone more than he did, or do you think he is also trying to save his sibling from evil geneticists?" She must have taken his silence as agreement and tossed him the phone without warning. He, of course, missed and had to pick it up from the floor of the car.

"And what am I supposed to do with this?" he asked, checking the rearview mirror in case the driver of the stolen phone had found them.

Athena looked at him like he was an idiot. "You expect me to risk my life without even knowing if your brother is in danger? Give the chump a call."

Romulus stared, dumbfounded, at the stack of papers thick enough to be a book lying innocently in front of him. "This is for real?"

"It is," the woman named Ms. Yang acknowledged, absently adjusting her glasses.

She seemed nice enough, but her posture, demeanor, and attire all reminded him of a praying mantis, silently waiting for you to draw nearer before pouncing. After being held prisoner for so many hours, two men had come to collect them. Romulus briefly fought, intending to knock them both out before taking Delilah and running, but a smack to the head cleared his mind of that train of thought. When entering the base, he had been asleep, the unfortunate victim of tranquilizers, so as he left the cell, he saw the facility for the first time. The walls and ceiling were made from a silver metallic metal and all the hallways looked identical to the one before. People raced back and forth down the halls, creating an atmosphere of panicked frenzy, and Delilah huddled closer to him. After what felt like hours, they'd entered a room where Ms. Yang had introduced herself before dropping a large bundle of paper, declaring it a contract for him to sign.

Delilah stepped forward and thumbed through the papers. "If he signs this contract, we get to leave?"

"Incorrect," Ms. Yang answered, not moving any muscles except her mouth. "You will get to leave, regardless of signing it. All this contract does is promise considerable help throughout your life—colleges, job careers, financial assistance, all your needs will be taken care of."

Romulus didn't care about any of that, though he felt he needed to pretend he did. He reached for the papers, but

Delilah slapped his hand like a parent slapping a toddler's hand away from a hot stove.

"Why would you people need a contract?" she asked, ignoring his look. "What does Romulus have to do and what do we get out of all this?"

Ms. Yang looked amused that Delilah had appointed herself Romulus' attorney, but her voice was nothing but professional when she answered. "The contract is broken up into several parts. The first, your absolute silence regarding everything you have seen and will see in the future."

"The future?" Romulus didn't like the sound of that.

"Ah, well, yes. Part two of the contract is that you will submit yourself to our tests for a year as you take an experimental but low-risk drug to help with your addiction problem."

"I don't have an addiction problem," Romulus protested.

At the same time, Delilah asked, "What does the drug do?"

Ms. Yang looked between the two before focusing on Romulus. "It is just a precaution. Imagine if you will..."

With a loud sigh, Delilah turned to Romulus. "The addiction problem is a cover up. That way they can say you're delusional if you decide to speak out against them. Get it?"

"Um..." Romulus started to say, but Delilah had already turned to Ms. Yang.

"Now what does the drug do?"

Ms. Yang blinked twice before her gaze burned into Delilah with renewed attention. Romulus didn't like it one bit and he stepped in front of Delilah to draw the other woman's attention. "What does the drug do?" he repeated loudly.

She was looking at him, but it still felt like her gaze was looking through him at Delilah. "It is a remarkable synthesis designed to unlock the true potential of the human DNA. Making you stronger and faster...able to perform the impossible."

"Steroids?" Romulus asked.

Ms. Yang threw back her head and laughed, a deep, hearty noise that sounded like the crackling of flames. "Steroids?" she scoffed. "You think all this secrecy is for the newest batch of steroids?" She shook her head before becoming professional again. "Actually, the best way to answer that question is to show rather than tell. And to that effect, I have arranged a quick tour of our establishments."

"I don't want a tour, I want to go home."

"Nevertheless, a tour is needed for your full understanding."

"I want to leave!"

"Why was Romulus chosen?" Delilah asked from behind him. In the back of Romulus' mind, he realized Delilah was asking all the questions he should be asking, and resolved to do better, lest Ms. Yang take any more interest in her.

"His blood analysis was very encouraging. The best we've seen. We believe him to be a perfect candidate for Ambrosia. The name of the drug," she went on to add as they exchanged looks of confusion.

"So you want me to be a human guinea pig for a year," Romulus summed up. "What about Delilah?"

"She will be treated to the same luxuries you have. Choice of colleges, financial assistance if needed. Even a job at one of our many companies, once done with college. Of course this all depends on you, Romulus."

"And if I say no?" Romulus asked, and Delilah drew back as if the question might send Ms. Yang over the edge.

"The young are so theatrical," Ms. Yang sighed. "We would take steps to guarantee our secrecy, but rest assured nothing as...permanent as the two of you are thinking. What I offer is an opportunity to become better than yourself. To that effect, take the contract home and think about it. You have twenty-four hours before I need a response."

"And if I sign the contract, will Remus be protected?"

Ms. Yang blinked. Just once. "I'm sorry, I thought you understood."

"Understood what?" Romulus demanded, denying the unsaid implication. "What?"

"Romulus, he's dead," Delilah said softly. She rubbed his shoulders, but Romulus angrily shook her off.

"No!"

"Romulus..."

"No!" It couldn't be. His twin, dead...the one person he'd known ever since birth. "These people killed him!"

"Athena killed him," Ms. Yang corrected. "Not to say we wouldn't have...or we might have used him as leverage. We'll never know now."

"Athena was your escaped prisoner!" Romulus shot back. He took a step towards Ms. Yang as Delilah tried to restrain him.

"Your father was going to have him killed anyway." The words stopped Romulus cold. He opened his mouth to deny it, but found he could not. "Oh?" Ms. Yang said curiously. "No argument? So you knew...or at least expected. Yes, he was going to kill Remus. Strangely enough, Athena saved him only to kill him later. From what I heard, she's very fickle like that."

"No," Romulus said dumbly.

Ms. Yang looked at him before reaching underneath her desk. "One of the reasons I decided to personally meet with you instead of delegating this task is because I have a special offer and didn't trust anyone else to state it." She procured a glass and a bottle of dark red liquid. Pouring it into the glass, she slid it over to Romulus. "I really do abhor drinking when discussing business, but this is a very special case."

Romulus hesitated. Picking up the glass, he briefly considering dumping the contents on Ms. Yang, but that one act of spitefulness might cause the end of his and Delilah's lives. He drank the shot in one large gulp, the liquid burning all the way down.

"Better?" Ms. Yang asked. Romulus coughed as a response. "Good. Your father is a power-hungry fool. Eventually, he will target you...perhaps try to convert those around you to his cause." Romulus felt Delilah bristle at the notion. "I have seen a lot of evil in my position, but your father is the most malicious—"

"Spare me," Romulus interrupted. "I get it. My father's the devil and you people are angels. What do you want?"

"To permanently remove your father from the equation."

Romulus' mind, which had been jumbled by Remus' death, now sharpened as Ms. Yang's words sank in. "You're going to kill my father," he said calmly. Surprisingly, and worryingly, he felt no emotion at the prospect.

"Only if you sign the contract, and only with your permission," Ms. Yang clarified.

The door behind them slid open, a guard walking through. Ms. Yang must have signaled him without Romulus noticing. She stood up. "Time is forever fleeting and I have so much work left to do. But it was a pleasure meeting the both of you. She stuck her hand forward to shake, but

Romulus only glared at it disdainfully. After a second, Delilah stepped out from behind Romulus and shook Ms. Yang's hand, the other woman nodding in her direction. "After the brief tour of our facilities, you will be taken home. I suggest you write down a list of questions for our next meeting."

"How will we contact you?" Delilah asked. Romulus should have asked that.

"You don't. In twenty-four hours, Romulus will be contacted by one of our agents for his decision."

She looked at Romulus for acknowledgement, but he couldn't bring himself to move. With a small shrug, she gestured at the guard who gently escorted them both away. As they walked, Delilah leaned in close and embraced him.

"It's okay, Romulus. You'll be okay," Delilah whispered.

Something in her words sounded cheesy, if not insincere, but Romulus forced himself to believe it and hugged her back. He'd be okay as long as he had Delilah by his side.

Chapter 53

Delilah made it a point to memorize everything she saw as they walked down the halls. Romulus was too dejected to speak to her, and honestly, she preferred it that way. Romulus was sweet and overly optimistic, two things she couldn't stand. Throughout the night, she'd been forced to listen to entire monologues on how they would be okay, and several times she'd come close to screaming at him to shut up

"This place looks like a prison," she commented to no one in particular.

"In a lot of ways, it is, ma'am," one of the guards replied. "It would be a catastrophe if the...people...of this place ever escaped."

"Why the hesitation?" Romulus asked, coming regretfully back to life. "You mean people actually live in this dismal place?"

"Calm down!" Delilah said sharply, and Romulus looked at her in surprise. "I can't stand anymore arguing," she said, quickly trying to cover her tracks. "I just want to go home."

Romulus nodded. Delilah had to get away from him before she made a major slip up.

The guard said, "I understand, ma'am. This place isn't meant for pretty girls like yourself."

Delilah gritted her teeth, but managed to offer an apologetic smile. "I guess so."

They turned a corner and Delilah spotted two men leading a girl, perhaps a year or two younger than her, into one of the many doors that lined the halls. She was darkly colored with jet black hair that was shoulder length and covered her ears. Mismatched cotton green pants and orange sweater made it virtually impossible to tell what type of figure she had underneath. A normal-looking girl, pretty but not re-markable enough to spare a second look, but the nervous-ness of the two men was interesting enough to have Delilah's gaze linger, searching for the cause of their anxiety. The girl stopped and glanced their way, her face blank of any emo-tions, and Delilah felt a shiver of fear down her spine that intensified when the girl spoke.

"You are the brother of the one who went with Athena," she stated.

Romulus jerked and nodded, even though it wasn't a question. The two men hovering around the eerie girl shared a look, and one gently nudged her towards the door while the other bent down to whisper something to her. To their obvious relief, the girl nodded and turned away, only to have Romulus call out to her, despite their guard's warning noise. "What do you know of her and my brother?"

The girl swiveled her head to look at him with big eyes that would have been expressive if any emotion was to fill them. The two men, who must have been her jailers, stopped beside her, clearly wanting her to enter the room but hesitant to push her in. One of them cast a reproachful look at Romulus. "I know nothing of your brother except his future. He will be killed, either by Athena's insanity or those wishing to capture her and silence him. That is his fate."

Delilah shuddered fearfully. The way the girl talked was the way a robot would talk if given sentience. It was unnerv-ing and frightening and Delilah just wished for the conversa-tion to end.

"But why?" Romulus asked plaintively.

The girl didn't blink. "Find someone else to satisfy your inquiries," she said softly. "I owe you no explanations." On that note, she shuffled into her room, the door closing behind her, and everyone breathed a huge sigh of relief.

Their guard whirled to face Romulus. "Kid, that was stu-pid!" he said angrily. "You trying to cause a bloodbath?"

Romulus looked taken aback, and Delilah hated his stupid expression of shock. "Bloodbath? We were just talking!"

The guard scowled, but his features softened marginally. "That's right, you wouldn't know," he said with a sigh. "That there was Selene, one of the many patrons of our facility. Caleb showed you those pictures, didn't he? Those men

Athena killed?"

Delilah flashed back to the bloody and broken bodies of the would-be assassins Maris had hired for Remus.

"Selene is like Athena, and is capable of the same thing."

Romulus opened him mouth, but the guard held up a hand. "Whatever questions you have, I can't help you with, even if I knew the answers. I'm telling you this much so you know not to talk to anyone you see unless it's one of the guards. Most of them are crazy and will attack if you even stare too long at them." The guard waited for Romulus' confirming nod before leading them down two more corridors, where they met up with another guard, a tall, lean man with glasses, whose gentle appearance looked out of place in the bizarre environment.

When he spoke, it was with a kind and understanding tone. "My name is Chris Burlington and I'll be driving you home," he said with a smile. "Also, Ms. Yang asked me to explain the general process of Ambrosia." In his hand he held two bags, which he presented to them. "Caleb told me to make sure you had something to eat, and he apologized for not having anything else. His exact words were 'I'm sorry it ain't gourmet, but it'll put a stop to your stomach rumblings.'"

Delilah tore through the bag, ravenous, learning from a young age that gourmet or not, food should never go to waste, for you never knew the next time you might have some. It looked like a turkey sandwich, completed with a Coke, and they even had a bag of M&Ms as dessert.

Romulus prodded through his bag.

"Is something wrong?" Chris asked.

"Nothing," Romulus answered, his face adopting Ms. Yang's unemotional mask, and Delilah perked up as warning bells rang. "Can we go?"

Chris nodded. "Yes, I know you're probably eager to leave. You can eat your food on the way, and you need not worry about any poisoning."

Delilah stopped. "I wasn't, until you said something."

Chris' smile was brief. "If you will come with me."

With every corner of the facility looking exactly the same, the walk out to the van was tedious until they ran into two more guards leading a man dressed all in black with a dark scowl on his face and even darker sunglasses that were out of place in the dimly-lit facility. The man glanced at them and huffed rudely.

"Don't..." Chris said warningly, but it was too late. Romulus, in a stellar display of his stupidity, took a step forward as if to confront him. Chris took a quick step forward and forcibly pulled him back by the arm, while the other man raised an eyebrow, grinned, and stuck up a middle finger. What made it truly terrifying was the hand he used for the rude gesture was nothing but a skeleton, absent of flesh and blood.

Delilah screamed and her view was instantly obscured by the two guards surrounding the freak, while Chris took her hand and Romulus' shoulder and frog marched them past the spectacle. Before they rounded the corner, she heard a voice complaining, "He started it! Why am I always being picked on?"

"That wasn't smart," Chris said when they were far enough away, a hint of strained anger in his voice.

Romulus jerked out of his grip. "What the hell was that?" he screeched. "The drug I'm supposed to take...is that what it's going to do to me? Make me one of these freaks?"

"Lower your voice," Chris demanded. "Some of them have excellent hearing and long memories." Romulus went quiet, but he was still breathing raggedly out of his mouth, finally realizing how royally screwed he really was. "You need to talk with Ms. Yang or Caleb," Chris started, his voice soothing. "But from what I understand, they created a new strain of Ambrosia." Delilah blinked and started paying attention. "The new drug won't have the side effects the old one has."

"So I won't become one of these?" Romulus waved his hand to indicate the many doors that lined the hallway, and Chris shrugged helplessly.

"That's how I understand it." Romulus opened his mouth, but Chris cut him off. "Go home, eat your food, and sleep on it," he said gently. "Things will look better tomorrow morning."

Romulus nodded, depression overtaking him and making him uncharacteristically quiet the rest of the way. Delilah, afraid her acting wasn't up to par, didn't try too hard to cheer him up. Three more dizzying turns later, Chris opened a door and suddenly they were outside, Delilah blinking in surprise as she stumbled into the cool air. There had been nothing to mark the exit door from any of the other identical doors, and she wondered if the indistinguishable doors and hallways were done intentionally to confuse would-be escapees and invaders. She almost mentioned her theory to Romulus, remembering only at the last second she was supposed to be a brainless airhead. Sighing, she glanced around, striving to memorize everything she saw and heard while Romulus looked down, still moping over Remus or perhaps over the drug.

Despite being outside and in a parking lot, they were still trapped, a tall and presumably electric fence boxing them in. Large towers protruded from the ground in two opposite corners and Delilah guessed there were snipers in each one. Loud chatter diverted her attention, and she saw two pristine white vans being loaded up with supplies and steel cylinders filled with god-knew-what.

"Is that our ride?" Delilah asked, visions of exploding vehicles on the 6:00 news filling her head.

Chris shook his head. "We're taking my car. Those vans are part of an operation that doesn't concern you."

The words, said with certain stiffness, instantly clued Delilah in, and she was amazed Chris could work for a secret organization with this level of incompetency when it came to lying. "They're going after Athena," she supplied, enjoying the shocked look on Chris' face, but dialing it down when Romulus also looked up.

"This way," Chris said, recovering fairly quickly, his refusal to answer her accusation the only answer she needed. She expected Romulus to speak up at this point, but he remained silent and she was grateful.

Chris started forward and Delilah quickly followed, grabbing Romulus' hand to lead him like a little kid. Now that they were so close to leaving, a feeling of anxiousness had tightened in her chest, for she knew from experience that just when you were at your goal was when the rug was yanked from underneath you. She kept a close eye on the men packing the vans, but other than a cursory glance, they seemed determined to ignore them. Chris stopped abruptly in front of an old Kia and Delilah ran into him before taking a step back with an apology on her lips.

"Do you have all your personal belongings?" Chris asked. "Wallet, jewelry, *cell phone*?"

Cell phone was said with a particular emphasis and Delilah picked up on it. Romulus nodded, his expression carefully blank, and Delilah shifted her gaze at him in trepidation. The idiot was hiding something he obviously didn't want her to know, which meant it was probably something stupid, and she refused to die for his stupidity. Instead of voicing her concerns, she endeavored to watch him even more closely.

"Good," Chris said, his face equally blank, and Delilah flustered at being left out of this grand secret. Chris opened the back door, gesturing for Delilah to get in, and she did, with Romulus scooting behind her, apparently not wanting her alone in the back. Chris walked around to the driver's seat, slid in, and they were off. The hulking gate loomed ahead of them and Chris picked up a radio on the dashboard, whispering something that Delilah couldn't quite hear, but what sounded like a bunch of random numbers. The gates slid open once he was finished. Then they were out and Delilah was elated before a sudden thought brought her back down.

"If you're letting us go, why aren't we blindfolded?" she asked, not caring that Romulus looked surprised at her inquiry. The need for survival far outweighed the need to keep up the façade.

"Pandora's Box now sees you as one of their assets," Chris said flatly. "In that regard, you are privy to certain secrets that regular humans cannot know without the threat of death hanging above them."

Delilah let out a shaky breath, fear making her grip Romulus' hands.

"Pandora's Box?" Romulus said, picking up on the wrong words. What he should have noted was Chris' choice of words when talking about "regular humans." Almost as if they were a separate race that he was not part of. Her fear was justified when Chris slowed the car, driving it onto the side of the road.

"Pandora's Box is the name of the facility that has held you captured for the last night," Chris answered, his lack of emotion frightening.

"Are you human?" Delilah blurted out. Romulus looked at her condescendingly for such a stupid question, and even in this desperate situation, she felt a second of pleasure when his expression changed to horror when Chris answered.

"Christopher Burlington is human," the entity that wasn't Chris clarified. "But I am not."

"Then what are you?" Delilah whispered at the same time Romulus asked why they had stopped.

"I am the Resident, Selene," Chris' mouth said, choosing to answer Delilah's question over Romulus. "We have met once before." Delilah flashed to the girl they had met in Pandora's Box and saw the same robotic persona she displayed then in Chris now. "We have stopped because I can go no further without losing control of this human, at least without the aid of Athena." The name Athena was the only word that had emotion behind it, and Delilah couldn't tell whether it was annoyance or exasperation.

"Why are you holding us?" Romulus picked up.

The puppeteer, Selene, swiveled Chris' head around to face them, his eyes unblinking. "I wish to aid Athena one last time, trying to guarantee her survival so that she may pay me my owed favor. In return, your brother will be helped as well, assuming Athena has not grown tired of his presence."

"My brother's dead."

"Incorrect," Chris said, but didn't elaborate.

Romulus' small breath of relief was an irritant to Delilah. "What favor does Athena owe you?"

Chris said nothing, simply staring at them until it was clear he...or more accurately, she...would not answer.

"What do you want from us?" Romulus asked, trying again.

"A message was delivered to you, hidden in the lunch Pandora's Box provided," Chris/Selene said. "You were meant to relay this message to Athena which meant, for whatever reason, Athena's mole believed she would get in contact with you. I do not trust you to deliver it, and so we will remain here until she finds a way to contact you, or I can no longer feel her mind, meaning she has died."

"But...you can feel her mind?" Delilah asked timidly, tensing up as Chris' gaze slid to her. It was like looking into a moving puppet's face. "Can you communicate the message to her without us?"

"I do not wish for her to know of my involvement," Chris/Selene said, once again sounding annoyed, and Delilah, not clear if the annoyance was directed at her, didn't ask any follow-up question. "You wish to know why I did not simply take over this other human's mind," Chris/Selene mused, pointing his head at Romulus, and Delilah felt her mouth go dry. Selene could read her mind. "It was my initial plan to do so, but he has a unique mind that cannot be invaded without utilizing a great deal of energy. In light of this, I chose Chris Burlington as my target. Ironic, as his mind has already proven a challenge, but given my other options and the alien feel of your mind, I concluded—"

"Why should I help you?" Romulus interrupted boldly, and Delilah whimpered as Chris/Selene's gaze seemed to intensify. Before Chris/Selene could answer, a phone rang out, surprising Delilah into a squeal.

Romulus fumbled for the phone, dropping it twice before finally securing it in his hand, glancing at the screen before glancing back up at Chris/Selene. "If I do what you say, will you let us go?"

Chris/Selene blinked, the first time he had done so in over three minutes. "Of course," Chris' voice said, detached.

At those words, Delilah felt herself shake as the cold reality set in. Chris/Selene would not leave any witnesses. She was going to kill them both, probably without a single shred of remorse.

Chapter 54

Athena winced as her head throbbed with agony. A reminder that overuse of her powers came with painful and severe consequences.

"Are you okay?" Remus asked, still clearly angry, but with real concern in his voice.

"Call your brother." Massaging her temples seemed to help with her migraine and made her a little less bitchy.

Remus hesitated. She could sense his mind working overtime as he wondered if she had any ulterior motives...which of course she did, but he need not know that until after the phone call.

"Athena..." he started, and she felt her temper begin to bubble.

"You're right." She smiled sweetly at him. "This is all part of my master plan. As soon as you call him, I'll have the tools to take over the world!"

"Petty doesn't become you," he retorted, and she raised a surprised eyebrow.

"You're joking. Petty is my default mode." Remus didn't crack a smile and a peek in his thoughts told her she was losing him. She thought of spouting out another quote, but after careful consideration, decided on sincere honesty. "I can't help unless I know what to expect," she said, an unfortunate migraine flare making her say the last part through gritted teeth, so that she seemed more frustrated than she was.

Not looking at her, Remus picked up the cell-phone and started to dial a series of numbers.

"You know, I read somewhere that talking on your cell

phone while driving causes twenty-six hundred deaths per year," she couldn't resist saying.

Remus placed the phone to his ear, his face changing as someone from the other side picked up. *"Romulus."*

Athena leaned back, content on resting her eyes when she heard what she assumed to be Romulus' voice. "Hello? Who is this?"

Athena sat up, surprised. He put it on speakerphone?

At her questioning look, Remus stared hard at her. *"You would have just read my thoughts later,"* he thought. *"And like you said, if we're going to rescue him, I need you fully informed."*

Athena smiled to herself. So that was it. Remus was checking to see if he had her commitment. Caught halfway between amusement and annoyance, Athena nodded.

"Hello?" Romulus called out again.

"It's me," Remus said quietly.

Silence. "Yeah, I figured it was. Do you know how much shit you caused?"

Asshole! Athena stiffened at Remus' potent anger. "I'm sorry I couldn't be a good boy and die when Maris wanted me to!"

"I didn't know Maris wanted to kill you...and I'm glad you escaped!"

"Really? Sounds like you're pissed!"

Their arguing was getting them nowhere, but Athena was hesitant to interfere. Never having any brothers or sisters, she had no idea how siblings' relationships were supposed to work.

"If you remember," Romulus was saying, "I tried to talk you out of your idea, but you were dead set on leaving home. You know our father. How did you think he was going to react?"

Athena's eyes narrowed of their own accord. Remus had been going to run away even before she got involved? Why didn't she know that? Remus saw her expression, briefly wondering what it meant before turning his attention back to his brother.

"Not once did I hear you say, 'Remus, our father plans to murder you.'"

"I thought he was going to rough you up a bit. I didn't know he was going to kill you!"

"He was going to beat the stuffing out of me, and you didn't think this was information I needed to know?"

"It's your own fault. You dug your own grave!"

Delilah. "Funny, that doesn't sound like something you would say," Remus said, clenching the phone. "Is anyone there with you?"

Romulus' voice was disbelieving. "You're talking about Delilah when you're running around with your bitch?"

Athena was glad she hadn't ended up choosing Romulus. Remus caught her expression, this time correctly interpreting it, and his lips twitched ever so slightly.

"Why did you call?" Romulus demanded, and the question seemed to startle Remus and he stared dumbfounded at the phone.

"Um...it was suggested to me that you might be in some type of danger. I was calling to see if you needed saving."

"*You* were going to save me," Romulus scoffed, and Athena felt anger, this time her own, at Romulus' underestimation of his brother. "That's rich. Yeah, we were in danger. Kidnapped by the people who wanted you. But I talked to them and they released us."

"*That doesn't make sense.*" Remus glanced at Athena for confirmation and she nodded her agreement. No way a simpleton like Romulus talked to Pandora's Box and gained his freedom.

"That's all you did? You talked to them?"

"Our dad was the one who ironed out the deal," Romulus admitted. "They came to some type of agreement. We even had to sign contracts."

"*Trick?*" Remus thought, still understandably dubious.

Athena shook her head. "No, there would be no point and it doesn't make sense. They would want you to think he was in danger so you would come running. If he signed a contract, then Pandora's Box is serious about it being legitimate."

"Who was that?" Romulus demanded. "Was that her? You're still with that psycho?"

"There goes my hope of your family accepting me," Athena said sadly.

"*Cut it out!*" "If it wasn't for her, I'd be dead."

For the last five minutes, Athena, despite her migraine, had been performing long range mind sweeps, and she finally found what she was looking for. She tapped Remus on the shoulder and mouthed, "Turn left, next light."

He gripped the steering wheel. *"Why?"* Athena stared him down until he relented and made the left.

"You know there's still hope," Romulus said urgently. "Give her up. Bring her in and Maris will have a talk with Ms. Yang—"

"Maris wants me dead," Remus said flatly.

"I'll talk with Ms. Yang then! We will figure something out."

"Who's Ms. Yang?"

Athena shrugged, keeping a close scrutiny of his mind. As of yet, he hadn't had any thoughts on giving her up. It was a possibility that, knowing she was listening, Remus was partially controlling his thoughts, an impressive feat even for a Class 5 Resident. Or maybe he sincerely did not wish to betray her, which would speak volumes for his personality. She couldn't quite decide which theory was favorable.

"So what are you going to do?" Romulus asked.

"I'm not giving her up!" He thought, leaving Athena with a warm feeling. She was definitely luckier than her karmic standing should have allowed at the mall. "I would never give anyone up to save my own hide."

"You've certainly become self-righteous," Romulus said stiffly. "I'm sure that's the girl talking and not you. For the record, sex doesn't mean loyalty."

Athena watched with amused interest as Remus' face turn bright red. "That's not it," he said, glancing quickly at Athena and, out of respect, she let his next couple of thoughts slide. She indicated for him to make a right.

"Well, like I said, we're doing fine on our own," Romulus voice rang out. "If that's all you wanted to know—"

"It was," Remus said abruptly. "I guess this was a mistake."

Athena's hopes sank until Romulus called out, "Wait! There's something else!"

"Hold on," Athena said quickly.

"What are you up to?" Remus wondered, but didn't hang up.

There was a long silence on the phone, and just when Athena began to think he was no longer there, "Upper back. Halfway up the left shoulder blade."

There was a click on the phone and Athena let out a long breath.

Remus looked at her sharply. "What was that?"

Athena ignored the question. "Are you now convinced of your brother's safety?"

"I can only assume," he said with obvious reluctance. "Now what was that?"

"Take a right here," she instructed. "I have fulfilled my end of the bargain and now you owe me one favor."

Amusement blossomed in Remus' mind, quickly dying when he realize she wasn't joking. "You didn't do anything!" he objected, but Athena was already shaking her head.

"The deal was to make sure your brother was safe for one favor. It could have just as easily have been me taking on another fifty men and ten Residents to ensure his safety, and you still would have only owed me one favor." He wasn't completely sold on her logic, but she pressed on determinedly. "Your brother was delivering a message from my mole on the inside."

"You have a mole?" Remus asked dubiously.

"War is not won by superior might, but by subversion, deceit and trickery," Athena answered, quoting one of her favorite sources, Sun Tzu. "Of course I have a mole, several actually, plus a Resident or two who are keeping a close eye on their investigation." She smiled at her own cleverness, but her mood soured when Remus' thoughts reminded her it was all for nothing, as Pandora's Box was able to find her almost instantly. "Anyway," she said in a more subdued tone. "My mole is probably the real power on why your brother is safe, not your dad."

"Then it seems I should owe your mole a favor instead of you," Remus muttered, catching Athena's ire. Before she could get properly angry, he took a deep sigh and relented. "So what is this favor you would have of me?"

With those words, Remus released all the tension Athena had stored in her shoulders and as her muscles relaxed for the first time that night, and with a grateful smile, she said, "Thank you."

In Pandora's Box, it was almost taboo to say those words, for it implied a debt that needed to be paid; Athena thought it was more acceptable to say in the human world, but considered she might be wrong when the tips of Remus' ears turned bright red and he shifted uncomfortably in his seat. "You still haven't named the favor."

"The next turn, make a left into the parking lot," Athena ordered, disengaging her still-not-recovered telepathy for the time being. She felt naked without it, but better to be without it now than in a middle of another fight with Ragnarok. Remus did what he was told and Athena waited for him to look up and pop the question.

"Why are we at a twenty-four-hour convenience store?"

Athena grinned, ignoring the dwindling pain in her head. "We're going shopping!"

Chapter 55

Mycheal tapped his foot impatiently, the action making a clicking sound on the metallic surface below him.

"You in a hurry to be somewhere?" For better or worse, Payton had taken a liking to him, and had now dubbed herself his wingman.

"We need to hurry."

"We need to be prepared," Payton corrected. "You heard what Athena did to the last guys who chased her?" She waited until Mycheal nodded grudgingly. "We're going after her with half the men."

Immediately after returning from Edward's house, Tyrone Froce, a man Mycheal hadn't decided if he liked or not, intensely questioned them before assigning them to a retrieval team dedicated to Athena's capture. Mycheal now waited impatiently in a large room filled with no more than twenty people.

"And what preparations are we making?" Mycheal asked gruffly.

Payton played with her curls, seemingly ignoring him, but then said, "That's a good question," in a way that implied he didn't ask very many of them. She gathered breath, and before Mycheal could stop her, she yelled out, "Hey Dominique!"

Mycheal winced as she yelled, her face inches away from his ear, and the idle chatter paused for a second before picking back up, everyone apparently used to Payton's outbursts. A man on the other side perked up, spotted Payton, and ambled over. Mycheal didn't interact with people very well, and he tried to hide his displeasure as the other man waddled forward, but must have failed for Payton grinned rather cheekily at him.

The man named Dominique smiled at Payton, who returned an even larger smile. "How are you, Payton?"

"Just fine," she said warmly. "This guy over here wanted to know what preparations we were making for Athena."

This guy? Since when did she start forgetting his name? Mycheal suspected she was doing it just to rile him up and he refused to give her the satisfaction.

"Certainly," Dominique said importantly. He grinned at Mycheal, and Mycheal returned it with a dark scowl. Dominique was a large man with glasses and a high-pitched voice. He seemed more equipped to be a computer programmer than a solider, and Mycheal took a disliking to him on general principle.

"Along with your standard equipment, each man will have a bulletproof vest and a gas mask. Why the gas mask, you ask?" Dominique said, not allowing Mycheal to get a word in. "Why, I'll tell you! Each van will also have two tanks of sleeping gas and—"

"Wait! Sleeping gas?" Mycheal interrupted, disbelieving. "You sure?" Payton bumped into him, reminding him not to be rude, but Dominique chuckled knowingly, which immediately got under his skin.

"Someone knows their science. Case in point, in history, there has never been a successful use of sleeping gas to knock out a large quantity of people except in comic books." Mycheal wanted to make a scathing remark on how Dominique was probably familiar with all the comic books, but swallowed it.

"What about general anesthetics and Pentothal?" Payton asked curiously, and Dominique turned eager eyes towards her.

"General anesthetics only work in a small scale area and Pentothal is a liquid chemical that needs to be taken as a shot instead of breathed in. The last recorded time someone attempted to take out a large crowd with sleeping gas was in Moscow, where a group of extremists took over a theatre and held everyone as hostages." Dominique was talking faster and Mycheal instinctively leaned in to try and understand him. "The government used an unknown chemical to knock out everyone within the theatre and it worked...but also killed one hundred and sixteen hostages in the process." Dominique's look of glee was out of place, and even Payton must have thought so, for her own smile was uncertain.

"But we're not using that, of course," she prompted for Mycheal's benefit.

"Oh, of course not," Dominique assured with a boisterous laugh. "Pandora's Box has been in possession of a working sleeping gas with no after-effects ever since the early nineties."

Mycheal crossed his arms. "If a workable sleeping gas really existed, wouldn't everyone know about it?"

"Did you know about Residents before you started working here?" Payton asked sensibly. He felt her elbow in his ribs, and he made an effort to calm down.

"If Athena is immune to drugs like they say she is," Mycheal started, trying his best to be civil, "then why would it matter if we carry sleeping gas or not?"

"To take away Athena's advantage," another guard said, sauntering up, stealing the question away from Dominique, who had already had his mouth open to answer. Dominique shut it, looking visibly put out, and Mycheal felt a fleeting gratitude to the new man.

Payton grinned and batted her eyelashes at him. "Hi, Omar."

"Always lovely to see you, Payton," Omar said. It dawned on Mycheal how much he disliked all of Payton's friends, but at least this one was more acceptable than Dominique. An athletic build with wide shoulders that almost guaranteed he enjoyed a good game of football, tanned skin that hinted at time at the beach, and brown wavy hair far too long for Mycheal's liking, all gave Omar the appearance of any of the many surfer boys that plagued the coast of California.

"Athena's advantage?" Mycheal asked, trying to draw his attention away from Payton. Omar's gaze flitted to Mycheal with a mirrored expression of dislike before returning to Payton. "Yep. Remember, Athena is a small blond whose only unusual trait is a particularly vibrant shade of grey eyes. As a result, she can blend in more easily than let's say a man dressed in a black bulletproof vest, wielding a gun."

He grinned as if he had said something extremely funny, and Payton laughed politely. Mycheal was on the verge of leaving the circus of men, and Payton, apparently sensing this, wrapped her arm around his; an action that earned them both frowns from all directions.

"Like I was saying," Omar said stiffly. "Athena will use the population to her advantage to block and deter us whenever possible. Just like she did at the hotel."

"So the sleeping gas gives us an edge," Dominique piped in. "By gassing a large area, we can take away Athena's advantage. It should be noted that there is a chance Athena will be affected by the gas, making for an easy pick up, and if not, she should be the only thing moving in a large area."

Mycheal hesitated, filled with questions, but loath to ask Dominique anything. "How big of an area are we talking about?"

"A radius of three hundred feet," Dominique supplied instantly. "And then the gas begins to dissipate. Everyone affected will fall asleep for about an hour, and will awaken with no nasty side effects besides a small headache." The words were barely out of his mouth before Mycheal bombarded him with another question.

"How do you know all this?"

Dominique straightened up, obviously feeling self-important.

"I helped fine-tune it," he said grandly, and Mycheal snorted, not at all discreetly. Dominique's smile looked pained, but he forcefully continued. "I have a master in bioengineering and a decade of experience creating toxins, and I must say, this is my best work yet. I can't wait to try it out...always wanted to gas someone."

Payton would later say he imagined it, but when Dominique was talking about gassing someone, Mycheal could have sworn he leered at Payton, leaving Mycheal to wonder why a master of bioengineering was disgraced into working with Pandora's Box.

Mycheal did not believe he could take another moment in Dominique's presence, so it was fortunate that Froce and Caleb chose this time to make their grand appearance. When Caleb entered a room, people paid attention, and it wasn't just because of his ridiculous western getup he insisted on wearing. Caleb had a presence that even the Residents respected. People looked to him for leadership and protection without consciously meaning to, and rumors had it he had once fought off two Residents by himself.

"Pay attention!" Caleb roared, walking to the front of the room, seeming not the least bit nervous about leading an illegal group to try and recapture a deadly monster. "This ain't a sorority!"

The crowd dispersed and positioned themselves near Caleb and Froce. Mycheal tried to sneak away from Payton, but she followed him, a look of dogmatic determination on her face. He sighed, coming to a stop and allowing her to catch up.

Froce spoke, his deep, gravelly voice conveying wisdom beyond his years. "In a few seconds, I'm going to explain the situation to you. We don't have much time, but I'll try to make this as explicable as possible." After pausing to look around, he continued. "Athena has been free for approximately sixteen hours. There have been two attempts to capture her and both have met with disaster. We might be the last chance we have of seizing her. In a few minutes, we're going to load up and go after her."

For a briefing, it was unrepentantly short and the crowd buzzed with unanswered questions. "Don't we need more men?" someone asked nervously. "The other team had fifty and they still failed."

Froce nodded at the obvious question that was going through everyone's minds, and said, "You have to remember, we have other obligations. Pandora's Box is falling apart, partly because of Athena's escape, and partly because there's no one here to monitor the Residents. There have been three riots since Athena's departure. We are too spread out as it is, and it'd be a shame to capture Athena only to come home to a full blown prison break."

Although a great chunk of them were disgraced soldiers, they were not stupid men, and all of them realized Froce failed to answer the heart of the question.

"So how are we supposed to capture Athena when we don't have enough men?" someone else prompted.

Froce shifted his stance in response to the slight hostility that was reverberating around the room. "Ideally, we're only there to track and keep tabs on Athena. If all goes as planned, she'll never even know we're there, and we can sit on our hands and wait for backup."

Mycheal wondered why Caleb, the higher ranking officer, wasn't doing the explanation instead of Froce. He whispered his question to Payton, who smiled. "Do you really want Caleb explaining the situation? It'll be hard to decipher with the twenty different curse words he'll be using." Mycheal conceded the point.

"Won't she know we're coming?" Omar asked the other obvious question. "Her being a telepath and all?" The fact that Athena could read minds had spread like wildfire and now everyone knew.

"Good question," Froce admitted, and with a start, Mycheal realized this was a hastily put-together mission with little forethought. "We're not sure, but we think she can only read your mind if you're directly in front of her."

"With all due respect, that sounds like wishful thinking," Omar said, instantly winning points with Mycheal. "What happens if she can read your mind from far away and she does discover we're there?"

"We deal with that problem if we get to it." Froce said.

"We don't have the time for anymore damn questions!" Caleb growled before Omar's mutinous attitude could infect others. "Everyone needs to be issued a gun, suited up, and inside a van in the next five minutes."

The employees of Pandora's Box began to shuffle towards the exits, some still grumbling along the way. Most of them seemed too depressed over the upcoming mission to focus on anything else, but a couple stopped to give Mycheal pointed looks, and in horror, he realized Payton had draped herself over his arm. He tried to shake her loose, but her grip was too secure. He couldn't break free without making a scene.

"Just relax," Payton suggested, digging her nails painfully into his skin. "Be good and, if we both survive, I let you take me out to dinner."

"Surely, a better consolation prize can be found."

Her nails were on the verge of puncturing skin and she refused to let go even as they made their way over to the equipment. "There's a nice little bistro just across from my apartment. Their venison is to die for and they make the most adorable little puffs of bread..."

Her babbling no longer gave him a headache and she was oddly charming; there were worse ways to celebrate a victory. "What's the price range?" he asked when she finally took a breath. He lived on macaroni and hot dogs, so paying a premium price for a meal was unthinkable.

Payton's smile was sweet. "I suggest you bring a credit card."

Chapter 56

Remus wondered how a store could possibly be this crowded when it was barely past five. It was discomfiting, for Athena still wore her bloodied pajamas, her hair was a filthy, stringy mess, and Remus smelled like piss thanks to Fides. A nasty gash to the back of his head plus a vomit stain that covered the right part of his shirt completed his disturbing appearance. How did action heroes do it? Go from fight to fight, never looking anything but perfect with not a drop of sweat on them? Athena smiled, probably at his thoughts, as they entered another aisle where a couple was examining screwdrivers. The couple quickly scurried away after taking one frightened look at them.

"Humans are rude," Athena commented offhandedly. A display of knives distracted her from getting too indignant, and she picked one up, gripping the handle to see how it would feel against her hand.

It bothered Remus the way she separated herself from the human race, as if the ability to read minds made her any less human.

"Not less...more," she corrected with a slight smile that made it impossible to tell whether she was joking or not.

Uncomfortable with the direction of the one-sided conversation, Remus looked away, only to spot the couple that fled earlier talking animatedly to a store manager with plenty of pointed looks in their direction.

"Care to spend five minutes in the bathroom sprucing up a little bit?" Remus suggested, worried that Athena might get the wrong impression, but all she did was nod without looking at him.

"If it will ease your mind," Athena said with an air of indifference as she placed the knife back only to pick up a longer one. "But you should know it's not the blood, puke, or stench that's attracting attention. People are just surprised to see a babe like me with a schmuck like you."

Remus snorted, Athena's ribbing releasing some of the pent-up tension in his neck. "I thought it was because of the bullet holes in your clothes and the trail of blood you left when you limped in here."

"I never limp," she responded with mock indignation. "I always enter a room with astonishing grace and dignity and with my head held high." Their banter was slightly ruined when, as Remus watched with great apprehension, she picked up a third set of knives to study them.

"You certainly like your blades, don't you?"

"They're quick and they don't need reloading," Sensing his discomfort, she dropped the knives in the shopping cart she was hauling around. "Don't get me wrong, guns come in handy, but it's impossible to get your hands on one at Pandora's Box, while knives are simply improbable. Plus, a man with a gun tends to be overconfident."

"Yeah, but a knife has no long-distance applications," Remus objected, and Athena raised an eyebrow, clearly surprised he was arguing with her. "Unless you throw it and then you're defenseless."

"True," Athena conceded while walking down the aisle, confident that Remus would match her step. "But remember, I'm not a powerhouse Resident—"

"How am I supposed to remember if I didn't even know in the first place?" Remus interrupted. "Exactly what does a powerhouse Resident looks like?"

"I'm not a powerhouse Resident," Athena repeated, ignoring him and casting a pointed look so that he knew it was intentional. "And thus, I rely on stealth and subterfuge instead of an all-out attack. A gun, even with a silencer, makes a loud commotion. With a knife and the right knowledge, I can dispatch all my enemies quietly." Remus realized how bizarre they must look and sound to the men and women passing them. Still, despite their appearance, anyone would just think they were a weird young couple out for some shopping. "I suppose," Athena said, not looking too pleased with his thought analysis. She lurched to a stop as something caught her eye and, reaching out, she picked up a hammer and weighed it against the palm of her hand. "This could be useful. You never know—"

The rest of Athena's words were drowned out by a loud ringing noise from inside Remus' head as the hammer triggered a flood of unwanted memories—Athena bashing Bruno's head in, a look of grim determination on her face; the explosion at the gas station that made burning corpses out of Ragnarok operatives; Athena brutally snapping Patrick's neck with callous indifference; and Fides' mental torture that came so close to snapping his mind in half.

His legs wobbled and Remus was sure he must have cried out as his memories threatened to overcome him. Athena roughly and painfully grabbed him by his arm. "Remus! Damn, I'm so stupid! Remus, snap out of it! Please!" she cried, and her intense panic mixed with desperation was enough to bring him to his senses. She was looking at him with such naked concern, and Remus briefly wondered what he had done to earn this degree of compassion from her. When Athena realized he had regained his composure, her grip loosened so that circulation could start back up in his arm. "You're okay," she told him, squeezing his arm one more time for added emphasis. "I promise you'll be okay."

"Resident attack?" he asked faintly.

His statement must have been the paragon of stupidity, for her affectionate gaze quickly transformed into one of exasperation. "No, it's not a Resident. God, we get blamed for everything! In Pandora's Box, a guard couldn't trip without blaming one of us! You were having a delayed panic attack, and given all that's happened today, all you've been forced to accept, it's not surprising."

Remus nodded, accepting Athena's explanation and feeling a rush of embarrassment for freaking out.

Athena hesitated as if wanting to say more, but settled on releasing his arm instead and turning around. "We're almost done."

If their attire hadn't attracted attention, their commotion certainly did, and as they walked through the shop, people gave them a wider berth than they would a chainsaw-carrying man with a hockey mask on his face. A greasy looking teen with MANAGER etched on a nametag hesitantly started to walk up, as if about to ask them to leave, but a blank stare from Athena had him fleeing in the other direction before he even got close.

"Not funny," Remus muttered as Athena chuckled softly. He insisted they change clothes in the bathroom, not wanting to stink up the car any more than it was already, and Athena relented after a few seconds of protest. The shop didn't have much to offer in terms of clothes and Remus eventually settled on a pair of khakis and button-up sweater, trashing his old clothes, before wiping his face and hands with a wet paper towel. He walked out to see Athena already waiting for him, looking more comfortable in a pair of jeans and t-shirt then she ever did in the dress he had purchased earlier for her.

"It was a hideous dress," Athena informed him, shuddering as if the yellow dress would forever haunt her dreams.

Remus didn't say anything as he led the way to the check-out line, but he did wonder how someone who'd lived their whole life isolated from any type of modern fashion, and who thought jeans and a t-shirt was stylish, could dare to critique his choices.

"You know," Athena began sullenly, "just because you think it doesn't mean I can't take offense to it."

"Of course it does!" The argument lasted their duration at the shop. In the end, Athena purchased a set of knives, a hammer, alcohol, cotton balls, several different types of paper towels, napkins, a whole row of gauze Band-Aids, and a lighter. If the cashier found these items odd, he didn't show it. He merely rang them up and wished them a nice day before moving on.

"It has to be considered rude to read someone else's mind without their permission," Remus said for the umpteenth time, and Athena was already shaking her head before he could finish.

"Who says that?" she shot back. "I have read a great deal of books and not once have I stumbled across any rule of etiquette that says it's impolite to probe into another person's mind."

"Because no one knows it's possible!"

"Humanity's oversight, not mine," she countered. "Who rides slow, must saddle betimes."

Remus spent the walk to the car trying to figure out her quote, and was growing more frustrated until he saw the twinkle in her grey eyes. "You're sprouting random quotes!" he accused, Athena's mock surprise immediately confirming it. She tried to mount an indignant protest, but ended up breaking into a fit of giggles. Remus watched her carefully. He couldn't see this Athena killing a man. This Athena had a sharp tongue and was extremely moody at the best of times, but other than that, she was a normal beautiful, caring girl. The other Athena, the one who killed and didn't look back...the Athena who would taunt a man for killing his brother just to manipulate him into doing her will...that one was the monster.

"We need an abandoned place," she said shortly, her mood transforming instantly.

Remus couldn't tell if she had picked up on his thoughts. "Why?" he asked suspiciously. "And how would you find it? If it's abandoned, then there's no way for you to pick up on anyone's thoughts."

Athena's mood lightened slightly as she glanced at him, impressed with his logic. "I saw a for-sale house ten minutes back." She waited for him to get in the Thunderbird and unlock her side.

"Athena, you do know I was serious when I said this wasn't my life?" he said cautiously.

"It will only take an hour, tops," she responded, not really answering his concern. "Ragnarok is too busy dealing with the hotel disaster to interfere with us."

"What about Pandora's Box?"

Athena nodded, recognizing his concern as valid, but at the same time, dismissing it. "Pandora's Box doesn't have the men or resources necessary to come after me. Plus, I have someone on the inside working against them. They won't catch me unaware."

Remus briefly wondered who it was.

"Can't tell you." She looked at him, and he caught traces of monster Athena smiling slyly at him. "If you help me, I'll split the rest of the money with you."

"That's my money!" he said indignantly.

"No, that was your father's money," she corrected. "Money that I stole fair and square."

"You stole fair and square?"

"That's right!" Athena said in a positively cheery mood.

"That's not right."

"Maybe not," Athena allowed. "But that still only leaves you with three choices. You can do me this small favor and receive over nine-thousand dollars, you can call the police and explain how you got your hands on illegal money, or you can try to take it from me by force." She smiled that damn annoying smile. "Which one is it going to be?"

The drive to the house took about fifteen minutes instead of ten, Remus thinking dark thoughts about Athena the entire time, and he figured that at some point she just tuned him out. She spent the time looking out the window, her mood having changed from cheerful to melancholy. He wanted to know what she was thinking about, but was too annoyed to ask, and she either refused to answer his thoughts or was too busy with her own to check on his.

"That's it," she said, breaking the silence and pointing to a small unassuming house surrounded by identical copies.

"Anyone here?"

"Nope," Athena said after a pause.

He followed her to the door where they discovered a new problem. "The door's locked," Athena said, frowning. "Why would they lock the door to a house they're trying to sell? I could be a potential buyer."

"Imagine that," Romulus said dryly. "So I guess we have no choice but to turn back."

He should have known better. Athena took a step back, took a breath, and kicked the door down.

"What are you doing?" Remus yelled. Athena put a finger on her lips and Remus lowered his voice to a whisper. "Do you want to get caught?"

"No one saw me," Athena said with the confidence that came from being a telepath.

"You can't just break down a person's door!"

Athena giggled. "Yes, that's the most serious offense I committed today. Go back and get everything we purchased. I'll be waiting inside."

He was getting sick of Athena telling him what to do and he almost refused, but at the end of the day, he still couldn't bring himself to leave, at least not without finding out what favor Athena wanted from him. He went back to the car to carry out her wishes. The envelope full of money was nowhere to be seen. *Figures.* She probably kept it on her at all times. So much for trust.

He returned to find Athena dragging a long table to the center of the room. "This should do." She fidgeted with her fingers, revealing her nervousness. "And I do trust you," she added as an afterthought. "If I didn't, I wouldn't let you do this."

"Let me do what, Athena?" Remus asked impatiently. "All you give me are cryptic riddles."

Athena took a deep breath. "You remember the last words your brother spoke to you?"

"Something about the left shoulder blade," Remus recalled. "I'm assuming you know what that was about?"

"Of course I do." Athena flicked a switch and the lights came on. Remus wished she had left them off. The walls were painted in overly bright colors and someone had seen fit to place a big smiley face clock in the center of a wall. Only a psycho clown would find the house comfortable. Athena looked up at the clock and cocked her head as if intrigued. "You remember when I told you I had help escaping?"

"You mean help from your friend who you refuse to tell me about?" Remus tried to put as much sarcasm as possible in that one sentence.

"What would you do with his name?" Athena inquired, repeating her question from earlier. She walked forward and now stood inches from Remus. "I doubt you've ever met him so it would do you no good."

"It's courtesy," Remus shot back. "I would like to know the name of the man manipulating my brother."

"First, when did I ever tell you it was a man?" She waited until he shrugged. "Second, why do you think he's manipulating your brother?"

Remus was tired of all the word games. "I wish you would stop treating me like an idiot, Athena. Center of the left shoulder blade; that's supposed to be the location of the tracker?"

Athena nodded, looking impressed, albeit puzzled. "Now how did you know without me knowing that you knew?" she asked, more to herself, before clearing her voice and saying louder, "That's my assumption. My friend must have discovered the information and found a way to pass this along to your brother, who in turn, relayed it to you."

Remus had figured as much, and briefly wondered what Athena was doing besides stalling and dragging out the time.

She moved forward a step, but hesitated when Remus took a cautious step back to maintain distance, and her eyes flashed with hurt.

"Fine, you want to skip to the conclusion?" she asked, her grey eyes brightening as they drilled into Remus. "I need you to take a knife, cut open my back, and remove the bug."

Remus felt like fainting.

Chapter 57

Too blunt, Athena thought regretfully as Remus' face turned a chalky white, which contrasted with his red hair magnificently.

"You're crazy!" Remus gasped.

"Only on even months," Athena said, hoping humor would alleviate some of the tension, but her awful joke only served to aggravate Remus instead of calming him down.

"I'm not a surgeon, Athena," he said slowly, spacing each word out, and though Athena appreciated the difficulty of his situation, she still felt a spark of irritation that he was talking down to her.

"I know you're not a surgeon, Remus," she said crisply, making sure she spaced the words out exactly like he did, and Remus' eyebrows knitted together as he realized she was annoyed. "But I wasn't one either when I took the first bug out of my arm."

She's serious! "But you're a Resident!"

"That doesn't give me a degree in medicine, Remus."

I can't possibly do that. "Athena..."

"It's not as hard as it sounds," Athena soothed. "We bought everything we need."

The most ridiculous thing I've ever heard! "Really?" Remus asked, and by his thoughts, Athena knew she was in for a wicked rebuke. "So it's going to be a piece of cake cutting and digging into your skin to get the bug? Of course this is assuming I can access it and it's not hiding under a bone, in which case I have to remove the bone, take the bug out, and graft the bone back in place. Tell me, did we buy everything we need at the convenience store for that procedure?"

"It's not going to be that difficult," Athena said, but this new train of thought worried her. Intelligent as she was, she didn't understand half the things Remus said until she peeked in his mind.

"And what happens when I open you up and find it's not in your shoulder blade?" Remus asked with enough derision to make her clench her teeth. "That this was all just a trick?"

"If that was the case, they would have had Romulus tell you he was in danger, instead of making up the location of the bug."

I have to change her mind! "What if it's a mistake?"

"My friend," she started slowly, thinking about everything she knew of her mole and concluding the trust she had for him was deserved, "wouldn't give me this information if he wasn't one hundred percent certain of it."

"And how am I supposed to stitch you up again?"

Athena tried not to grin, but failed. "Well you can try to stitch me back up or we can use the heavy duty Band-Aids I bought!" Remus did not crack a smile. "My body will heal itself," she added. "No more than a day."

"So to recap, you want me to cut you up when I have no idea what I'm doing?"

Her patience, which had been strengthened by years of speaking only in quotes, was being severely tested, and she wondered what exact aspect was making her lose her temper. "I'm a telepath. I can read your mind, know what you're doing, and guide you."

"Guide me when I'm cutting you up?"

"Correct, and please stop using the term cutting you up. It sounds vulgar."

She asked me to cut her up and she's worried about my manners? "Why can't we go to a real hospital?"

Athena didn't answer. Instead, she waited for Remus to figure it out on his own.

That would mean telling the doctors that she's bugged, and even if they believed us, they would certainly call the police."

"You ready to do this?" Athena asked.

"What about infection?" Remus cried, desperately grasping at straws.

"I don't get infected," Athena stated firmly with enough confidence to close that line of questioning.

"But what about—"

"In examinations, the foolish ask questions the wise cannot answer." The quote was a bit rusty, but it did convey her point. While Remus paused to work it out, Athena pressed the advantage of his silence. "If you think this plan reeks of desperation, it's because I'm desperate. If you believe fear is driving my actions, it's because I'm afraid. If I can't remove the tracker right now, then I have lost..." She was going to say "the game," but though the term would alienate Remus. "My freedom," she finished, and when Remus still looked askance, she asked, "Earlier, you thought it would be tragic if Pandora's Box got their hands on me. Do you still feel that way?"

"You're asking me if I still think you should be allowed to live free even after all that happened?" Remus asked. "Even after the destruction you wrought at the hotel?"

Athena's temper flared, but with it came realization. Her lack of patience for Remus was driven by a need to be understood, and she paused to ponder why it meant so much for this boy to accept her. Remus took her silence for anger and a tremor of fear passed through his mind, which did succeed in enraging her, and with the anger came a sense of hurt and bitterness.

"Humans are obtuse creatures," she remarked, keeping her tone playful to cover her resentment. "All of you so judgmental when something doesn't fit your preconceived notions of right and wrong. You don't know me and yet—"

"I know you," Remus cut her off, determined, and Athena laughed manically, a harsh sound that always had the guards of Pandora's Box running, but Remus stood his ground. It was such a rare occurrence when someone would dare stare her down that curiosity took the edge off her anger. "You can be cold, cruel, and calculating," Remus accused aggressively, and continued before she could open her mouth in protest. "You're beautiful and you're extremely intelligent, so you know how to use your beauty as a weapon. You're always watching for the next threat, and the only times I see you truly relax is when you're eating or sleeping."

Athena blinked. She hadn't been aware that Remus had been watching her on that level, and it disturbed her that she had missed him scrutinizing her. Once again, her telepathy had partially failed when it came to Remus, confirming her suspicions of his uniqueness. "That's quite a critique," she remarked.

"I'm not done yet," Remus rebuked, and Athena resigned herself for another barrage. "You can be manipulative, ruthless, and, at times, cold-hearted. In the forty-eight hours I have known you, you've killed more than three times the amount someone needs to kill in order to be classified as a serial killer." Remus took a breath as Athena did some quick math and regretfully realized he was right. "However, one could say you did it only to defend me and protect yourself." The words were said with great reluctance, but he was making an effort to understand her and that was more than she expected. "There are times when I've seen you show compassion, although it's really just with me. It's been a..." He paused as if searching for the right word. "Joy to see you discover new things like the night sky or raindrops...and even watching you eat a whole pot of spaghetti or watching you try to work a gas nozzle." His lips twitched at some memory replaying in his head. "As hellish of a trip as it's been, those are some of my best memories." He winced. "How sad is that?"

"It's pretty sad," Athena answered honestly. By his posture, Athena could tell he had come to a decision, and for the first time in years, she found herself too afraid to use her telepathy.

"I think I will regret it for the rest of my life if I walk away now," Remus concluded. "I don't want you to be captured again...and I don't want to be a coward anymore. God help me, I'll do it. I mean, I'll try."

"Ridiculous!" Athena scoffed, and Remus jerked back as if he had been kicked. "That you think yourself a coward is the most ridiculous thing I've ever heard." Remus tried to look modest, but Athena knew he was pleased with the compliment, and she wanted to tell everything else she admired about him, but a deep, uneasy feeling had gripped her and she wanted the bug removed immediately, even if there was only a minimal chance that Pandora's Box or Ragnarok would make a move so soon after their attempt at the hotel. "There are so many things I wish to thank you for, but time escapes us." She took off her t-shirt.

Remus naturally averted his eyes.

"Remember, the left shoulder blade. The cut should be no

deeper than two inches."

He already looked like he was having second thoughts. "Are you sure this is the only way?"

"No, I just thought this way would be the most fun." His face flushed and Athena amended her tone. No sense getting him angry when he was doing her a favor. "This is the only way, and it's really not major surgery. You can do this."

Remus nodded, but didn't look entirely convinced. Athena rummaged through their stuff and handed him a knife, and he looked even less convinced. "Is this supposed to be my scalpel?"

"It will do." Comforting was not really in her skill set, and she could think of nothing else to say except for a couple of handy quotes, but one look at Remus' face made it clear he wasn't in the mood. Athena scooted herself up on the table. "We also have paper towels to wipe away the blood."

"You don't wipe away blood with paper towels!"

"What do you wipe it with?" she asked, curious.

"Not paper towels!"

She turned so that her back was facing him, and that's when her own fear hit. She was willingly going to let someone whose hand she didn't control take a knife to her back. "We're wasting time," she said, making sure Remus couldn't sense her nervousness. "For starters, do feel free to look at me. I'm wearing a bra and, from what I understand, they cover just as much as a bikini would."

Now she thinks I'm a prude, Remus thought sourly. "Okay, what's next?"

"Make a...make a three-inch incision just above the center of my shoulder blade," she answered, her voice faltering.

She almost flinched as Remus' cool hands touched her back. "You're sure about this?" he asked, nervousness coloring his voice.

"Let's not start that again."

"Your shoulder strap is in the way. I can't..."

Athena shrugged her strap off before Remus could say another word, and at any other time, feeling his embarrassment would have made her laugh, but Remus' main problem was his self-esteem, and he needed to believe that she had nothing but the absolute faith in his abilities for him to succeed.

"Do it now." Athena closed her eyes as she felt momentary pain, then she opened them with a sigh as she read Remus' mind. The cut was way too shallow and both of them knew it.

I can't do it! "I don't think I can do it, Athena."

"You never told me why you wanted to leave home," Athena said, changing tactics.

"Is this the most appropriate conversation?"

"Tell me, and while you're at it, try doing the incision over again."

Why the hell not? "I wanted to leave because I was sick of my life. I was tired of my dad. I didn't see a future...no, that's not it. I wanted to leave because I met you."

Athena ears perked up at this, but before her question could be formatted, she felt a slicing pain.

"There's a lot of blood!" Remus said, on the verge of panic. "What do I do?"

"Wipe it away!"

"With the paper towels?"

In hindsight, getting something as inefficient as paper towels seemed absurdly stupid, but she would never admit to it. "Yes with the paper towels!"

"Shouldn't I have gloves for this procedure?"

Athena briefly wondered how one man could be filled up with so many annoying questions. "I can't think of every-thing. I don't have anything and you can't get anything."

"There's blood on my hands!"

"Ignore it. Do you see the bug?"

A pause, and Athena read his answer before he gave it. "No. I don't see it."

Athena held back her frustration. "Make another incision below the first one."

What? "You want me to make another cut?"

"We need to find it, Remus. You can do it." Athena felt like she was walking a tightrope with Remus. The wrong words or move would render him incapable of helping her. "Finish telling me your story. I was the reason you wanted to leave? Because I stole the money?"

"No, the money had nothing to do with it—oh, and thanks, by the way, because of you, I had a delightful con-versation with Mr. Bob."

Athena dove into his mind to figure out what he was blaming her for, at the same time assessing his mental state.

Remus was steeling himself to make another incision and she knew he was glad for the distraction.

"I had given up. Resolved myself to living a miserable life, forever under my father's thumb, every day a horrible existence. Before that day, I can't remember the last time I really laughed. Or the last time I held a conversation that wasn't strictly cordial. I can't even remember the last time I made eye contact with another human being that wasn't forced."

It took every ounce of control that Athena had to not move away from the blade as it made another cut through her flesh. Sweat began to pour down her face and she asked in the most normal tone she could muster, "Anything?"

"No, it's not here." Remus sounded defeated. "I'm sorry, but it's not here."

"Try again."

"No," Remus said firmly.

"Again!" she growled. "We didn't get this far to quit now."

"I won't do it." *I won't hurt you again.*

Athena barked out a laugh that sounded cruel even to her ears. "You think you're hurting me? Imagine what Pandora's Box will do once they get their hands on me?"

Athena felt the truth register with him. "Where should I look?"

Athena was going to suggest directly under his last incision, but changed her mind at the last second. "You choose the place." Oddly enough, Remus didn't argue with her. "So you were committed to a dismal existence. Then what?"

"Then I met you." She felt him dab away some of the blood with a paper towel. "I had never met someone like you, Athena. Filled to the brim with confidence. Never met someone as smart and witty as you. Never met someone who could be so sarcastic and charming at the same time. Someone who could set my teeth on edge and, at the same time, made me want to kiss her."

Athena squirmed a little bit. Not because of the pain in her shoulder, but because Remus' words were making her intensely uncomfortable. "You thought all that even after I stole the envelope?"

"I was pissed to be sure," Remus allowed. "But that didn't change the fact that you were the most amazing person I'd ever met. In my current life...the one that I was destined to live underneath my father...I was certain I would never meet another girl like you, and I found that thought unbearable."

The slice came so unexpectedly that she cried out more in surprise than in actual pain. The cut was much lower than the second one, and she felt a pang of regret for allowing him to choose the spot. It couldn't be that low.

"But you know what sealed the deal?" He went on as if he hadn't just stuck a knife in her. "It was what happened later. There was a man named Mr. Bob."

"Mr. Bob?" Athena asked skeptically for his benefit. She had already read his mind and knew who Mr. Bob was.

"Yeah, I know. He was the *real* contact that I was supposed to deliver the money to. He wasn't full of cheer when I told him I gave the money to you."

"So what happened next?" Athena asked, interested as to where this was leading.

He chased me down the mall and down the escalator and, get this, fell on the escalator and broke his hip." Remus started to snicker. "Can you believe it? *He* broke his hip."

Athena remembered the conversation they had about Remus possibly breaking his hip and she saw the irony in the situation, but failed to see why it was so funny. She was about to ask when Remus' voice changed. "I found it, Athena. I found the bug."

Chapter 58

After hanging up from Remus, Romulus looked at his phone before half offering it to Chris/Selene.

"It is your phone," Selene said through Chris' mouth. "I have no need for it."

"What are you going to do with us now?" Delilah asked, her voice nothing but a frightened whisper.

"Chris Burlington will drive off and, in a couple of minutes, you will be outside my range of control. Whatever fate befalls you after that is none of my concern." The words sounded good, yet Selene/Chris made no move to shift the car off the side of the road. Looking at all the dense woods surrounding them, it occurred to Romulus this would be a perfect place to dump a couple of bodies.

"Then why aren't we moving?" Delilah asked, her thoughts similar to Romulus.' "Please...you don't want to kill us!"

"It is presumptuous for you to make assessments on my behalf," Selene/Chris said, his voice still a flat, robotic monotone.

"If you kill us so close to where you live, won't people get suspicious?" Delilah said quickly. While she was talking, Romulus saw her discreetly try the backseat's door handle.

"Killing you would draw unwanted attention," Chris/Selene acknowledged. "As would your disappearance."

"Then what do you plan to do with us?" Romulus asked, reaching out for his door handle.

"Chris Burlington has safety locks installed in his car," Chris/Selene informed. "Your efforts to open them are futile." He waited for Romulus' hand to drop in defeat. "I have told you once before and my intent has not changed. You will be released."

Delilah was shaking and Romulus placed a comforting hand on her shoulder. "Then why are we still here?"

"My previous aid to Athena has already depleted my energy greatly," Chris/Selene admitted. "I require a minute if I wish to erase your memories."

"Erase!" Delilah repeated, aghast, bringing her knees up to her chest in a defensive posture. Romulus shared her sentiment. To have someone violate them so intimately seemed ethically and humanly wrong, and the way the mind controller talked so casually about it was terrifying. Romulus tried the door handle, not caring what Selene/Chris thought, and when he found it wouldn't open, he scooted closer to Delilah, wanting to protect her, and said angrily, "You will not erase our memories!"

"Yes, I will," Selene/Chris said, her tone not argumentative but factual.

Romulus squeezed Delilah's shoulder and she flinched, the unexpected action startling her. "Why?"

"You wish to know even though you will not remember?" Selene/Chris inquired. Throughout the whole conversation, Selene/Chris had not once looked back at them, instead staring straight ahead, and this somehow enhanced the puppeteer's inhumanity. "Very well. If word of my aid tonight was to fall into the wrong hands, my continual safety would be put greatly at risk. You need to forget so that I may survive."

Romulus had seen enough of Maris' organization to know there were always different factions vying for control. Athena represented a side, Ms. Yang another side, and Selene was probably playing both sides as she looked after her own interests.

"You understand quickly," Selene/Chris observed.

"What if you let us go and we promise not to tell anyone?" Romulus asked, trying to see this like one of his father's deals. Selene probably wanted something badly enough to let them go with their memoires intact, and it was up to him to figure out what that was.

"There are several reasons why that scenario is not viable," Selene/Chris spoke, and though it seemed like a refusal, Romulus' hopes soared because the fact she was willing to talk meant a deal could be made. "The most obvious is that I cannot trust you to keep your word once you leave my area of control."

"If I tell, that means my brother is in danger and I won't do anything to risk his life," Romulus argued.

"You have already." Those words had been bouncing in Romulus' head ever since he passed up the chance to warn Remus of their father's intention to harm him, and the truth hurt even more when said out of the mouth of a heartless monstrosity. If Selene, whose world existed without emotions, thought he'd betrayed his brother, then it had to be true.

"That's not fair," Delilah argued, coming to his defense. "He did it to protect us!"

"And you believe the humans who keep me prisoner are more lenient than your dad?" Chris/Selene asked logically. "That reason aside, any minor telepath could easily read your mind to discover my actions."

"But still..." Romulus began, but had to stop, as he couldn't think of a single thing to say in his defense. "Delilah and I can be trusted," he concluded lamely, and Selene mercilessly attacked his logic.

"I have already previously stated that your claim of reliability means nothing in the face of telepaths and your previous duplicity," the puppeteer said, sounding almost annoyed. "It should also be noted that the one you know as Delilah Lane, if her memory is not erased, will instantly report this to Ms. Yang and your father."

Delilah stiffened in her seat before looking pleadingly at Romulus, and he opened his mouth to defend her. "You don't know what you're talking about!" he screamed angrily.

Selene/Chris didn't move or speak for the next three minutes, and in that interval, Romulus had time to reflect on his outburst and to conclude he might have made a fatal error. Just because the monster sounded like she was driven by logic didn't mean she didn't have a temper. The two guards who escorted her to her cell were terrified Romulus would say something to set her off, and perhaps their fear was based on past experiences.

Delilah's cry of alarm tore Romulus away from his thoughts, and when he looked up, his heart leapt to his throat. Chris/Selene had turned around in his seat and was looking back at them, his glasses reflecting the moonlight eerily. It was almost impossible to describe why this new development was so alarming. When the monster wasn't looking at them, it was easy for Romulus to imagine he was simply talking to another ordinary human, one who followed a basic moral code, but with Selene looking at him through the dead gaze of her puppet, there was no way he could pretend that there was anything normal about the circumstance. His and Delilah's lives rested on this creature's wishes, and he might have just angered her.

"I'm sorry," Romulus apologized.

Chris/Selene didn't blink as he spoke. "Your apology is unwarranted. Your point, though motivated by childish emotions, was nevertheless accurate. I did not know the one you know as Delilah Lane and so, as I gathered energy for the erasing of your mind, I dwelled within her thoughts."

"Stop her!" Delilah cried fearfully, tears beginning to trickle down her cheeks. At the same time, Romulus shouted for Selene to leave Delilah alone. Selene ignored them both.

"Her real name is Annette Spring and she is a mole, sanctioned by your father, to spy and control your actions."

Romulus was stunned, but then anger took its place. "You filthy liar!" he spat at Chris/Selene. "How dare you...how dare you insinuate..." His hands clenched in fists as he thought about punching Chris/Selene.

Chris/Selene blinked for the first time and Romulus didn't know whether that was significant or not. "You would attack, even knowing you cannot win, just to prevent me from continuing my assessment of Annette Spring?" Selene said, with just the barest hint of curiosity. "Why? Even if what I say are lies, they do not physically harm Annette in any way. Why throw your life away for something so insignificant?"

"Her name is Delilah!" Romulus shouted.

"It is not."

"Why should I believe anything a monster like you has to say?" Romulus challenged.

"Again, you seek to provoke, even though I can kill you easily," Selene/Chris observed, and although it didn't have the air of a threat, it still chilled Romulus' blood. "Some of the other Residents, especially Athena, act in the same manner, but I assumed it was their unpredictable and sometimes fragile mental state that caused them to lash out at impossible odds. Perhaps it is the lack of control of one's emotions?" Selene/Chris looked deep in thought before blinking again.

"Regardless, I do not care if you do or do not believe me, for the opinions of humans are worth little and, once I'm done, you will not remember this conversation."

"Wait!" Delilah cried out, raising her hand. Chris/Selene did not move his gaze from Romulus, but he felt the monster's attention shift to Delilah. "You say we won't remember anything?"

"Correct."

"And you can erase our memories now?"

"Yes, curiosity was the only reason why I have not acted up to this point," Chris/Selene admitted.

"Give us one more minute," Delilah pleaded, and Romulus thought she wished to say something comforting or stall Selene until they could come up with a plan, but when she turned to him, her mouth was set in a cruel line and her eyes oozed hatred. "You whiny little bitch!" she shot at him, and he flinched as if he had been slapped before looking angrily at Chris/Selene.

"Stop controlling her!"

Chris/Selene frowned, the first expression that Chris had made since Selene took over. "I have read his mind and still do not understand," he said, and Romulus realized he was talking to Delilah. "Is it love that makes him so resistant to the truth?"

"No, it's 'cause he's stupid!" Delilah answered coldly, and Romulus, through his incredulity, caught the slight traces of a southern accent. "You think he's dense now, try spending hours with him." Her voice became high and mocking. "Oh, Delilah, do you think I'm a good person? Oh, Delilah, do you think I'll ever be free of my father? Oh, Delilah, I will make you so happy!"

Romulus was numb, not believing...knowing that this was not the Delilah he knew. She must be stalling...giving him a chance to figure out how to beat Selene.

"He still does not believe you," Chris/Selene observed, changing from kidnapper to interested watcher.

"Of course he doesn't," Delilah agreed. "I told you he's a moron! And you know the worst part of it? I have to pretend to be a bigger moron than him!"

"Why?" Chris/Selene asked.

"Because men don't like it when their women are smarter than them," Delilah answered, her southern drawl becoming stronger. She looked ready to shout more abuses at him, but a thought must have hit her and she glanced at Chris/Selene. "Is it different for your kind?"

"Our gender has no bearing on our status," Chris/Selene answered, and Delilah sighed wistfully.

"Must be nice."

"This can't be real!" Romulus whispered, but doubt was beginning to worm its way into his mind.

"Remember the first time we officially met?" Delilah asked. "In the park where I tripped and fell into your arms? I practiced that trip over a dozen times before I tried it on you. Man, was I nervous!"

"But..." Romulus stammered.

"My love of baseball? Never seen a game in my life. Spent a day memorizing the Wikipedia page. And I hate every one of your stupid impressions! I hate everything about you really," she added, as if the thought had just occurred to her. "Every hour I spend in your company is like a day in hell. Your brother is far more interesting."

"My brother?" was the only thing Romulus could think to say as his world crashed around him.

"Maris originally had me go after Remus," Delilah explained, clearly enjoying the look that shot across his face. Enjoying how badly she was hurting him. "We went on three secret dates before he dumped me. Never told you, did he?" Romulus opened and closed his mouth, and Delilah laughed cruelly. "If you only knew how much of an ass you look like right now!"

Romulus looked at Chris/Selene.

"I can find no deceit within her words," the monster said, seemingly forgetting that she was supposed to be erasing their memories.

Romulus looked back at the gloating Delilah and accepted what she said was true. He took a deep breath and leaned back.

"That's right," Delilah taunted. "Lean back and take it. You're so good at—" She shrieked as Romulus lunged at her, pinning her against the door with his hands around her pretty throat.

"I would have sacrificed my brother for you!" he screamed at her, his rage making him see red. "I put you above all else. I would have given my life to see you happy!"

Delilah was laughing as he shook her. "You're so full of it that you believe your own crap! You would have sacrificed Remus for *you*! Even if you knew Maris was going to kill Remus, you wouldn't have done a damn thing! It's all so that you can hold on to all the respect and power your father gives you! You only love me as long as I'm a perfect shallow doll without an independent thought or personality of my own!"

"You—"

"You would make an interesting Resident," Chris/Selene observed, and it was unclear as to who she was talking about.

"Remus," Delilah continued, her voice hoarse from the lack of air. "Sweet, stupid Remus is the best of you Sylvias. At least he doesn't make excuses for what he is. You want to know why Remus dumped me and you didn't?"

Romulus wanted to ignore her words, but found the answer was terribly important to him. "Why?" he asked, releasing her. Delilah didn't answer. Instead, she looked up at him with a dazed, confused expression. "Why?" he screamed at her.

Delilah jerked from his shoulder where she had been sleeping, and Chris Burlington pressed hard on the breaks, the car squealing to a stop. Chris turned around, checking to see if they were okay while Delilah rubbed her blurry eyes.

"Why what?" she asked sleepily, a note of irritation creeping into her voice at being so rudely awakened.

Romulus blinked, suddenly uncertain, and he ran a hand through his disheveled hair as he tried to get his bearings. "I think I was sleeping," he said slowly, trying to recall the exact content of his dream. "Having a nightmare."

Chris nodded empathetically before turning back towards the road, accelerating slowly until they were back up to normal speeds. "I've been there. The first few weeks of knowing what you now know, I didn't sleep a wink."

"I, however, was sleeping peacefully," Delilah grouched, her complaints losing their weight when she placed her head back on his shoulder. "What were you dreaming about?"

"I don't know," Romulus admitted, his beating heart still going about a million miles per hour. "Whatever it was...it was terrifying."

"It's been a long day," Delilah consoled. "Things will look

better in the morning."

Romulus didn't see how. Tomorrow would change nothing; he would still be expected to sign a contract, making him a test monkey for a drug that made monsters out of humans, but he knew Delilah was only trying to help.

"You're right," he agreed, and she beamed up at him.

"We're here," Chris said, and Romulus blinked in surprised as his house came into view. He must have been really out of it if he'd slept through the entire trip home. "Where do you want to be dropped off at?"

"In front will do." Romulus was about to thank him, but hesitated. Was it really okay to show gratitude to a man that was part of the organization that kidnapped them in the first place?

Chris, apparently sensing his dilemma, smiled and said, "On behalf of my group and the people I work with, I want to apologize for our actions tonight."

"Thank you," Romulus replied as the car slowed to a stop. He reached and pulled the handle, but the door refused to open.

"Children's lock for the kids," Chris explained, and though the explanation was plausible, Romulus still felt a wave of unease. "Here, I'll get it for you."

"Can you drive me home as well?" Delilah asked. "Please," she added, her voice growing louder to drown out Romulus' immediate rejection.

"I don't see why not," Chris said cautiously. "In fact, it will give me something to focus on, instead of picturing all the horrible things Athena is doing to my comrades." The comment seemed out of place coming from the mild man.

Delilah glared at Romulus, who braced himself for an argument. "Romulus, you will be up all night with your father and my presence won't help matters. Chis will drive me straight home and I will call you as soon as my mother stops yelling at me, okay?" Romulus hesitated and Delilah leaned in to give him a kiss. "Don't worry about me. Nothing bad will happen."

As they had been talking, Chris had exited his seat, walked over to Romulus' side, and opened the door for him. Romulus hesitated before glaring hard at the older man and saying as forcefully as he could, "Don't let anything happen to her!"

If Chris found his words to be lacking force or his attempt to give orders ridiculous, he didn't show it. "I promise she will not come to any harm under my care," the soldier said sincerely, and Romulus had no choice but to believe him.

Romulus watched from the lawn as Chris drove off and, from the backseat, Delilah blew him a kiss. He stood for a second, not wishing to face his father, but knowing he would need to eventually, and so with a long, heavy sigh, Romulus started up the driveway.

"You would make an interesting Resident."

Chapter 59

Remus stared stupidly at the little blinking light wedged in Athena's muscle, barely seen over the blood pouring through the wound.

"You found it?" Athena asked, sounding just as shocked. A few seconds passed in which he assumed she was reading his mind. "You did," she breathed. "I would never have imagined the location would be that low. How did you guess?"

"I got lucky," Remus said in way of explanation, not really understanding it himself. A hunch, more like a premonition, had directed his hand when he made the last cut, and though he felt like he accomplished the hardest task by simply finding the tracker, he drowned out the feeling of success with caution. "So how do I take it out?"

"Any way possible," Athena responded vehemently, as if she had a personal hatred for the tracker itself. "The easiest way might be to pry it out using the knife. If that doesn't work, feel free to smash my shoulder with the hammer until you destroy it."

Remus started to laugh until he realized she wasn't joking. "I think I'll try the least drastic way first."

"If you think that's practical," Athena said, with far too much confidence in his abilities to make him comfortable. When he shifted nervously, she added slyly, after obviously reading his mind, "I have *complete* confidence in your ability. There's no way you can mess up now!"

"You think that's wise, taunting the man doing surgery on your back?"

Annoyed at her immature antics and not waiting for her half-apology, he focused on her back, where only part of the bug was uncovered. In order for him to have the slightest chance of removing it, he would need to widen the incision. He raised the knife, but at the same time, either through fear or pain, Athena shivered involuntary, and the movement sent cold fear coursing through Remus. What was he doing? He didn't have a clue as to how someone would widen an incision and Athena's back was already covered with blood, the paper towels doing nothing but smearing it around. What if she was wrong? What if her healing factor only worked to a degree? He could be doing serious irrevocable damage to her and not even know it. His hand began to shake, and he knew he was on the verge of being completely immobilized by his uncertainty. Athena, being who she was, recognized his predicament.

"It was rather childish of me to tease my savior," Athena said theatrically, her new label for Remus not making him feel any better. "How about this, I give you a reward for all the help you given me so far."

"Is this a ten thousand dollar reward?" Remus asked, surprising himself on how easily he could banter with her.

"I'm afraid not. But if you're curious, I'll tell you why I chose you."

He had meant to ask Athena this question after the hotel, but there hadn't been an opportunity as she was nearly dead directly afterward and when she recovered, her only thoughts were of removing the tracker. Remus was aware that his body had stopped shaking and he placed his hand on Athena's shoulder to steady her for the next cut. "You're going to tell me why you needed a companion on this little trip of yours?"

"That's not what I said. I said I would tell you why I chose you, not why I wanted a companion in the first place."

"Okay. Why me, Athena?" He made a small but deep incision where he assumed the rest of the bug was hiding, and felt like an ass as Athena hissed in pain. He connected the incision with the previous one so that it now looked like someone had carved a sideways T in her skin. The bug was now easy to spot. Remus couldn't distinguish the color because of all the blood, but it was approximately two inches wide and three inches tall. It must have been placed in her when she was young, for muscles had grown around it, which meant it would be impossible to remove without causing agony to Athena.

Athena tried to disguise the discomfort in her voice. "I almost chose your brother."

Remus wasn't sure Athena talking to him was helping anymore, but it seemed to be helping her deal, so he responded with, "Romulus? When did you meet him?"

"Meet?" Athena shook her head, but stopped when Remus made a warning noise. "No, I wouldn't call it a meeting. I saw him at the mall and wanted to check him out."

"Check him out for what?" Remus studied the bug. The only way he could think of prying it out was to get the knife behind the bug and use it as leverage to pop it out, but it meant digging the blade into her muscles.

"For the right traits. I wanted to see if he had the right personality to..." Remus didn't miss the hesitation. "Come with me."

"And did he?"

"Who knows? Some jerk knocked me down before I had the chance to find out."

A laugh escaped Remus. "So you chose me because I tackled you?"

"My dear Remus, if I was to choose someone simply because they knocked me to the ground, I would have a whole entourage by now." She let Remus ponder that statement for a second. "No, I had to do a sweep of your mind. See how you responded to certain statements and questions."

"And?"

"I found you to be gullible, depressed, and uncertain of your capabilities." Remus winced as he heard the ring of truth in her words.

"Guy with a knife," he reminded her sourly, only belatedly realizing how threatening it sounded, but Athena, knowing he didn't mean anything by it, responded defensively.

"It's the truth! If I'd had more time, I would have passed over you in search of someone else, but since I didn't..."

"So you had to settle for me?" Remus couldn't keep the bitterness out of his voice.

"Initially, yes," Athena agreed. "But you became so much more than that." She shrieked as Remus sank the blade into her muscle in an attempt to get the knife under the bug. For the first time, she instinctively tried to move to get away from the pain, moving against Remus' hand on her shoulder, but quickly mastered her instinct and settled down so he could continue. "I was dead asleep after the events of your house," she continued through gritted teeth. "You could have left me and took the money, but you chose to stay. You claimed it was for your brother, and I suppose that was part of the reason. But it was mostly because you didn't want to leave a helpless girl by herself, even one you didn't particularly like at the time."

"It's not that I didn't like you..."

"Mind reader, Remus!" Athena interrupted ferociously, pain making her cranky. "You hated me, but not because I stole the money and blew your life to hell. You hated me because I had the audacity to kill the thugs your father hired to kill you!"

Remus was so enthralled by Athena's story that he barely knew what he was doing to her back. The flat of the knife was now securely set under the bug and all he needed to do was apply enough pressure...

"It was the same with the soldiers at the gas station." Athena no longer tried to hide the pain in her voice. Her babbling seemed to help her, so she continued. "Your biggest offense is that I killed them, even though they would have killed us both, and that frustrated me, Remus." The last words ended up in a growl. "Frustrated me because I couldn't understand it! I wasn't raised to understand it."

"You didn't understand that I valued life?" The bug refused to budge, so Remus applied more pressure and it started to move.

"Valuing life over your own," Athena corrected. "Especially those trying to kill you...it's not natural. My first theory was you had an inferiority complex. I even went so far as to think you were like Fides and wanted someone to kill you." Remus was too busy concentrating on her back to comment and, at times, he tuned her words out, but he got the gist of what she was saying. "After the hotel, I realized how wrong I was," she was saying. "The answer was so simple that it bordered on the lines of idiotic."

"And what was the answer?" Remus asked, deeply intrigued. *Pop!* The bug flew out of Athena's skin and bounced harmlessly off his chest. It made a small clinking noise as it hit the floor.

If Athena realized he had succeeded, she didn't

acknowledge it. "The answer was that you simply valued human life. It ate at you every time someone died in what you thought was an unnecessary death." She laughed, and her laugh had a slight craziness to it that Remus didn't like. "How someone with your childhood could have such noble values still escapes me... *Smash it!*"

She said it with such venom that Remus actually jumped back. "Smash what?"

"The bug, you idiot! Use the hammer and smash the bug!"

I went from having noble values to being an idiot, Remus thought sardonically.

"You can be both!" Athena snapped. "But...I called you an idiot out of anxiety. I apologize."

It sounded sincere enough. "Apology accepted." Remus picked up the bug from the ground and placed it on the table far away from where Athena sat. He then searched the bag for the hammer.

"And that's the other thing. If I was to consider your value of life your best quality, the second best would have to be your chivalry."

"Plenty of guys are chivalrous." Finding the hammer, he raised it up high so he could smash the bug out of existence...and missed. His hands were shaking too much.

"Plenty of guys act chivalrous," Athena argued, kindly overlooking his folly. "But most guys aren't."

"And you're saying I am?"

"You have me with my shirt and half my bra off and you have yet to think of jumping my bones."

"I just cut into you!"

She laughed the same crazy laugh as before, and Remus began to worry about her.

"I suppose you have a point," she said. "Although...no, never mind." Athena lapsed into silence.

Remus raised the hammer again, and this time succeeded in smashing the bug, but the light continued to blink. It was a durable little device.

"You didn't leave me," Athena said, so softly that Remus wondered if she wanted to be heard. "Not when I was sleeping, not at the hotel, and not now. You cared for a poor girl's wellbeing. A girl you met only days ago and risked your life to see that she was okay. You cannot imagine how much I appreciate that. How much your acts of kindness touch me. One more time with the hammer ought to do it."

The slight insanity that had plagued her earlier seemed to have vanished, and Remus was glad to see it go. He struck again with the hammer and the bug shattered to pieces. "It's done." He felt a great weight lift from his shoulders and, though happiness was uncertain with the universe always lurking around, he did allow the tension from his muscles to ease out. "They shouldn't be able to find you again. Unless there's another bug hidden in you somewhere."

Remus meant for it to be lighthearted, but Athena answered seriously. "I doubt it. I believe my friend would have investigated this line of thought and warned me if your concerns were valid." She looked confused for a second. "Where was I?"

"You appreciate me and my acts of kindness."

"That's right, I do. To recap, I was unsure of you in the beginning, but the more I got to know you, the more I realized how extremely lucky I was to have you in my life." She hesitated. "Boy, does this sound sappy...whatever. You earned it. You were everything I could have wished for, Remus, and so much more. I'm glad to have traveled this far with you and, whatever happens, I want you to know that."

If Romulus had been in his place, he would have said something touching and sincere to complete the moment, to make it perfect. But Remus was clumsy and didn't know the right thing to say, so he said nothing until the silence lengthened into awkwardness.

"Athena..." He hesitated.

"Forget it, the mood's ruined," she said, and Remus was disappointed until he realized she was teasing him. It seemed impossible for her to stay serious for very long. "Hey, do you mind patching me up?"

With horror, Remus realized he had been allowing her to bleed out on the table, and he rushed to find the gauze Band-Aids while rambling apologies. He had serious doubts that Bands-Aids, no matter how heavy-duty they claimed to be, were going to fix the problem. At the very least, she needed stitches, but when he returned to the wound, box in hand, he found it already beginning to heal, the blood loss having subsided immensely.

"Incredible," he murmured, awestruck.

"It has its uses," Athena said, making light of it. "Still, it's going to be a couple of hours before I can move around."

"I'll stay with you until then."

Athena laughed, and Remus wondered if it was at his expense until she said dreamily, "And you thought you couldn't say the right thing."

Chapter 60

Brandon Badger was not an idiot. He knew by the time the sun rose tomorrow he would be dead, but try as he might, he could not bring himself to care, his anger towards Ragnarok smothering all other emotions. Throughout Ragnarok's history, many men, either to save their own hide or simply striving to do the right thing, had gone to the press with stories of enhanced humans and monsters and the end results were always the same—a very tragic and horrendous death, one that served as a warning to anyone else who harbored thoughts of betrayal.

"So, let's go over it again," the detective said. He was a beefy man with a thin mustache, and Brandon instantly disliked him because of his appearance. His shirt was half tucked in, his hair uncombed, and there were numerous ketchup stains on his pants. "Mr. Titanos, one of the richest men in the world, sent a squad of hired assassins to kill a teenage girl because..."

"I don't know, sir," Brandon answered, knowing that the truth would be dismissed as the ranting of a maniac. The rickety chair creaked loudly as he shifted in an effort to try and get comfortable. It had been seven years since he had abandoned law enforcement, and none of the interrogation tactics had changed. They still sat the suspect in an uncomfortable chair away from light switches and thermostats to convey a sense of powerlessness. The detectives had started with some light off-topic conversation, trying to connect with Brandon before launching into some aggressive and hostile questions. "For some reason, he wanted this particular girl dead. I figured she was a daughter of some affair he had and he wanted to tie up loose ends."

The detective leaned forward and Brandon wrinkled his nose at the strong odor of tobacco mixed with the stench of a man who believed showering was something you did every three days. "Do you always agree to murder little girls for the sake of your employee?"

"Sir, he signs my paychecks. That's all I care about." The second detective, an older man with greying hair, had been mute and expressionless up to this point, content on allowing his sloppy partner to take charge, but at Brandon's statement, his face twisted to unmistakable disgust. Brandon couldn't blame him; a man who killed women and children to pay his rent was not a man to be respected.

"You know I contacted Mr. Titanos," the detective continued, his putrid breath assaulting Brandon every time he opened his mouth. "He said he never heard of you."

"Did you think he was going to admit to it?" Brandon scoffed, infuriated when the detective shrugged carelessly. "He probably offered you a generous amount of money to close the case in his favor."

The detective's eyes flickered, confirming Brandon's suspicions. His dislike for the detective intensified. "Are you on any medications?"

Brandon sighed inwardly, unsurprised they were trying to establish a claim of mental instability. "Only for my kneecap," he answered, his leg convulsing slightly at the mention. It was in question whether he would ever be able to walk without a limp.

"Do you have a personal grudge against Mr. Titanos?"

"Yes, sir, I do," Brandon answered honestly. "But that doesn't make my testimony any less reliable."

"And what would be the nature of that grudge?" the detective asked, his curiosity obviously faked.

"My brother died because of him."

The detective frowned, as if puzzled by a great mystery, shifted through the pages in front of him, and shook his head slowly. This was supposed to be an intimidation tactic. Make Brandon nervous so he started babbling out all his secrets. The detective had also neglected to mention his name even after Brandon asked, another psychological tactic but one that was illegal, which meant everyone involved was confident the case would never make it to trial "Approximately fifty men showed up at the hotel. Doesn't that seem like overkill for one little girl?"

"Mr. Titanos likes to be efficient."

The excuse sounded lame even to his own ears and the detective smirked at his aging partner, but the gesture wasn't returned. "I bet he does." The detective fixed him with what was supposed to be a menacing stare and Brandon looked back, unconcerned. "You want me to tell you what I think really happened?"

"No, sir, I do not."

The detective paused, momentarily thrown off his game, but forged on. "I think this whole operation is your idea. I think you're all delusional maniacs looking for something to cut up or kill. You went to the hotel looking for a good time, maybe to kill this fictional girl, or maybe you just love the sounds of people screaming for their lives. Except along the way, maybe some of your comrades started questioning you. So you shut them up by shooting them up." He smiled as if he just made a funny joke.

"That's the stupidest thing I've ever heard," Brandon said, refusing to let the man get a rise out of him. "People with my training don't shoot at crowds of civilians for kicks and giggles."

"But you kill little girls to pay your bills," the elder detective asked, speaking for the first time, and the words stung all the more because of the grain of truth in them.

"Ballistics and forensics will show that I had nothing to do with the death of my own men."

"I wonder if you killed your kid brother too," the sloppy detective mused, tapping a pencil on the desk, and Brandon recoiled in disgust as he saw the pencil had bite marks on it. "You said his name was Anthony?"

Even with his injured leg, it would be the easiest thing in the world to reach over the desk and strangle the detective. He bet he could kill him before his partner could react. "Like I said, the forensics and ballistics reports will clear me."

"Of course, I wouldn't be too upset if you killed your precious brother," the detective said with a sneer. "You were doing the world a favor, removing scum like that."

The detective never saw it coming. In the blink of an eye, Brandon grabbed the detective's crooked tie and pulled him in so that he could pummel him. In three seconds, Brandon had broken some of the detective's teeth. In the space of ten seconds, he could have had the detective's face looking like raw hamburger, but before he could get that far, the other detective's hands wrapped around his torso in an attempt to wrestle him to the ground and that's when backup entered.

"Get on the ground!"

Now he really did look like a madman. The most infuriating thing was the detective's smile, his missing teeth easily displayed. The dick had planned this and must be receiving a hefty sum from Ragnarok to be this happy, even after losing two incisors. He would have no problem closing the case and putting the blame solely on Brandon's shoulders. Brandon struggled against the hands attempting to bring him to the floor. And then...it all stopped.

Brandon looked up to see three cops frozen in midstance, their arms still reaching for him, their eyes unseeing. Slowly, he dislodged himself from their grasps and his heartbeat quickened as he realized what this must mean. Ragnarok had already sent a Resident to eliminate him. He had known it was coming, known his time was limited, but he hadn't expected it this soon. And, judging by the frozen men and women around him, it was obviously a very powerful Resident. Brandon reached into the detective's holster and pulled out his gun. He wouldn't go out without a fight.

"My, aren't we hostile?" a whimsical voice boomed over the intercom.

Brandon jumped and looked around for the enemy, finally settling on the observation mirror, and said, "You would be too if you'd had the day I've had."

"I heard about that." The voice was female with a very distinct English accent. "I'm sorry for your loss."

"Bullshit." Brandon edged for the door, his eyes constantly scanning. He accidentally bumped into one of the cops and the man slowly tilted forward with unblinking eyes until he fell face-first onto the floor, making no moves to catch or soften his fall with his arms. "What did you do to them?" Brandon demanded. He had never seen any of Ragnarok's Residents accomplish this.

"You mean the men in the room with you? I didn't do a thing. A very dear friend of mine did that and she would do anything to protect me, so I suggest lowering your gun before I come in."

"I'm not going out without a fight!" Brandon huffed, recognizing how cheesy it sounded a split second after he said it, and what was worse was his assassin thought so too and laughed merrily over the intercom.

"My, aren't we a cowboy?" she commented after she finished laughing at his expense.

There was only one way out of the interrogation room and the door required a keycard. He could take one off one of the frozen cops, and he reached for the sloppy detective's pocket, intent on doing just that, when another plan occurred to him. A desperate plan with only about a five percent chance of success, but that was better than no chance at all. Meanwhile, the British accent was taunting him.

"You asked what happened to those men you see around you."

"That does have me curious," he admitted, speaking to the two-way mirror. In the precinct he worked at, the button controlling the intercom was located on the right side of the mirror, and if this was the case for this building, then he knew approximately where the Resident assassin was. The glass wasn't bulletproof, and Brandon, as casually as he could, took the safety lock off the stolen gun. He would literally only have one shot at this, for if he missed, the assassin would stop toying with her prey and freeze him as well.

"Think about it like being frozen in time," the voice was saying. "They see nothing, know nothing, and when my friend awakens them, they won't even be aware any time has passed. It would be child's play for my friend to freeze you, slit your throat, and escape. The cops will awaken to see you dead and with no reasonable idea as to how you got that way, though I'm sure they'll find an adequate way to cover it up."

"What's the point of all this?" Brandon demanded. If he was to die, it wouldn't be without taking at least taking one Resident with him, so he tilted himself so that he had the perfect angle to shoot out the glass and hopefully hit and kill the assassin.

There was a loud sigh over the intercom. "Why am I always stuck recruiting the stupid ones?" she complained. "Just once, I would love for someone to say, 'Wow, Andraste, you really saved my life. Thank you so much!'"

Brandon's muscles bunched up as he prepared to act, but

the assassin's voice held him captive.

"The point, as it should have become obvious to any normal person, is that we're not here to kill you. If we were, you'd be dead."

Her words made sense, but he still didn't want to relinquish his gun. "Recruit me for what?" he asked, not completely giving up on his desperate plan, but at least wanting to hear what the Resident had to say.

"Uh-uh. No more freebees. If you want answers, you're going to have to throw your gun away."

"And if I refuse?"

"I'll have my friend unfreeze your friends. Of course, seeing how you're wielding a gun, they'll probably fire first and ask questions never." It seemed all Residents shared the same twisted sense of sadistic humor and bad jokes.

"Fine." Brandon didn't see any other choice and he hated that he was backed in a corner. He dropped the gun and kicked it away, keeping a careful eye on where it skidded to a stop.

"That's a good boy," the voice said approvingly, complimenting him like one complimented a dog. "My friend and I can't wait to meet you!" The door opened and Brandon braced himself for the worst scenario. Instead, a pretty brunette walked in. Even more unusual, she was carrying a small child, no older than four, and with her one free hand, she waved cheerfully to him.

"You're the Resident?" he asked, taken aback.

"Not what you were expecting?" she asked, a wide grin on her face, clearly enjoying his shock. "I don't see why," she continued in an accent that was so British Brandon almost thought she was faking it. "It's not like Athena looks particularly hideous."

"That child shouldn't be here," he stuttered, grasping onto the only thing that made sense.

The woman never stop grinning as she patted the child fondly on the head. The child had blond hair with green highlights at the tip of each strand of hair; someone must have thought that was cute. She had rosy red cheeks that still held a trace of baby fat in them, and a curious, innocent gaze that would unfortunately fade as she spent more time with Residents. A ridiculous notion entered Brandon's head and he shot a look at the Resident, who nodded in confirmation.

"Yep, this is the friend I was telling you about," the Resident verified. "Quite a special little tot, she is. Can do all this—" she waved her hand airily, indicating all the frozen men "—without even breaking a sweat.

"You're lying," Brandon said, his confidence wavering as the Resident shook her head pityingly. "There's no way that a little girl could be a Resident. There's no way!"

The child responded to the anger in his voice and hugged the woman fearfully.

"Shhh," the woman said, patting the child's head reassuringly and, at the same time, shooting Brandon a reproachful glare. "Don't raise your voice, you oaf! You'll scare her."

"She's too young to be a Resident!" Brandon continued, lowering his voice so as not to upset the kid. "Ambrosia takes years to affect the DNA structure; the youngest anyone has ever presented powers was at the age of eight!" The child seemed to have calmed down and was now trying to tug on the Resident's hair, giggling when the woman would tilt her head so that the toddler would almost get a handful before jerking it out of reach at the last second. The scene, so normal and adoring from regular humans, was unsettling when Residents attempted it, especially in the middle of a room full of people frozen like corpses. "This is impossible," he reiterated.

The woman stopped moving and the child grabbed a fistful of hair, squealing in victory as she did so. "After all you've seen, you still talk about the impossible," the woman said with a touch of sadness. "You disappoint me, Brandon Badger."

Brandon jerked when his full name was mentioned. "It seems like you have me at a disadvantage."

The woman slapped her head in mock astonishment. "My gosh, where are my manners? My name is Andraste and unless you're completely ignorant, you know that's the Celtic goddess for victory."

In truth, Brandon didn't know, having never studied Celtic mythology, but saw no need to share that.

"And this delightful little child here," Andraste said, indicating the child in her arm, "is Medusa."

"The snake monster," he blurted out.

Medusa's eyes welled up with tears and Andraste looked at him angrily. "Not very tactful, are we?" she said scathingly before adding, more for Medusa's sake than his, "For your information, Medusa was the powerful queen of the Gorgons."

The child looked slightly mollified.

A thought occurred to Brandon. "At the hotel, my men found a woman and her four-year-old child with the boy. Was that you?"

Andraste was already nodding yes before Brandon finished. "The boy's name is Remus Sylvia. You should at least give him that, seeing how he outsmarted the lot of you. And yes, that was us at the hotel. Horrid place! There was a distinct odor in our room that reminded me vaguely of..." She stopped short as Brandon took a couple of hobbled steps towards them, the pain from his knee preventing him from lunging at her and perhaps saving his life.

"You're the one who helped them out," he snarled, spit flying out of his mouth. "It's your fault my men are dead. You're the ones who killed my brother!"

"Don't be a fool, Mr. Badger. We did not kill your brother. You did!" Andraste said sharply, matching Brandon's anger perfectly. "Your arrogance and Athena's ruthlessness killed your brother. Not me, and definitely not Medusa. We were sent to keep an eye on things and we did our utmost not to interfere, one way or the other."

"Then why were you with the boy? And who sent you?" Brandon took another step towards them, ignoring the agony his knee was sending him. Andraste looked wary, but didn't make a step in any direction.

"I must confess, my curiosity did get the better of me. Everyone was so concentrated on Athena that people completely overlooked Remus."

"He's just a pawn of Athena," Brandon dismissed.

"As a former detective, you should know how important the meaningless details can be," Andraste chided. "Besides, I wanted to know what type of man voluntarily agrees to go with a monster even after knowing exactly what she was. Did Athena trick him? Is he a danger junkie? Does he find being near a monster erotic?"

"Monster?" Medusa whispered, speaking for the first time. Her grip on Andraste's hair tightened and the British woman winced.

"Pardon me, darling, I meant to say Resident," Andraste cooed, disentangling herself from Medusa's grip. "I only used the word monster for emphasis."

"So what did you find?" It was true; they had dismissed

the boy as unimportant.

"I found him to be a decent human being. Not quite sure if he's special or not, but at the very least, he's a refreshing change in our hostile world. Perhaps she just wanted the company."

Brandon waited for more, but when it became clear that was all she was going to say, he became enraged once more. "That's it?" he yelled. "What about who you work for?"

"You're quite a brute, aren't you?" she said, disgusted. Brandon was ready to kill her if she said "aren't you" one more time. "And not the least bit smart. I would think it should be obvious."

In truth, Brandon had his suspicions. "Avalon?"

"Well look at that!" Andraste exclaimed scathingly. "The monkey can use his brain!" Medusa smiled at her comment

"Why would Avalon be involved in this?" Brandon asked, determined to ignore her insults until he got the information he needed.

"First off, it's always a good idea to watch your competition try to correct a mistake. You gave us some prime footage at the hotel. The boys back at Headquarters will be laughing at this for quite some while."

"You think this is funny?" Brandon roared.

Medusa buried her face in Andraste's shoulder and Andraste fixed him with a withering glare. "This is the last time I will ask you, Mr. Badger. *Lower your voice.*"

He ignored her demands. "You were right the first time. The term is monsters. That's all you are. Creatures that should never have existed. Animals that should be—"

"If you finish that statement, I will kill you," she said in a quiet tone. "Which would be sad, because Avalon had such high hopes of bringing you in alive."

Her tone was somber, as if saddened by the prospect of killing him, but still completely serious, and Brandon had little doubt that, if he continued, she would kill him and not glance back. He couldn't let that happen. He had to stay alive for his brother because if he didn't get justice for him, no one else would.

"Good," she said when she saw him settle down and Medusa peeked at him from behind her arms. "Now, like I was saying, it's always a good idea to capitalize on your competition's mistake, but our boss seemed to have another reason for wanting us there."

"What other reason?"

"Well how should I bloody know?" Andraste snapped, re-verting back to the imbecilic behavior she had first shown when walking into the room. "It's not like I'm chummy with the boss. The boss told us to watch Athena at the hotel and, by golly, that's what we did. The boss told us to offer you a deal and that's what we're doing now."

Finally, the reason why they were here. "What deal?" He had known they wanted something from him once he real-ized they weren't here to kill him.

"We get you out of this joint, and you come work for us in our neck of the woods," Andraste said, once again cheer-ful. "We offer much more than Ragnarok's paying and our dental plan is phenomenal."

"Dental plan?" Brandon repeated angrily, and Medusa smiled at him, showing all her teeth as if to emphasize An-draste's point.

Andraste's smile disappeared and Brandon caught a glimpse of the calculating mind lurking beneath. "We're also the best chance you have of avenging your brother, and if you don't take this opportunity, you'll be dead by this time tomorrow, killed by your own employees."

He was trapped and she knew it. Even if he managed to somehow kill her and escape, he would forever be on the run. Not that it would take a particularly long time for Ragna-rok to track down his location and kill him; the organization was nothing if not thorough. "I don't have much of a choice," he said. It was a struggle to admit his own helplessness, but Andraste visibly relaxed at the admission. "As long as our goals agree, I'll be your man."

Andraste grinned broadly. "Well that's brilliant!" she ex-claimed. "Truth be told, there was a poll going on whether you would agree or not. You won me three hundred bucks!"

Brandon ignored her foolishness. "When do we leave?"

"Impatient, aren't we?" she observed, absently rocking Medusa as the toddler, growing tired of being in one place, started to fuss. "I suppose we can leave now. We have a pickup truck in the parking lot. I'm afraid that's as fancy as it gets."

"Wait a minute," he said as she turned around to leave. "We're just going to walk out?"

"Well, I hope you weren't expecting a magic carpet," Andraste admonished. "Come on now, use your legs." She glanced down and covered her mouth in embarrassment. "Oh, how silly of me! I completely forgot that Athena did a rather bloody number on your knee." Brandon ground his teeth together, knowing full well Andraste had not overlooked his barely operational knee. "Well this won't do," she continued. "It will take forever to for a bloke like you to walk to the truck and I certainly can't carry you! What in heaven's name am I supposed to do?"

Brandon was about to utter a cruel jape when Medusa spoke up. "Heal him," she suggested timidly. Then with more confidence, "You can heal him!"

"Splendid idea, love," Andraste exclaimed. Obviously, the whole performance was for the child's sake. "No wonder I bring you along."

Medusa raised her head with pride and grinned shyly at Brandon, whose immediate unconscious response was to grin back. Andraste took three quick steps towards Bandon and touched him lightly on the leg. He slapped her arm away, but by that time, it was too late. An intense heat washed over him, and he screamed in agony as all the pain receptors in his leg fired at once. The pain was the most intense he'd ever had, and his only solace was that it only lasted for a few seconds. Andraste didn't say anything else. Instead, she waited in silence as he tested his knee and, besides a lingering pain, found it to be completely healed. After he stood, she beckoned him silently to follow her out of the room.

Walking out the door, Brandon looked around in wonder at all the men and women frozen in place, surprised to find Medusa's powers extended outside the room. He saw a cop discreetly reaching for a female officer's butt, two immobile cops frozen in the middle of a laugh, and one in mid-yawn, his hands stretched over his head.

"She's impressive, isn't she?" Andraste said, reading his face, and Medusa beamed at the compliment. "If we're going, we should go. She can't hold this forever."

Useful information to know. Brandon walked behind Andraste and Medusa. He made a mental checklist. 1: Call his other brother and tell him about Anthony. 2: Bring Ragnarok down to its knees. 3: Kill Athena.

Chapter 61

Freedom—a concept that no human ever thought of un-less making political arguments or unless their own freedom was infringed on, but for a Resident, it was one of the most important and sought-after ideals. Athena remembered three years ago when some idiot guard was complaining the gov-ernment was taking away his freedom simply because he got arrested for giving the finger to a cop. She remembered breaking both of his middle fingers with great delight so that he wouldn't have to deal with that problem any time in the future.

"What are you giggling at?" Remus asked, snapping Athena back to the present. Once again, they were on the road, looking for one last safe house before Athena would be forever free of Pandora's Box.

"Just happy to be free," Athena lied, wisely concluding he wouldn't find the man's broken fingers nearly as comical as she did. "Take a right at the next light." She needed to rest, but to stay at the last-known location of the tracker was folly beyond measure. They had left, Athena wanting to get as far away as possible from her last connection to Pandora's Box. After an hour on the road, however, all the bumping and swaying of the car had aggravated her wounds to unbearable portions. Remus had tried to patch her back together as best as possible, but he would never be a surgeon, and every little bump brought a fresh wave of pain. She had started scrying the minds around her, looking to see if anyone knew of a nearby empty house. After fifteen minutes, she found one in a relatively quiet neighborhood.

"Take a right," she told Remus. "Then..." She stopped as

she thought she felt the presence of a Resident's mind. It lasted half a second before disappearing, and she was forced to wonder if she had imagined the whole thing.

"Selene?" she thought out, staying alert for a response. No answer, and though it cost her energy she didn't have, Athena did a wide-sweep, examining all the minds around her and making sure a Resident hadn't taken over one and was using it to follow them.

"Athena!" Remus screamed.

Athena jerked up, adrenaline already flowing for the up-coming fight. "What?" she asked, scanning for the threat.

Remus was gripping her shoulder where he had been shaking her. At her wince of pain, he withdrew his hand, but his tone was anything but gentle. "You fell silent in the middle of a sentence. I started calling your name, but you didn't answer for like five minutes. I thought...I don't know...I thought you might have fallen into a coma."

"A coma?" she scoffed, which only aggravated Remus more.

"Yes, Athena. I thought 'the girl bleeding out beside me has entered a coma. How funny is that?'" It was more disdain than Athena was used to hearing from him, and she wasn't sure how to respond. Fortunately, Remus seemed to have more to say. "You can't check out like that...not without telling me. I didn't know what was wrong and you already looked mostly dead, so when you fell silent..."

"Okay, I get it," Athena said, subdued. "I'm sorry."

It seemed like Remus had more to say, but at her apology, he deflated, gesturing in front of him. "Is this it?"

Athena looked out the window to see they had arrived at a small one-story house with a FOR SALE sign in the front yard. The area was a bit more woodsy than the last house, which gave enemies a better chance of approaching unde-tected, but the risk was manageable. It also wasn't as up-scale; empty bottles littered the front yard and the paint was badly peeling.

Remus was scowling at her and she answered quickly. "No, I haven't checked out. Yeah, this is it."

Remus exited the car, walked around, and opened her side door, extending a hand to help her out. She raised an eyebrow at him, long enough to see him blush before grabbing his hand for support as she exited the car. As soon as her feet hit the ground, she instantly stumbled, but Remus was there to catch her before she fell on her face.

"So much for ultra-healing."

"I never said it was instantaneous," she protested, though, in truth, she was healing at a slower rate. The results of her body reaching its limit. Remus slid an arm around her waist, propping her up as they headed for the door. On top of a nearby tree, a raven was crowing and Athena's gaze lingered on it.

"What's going on?" Remus demanded, noticing her distracted attention.

With one last squawk, the raven took off, Athena watching it leave. "I'm just thinking. Thinking about a life without Ambrosia, without being trapped in the same room day after day, without the pointless and demeaning tests that were forced upon me. It's all over." She sighed blissfully, but a feeling of unease wormed itself into her mind. "It almost seems too easy, doesn't it?"

"Too easy!" Remus spluttered. "You think we had it easy? The fight at my house, the explosion at the gas station, the small army at the hotel, not to even mention—"

"I get it!" she cried, exasperated. "My gosh, your kind gets so cranky after a few small explosions and assault teams."

Instead of rising to the bait, Remus felt silent, prompting Athena to risk a peek inside his mind. He had agreed to take care of her until she could fend for herself, but he still had no inkling as to what he would do afterwards, and even thought Athena loved his sense of duty, she had trouble justifying a partnership with a human on that alone.

The door loomed up before them. Athena pushed off Remus, ignoring his cries of protests. She squared herself and aimed a kick for the door, but when her foot left the ground, she experienced a wave of dizziness, causing herself to lose balance and stumble back to Remus' waiting arms.

"Stop that," he reproached. "You lost too much blood to be an idiot."

"Are you calling me an idiot?" Athena demanded, feeling heat rise to her face. "Obviously you are disregarding the cleverness of how I..." She stopped as Remus, still holding her arm with one hand, used his other to open the unlocked door with ridiculous ease. He then glanced at her, obviously wondering if she would acknowledge his victory. Athena shut her mouth and nodded. "Perhaps lack of sleep has caused me to behave irrationally," she admitted, trying to be gracious.

"Can you walk?" he asked, noticing her swaying back and forth.

"Sure. Just give me a...what are you doing?" She cried in horror as Remus scooped her up and carried her inside. "Back in the day, I would have killed a man for such an offense."

"You let me slice you up with a knife, yet you feel uncomfortable with me carrying you?" Remus asked, bemused. By luck, the house had furniture and, after a minute of searching, he found a couch and set her down gently. Athena grudgingly admitted the couch was far more comfortable than collapsing on the floor. However, there was still one more thing that had to be done and had to be done quickly lest she lose her nerve.

"I need you to go," Athena said as harshly as she could, and Remus jerked up, the anger and hurt on his face enough to sadden her.

"So that's it?" he asked stiffly. "You got what you wanted from me and now I'm no longer needed."

The original plan had been to be as mean and cruel as possible, to make Remus flee from her side and never look back. As a telepath, she could easily say the right things to make him hate her. But ultimately, she was a selfish person and couldn't stomach the thought of Remus forever holding her in contempt. "I would like nothing more for you to stay," she said honestly. "But you're only doing so out of obligation. It makes no sense for you to stay now if you're just going to leave later."

Remus looked away, not bothering to deny it. "So you read my mind?"

"A few minutes ago," she admitted. "I couldn't help it. I've done it so often, its subconscious."

There wasn't enough room on the couch, so Remus walked over to the adjacent love seat and sat down. He was quiet for a long minute; the only sound was that of a ticking clock that the previous owners left, and Athena was on the verge of taking a nap when Remus spoke, his voice nothing but a soft whisper. "I want to go with you, Athena, but I can't."

"It's not me, it's you," Athena concluded dryly. "Honestly, just because I was sheltered doesn't mean I haven't heard all the break-up lines."

Remus glared at her, and Athena was sure a retort was coming, but something about her lying wounded on the couch quenched his fury. "I'm not even sure what you're looking for." Not understanding his statement, she reached out for his mind. *I'm not good enough.*

At Remus' ridiculous notion, Athena's giggles became hysterical and Remus, thinking she was laughing at him, which she technically was, leaned back in the chair, waiting for her episode to conclude.

"There you go again," Athena said, wiping a tear from her eye. "How pathetic is it that you don't know your own self-worth? Do you really enjoy being this miserable?"

"Do you enjoy being this cruel?" Remus shot back, her vulnerable state doing nothing to alleviate his anger this time around. "This cold? Can no one have a problem to work out unless sanctioned by Athena?"

"If you were an asshole, I would understand. If you were a jerk, I wouldn't care. But you're an amazingly wonderful guy, and it kills me that you don't see that."

Remus' face flushed a deep maroon, but he said nothing, and Athena, getting fed up with this drawn-out conversation, reached again for his mind. *She doesn't understand.*

"No, I don't. I'm a mind reader and I still don't under-stand. Make me understand, Remus."

"Stay out of my head!" Remus barked, his patience snapping. He leapt out of his seat and Athena stared, unim-pressed. Residents had tried to kill her in the past because they were mildly annoyed. Remus throwing a tantrum was nothing.

"Then tell me or I swear I'll drain you dry of information!" she promised. There went not making Remus hate her. She sighed inwardly; maybe she should start with a dog compan-ion before moving on to a human.

Meanwhile, Remus was pacing back and forth, only halt-ing when Athena threatened to bean him with a pillow unless he stopped. Still he said nothing. Athena was reaching for his mind, grimly determined to find the truth when it happened. "Everything I touch withers and dies!" The words seemed to be wrenched from his gut, and he took a breath before continuing. "Every attempt I make to succeed fails horribly. Every time I try to help someone, it goes so horribly wrong." *Romulus, Delilah, my mom...*

"I think I get it," Athena said, once she was sure he had finished. She was going to add something else, but he opened his mouth to speak and she fell silent. After all, he had listened to her rant without judgment.

"I always mess everything up, Athena, and if it isn't the universe's fault then it has to be mine. So what do I do?" He walked forward, towards Athena, and kneeled down so that he was at her eye level, his face only inches apart from her own. Normally, this would be too close for personal comfort, but she didn't mind as much with Remus. "What do I do when everything I touch turns to ash?"

"We had this conversation before," Athena said with a frown. She flicked him hard on the forehead and Remus rocked back, rubbing the injured spot with his hand while looking at her resentfully.

"I don't quite remember what was discussed."

"You have to keep trying, Remus. You can't stay still just because you're afraid of failing. It's not healthy, and it's unfair to you and everyone around you." Athena wasn't a big lover of motivational speeches, and thought she did okay, especially considering the agony from her healing back and the fact she hadn't slept for more than 24 hours.

Remus shook his head as if trying to shake her words from his mind. He stood up and took a step back from her. "I have to go."

"I left your half of the money in the glove compartment," Athena said, making a tactical retreat. She had planted seeds in his mind and hopefully that would be enough. "Take the car, seeing how I can't use it. I'll be here for at least another six hours recovering."

"Are you sure that's smart?" His sincere concern for her was touching, but at the same time, Athena was worried he was starting to see her as a perpetual damsel in distress.

"We're far enough from the tracker's last signal, and in all honesty, I can't see them organizing another team this quickly anyway. I left a diary at Pandora's Box of all the places I wanted to go. They will, no doubt, spend countless hours on it." She paused to gather her thoughts. "Like I said, I'll be here for another couple of hours, so if you feel like coming back..."

"Yeah...I'll keep that in mind." He looked regretfully at her. "Goodbye, Athena, and I wish you the best in life."

Remus left, leaving Athena to her thoughts. She was sur- prisingly optimistic. Remus was already having second thoughts and, if he didn't return, it wasn't the end of the world. Her eyes drew heavy and, once again, she was im- pressed with how tired she was. She'd only had a couple of cat naps since her escape, and her body was aching for a real sleep. It would be great if when she opened her eyes, Remus would be there making another large pot of his deli- cious spaghetti. And if he wasn't...well, maybe it would do her good to be out by herself. The most important thing was that her enemies would no longer be able to find her. She had obtained freedom.

Chapter 62

Ms. Yang did not have the time nor the patience to deal with this newest bump, yet it couldn't be ignored either. Chris Burlington stood at attention as Matthew Titanos questioned him for the third time. Ms. Yang was doing busy work on her laptop, keeping a keen ear in case she heard something that needed addressing.

"Are you *sure* she didn't say anything else?" Matthew asked suspiciously.

"Yes sir," Chris repeated again. His tone was meant to be professional, but someone with Ms. Yang's hearing could easily catch all the murderous undertones beneath it. Even if she couldn't, the aggression in Mr. Burlington's stance was warning enough.

Matthew, having neither her hearing nor her brains, continued blithely on. "Did anyone mention our situation to her?"

"I doubt any of the guards would. Selene made mention of Athena in regard to Mr. Sylvia's brother. Something along the lines of anyone who got close to Athena was destined to die."

"Are you sure she didn't say anything else?" Matthew asked for the fourth time.

Ms. Yang had to admire Mr. Burlington's restraint as he paused for only a second before replying civilly, "No, sir."

Twenty minutes ago, Chris Burlington had barged in with a new tidbit of information. He had been charged with taking Delilah Lane home, which should have been an easy task. According to Mr. Burlington, Ms. Lane had waited until she was clear of Mr. Burlington's vehicle before shouting that she knew exactly where Athena and Remus were heading and that the two had been planning this caper for years. She said she would explain further in an hour's time, but only to the man in charge, and at a location she had chosen before quickly retreating into the relative safety of her apartment complex.

Matthew was leaning back in his chair with his hands together in a gesture that was supposed to convey intelligence. "Can it be true?" he mumbled to himself while discreetly glancing at Ms. Yang for her thoughts.

Athena's escape was still a conundrum, and until they figured it out, Pandora's Box could not be considered secure. It would explain away a lot of questions if Remus Sylvia had been in on it from the start, but from talking to his brother and father, Ms. Yang didn't get that feeling. Trusting her intuition, she adjusted her glasses in a secret code she and Matthew had long since worked out.

"No, I don't think so," Matthew mused out loud. "Still, to cover our bases, we need to have this meeting with this girl. Better safe than sorry."

Ms. Yang cleared her throat. "Sir, I can delegate this task to one of our guards. Dress him up like he's a top-ranking person, and Ms. Lane would never know the difference."

"Do it," Matthew said before she had even finished. "Please," he added when he felt the rush of heat radiating off her. "Mr. Burlington, you're excused."

Chris nodded to Matthew and left, but not before shooting an unreadable glance at Ms. Yang. As soon as the door slid shut, Matthew got up, walked to the door, and peeked outside. "I saw Tyrone Froce loitering around the last time we met," he explained to Ms. Yang's raised eyebrow. "Eavesdropping."

"I'll look into it," Ms. Yang promised. She had narrowed down the candidates for the mole to only a handful of people and Tyrone was near the top of the list.

Matthew plumped back in his chair, looking bone-tires. "Can you give me a status report?" he asked, a hint of whine in his voice.

Ms. Yang struck a few keys as she wondered how much to tell him. "Athena managed to remove the second tracker, which means either she telepathically found out, or someone got her the information." Matthew's head dipped even lower. "The news isn't as bleak as it sounds. One of Ragnarok's Residents has her in his sights and Athena is unaware of his presence. We know her exact location and status."

The news pepped Matthew right up and he smiled a winning smile. "Excellent work!" he complimented.

"However, there is a problem," Ms. Yang continued, watching the smile disappear again. "Our Ragnarok Resident is keeping track of her with a unique version of remote viewing, and he's nearing depletion of his energy. He won't be able to watch her for long."

Matthew slumped back down again. "If it's not one thing, it's another."

"But..." Ms. Yang went on to say, and Matthew fixed her with an accusatory stare, obviously wondering if she was messing with his emotions on purpose. "Caleb and his team have been following the tracker's last known location and are close enough to intercept."

"And you think they're capable of taking her down?" Matthew scoffed. It was a legitimate question.

"Athena has suffered numerous wounds since her escape. The Resident's opinion is that she is incapable of putting up much of a fight."

Matthew stared. "Do whatever you want," he finally said with an air of surrender.

Ms. Yang had planned to, but she nodded as if she needed his permission before closing her laptop and standing up. Matthew followed her progression out of the room through half-shut eyes. "What should I do?"

"Stay here, take a nap," Ms. Yang said indifferently. "By the time you wake up, the situation will be..." She paused, as the words sounded painfully similar to the ones she uttered when she thought Badger's team would capture her. "Resolved," she finished when Matthew looked at her questioningly.

The door slid open, but Matthew's final question stalled her. "You hate me?"

Ms. Yang left without answering. She would not be a part of Matthew's self-pity monologue, especially since she was doing ten times his workload with none of the credit. And if they failed to capture Athena, it would be her who suffered the consequences, not him.

Out in the halls, she found the hysteria that had gripped Pandora's Box had calmed down, as even Residents needed to take a break after a day of mischief. Still, the atmosphere was bleak; there really weren't enough guards to stop a full-on riot, and rumors of Mr. Titanos purposely sending a team to die against Athena was beginning to surface.

"Pathetic."

Ms. Yang stopped, adjusted her glasses, and turned to face Horus who was looking around with a palpable air of disgust. "I asked you to stay in the car."

"Didn't want to," Horus said, and the raven on his shoulder crowed its agreement.

Horus respected and listened to no one, but long years of working with Ms. Yang had made him lukewarm towards her. He once said it would be a pity if she died, for someone truly incompetent might take her place...it was the closest thing to an affectionate statement one could expect from the Resident.

"And you managed to make it here without confronting any of the guards?" Ms. Yang asked hopefully.

The raven squawked as if she'd made a joke, and Horus shot it an annoyed look. "Those who removed themselves out of my way were allowed to continue on whatever menial tasks assigned to them. Those who didn't..."

"How many?" Ms. Yang prompted.

"Three." Ms. Yang closed her eyes. "None of them are dead," Horus added, his tone indicating he should be thanked for his benevolence.

To rebuke Horus would only lead to a long screaming match, which would only waste time. "Athena's status?" She had been on her way to ask him anyway.

"Injured and alone."

"The boy?"

"He's doing what a human does best...fleeing as fast as he can."

Horus' voice carried, and several officers had overheard. Ms. Yang ignored the gawking and hostile glances. "Why would he leave her now?" she wondered.

"What a stupid question," Horus sneered. He backed away from the sudden rush of heat radiating from her, but still he persisted. "Obviously, with her injuries, this is the best chance he got at getting away from her." It was a plausible explanation, but Ms. Yang's instincts said otherwise. "Hold," Horus said as his raven squawked. "It appears he's heading back to her."

Interesting, but not her greatest concern. "How long can you maintain the remote viewing?"

Horus huffed as if she was personally questioning his masculinity, but after a minute, he said, "Fifteen minutes. Perhaps twenty."

"Keep an eye..." Ms. Yang stopped as his eyebrows were already furrowed in challenge. "I really need help. Could you please keep an eye on Athena?"

Horus nodded, appeased. "And you?"

"I...I have to meet a teenage girl to see if she knows how Athena escaped."

Horus laughed, a boisterous sound that scared those around him and, at the same time, the raven shook its head in pity. After a few seconds, it nipped at Horus' ear to tell him they had properly showed amusement at her situation. "All this because a slip of a girl managed to escape?" Horus asked.

"This slip of a girl escaped from Pandora's Box, defeated two teams sent after her, killed Fides, and managed to free herself of the trackers. I need to know how so it won't happen again."

Horus stilled, and Ms. Yang wondered what she had said. "She killed Fides?"

"I..." It truly showed how tired she was that she'd forgotten to pass this information on. "Yes, Fides died trying to recapture her."

Horus and the raven exchange glances. "Well, this has become interesting," he stated. "Once captured, I wish to meet with this Athena."

Not a chance in hell, but Ms. Yang was still curious. "Why?"

Horus flashed a grin that showed every single one of his white teeth. "To thank her. I hated Fides; eventually, he would have died at my hands, which would have caused a rift between you and me, and would ultimately have led to your death."

Before Ms. Yang could show her displeasure, the lights flashed red and the alarm started up again. It seemed like the Residents' break was over.

The tracker beeped one last time before forever falling silent, causing contrasting feelings within the lead van. Caleb glanced at the faces surrounding him in the vehicle. On the one hand, there were the men and women who were depressed because it looked like Athena would escape, and they felt responsible for releasing such a monster into the world. On the other hand, they were cowards who were relieved because they didn't have to face such a dangerous monster themselves. Before anyone could meekly make the suggestion they head back home, Ms. Yang had called with precise directions to find Athena and damned if she wouldn't share how she'd gotten the information, despite how much Caleb barked at her.

She hung up with the excuse of having to attend a very important meeting, leaving Caleb fuming for a good minute.

Omar cleared his throat. "So, do we—"

"Yes, we follow her damn directions!" Caleb snapped. "Ain't much else we can do."

"We can leave?" someone had the gall to ask from the back.

Caleb thought of ignoring it, but, figuring that would be too kind, craned his neck so that he could clearly see Dominique fidgeting nervously in his seat. "Sure, someone can slide the door open and you can jump out." The van increased the speed, emphasizing that it would not slow down to accommodate him. "And if you somehow manage to make it unscathed and back home, don't even think of coming in the next day. You won't be welcomed." Caleb wanted to say more, but oddly and annoyingly enough, Pandora's Box did have strict protocol on how to treat employees, and he didn't want to be stuck taking another anger management class.

Dominique looked around to see if anyone would come to his defense. When no one did, he fell silent.

With Dominique satisfactorily snubbed, Caleb turned his attention to the front where Omar was driving. Caleb usually preferred to drive, but his eyesight had been waning the last couple of years. No one knew except a few trusted friends, and Omar was among them.

"How close are we?"

"From Athena's last known location? About twenty minutes."

"Do it in fifteen," was Caleb's response. Omar nodded, but Caleb caught his smirk. They didn't think he knew, but for years, he and the others had been padding the time table for their tasks so that when Caleb demanded they do it quicker, it was easier to manage. Caleb allowed them to think they were getting away with it because it relieved stress for them to think they were getting one over on the boss. Omar glanced out the window and did a double-take.

"What the hell is wrong with you?" Caleb snarled as Omar nearly rear-ended another car. "You trying to kill us before Athena has the chance to?"

Omar hesitated. "Sir, I just saw Remus Sylvia driving in the other direction. He's the boy—"

"I know who Remus Sylvia is," Caleb snapped, his heartbeat quickening. He glanced at his watch. It was now 6:50. "You better be damn sure it was him."

"Positive, sir." Omar was one of the guards assigned to the mall project where Athena and Remus had supposedly first met. There were some who thought they had been in contact for years, but no one had yet to come up with a valid theory on how they'd done it, if they'd even done it at all.

"Did you see Athena with him?"

"No, sir. I saw no one but Remus. Doesn't mean she wasn't there."

If Omar said he saw Remus, then he saw Remus.

"Does the gal know we're coming?" he wondered out loud.

"Sir?"

"We never officially determined how long a range Athena's telepathic skills are. She might already know we're coming, and it would be just like her to send a diversion to split us up."

"Divide and conquer," Jack Nellar, a reasonably reliable man blurted out, then winced, expecting a severe reprimand from Caleb.

Fortunately, Caleb was too deep in thought to respond. "Of course it's not impossible to think she's hiding in the backseat. She could be making her escape right now."

No one envied Caleb at the moment. He was stuck between two impossible choices, either of them potentially leading to disaster, failure, or death. What was worse, he had to make the decision now, before Remus got too far away.

"Sir?" Omar asked. "We need a decision."

"Screw it," Caleb muttered. "Omar, turn this van around and find that kid. If you're wrong, my last task as your superior will be kicking your ass! Someone call Froce and tell him what we're doing. If he starts to give you too much lip, tell him Caleb said to deal with it. Gentlemen," Caleb said with an uncharacteristically broad grin on his usual scowling face. "I always wanted to say this... Follow. That. Car!"

Chapter 63

Remus was dizzy with the same thoughts going over and over in his head, so much so that twice he had to pull over as intense nausea threatened to have him vomiting. Twice he had turned around to go back, but then changed his mind at the last second. She was expecting him to come back; that manipulative little witch expected him to come running back, despite all the horror and pain he had endured because of her. He seethed, gripping the steering wheel until his knuckles hurt; it was very easy to be angry at Athena for dumping such a huge and immense decision in his lap...but at the same time, it was kind of touching that she had such absolute faith in him. No one had ever trusted him to this extent, and he wasn't sure if he liked the feeling of being relied on so heavily, even if it was by a girl who could easily take care of herself without him. It wasn't fair. Of all the people he could have bowled over at the mall.

His self-pity was interrupted as a car horn blared loudly behind him. It seemed he had attracted a fair amount of ill-will by only going fifteen mph and, like an idiot, the car behind him continued to press down on the horn until Remus drove to the side of the road, allowing the impatient car to pass. He took the keys out of the ignition and pocketed them before reclining the seat so that he was staring at the roof of the car. Driving was not an option, at least not until he got his head on straight. Not only that, he was both physically and mentally spent; the day he'd spent with Athena seemed more like a month. How did she think he could last a week in her company if he couldn't even keep his eyes open after just one day?

A car slowed down, checking to see if he needed assistance, and Remus sat up and waved them off before reaching for the glove compartment as a sudden suspicion leapt to his mind, but no, the half of the money Athena promised was in an envelope just like she had said it would be. He started to count it, but his heart wasn't in it and he stopped at three thousand. With a sigh, he dumped the money back in the glove compartment and slammed it shut as anger got the better of him.

"How dare she dismiss me!" he seethed, ignoring the small detail that he was talking to himself. "I said I would stay until she was better. She had no right to tell me to go. She didn't stop to think...if she dies it means it's on me, and I won't let that woman turn me into a killer!" With indignant anger and flimsy excuse in place, he put the keys back in the ignition and prepared to drive back to Athena and give the telepath a verbal piece of his mind.

It always happened. As soon as Remus made a decision, the universe always intervened, knocking the confidence out of him and replacing it with misery. This instance was no exception. Remus had just turned the key to start up the engine when a dark van screeched to a stop directly beside him. The van door opened, revealing a hoard of men, and though they were dressed in regular clothes, unlike the army at the hotel, Remus had no doubt about who they worked for.

"Turn off the engine and get out!" one of them screamed, pointing a very impressive gun at him. Remus didn't know much about guns, so he couldn't tell what type the man was carrying, but imagined any type that shot bullets were probably to his disadvantage. "Get out!" the man screamed again.

Back in his naïve days, before Athena, Remus would have followed his instructions and hoped for the best, but a mere day with the grey-eyed Resident had taught him the stupidity of such action. He shifted the car into reverse and gunned the engine. The car flew back, clipping one of the men who had been trying to sneak up behind him, and he felt a disturbing lack of sympathy or pity. They were planning on killing him after all.

"Shit!" he yelped as a bullet shattered his front window, instinctively covering his eyes to avoid debris, but still with his foot on the gas.

"Damn it, we want him alive!" a voice screamed, which was promising, but not enough to make him stop. Another shot rang out and Remus ducked low while sharply turning the steering wheel, forcing the car to go across the road backwards and directly across the path of a random truck.

Remus thought—knew—he was about to die as the truck's headlights barreled toward him. His whole life was supposed to pass before his eyes, but instead, only the last twenty-four hours played in his head—Athena's mocking smile, his success in convincing a whole room he was a Homeland Security agent, the spaghetti meal that Athena had all but inhaled, making Athena laugh, the way her cheeks puffed up when she was annoyed with him, the surgery he had performed on her shoulder and her calming him down throughout it despite the intense pain she had to have been in. It wasn't his entire life, but he didn't feel cheated for focusing on his time with Athena; the rest of his life wasn't really worth watching over again.

The universe must have had different plans for him, because, whether the truck was able to slow down or Remus managed to speed up in time, the collision was avoided by the slightest of margins, the front of Remus' car kissing the side of the truck as it scooted by. Forgetting to take his foot off the gas, Remus fell into the ditch between the two lanes, the crash jolting him roughly in his seat. Before he could recover, his car was surrounded by men, their anger evident on their faces.

"Get out or die!" one of them ordered, confirming Remus' belief that these were not friendly cops bent on asking him a couple of questions.

"Perhaps a third option is available," Remus suggested, even as his door was opened and hands forcibly pulled him from the car. He was quickly patted down and shoved face-first inside the van, which had driven alongside the ditch separating the two lanes. He stumbled inside, tripping over a bag and landing painfully on his left arm. "Was I really going that slow?" Remus huffed as he struggled to an upright position, looking around as he did.

Instead of being arranged like an ordinary vehicle with seats occupying the space between the two doors, the seats, more like long cushioned benches, were placed alongside the van's walls, creating a relatively wide space between them. Near the back doors there were around five-to-six silver canisters, all of them over four feet tall. The canisters, along with the crate of gas masks directly beside them, had Remus wondering how far these people would go to reclaim Athena.

A man laid a hand on Remus' shoulder, gripping tightly when Remus struggled to throw him off. Another man brutally shoved him, driving Remus into one of the benches, where two more hands grabbed his arms and forced him down into a sitting position as the rest of the men piled back in.

"I suggest you stop struggling," one of the men said, in what Remus assumed was supposed to be an ominous voice, but in actuality just sounded quite cheesy, and Remus responded boldly even as a couple of the mysterious organization's operatives sat beside him on both sides, wedging him in.

"I'll take your suggestion into consideration. Who the hell do you people think you are?"

"Gutsy," a voice said approvingly. "I wasn't expecting gutsy. I figured you'd be more of a hide in a corner until Athena kills all the bad people type of guy."

Remus looked directly across the van at the man speaking and had to snicker. The man had obviously watched too many John Wayne movies when he was a kid. He was a slightly beefy guy dressed in traditional cowboy garments, complete with a hat, thick bushy mustache, and a dark pair of sunglasses.

"That's funny. I figured you people would be a bunch of idiots that wouldn't have enough sense to recognize when they're beat, and look at that! I wasn't disappointed!"

There was stillness in the air, and Remus realized it had more to do with who he'd said the insult to rather than the insult itself. There appeared to be a healthy fear when it came to the cowboy, and in a world where anyone could be hiding destructive and impossible powers, it paid to watch what you said.

"Funny." The cowboy grinned, at ease as he leaned back in his seat. "Dominique, why don't you radio Froce and tell him we got the boy?"

Remus figured he needed to display a confident attitude if he wanted to get out of this mess alive. "I'm getting sick and tired of being known as 'the boy.' My name is Remus Sylvia. And you are?"

There was almost a collective gasp from the flunkies, and though Remus was absolutely terrified, he felt a sense of fun as he antagonized a man that everyone else was afraid of. The cowboy, however, took it in stride. "Caleb, since you asked."

"Good for you."

"There's a fine line between gutsy and annoying," Caleb warned. "Make sure you don't cross it." Even though he used a light tone, there was a power in his voice that seemed to demand respect, and Remus swallowed, suddenly nervous. Still, he refused to be daunted.

"You act like crossing another line will make a difference. I'm dead anyway."

"You don't have to be."

Remus stared hard at Caleb, but the man's glasses hid his thoughts. The van started to move forward, picking up speed as it did so, and Remus wondered if the police were on their way. Surely someone had seen him get kidnapped in the middle of the street. "I have known for quite some time that if you captured me, you'd kill me."

"Who told you that?" Caleb pressed. "Was it Athena?" Like before, they were trying to establish a claim that Athena was the lying monster and they were the ones trying to protect society from her.

"George Hacker tried to kill me. Fides took a whack at me also. Do I need any more proof?"

"George Hacker was a dick," Caleb said, and a couple of the flunkies nodded their agreement. "And I don't know who this Fides is, but I'm guessing it's a crazed Resident. Plus, they were both working for another organization, separate from ours."

"Ragnarok?"

Caleb looked surprised, but nodded. "Correct."

"And so you're Pandora's Box?"

"Damn, it seems Athena's shared a lot with you," Caleb observed, and Remus could tell it wasn't a good thing. "But we're not them. We have no problem returning you in one piece to your family." Remus felt sick to his stomach. That was the last thing he wanted. If he never saw Maris again, he would consider himself lucky. Fortunately, Caleb mistook Remus' silence for consideration. "And all you have to do is tell us where Athena is. I'll give you my word that if you assist us, you will not be hurt and, boy, I'm a man of my word."

Remus believed Caleb's conviction. It was impossible not to. If he told them everything he knew, they would ship him back to his dad alive. Maris wouldn't dare risk another assassination attempt. He would be safe in his father's home. The decision had to be the easiest decision in the world.

"No."

There was a stirring in the van. "And why the hell not?" Caleb growled, his sunglasses hiding his reaction. "It sounds damn reasonable to me. You do your patriotic duty and you'll be set free."

"Because I'm not so sure it's my patriotic duty."

Caleb rubbed his greying mustache, expecting him to say more, so Remus said the first thing that popped in his head.

"It feels more like...betraying a friend."

"Betraying a friend?" the man named Dominique scoffed. "She's a Resident!"

Remus shot him a look and Dominique shrunk back. In the back of his mind, Remus realized the change. Before he'd met Athena, he couldn't even make a five-year-old in a wheelchair cower in fear; now he was scaring fully armed soldiers. In the past twenty-four hours, he had required a toughness he'd never possessed before.

"What does being a Resident have to do with anything?" he asked. "Are her grey eyes enough to categorize her as a subhuman? Does her physical abilities make her some type of monster? So what if she can read minds or shoot lightning, she's still a human!"

"She can shoot lighting?" someone piped up. Remus mentally kicked himself.

Caleb spoke, his voice snuffing out all others. "She's also unhinged, boy. I'm sure you noticed. Sometimes she ain't entirely there."

"True," he conceded. "But that's only because you made her like that. What gives you the right?" he demanded, suddenly angry. He leaned forward as best he could, but the guard beside him placed a restraining hand on his arm. "What gives you the right to take a girl, experiment on her for most of her life, then call her a monster and hunt her down when your experiment succeeds?"

Remus didn't know where Pandora's Box got their soldiers from or what type of training it took to make them adequately efficient in dealing with forced human mutation, but whatever it was seemed to drain all concept of pity from them and they took his rant with stoic postures along with a slight sense of ridicule. As if he was complaining there was a lack of cookies for Santa Clause to eat.

Caleb, in particular, remained unmoved. "Kid, I don't got the time nor patience to debate philosophy with you. In a couple of minutes, a van of my men will enter Athena's current location, and I don't want another incident like the one at the hotel. Is she still there? Why did you two split up? Does she know we're coming? Did she set a trap?"

Caleb's questions revealed a surprising amount of information. They were heading toward Athena, which meant they knew her location, but little else. How were they finding her? It seemed ridiculous to believe there was a third tracker, but it had to be considered. Pandora's Box knew she had telepathy, but seemed to be clueless as to the range and strength of it. All of this would have been relieving if Athena wasn't wounded because of a crude surgery he had performed.

"Answer my questions!" Caleb barked. Remus' heart began to beat heavily, his mouth became dry, and he had a difficult time swallowing.

"No," Remus murmured. Then he repeated it louder as Caleb leaned in, pretending not to hear him. "If your men are stupid enough to ambush Athena, then they deserve whatever happens to them."

He had crossed the line Caleb was talking about. Nothing observable happened; Caleb made no sudden move, but the aura around him changed to something a lot more menacing, eerily similar to Athena's aura when she had killed Ragnarok's men at the gas station. Remus leaned to the side in a futile effort to put as much space between him and Caleb as possible.

"Stop the car," the cowboy ordered, his voice low and guttural, and the van immediately responded to his wishes, driving off the road and lurching to an abrupt stop. Caleb had to do a fair amount of maneuvering to dislodge himself from all the men crammed on his seat, but eventually, he stood up.

"What are you doing?" Remus asked, his sudden confidence vanishing as Caleb loomed over him.

"Stand him up." Remus was shoved from his seat and

stumbled awkwardly forward, barely managing a collision into Caleb's chest. "Tell Froce not to make a move until we get there." Caleb cracked his knuckles in a very menacing manner. "If he argues, tell him to shut it. I ain't letting us walk into one of her traps. Last chance," he said, talking to Remus. "Spill what you know."

"You think you're scary?" Remus scoffed, proud that his voice didn't shake when he spoke. "My father has been intimidating me for—" He barely saw Caleb's hand moved as the soldier punched him, the blow rocketing off the left side of his face. Remus reeled away, but before he could react, Caleb jabbed him in the throat. As Remus struggled for breath, the cowboy wannabe grabbed him by the shoulders and pushed him towards the back of the van, where he tripped over one of the canisters and landed on his back, his head bouncing off another canister.

"Sir?" Remus heard one of the other guards asked tentatively, and Caleb answered gruffly.

"It's fine. Everybody stay where you are. I don't need no help with a whelp like this."

Remus heard the clatter of Caleb's feet as the man approached and he scrambled to his feet.

"Smart," Caleb approved. "Don't ever let the enemy catch you when you're down." He raised an eyebrow over his tinted sunglasses as Remus grabbed one of the canisters by the top in an attempt to throw it, but it proved to be too heavy. It still didn't stop the rest of the van from issuing a collective murmur of alarm, alerting Remus that whatever was in the canisters was probably something he didn't want out. Caleb darted forward and Remus covered his face only to be punched in the chest, the force sending him backwards. Remus lashed out with a wild punch of his own, but Caleb blocked it with contemptuous ease before attacking with a jab. This time it missed, as Remus backpedaled, his momentary victory ruined as he hit the double doors at the back. He ducked as Caleb punched, the cowboy's fist hitting the back of the van where Remus' head used to be. Caleb hissed in pain, but at the same time, he kicked, his leg connecting with Remus' temple, and Remus slammed into the ground with no more energy to move or defend himself. This was the extent of his ability—a three-minute fight with a regular human years past his prime. And he thought he could handle Athena's company when he couldn't even handle a decent fight; the universe laughed at his stupidity.

"Watch out, kid!" Caleb warned, and Remus looked up to see one of the silver cylinders tilting forward. He rolled over just in time to avoid being crushed by the container. "Close one," Caleb whistled as Remus felt his knee press hard against his back.

"Sir?" a voice called out. "Froce is threatening to face Athena by himself if you don't hurry up."

"Damn it!" Caleb yelped. "Tell him he better not if he knows what's good for him. If Athena don't do him in, I will!" The pressure from Caleb's knee increased. "All right, kid, enough playing around!"

"Playing around?" Remus asked incredulously. "I thought I was fighting for my life!" He could have sworn he heard soft snickering from the front, but Caleb's actions diverted his attention; Caleb's hands were on the silver cylinder that had toppled over, and as he watched, he realized the soldier was messing with the valve, trying to release the contents within. Whatever it was terrified the rest of the guards, so it couldn't be anything Remus wished to breathe. He opened his mouth to demand to know what Caleb was doing. A sharp slap to his face and Remus craned his neck, looking at his mirrored reflection in Caleb's sunglasses. The cowboy mouthed something, the words not at all clear but the meaning obvious. He wanted Remus to stay silent.

From the viewpoint of everyone else, it simply looked like Caleb was leaning in to threaten him, the other canisters and boxes obscuring their view. Remus swallowed, sweat beginning to pour down his face as Caleb continued to try and release the valve. It only made matters worse when the canister began to hiss. Remus, being the closest, would be affected by the gas before it affected anyone else.

"Last time I'm asking," Caleb yelled, raising his voice and trying to drown out the hiss of the gas slowly creeping in. "What is Athena up to?"

"I don't know!" Remus answered, matching his voice so that it was as loud as Caleb's. A sudden inspiration struck him, a recourse that Athena would think of and implement. "She knew you were coming and made a call!"

"What call?" Caleb demanded. The pressure in Remus' back lessened as Caleb raised his knee, an acknowledgement that he knew Remus was working with him. "A call to who?"

"I don't know! She didn't tell me her plans." Already Remus was growing disoriented as he breathed in the odorless gas, and still he forged on. "When I left, and she told me to leave, she was making a call. Planning some type of trap...and I'm pretty sure I heard her mention C4," he added for good measure.

"Tell Froce not to enter!" Caleb ordered, his voice becoming harder and harder to comprehend from the gas fogging up his brain. "Tell him we think they're might be explosives!"

"How do we know he's telling the truth?" someone asked.

Caleb said something scathing, but Remus could no longer understand it. His eyelids became heavy as death crept up on him. Had he beaten the universe? He didn't want to die, but at least he would die protecting Athena; perhaps it was a stalemate. Remus closed his eyes, intent on only resting them for a moment. And then...

Chapter 64

"Athena, are you there? Athena? Avalon says you're a telepath and that you might be able to send your thoughts as well as receive. If this is true, please answer me. I'm on your side."

No answer.

"Perhaps you're skeptical because I mentioned Avalon. Avalon is not your enemy; it's your ally...kind of. Excuse me if I'm not making any sense. I've never tried to have a conversation with a telepath before, and it doesn't help that I feel stupid talking inside my head. Let me start from the beginning. Avalon and Ragnarok have been at war for over three decades. Pandora's Box is only a side note in this war, with little value for either side. Think of it like a pawn in a game of chess. Anyway...it just occurred to me that you might know all this, being a telepath. Crap, this is hard! It would help if you could talk back... Nothing? I guess I'll continue. So Avalon and Ragnarok are at war; that's the main point you need to take away from it. But not like a war as you know it, more like a cold war. Do you even know what a cold war is? Not trying to insult, but spending your whole life in Pandora's Box probably led to some gaps in your education. Instead of all-out battles, this war is more about subterfuge, assassinations, sabotage. We do this because neither side wants the humans of the planet to know about us, and they would notice a Resident battle. Trust me.

"That's why we intervened at the hotel. Everyone frozen? That was one of our Residents. I know. Pretty cool, right? We did this not to help, but to keep our existence a secret. Understand? Hope so, because here's where things get interest-

ing.

"*Avalon knew about your escape and thought you would soon be captured. Sorry we underestimated you. Or maybe you're proud we underestimated you. Anyway, you have piqued our leader's interest and she wishes to help you escape. Good news, right? Problem is that she can't help directly. You see, Ragnarok and Avalon have rules set up for their war and one of them is no direct interference with the other's Residents. Don't get me wrong, both sides break the rule all the time, but they never get caught, and sadly, although you'd probably disagree, you're a Resident of Ragnarok. Sorry. However, I can offer a small amount of help...crap! I forgot to explain who I am!*

"*I'm an Avalon Resident working undercover at Pandora's Box. You have no clue how tough it was to sneak me into the good graces of Pandora's Box...but I digress. The point is Ragnarok doesn't know I'm with Avalon, nor do they know I'm a Resident, and it has to stay that way. Sorry. Your freedom is not worth my position at Pandora's Box.*

"*So what can I offer? A small chance, a slight shift in the odds that are currently against you. You might not even need me; your own mole did a good job taking out one of the vans, but I'll be here if you do require my assistance. Athena? I hope you heard my whole spiel. Andraste assured me your telepathy has a mile range, and if she's wrong, and I did all this for nothing, I swear I'm going to place my foot up her...*"

Chapter 65

"Sir, we lost contact with the other van," Payton informed, her voice cracked with tension.

"Damn it!" Froce didn't bother to hide his fear. Only a fool wouldn't have a healthy fear of Residents, and Athena was shaping up to be the worst of them. Plus, the last information about C4 and Athena possibly calling in outside help was enough to have him second-guessing every move he made.

"Sir?" the driver, whose name Froce couldn't quite remember, asked.

Upon Caleb's instructions, Froce had the van pull off onto the side of the road with the understanding that they would eventually get moving once the cowboy caught up, but now that was looking less and less likely.

"Sir?" the driver asked again, and Froce silenced him with a semi-hostile look.

"Try again."

Payton Trist spoke into the radio, waited a moment, spoke into the radio again, this time more urgently, before glancing at Froce with a negative shake of her head. Froce cursed silently under his breath as he contemplated his options. The neutralization of Athena was the main objective. Her capture or death took precedence over the life of Caleb and his men, but abandoning them to their fate when he might be able to save them was an action he could not do without thought. And there were other factors to consider. Like Athena calling for help.

"Who would Athena call?" Froce mused out loud. "For that matter, she's been stuck at Pandora's Box her whole life without access to a phone. How would she call someone in the first place?"

His question was half-rhetorical, but Payton answered seriously. "Perhaps she didn't use a phone. If she is a telepath, could she maybe make contact with others using only her mind?"

"There are other organizations that use Residents," David Tomoghan said quietly. David had found religion after joining Pandora's Box, and saw the Residents as demons that, if released, would inflict apocalyptic horrors on the earth. He wasn't the first man to think this, but these types of people made Froce uncomfortable. They had no concern for collateral damage when it came to dealing with Residents, easily justifying the deaths of twenty men to kill one of them. "Perhaps she came into contact with one of them."

It made a certain type of sense, yet... "I think it's a lie," Froce declared, going with his instinct that had saved him countless times over the years. "I think that's what Athena wants us to believe, which means she's stalling for time, and that's the one thing we can't afford to give her." Damaged pride was an easy price to pay if it meant the life of his men and success of his mission, so he made a phone call he really didn't want to make.

"What is it?" Ms. Yang demanded without preamble, and Froce answered in the same manner.

"Caleb and his van went dark after capturing Remus. Athena might have C4 with her. What does your source say about this?"

A lengthy silence followed. "Wait," she ordered. A minute went by. "There is no C4, Athena is alone."

"And Caleb?" Froce demanded.

"Don't know. The Resident in question only has strength for one remote viewing. He can't check on Caleb without taking eyes off Athena, and that's unacceptable." There was a stir in the van. Everyone suspected they were tracking Athena through Resident means, but to hear it stated out loud caused discontent. "Continue your mission to apprehend Athena. Afterwards, we can check on the safety of your comrades." She disconnected the call before Tyrone could respond, and he made sure to hide his anger at the dismissal.

"We're moving out," he ordered. "Everyone keep your wits about you."

"What about Caleb and the others?" Payton asked.

"I have given my order!" Froce responded sharply, a reprimand in his voice, and Payton lapsed into a sullen silence. "We'll go back after we've checked out Athena's last location."

The silence stretched on, Froce checking his gun three more times and radioing Caleb six more times. Their numbers had been cut in half before the fight had even begun, and depression rolled around the van. "Sir, we're here," the driver said. Herman. That was his name, Herman.

Froce looked out the window at the dark house with the foreclosed sign in the front yard. No movement from within, but of course, if Athena knew they were here, there wouldn't be. "Park out of sight. She may know we're here, but if she doesn't, no use advertising it. We split up into two teams. Team A goes in and Team B hangs back in case she tries to sneak out. Herman, keep trying to reach Caleb, and if you establish contact, direct him to this location."

Team A consisted of Mycheal Lawyer, David Tomoghan, Delmon Roache, and Payton Trist. Mycheal was a relatively new employee with a brusque personality, but his military record was very impressive. He'd had very few dealings with Residents, which could be a liability, but more importantly, Mycheal had had virtually no dealings with Athena and didn't know about her barbaric years, which meant he didn't feel that twinge of fear every time someone mentioned her name. Tomoghan spent his days trying to convert others to his cause against Residents. In spite of his beliefs, he was one of the more levelheaded individuals at Pandora's Box. He could possibly be a good defense against Athena's mind games. Roache was an ex-mercenary and everything his last name suggested. He was one of the sleaziest, most dislikeable men Froce knew, and he didn't appreciate the way Roache looked at some of the younger Residents. Froce had chosen him because he had an efficient, if not brutal, way of dealing with unruly Residents at Pandora's Box, and if Athena needed to be put down, Delmon would be the one to do so without hesitation. Payton was the last member, and from her record, Froce knew she'd spent several years in the Marines before being discharged for failure to comply. It was rare to find females at Pandora's Box, and even rarer to see them last as long as Payton had. He was betting a female might have a better rapport with Athena, and he still wanted to bring her in alive.

"There's a good chance she's already left, but if she

hasn't, I prefer to take her in alive." Froce cleared his throat and made sure his next words were very clear and precise. "That being said, if Athena comes at you, or does anything remotely threatening, shoot her. Shoot to kill and don't dare hesitate." He looked at each man to make sure they understood. "She might try to charm you, and she certainly looks sweet and innocent, but I can't begin to count how many people she killed today alone."

Nothing more needed to be said, and he tried not to dwell on the fact that his tactics were eerily similar to Brandon's, the leader of the Ragnarok squad that had failed so epically at the hotel. The walk from the van to the house took a minute, as Froce had the van parked so that Athena couldn't look out the window and easily spot it. Learning from Brandon's mistake, everyone wore concealed bulletproof vests under street clothes and carried only weapons that could be concealed, trading firing rate for stealth. They might have made a strange-looking bunch, all of them walking in a line with different degrees of nervousness on their faces, but no one would think of them as terrorists and call the police.

Froce was just starting to believe they could pull this off when a hissing sound erupted from the side.

Mycheal was the first to react. "Duck!" he screamed, diving to the ground as he did so. A second later, he was sprayed with water as a neighboring lawn's sprinklers switched on.

"Mr. Lawyer, please get off the ground. We have work to do," Froce said with far more patience then he actually felt. At least the man had good reflexes. To his squad's credit, no one laughed as Mycheal stood up, his face flushed with embarrassment. Payton did give him a good-natured pat on the back, which only served to deepen the man's scowl.

A couple of feet later, David almost tripped over an empty bottle, the soldier regaining has balance at the last second. Froce tried to squash the feeling that he was in a comedy movie and that Athena would trounce them in painful but hilarious ways. The rest of the way went without incident, and Froce approached the door, casting one last look behind him, hoping to see Caleb drive up with his leather boots and glasses ready to "kick some ass." When his hopes failed to materialize, he kicked the door in, not caring if Athena heard. Stealth hadn't worked for the last two teams, so he doubted it would be of any help now.

The house was still, with no movement or sounds coming forth. The walls were bare, absent of paintings or pictures of loved ones. The hallway was painted a grotesque pink and seemed to beckon ominously for Froce to come in and meet his fate. Froce mentally shook his head; working at Pandora's Box tended to make the average man see monsters and dire symbolisms in everyday life.

His squad quickly dispersed, spreading out in pairs, and Froce felt a sense of pride. Pandora's Box didn't train their operatives for raids, but his team was on par with the covert squads he used to lead years ago.

"Clear!" Mycheal yelled after checking the kitchen.

"Dining room's clear," Payton said without Mycheal's enthusiasm. "Moving on to the bathroom."

"No need," Delmon said. "We found her."

Delmon's oily voice lacked urgency, but Froce still sprinted to his location, readying his pistol in case the Resident was currently choking the life out of him. Instead, he found Delmon and David, both still alive with eyes pinned on a motionless figure on a red couch. Froce feared it was one of Athena's victims until he drew nearer and discovered it was Athena, sleeping or pretending to be asleep, her small frame looking incredible fragile. The terrifying Resident that had all of Pandora's Box fearing for the world's safety was taking a quick nap, unaware that her captors had come to take her home. The most bizarre part was that she snored. Badly.

"What happened?" Froce was too cynical to believe it would be this easy.

Delmon shrugged, his gun never wavering far from Athena's face. "She was like this when I came in." He didn't miss the way Delmon's eyes went up and down Athena's frame, stopping momentarily at her chest. Pretending not to notice, he made a note to keep Delmon far apart from Athena on the ride home.

Footsteps from the left, and Froce's hand drifted to his gun. Payton rounded the corner with Mycheal only a beat behind him, and both stopped and stared with distrustful eyes. "She's asleep?" Payton asked with a mixture of surprise and wariness.

"That certainly makes our job easier," David observed.

"Are we sure this isn't a ploy?" Mycheal asked, voicing Froce's concerns. "This seems too easy, and we still haven't heard back from the other van. For all we know, she wanted us to find her."

"Hmmm, you're back," Athena said as she stretched lazily on the couch. Instantly, every eye and gun was pointed in her direction. Athena opened her eyes and blinked a couple of times in surprise. "Well, you're not who I was expecting," she commented mildly.

Froce took lead. "Athena, I'm authorized to shoot if necessary. In fact, after the damage you caused, they'd prefer if I shoot you, so if you make one move I don't like..."

Athena looked him straight in the eyes and uttered only one word. "Remus?"

Payton and David shot each other quick glances of surprise. Mycheal, the professional soldier, never took his eyes off the target. Neither did Delmon, but for different reasons. Still, it was a given that everyone was thinking the same thought.

"I see," Athena said, closing her eyes. "Caleb picked him up and you haven't heard from him since."

Froce was taken aback, but never allowed his gun to waver. "You can read minds!"

Athena's eyes opened, her gaze mocking, as she looked at him. "I didn't realize my abilities were still in dispute." She was needling them and seemed to be enjoying it. Athena looked them over and smiled a menacing smile. "Tell you what. Why don't you try *not* thinking about your deepest, darkest inner secrets?"

Froce refused to let Athena's taunts unnerve him. "Your only choice is to cooperate. Failure to follow my precise orders will result in death."

Athena did not look impressed. She wrinkled her nose as if a foul smell was in the air. "Can you please get that man away from me? His thoughts are disgusting!" Froce cast Delmon a look. "Not him," Athena said smugly. "The other one. David."

"It's not true," David said tightly, looking around at them. "Lies from the devil meant to deceive us."

"For a man of God, you have some really dark impulses," she taunted before frowning. "Wait a minute...I think I got my wires crossed. Yep, Delmon is the one with the dark impulses, not David. So which one of you is the suicidal one?"

"Enough." Froce wished Caleb was here. Even at her

worst, Caleb still had some degree of control over Athena. Which reminded him... "Athena, do you know what happened to Caleb's van?"

"No idea," Athena said airily. She made no move to sit up, which was odd as she was at a disadvantage. "They're outside my limit of telepathy. Maybe Remus killed them all. He's much more resourceful than you give him credit for."

"If you're not up in the next ten seconds, I'm going to kill you."

Athena's smile dimmed, as she must have read his mind and found him to be completely serious. The more she talked and stalled them, the more likely she'd figure out a way to escape. "That was my thinking," Athena admitted. She struggled to get up. As she was doing so, her shoulder rubbed against the couch and she wasn't quite able to mask the flash of pain that crossed her face.

"You operated on your shoulder," Froce blurted out with dawning realization. The look Athena gave him was hateful. "That's how you disabled the bug."

"Correct, if you replace 'you' with 'Remus,' and if you replace 'operate' with 'butcher.'" She smiled as if she'd said something particularly funny, all animosity towards Froce vanishing. "Swell guy, but he's not growing up to be a surgeon."

"Mycheal, search her and cuff her," Froce ordered. He didn't send Delmon or David because he feared Athena's influence on them, and if she managed to get her arms around Payton, she would have herself a female hostage. "If she makes any sudden moves, get the hell out of there. Athena, any sudden moves and you know what will happen."

To his credit, Mycheal didn't even hesitate. Froce was half-expecting him to protest, but the man simply handed both his guns to Payton—they all knew the risks of allowing Athena to get close to a weapon—and crept forward where Athena sat motionless. She cocked her head to the side and gave him a playful look before standing up, her movements less awkward than just a moment ago. "Didn't I threaten to kill you if I ever saw you again?" she pondered, her question more inquisitive than rhetorical.

"Yes, ma'am, you did," Mycheal said coolly, and Froce's respect for the man grew. He quickly patted Athena down, and when he didn't find anything, he took out a pair of handcuffs. "Ma'am, if you will turn around."

Athena looked up at the ceiling deep in thought. "You present me with a dilemma, Mycheal Lawyer. I quite clearly promised you if I ever saw you again, I'd kill you, and I haven't broken a promise yet."

"If you can hurry up and make a decision so we can go home," Mycheal said, never once giving the impression that he was anything but in control. "I haven't slept in twenty-four hours." Athena smiled warmly, her eyes flicking from Froce to Mycheal, and Froce could almost believe she approved of Pandora's Box's newest recruit.

"Surrender your life serenely," Athena quoted, spinning gracefully around so that her back was facing Mycheal. Her movements were definitely getting faster. Mycheal hesitated, thrown off by her compliancy, and his confusion increased as Athena placed her hands behind her back without being asked. He glanced at Froce for instructions, and when the other man nodded, he proceeded to cuff Athena. And there it was. Nineteen hours and three teams later, Athena was back in captivity without so much as a scuffle. "As serenely as the one who takes it from you."

"What?"

Athena spun around, and Mycheal immediately took a step back, reaching for his gun before remembering he had given it to Payton. Delmon raised his own pistol and would have fired if Froce hadn't held up a hand, forestalling him. "Surrender your life serenely, as serenely as the one who takes it from you," Athena repeated, her head bobbing.

"Pipe down, Athena," Froce warned, not liking how the Resident seemed to be enjoying herself. "All right, let's hurry up and leave. David, I want you and Mycheal to stick with Athena like glue. If she so much as scratches her nose, shoot her."

"Great, now that you said that, my nose is itching like crazy," Athena complained. "I don't suppose any of you are willing to help out a lady in need?"

"Payton, up front," Froce continued, as if Athena had never spoken. "Delmon, you and I will hang in the back." Out of the members of his squad, Payton would have the most misgivings about shooting Athena, so Froce wanted her as far away from that decision as possible.

"Sir." David spoke up, his voice soft yet menacing at the same time. "Sir, I regret that I cannot obey that order."

This had to be worst time for insubordination, and Froce made the mistake of glancing at Athena, who was staring at him, her eyes turned comically big with righteous indignation when their gazes met.

"You're kidding!" she exclaimed. "You want me to read his mind to figure out why he's refusing your order? I'm not going to help you. Figure it out yourself!"

Of course, it wasn't true. Froce glanced at her, trying to figure out if the telepathic Resident was controlling David's actions, but now his whole team thought he needed guidance from her to keep order. Athena winked at him before giggling. Froce couldn't tell if she had a plan in motion or if she was just crazy; with Athena, it didn't necessarily have to be one or the other.

"You better have one hell of a problem, Tomoghan," Froce threatened, momentarily channeling Caleb.

"Sir, weren't our orders clear?"

Athena's head was going back and forth between the two as they spoke so it looked like she was following a tennis match. Mycheal was keeping a careful eye on her. At the same time, Payton shuffled closer, which instantly earned her a suspicious glance from Athena, and the other woman nodded understandingly in her direction. Just like Froce figured, Payton was trying to establish a connection with the female Resident. Doubtful it would work, but if she succeeded, it would make the rest of the mission a hell of a lot easier.

"We were given permission to kill her on sight," David was saying, and his words hung in the air. "Would that not be easier than carrying her the long miles to Pandora's Box?"

Not surprisingly, Athena was the first to respond. "He's right," she said, sounding positively gleeful. "It would be easier just to snap my pretty little neck!"

Froce spoke up to reassert his authority. "I'm in charge, so I get the last word. We have her in handcuffs and we're taking her in."

"With all due respect, handcuffs aren't enough," David argued. "Sir, I don't think it's a freak coincidence that we lost contact with the other van. I believe she knew we were coming and didn't want to move because of her injury. So she sent Remus ahead to distract us. And maybe Remus had a bomb and was prepared to sacrifice himself for her. Caleb and the others could all be dead."

"They could be," Athena agreed, her annoying comments almost enough justification for Froce to consider David's words, but at the same time, Payton shouted her two cents.

"That's farfetched," she protested.

"So, it's not farfetched to think all their radios miraculously malfunctioned at once?"

"We won't know what happened until we check it out."

"And by that time, Athena could already be miles away using whatever escape scheme she's concocting now."

"I already thought up two and I'm working on the third one now!" Athena said brightly, not able to resist butting in.

Froce studied her closely. There was something off about her. Froce had seen her this way a couple of times, and now was the time you were supposed to holler for Caleb. Sometimes Athena crossed the lines of sanity, and it usually took Caleb to bring her back. She was at her most dangerous in this form because she was so irrational. It might be in everyone's best interest to kill her now.

"Froce has decided it *might* be okay to kill me," Athena informed everyone. "Along with David, that's one and a half."

Payton looked shocked. "Sir, no! She's handcuffed and unarmed. She's not a threat to anyone. Killing her now would be nothing short of murder."

Delmon laughed abruptly. "Don't kid yourself, babe. She's a living threat as long as she's alive and it's not murder if you're doing it in defense. Do you want to go down in history as the dicks that let the monster get away, simply because we were too squeamish to kill it?"

"That's two and a half," Athena said with a giggle. "If I was in my right mind, I'd be worried. It looks like Mycheal is the deciding factor."

"This isn't a democracy!" Froce said.

"In that case, it's up to you, which means it's still a toss-up." Athena yawned as if bored with the whole event. Tyrone's phone rang, almost making him jump, his heartbeat quickening as he noted Athena's smile and her twinkling eyes. "Watch her," he ordered before answering.

"Froce!" Ms. Yang said with a clear note of panic. "Where are you?"

"I'm standing beside Athena. What's wrong?"

Ms. Yang hesitated. "There has been a change of plans."

Chapter 66

Eris Yang walked down the street, feeling like a commoner; another pretty face among the multitude of humans who thought their lives and problems were the center of the universe. How she hated them all.

Her hands burned with energy, and the itch to light something on fire intensified. Everyone had vices, but hers was unusual. She loved to see stuff burn. She *needed* to see stuff burn. To watch her flames eat away at an object fulfilled her like nothing else could. Little things like paper or dolls would only satisfy her for a couple of hours. Couches or sofas would sustain her for a day. Of course, living things were the best—a cat that wandered too close to her house, a dog that was in the wrong place at the wrong time. Animals usually allowed her to go through a week without temptations. So did houses, for there were very few things as magical as seeing a house explode into flames, the memories and lives that some poor insignificant humans had built gone in a matter of minutes. But, of course, the best treat was humans. To see a human go up in flames and watch as they danced around while their arms flailed in what could be mistaken as ecstasy...nothing else compared, which was why she hated the administrative position Cronus had put her in. She longed to be out there, busting heads with Horus, but they all needed to sacrifice for the greater good.

Her hand itched, and she frowned, knowing that scratching it would not alleviate the need. A few days ago, she had bought a litter of mice from a pet store and, after the fiasco with Athena was done with, she would burn them in celebration. She suddenly veered into the alley that Delilah wished to meet her in, and after waiting a few seconds, she leaned against the wall. "I see no reason to pretend I don't know you're there," she called out into the darkness. "Thus, I see no reason for you to continue hiding."

"I wasn't hiding," the darkness answered back. "I'm being discreet."

A lie. She was afraid. Eris could easily tell by listening to her rapid heartbeat. "I'm alone," she offered in an effort to hurry things along. With Caleb's van unreachable, and a possible traitor in their midst, she needed to get back. "Come out."

"I prefer talking to you where I'm at," the other woman said. It was a damn taunt and Eris felt something snap within her. An explosion of fire erupted in the darkness and, with a shriek of terror, Delilah Lane stumbled out of the shadows, falling on her knees in front of her and looking back fearfully, but by then the anomaly was gone.

"Ms. Lane," Ms. Yang said with the pretense of composure, even as she realized she'd made an egregious mistake. "You wished to speak to me?"

"No," Ms. Lane breathed, still looking over her shoulder for the flames. She finally looked towards Ms. Yang, but instead of fear, there was awe. Almost a reverence that Ms. Yang didn't appreciate. "I was hoping the head honcho would come, but this...this is so much better." Ms. Lane stood up and walked slowly towards her. Her foot kicked a bottle and she paused as if afraid the sound would scare Ms. Yang away.

"You had news that Remus has been working with our ward," Ms. Yang said, feeling a sense of unease. Not fear—this girl could never threaten her—but discomfort at the almost-lust in Ms. Lane's eyes.

"Oh...that was a lie to get your attention." Though she said it dismissively, Ms. Yang sensed Delilah's heartbeat speed up, obviously afraid the admission would get her killed. Ms. Yang did consider it.

"And now that you have it, Faust, what are you going to do with it?"

Wrinkles appeared on Ms. Lane's forehead. "Faust?" She hesitated before her face cleared. "The German story in which 'deal with the devil' originated."

Ms. Yang was mildly impressed. "You know the story."

Delilah scoffed, her heartbeat slowing down as she concluded Ms. Yang was not going to kill her in this dark alley-way, and at the same time, Ms. Yang concluded that Delilah was not the idiot she pretended to be. "Are you saying you're the devil?"

Ms. Yang had a response ready, but then remembered she didn't have time to banter with children. "Why did you call me out here?"

"Oh, um..." Delilah took a breath, finding her composure. "Maris Sylvia pays me to be the perfect girlfriend for his son," she said, challenging Ms. Yang with her eyes to judge her. "Then I report all I have seen back to Maris Sylvia."

"Explains why you gave off a different impression than before." She got the sense Delilah was disappointed that she didn't show any shock. "But why does Maris go to such extremes?"

"Because he's scared of losing control of his heir, and he's also a giant massive prick."

Ms. Yang had only met Maris once, but fully concurred. She'd had people research Maris and they somehow had missed this fact. Someone was sure to get fired...perhaps literally. "True, it's interesting gossip," she conceded, "but I don't see why you have to drag me all the way out here just to tell me."

Delilah blinked, apparently thinking Eris would want to know more about her, but recovered quickly. "Maris pays well, but I could do with some more cash. And I never claimed to be exclusive."

It took Eris only a second to get what Delilah was suggesting, and she had to laugh at the nerve of the girl. "You're suggesting I'd pay double what that creep is paying you just so I can get the same information?"

"You'll pay me triple," Delilah stated firmly, although her lips twitched when Eris called Maris a creep. Eris was starting to like this girl, and the desire to see her burn lessened to more manageable levels. "And I'll be spying on Maris as well as Romulus."

Because she liked Delilah, Ms. Yang did the kindness of considering her proposal before shaking her head. "Why should I shell out what I'm sure is going to be an exorbitant amount of money just to keep tabs on two insignificant people?"

"Romulus must be very significant or else he wouldn't be

alive right now," Delilah pointed out, proving once again that she wasn't an idiot. "And you don't know Maris. He hates to lose, especially to a woman. Rest assured, he will be plotting and scheming behind your back."

A thought occurred to her. "Are you and Maris...?"

"Every now and then," Delilah said in an almost defiant tone, as if daring her to criticize. "When he wants to feel young, he comes to me."

Her blunt and defiant manner, along with her obvious ability at deception, was an interesting mix that Ms. Yang found endearing. It reminded her of a young Andraste, a childhood friend. It was also true that Romulus was a huge investment; very few people had the right genetic code to be so susceptible to evolving. If the new version of Ambrosia was successful, then he would be exhibiting abilities within a year, and it would be helpful to have someone on the inside carefully studying Romulus, taking notes and reporting back to her.

Delilah seemed to sense she was weakening and added, "I'll tell you what. As a show of good faith, I'll give you a freebie. You have a traitor in your midst."

Eris' ears perked up. There was no way Delilah should have known. "Your reasoning?"

"Romulus was acting strange, so I checked his bag. You know, the one they packed with a measly sandwich because we were kidnapped and held hostage without food or water?"

"Five-star treatment compared to some of our more permanent guests," Eris answered, not knowing if Delilah wanted an apology or was simply looking to provoke a reaction, but deciding either way not to play her game.

"Well, there was a note inside the bag." Delilah paused, and Eris tapped her foot impatiently, the toes of her shoes making a distinct clicking noise as they hit the pavement. She knew Delilah was deciding whether or not to hold the pertinent information until a deal was made, but hoped the young human was smart enough to realize what a horrible blunder that would be. She found the girl to be more tolerable than other humans, and hoped she wouldn't have to burn up a leg to get her to talk. "There was a note," Delilah repeated quickly, licking her lips. Somehow, she'd realized how close she'd come to being disfigured for life. Excellent survival instincts. "'If you want to save your brother, tell him it's in the left shoulder blade.' That's what it said."

Eris stilled her foot, and it was with great effort that she kept her face as blank as possible. If Romulus had somehow passed the information along, via his brother, it would explain how Athena had known where the location of the second tracker was. But who could have done it? Tyrone, Caleb, Chris...the only suspect it ruled out was Dr. Pluck, as he had been in isolation and thus incapable of passing a message.

Delilah cleared her voice. "Does that mean anything to you?"

It was a bold question, above the human's need-to-know, but Eris found herself answering anyway. "Yes. I can do a lot with that information," she admitted. "It proves beyond a shadow of a doubt that there is, indeed, a traitor at my organization. And since only a few people knew this information, it narrows down the field of suspects significantly."

Delilah blinked, obviously surprised she would share so much information with her. "I think the driver might be involved in it," she offered tentatively, possibly aware that she was stepping over boundaries.

"I'll make sure to check it out," Ms. Yang dismissed. Her hand was itching to the point of being painful and she knew if she didn't burn anything soon, she would lose control. Delilah's eyes fell to her twitchy hand, and she leaned forward as if to grab it.

"Can anyone obtain that power?" Delilah asked with a hopeful longing that seemed uncharacteristic for such a disillusioned girl.

The correct course of action would have been to pretend ignorance. Instead, Ms. Yang raised a finger as if pointing to the sky. "Only the selected ones."

Delilah stared uncertainly before looking upward, and as soon as she did, Ms. Yang released pent-up energy, a burst of flames exploding overhead and momentarily lighting up the alleyway. Delilah gasped, her expression of desire illuminated by the red and orange light that fell across her face. A cat halfway down the alley screeched its displeasure at the sudden light. It was a sober reminder that there might be other witnesses, so Ms. Yang allowed the ball of fire to dissipate.

Delilah continued to look at the spot where the fireball had appeared, as if expecting an encore. Eventually, she looked back at Ms. Yang, and it was the naked desire on her face that was the final selling point. "Can I..."

"I accept your offer," Ms. Yang interrupted. "Three times what Maris is offering for your loyalty and information regarding both his and Romulus' movements. Correct?"

Delilah nodded, not looking at all happy that she was getting the exact deal she wanted.

"I'm pressed for time, but will make the arrangements and contact you shortly."

"Okay...bye," Delilah said, at a loss for words. It had crossed Ms. Yang's mind that Maris had sent Delilah to worm her way into Ms. Yang's good graces, but if that was true before, it was no longer the case now. Delilah wanted the Ambrosia, which meant her loyalty belonged to Ms. Yang.

"Oh," Ms. Yang said with deliberate nonchalance. "About what you saw right now..."

"What do you mean?" Delilah interrupted, doe-eyed. "We just had a conversation about my boyfriend's wellbeing and how I was very concerned about him."

Ms. Yang nodded brusquely and quickly walked away without a backward glance, leaving the human to fend for herself. She had parked her car three blocks away, and for every step she took, she regretted coming to the meeting with high heels. Halfway there and with feet throbbing, her phone went off.

She stiffened as she saw the number, and stared at the phone as if waiting for it to explode. Finally, with an air of resignation, she answered. "Hello?"

"Want to explain to me why my son is telling tales of you unable to control yourself at Pandora's Box?" Cronus asked, his voice stern and unforgiving.

That little bitch. After she'd downplayed Matthew's involvement in Athena's escape, he'd gone behind her back to inform his father about how she'd raised the temperature a little when she temporarily lost control of her powers. No one had even noticed. "I'm sorry, sir. It was a very stressful time and I lost control." If he ever learned the display of power she had just performed, she would be toast.

"Tell me about Athena," Mr. Titanos demanded.

"Sir, she disabled both trackers with the help of Remus Sylvia and a traitor in Pandora's Box. I believe this very same person also helped her escape."

"And do you know who this person is?"

"I have my suspicions, but no definite proof. Horus is currently watching over her, and as we speak, a team is traveling to collect her."

"I know. They found her." Ms. Yang didn't doubt his claim. It wasn't unusual for him to know information that he had no way of knowing, but what should have been good news was spoken more like a rebuke. "Tell me, why are they under the impression they have permission to kill her?"

"Because I gave the permission, sir," she said, not comprehending. There had been numerous times that she'd issued a kill order on a Resident she found to be too bothersome, and she'd never had to run it past Cronus before.

"Recall it immediately. Athena can't die."

"I don't understand, sir. Isn't she just a Level Two Resident who got lucky?" Cronus didn't allow anyone to contradict him without punishment, but questions were acceptable and even encouraged. As long as Eris phrased her statements in the right way, she could usually avoid his anger.

"Perhaps," Cronus humored her. "But there's a chance she could be something more...unique."

Ms. Yang chose her next words very carefully. Even with the correct phrasing, there was only so much lip her boss was willing to take. "Besides her miraculous escape, there's no proof to suggest she's anything special. Fides confirmed as much before he died, so unless I'm missing a crucial piece of the puzzle, I'm force to conclude that Athena is nothing more than a troublesome nuisance."

There was a long silence during which Eris was sure she had ventured too far. Then an unexpected laugh. "You've come a long way from who you used to be."

"Thank you, sir."

"I could make a case that the same Resident who confirmed she was unremarkable is the same Resident that died in the middle of a hotel parking lot by her schemes," Cronus mused. "But no, I will answer the question you are too afraid to ask. Sixteen years ago, both I and the director of Avalon were frustrated with our lack of success with Ambrosia. Either the Residents we created would take too long to develop, or develop quickly but not without mental instability. In a moment of weakness, we decided to cooperate together to make a new class of Residents."

"I don't remember hearing about this, sir."

"You wouldn't have. It was done in complete secrecy, and it didn't take me long to regain my senses and break up our alliance. However, this partnership did yield two children. I took one and Avalon took the other.

"Athena was one of those children? Why not place her in Ragnarok instead of Pandora's Box?"

"Because she was utterly unremarkable," Cronus snapped, and even though his frustration wasn't directed at her, Eris flinched all the same. "You can't imagine my disappointment when the first initial tests came back, placing her Residency below mediocre. I still kept tabs on her, though. I hoped she might have been a late bloomer, but after twelve years, I classified Athena as a failure and moved on."

"But now that she's escaped, you're wondering if you were too hasty in your conclusion."

"Indeed," Cronus said dryly. "Bring her in alive, Ms. Yang, or I might wonder if I was too hasty in promoting you."

Cronus disconnected and Eris clutched the phone, knowing with only a little effort she could send it bursting into flames. With a sigh, she started to dial a number. The mice would have to wait until later.

Chapter 67

"Wake up, kid!"

Remus dreamed, not specifically of Athena, but of his life back home with his father and brother. But instead of being miserable, in his dreams he was content, happy even.

His father was not a thug pretending he was a politician; he was an honest small-time business man. Remus and his brother were the best of friends, and they both planned on attending the same college together. Delilah and Romulus were happily engaged, and in his dream, Remus didn't feel a sense of foreboding, for he knew Delilah loved Romulus and was dating him for the right reasons.

"Damn it, kid! You were supposed to be up by now. I need you!"

In his dream, his mother had never left. She spent her days planting flowers and helping Maris around the office. In his dreams, there were no such things as Residents, but Athena was there. She was going to the same college Remus planned on going to, and in his dream—

"Oh, for the love of God!"

A staggering flash of pain and suddenly Remus was awake. His eyesight was blurry, but he could still make out the image of Caleb above him, his hand raised to hit him again.

"I'm up!" Remus yelled, defending his face with his hands. "Stop hitting me! Why is your first response to everything to hit it?"

Caleb lowered his hand, and Remus noted he seemed to do so with a great amount of disappointment. "You were taking your sweet time getting up, even after the adrenaline shot," he growled, watching as Remus struggled to stand, not once offering a hand. "And we don't have no more time to be wasting."

Finally, after a tremendous struggle, Remus made it to his feet, but his legs were so wobbly he had to lean against the back doors to avoid collapsing again. He was going to say something, but then looked around and realized the van was littered with the sleeping body of Pandora's agents. At least he hoped they were sleeping and not something much more permanent.

"They'll be okay," Caleb said, interpreting Remus' expression while still studying him from behind his dark-tinted sunglasses. "Not that they won't be plenty angry when they wake up."

Remus nodded, but that act alone made him nauseous, and as the room spun, he tried to piece the facts together. He had been captured by a team from Pandora's Box. Caleb had goaded him into a fight to cover his actions of releasing a mysterious gas from one of the tanks stored in the back.

"You're Athena's mole?" he guessed. When Caleb made no move to confirm or deny, Remus tried another theory. "Or are you a spy from Avalon?"

At this, Caleb's expression scrunched up in disgust. "Now how the hell do you know about Avalon when I've been with the company for twenty years and only heard about them today?" he demanded. Remus shrugged helplessly and Caleb snorted. "No, I ain't no Avalon spy and I don't reckon Avalon would be too interested in our gal."

"Our gal?" Feeling his energy returning, he gingerly pushed off against the back door and found that he could stand without its support. He still felt anxious to the point of being nauseous, his heart hammering too fast. He tried to believe it was simply fear, except if he didn't react like this when there was a van full of people willing to kill him, why was he having this reaction now?

"Adrenaline shot," Caleb commented, answering his unspoken question, and Remus had to wonder if Athena wasn't the only telepath. "What I used to get you up. And yes, our gal." Caleb stopped to scratch his beard. "Unless your big speech on how she should be free was nothing but hot air."

"It's not my support I'm questioning, it's yours," Remus retorted, the adrenaline flowing through his bloodstream making him uncharacteristically reckless. "I have nothing but your word that you're her friend."

Whatever retort Caleb was about to make was lost as another voice rang out. Remus, for reasons unknown to even him, ducked with his hands above his head. It was only after Caleb breathed a tired sigh that he realized the owner of the third voice was not actually in the van with them.

"Repeat, this is Herman Mcannan. Is there anyone there? Froce is requesting immediate assistance dealing with target." A moment of silence before the voice added pleadingly, "Anyone?"

"They're still calling for assistance," Caleb stomped over to the side door and pulled it open. "Which means our gal is still giving them hell."

"There's that 'our gal' comment again."

Caleb ignored him, choosing instead to bend down and grab one of the sleeping soldiers by the arm. With a grunt, he pulled the unconscious form up, and then shoved it out the door.

"Stop!" Remus yelled, which only earned him a scornful look from the other man.

"Damn, you're a bit sensitive to be around Athena." Caleb walked over and grabbed another man by the arm. "Listen, kid, with or without you, I plan on rescuing Athena, and I can't do so if I'm worried about these folks waking up and stopping me."

"What about witnesses?" Remus countered. "If someone drives by and sees you dropping bodies, they're bound to call the police."

Caleb stopped momentarily. "Good thinking," he said grudgingly. "However, I already thought of that. I drove us a little bit and we're now in a small parking lot. At this hour, there won't be much traffic going through." Remus opened his mouth to argue, but Caleb forestalled him. "Yeah, it's still plenty risky, but it's the best I could do with the time we got left."

Remus thought it over, which was difficult, as the adrenaline was screaming for action. He walked forward and grabbed the legs of the man Caleb was attempting unsuccessfully to haul out.

"We need to hurry then," Remus summarized when Caleb glanced at him questioningly and the soldier huffed indignantly.

"I could have done it alone!"

"Of course," Remus answered, having known enough of Caleb's type to recognize the best way to deal with them. "I just thought in the spirit of saving time, I'll give some minor assistance."

Caleb scowled, but didn't protest further, and together they worked to clear the van of Pandora's operatives."

"You sure they're going to be okay?" Remus asked as they threw another man onto the side of the road. He winced as the body hit the ground.

"They'll wake up with a headache, but they oughta be okay."

"Ought to," Remus corrected for no particular reason.

"Did Athena pick you because of your stellar English skills?" Remus dropped the legs of the body they were carrying, causing Caleb to stumble forward clumsily.

"I know why she chose me." Sudden anger was threatening to overcome him. "What I don't know is how you did this to her." Remus' voice picked up in volume. "While you're explaining that, maybe you can also explain to me why you're experimenting on humans, why you're helping her, and last, but certainly not least, why are you wearing sunglasses when it's completely dark outside?"

"That's the adrenaline shot talking," Caleb warned. "We don't got the time for your whining. Not unless you want to see Athena dead, which reminds me..." Caleb dragged the man he was carrying into the van's entryway and tossed him out. He then stopped to glare at Remus while pretending he wasn't nearly out of breath. "Why the hell are you here talking to me when she's off fending for her life?"

"She told me to leave!" The words slipped from Remus' mouth, and he instantly wished he could take them back. Caleb's dark look left nothing to the imagination about what he thought of him. "I mean...I needed to clear my head for a bit. And she told me you wouldn't make another attempt on her this quickly."

"Foolishness on her part," Caleb barked. "Once she gets a notion stuck in her head, she rarely goes about changing it. Arrogant is what she is. But you!" Caleb pointed a long finger at Remus. "You're gonna need more of a spine if you're going to be traveling with her."

Remus walked over to the last body, and reaching down, he grabbed the legs. After a moment's hesitation, Caleb grabbed the arms and together they carried the body to the doorway. "What I don't know is why she risked her escape by bringing me along." Caleb feigned ignorance and Remus, not about to let him off the hook, clarified impatiently. "Athena. Is she looking for a traveling companion, a partner-in-crime? What does she sees me as?"

Caleb scratched his beard and shook his head. "Kid, we don't have the time to get into this. Get the driver."

Remus was sick of these people giving him orders and not giving any information in return. Still, if it would help Athena... Remus walked over to the driver's seat, opened the door, and dragged the driver out by the arm. He found it difficult to muster up sympathy when the soldier's head hit the pavement. These people had shot at him after all. Still, to be safe, he dragged the sleeping man a couple of feet so that, when it was time to go, the van wouldn't accidentally run over him. He walked back to Caleb, who was rummaging around in the back.

"You ever used one of these before?" Caleb asked, pulling out a pistol.

"Yes, I make it a hobby to play with deadly guns in my spare time." Remus decided to cut back on the sarcasm after the look Caleb gave him. "My father took us to the shooting range a couple of times. I know how to fire a weapon." Remus hated guns, but the time at the shooting range had been some of the most tolerable memories he had of his family.

"Good. Just in case, you get the tranquilizer gun." Caleb pulled out a different pistol. The only difference was the barrel was longer. "It handles exactly like the real thing 'cept you're gonna have to reload after every three shots. Here, come take it."

Remus walked towards Caleb, and though the man held out the gun for him, Remus refused to grab hold.

Caleb raised an eyebrow and said derisively, "Is this where you get off?"

"I don't think of her in the romantic capacity," Remus confessed, taking the surprisingly light gun from the other man. "I mean, not since the first day I met her and she stole my money and made my life a living hell." Caleb may or may not have smirked at that, Remus couldn't quite tell. "But she's closer than any mere acquaintance," Remus continued. "I don't know if she did some voodoo or some Resident trick on me, but in the period of a few short hours, I went from fearing her to risking my life for her, and I'm guessing that's what you're going to want me to do in a few minutes. Before I do, I need to know where I stand. Am I her friend or her pawn?"

Caleb's expressions were hard to interpret already, and the sunglasses only made the task more difficult. "Kid, with her, the two are often the same."

Caleb made as if to approach the driver's door, but Remus beat him to it, sliding into the seat. "I'll drive. I know exactly where she is."

"You don't know where we are," Caleb argued, but despite this excellent point, he hurried over to the passenger's seat, relenting surprisingly quickly. The cowboy plopped into the seat with a heavy grunt and handed the keys over. "Take a right after you exit the lot and then take an immediate left, which should get you on the main road." He waited until Remus made the first right. "Did she tell you about her life at Pandora's Box?"

Obvious who he was talking about. "Bits and pieces. She told me she read more than a dozen books and that's how she was able to conform so easily to the outside world. I got the impression she didn't have many friends."

"She had a couple. Guards like me were supposed to be polite with the Residents, and we tried to have a mutual relationship with them, but there was no room for friendships. It's hard to be friends with a person that would rip your head off at any moment. For a time, Athena was the worst."

"Athena?" Remus said, confused that Caleb would choose now to joke around. He made the right and was immediately in familiar territory. It would take about seven minutes to reach Athena...five if he blatantly ignored all traffic laws. "I've seen Fides, and I witnessed as a Resident paused time, yet you're telling me Athena was the most dangerous person at your facility?"

"You better believe it. Before the age of eight, she was an angel." Caleb smiled as he reminisced. "Sweetest girl you ever seen. So intelligent too. She would engage you in hours of conversation." Caleb's face twisted. "But then on her eighth birthday, this jackass of a doctor decided she wasn't making enough progress, so they injected her with the newest form of Ambrosia. Two weeks later, she killed four guards."

"Jesus Christ," Remus whispered.

"I found her sitting in the middle of the room, covered in blood, crying her eyes out, the bodies piled around her."

"Did they take her off the Ambrosia?"

"No!" Caleb snapped, glaring at him as if he was the one who had committed those horrible acts. "This doctor was actually impressed that Athena was able to kill four fully grown men. So he upped her dosage."

Remus felt a mixture of dread and rage, and wondered what he would do if he ever met this doctor. "You couldn't stop him?"

Remus was expecting a defiant answer, but instead, Caleb looked at the floor. "I tried, but not nearly hard enough. It was easier for me to remain in my ignorance. Year after year, Athena got more violent. She became nothing more than a wild animal, and at the height of her brutality, she killed eleven guards in the space of fifteen minutes." Caleb smiled bitterly. "Well, you can imagine that the big bosses didn't take kindly to that. In fact, I'm surprised they waited that long to take action. They gave the doctor two choices. Get Athena under control, or resign from his position. You wanna know his solution? A lobotomy."

Remus almost couldn't breathe as fury filled his veins. "But they didn't."

"No, I got to her before he did."

"What did you do?"

Caleb checked his gun. "I gave her a copy of *Romeo and Juliet*. I remembered her talking about it when she was younger, and I didn't have a better suggestion. Imagine my surprise when the next day I entered the room, accompanied with the usual small army we brought to her door, and found her not screaming death threats. What's more, she was actually cordial. Even using complete sentences. We had a short conversation and she requested another book. So I bought her *Macbeth*. And the day after that, *Hamlet*. Then she told me that if she received a hundred books by the end of the week, she promised not to harm anyone for the whole year. I told the other boys about this and they couldn't rush to the bookstore fast enough. At the end of that week, she had one-hundred and seventy-two books stacked in her room. The doctor was enraged and said the books were a security risk. Who knew what kind of dangerous objects they were hiding, but I shouted him down and contacted his boss before he could. They said as long as Athena towed the line, she was free to keep as many books as she liked, provided that each one was checked before being handed to her."

"And she didn't hurt anyone else?" Remus asked hesitantly. Caleb's face became unreadable, and Remus realized he had said something that didn't sit well with the man, but for the life of him, he couldn't figure out what it was. Still, after a second's hesitation, he answered.

"She was the perfect lady for the year. Guards still brought her books to solidify the deal, and after the second month, she started speaking in literature quotes."

"She needed to find new ways to keep her mind sharp," Remus speculated, more to himself than to Caleb. He ran a red light, barely caring that a car almost sideswiped him. "New ways to fight back the madness the Ambrosia was forcing on her."

"I reckoned as much. The end of the year is when she told me she had to escape or else Pandora's Box would drive her mad. That's when we started plotting."

"Why did you decide to help her?"

"That's my business and not yours," Caleb responded gruffly. "We originally planned the escape for her eighteenth birthday. The strategy was to convince the bosses that Athena was completely harmless, and that all she needed was a half hour a week at the mall to become their stellar Resident. Except this asswipe of a doctor came up with another new form of Ambrosia that he wanted to try out on her. We had no idea what this new drug would do, and didn't want to risk any more harm to her psyche. So we moved the plan up. She stalled for three months while I laid out all the preparations, which only left her with one chance to find the perfect candidate at the mall."

"And that's where she found me," Remus finished. He was glad Caleb had shared Athena's backstory, but nevertheless, impatient to finally receive an answer to his question. "But the perfect candidate for what?"

"She wants a friend," Caleb said, as if it was the simplest

concept in the world. "Or maybe she needs a friend. She needs someone who will stick with her throughout all the craziness and despair. Someone she can be completely honest with. Someone who can ground her and bring her back when she gets too close to the edge."

"She expected to find someone like this at the mall?" Remus demanded. It seemed odd that an ingenious and calculating mind like Athena would depend on such an unpredictable variable.

"I tried to talk her out of it a couple times, but she was dead set. She seemed convinced she would find the perfect friend at the mall, and like you said, that's how she ended up with you."

Remus ignored Caleb's subtle insult. "Why didn't she just take one of her friends from Pandora's Box?"

"Her two closest and most reliable friends are a forty-year-old man named Thor and a fifteen-year-old girl name Selene."

"What's wrong with Selene?"

"On occasion, Selene will try to kill Athena for no other reason than the fact that she's there. Sound like a good buddy to you?"

Remus asked his last question. "What would Pandora's Box do if we fail to save her?"

Caleb scratched his beard. "Assuming they don't kill her, they would take her back to Pandora's Box where one of three outcomes would happen. The doctor would finally have his way and lobotomize her, Athena reverts back to an insane animal, or she kills herself to stop option A or B from happening."

"That can't happen."

"Yep. So you understand why I don't got no more time to waste," Caleb huffed, glancing at his watch as if it would show the exact moment of Athena's demise. "Damn it all, we ain't there yet?"

"You don't see her on your right?"

Caleb's head snapped to the side, looking out the window for far longer than he should have before craning his head to glare at Remus. "Sick sense of humor you got there."

It wasn't meant to be a joke. It was meant to test out a theory Remus had come up with due to Caleb's ridiculously dark sunglasses, the fact that he allowed Remus to drive, and that he was convinced he needed Remus' help. "You're blind!" Remus accused.

Caleb made a protesting noise, but then stopped. "I manage to hide it from the most covert organization in the States, but got it figured out by a kid not old enough to smoke."

"How bad?"

"I can clobber anyone right in front of me, but shooting at far range is impossible. In Pandora's Box, Athena helped me out by building up my reputation and making deals with the other Residents not to make trouble, and even to pretend to be afraid of me." It was difficult not to be discouraged. What Remus had hoped to be an elite fighter was in reality, a blind, aging man. Caleb cleared his throat. "Kid, I can't say I'd entirely blame you if you want to bail. However, I need—"

"I'm not leaving Athena."

Caleb paused. "How close are we?" he said with something akin to respect.

"A minute, but I'm slowing to a stop until you can tell me your plan."

"The plan is we see if an old man and some young upstart can battle our way through Pandora's best and brightest," Caleb said, and Remus didn't dare remark on how his plan was more of a goal and lacked the crucial "plan" aspect.

Remus glanced in the rearview mirror, painfully aware that each minute they wasted put Athena closer to capture or death. "The injection you gave me. How long does it last?"

"The epinephrine? Fifteen minutes, give or take."

"Do you have any more injections?"

"Bout seven or eight," Caleb answered, checking his pistol one last time before being satisfied that it would do its job as best it could. "Reckoned I wouldn't need no more than that."

"How long does the gas linger?"

"Dissipates 'round two minutes." He was now looking at Remus, aware that the questions were leading to something.

"Once you breathe in the gas, how long does it take to lose consciousness?"

"Start feeling the effects 'round the first minute. You're out by the second one." When Remus fell silent, Caleb asked impatiently. "You're wasting daylight, boy. Whatcha thinking?"

Ever since Remus first found out Caleb was a mole, a question had been nudging him and he had been too afraid to ask, for the wrong answer would change his whole plan and drastically lower his and Athena's chances of escaping.

"What about you?" Remus asked, hoping against hope that the universe would give him this one. "After you help me rescue Athena, what will happen to you?"

"None of your business!" Caleb snarled.

It was the wrong answer. He should have known the universe would not have the slightest bit of mercy on him. Closing his eyes, he asked almost desperately, "Can't you run? Or come with us?"

Caleb shook his head. "I'm too old to run and, besides...I have kids, and they'll use them to draw me out. Naw, I stay here and take my lickings."

They would kill him. "This is not what Athena would want." Remus counted out the minutes in his head. He had been up for about ten minutes. If Caleb took an adrenaline shot before he released the gas then that meant the shot was nearing its fifteen minute run-time.

"Pawns and friends," Caleb reminded him. "She might not be too keen on the notion of me dying, but she'd sacrifice my life in a heartbeat if it meant saving hers."

"You're wrong."

Caleb chuckled darkly. "I've known the gal her whole life, you've known her for a minute, yet you think you can tell me what she wants." He shook his head. "We waste any more time and she's dead. Here's the plan...I walk in. They won't be suspicious of me so I'll be able to fire some shots off. Athena will read my mind and know what I'm up to. During the diversion, she'll run out to you, waiting in the van. Then you both escape. Got it?"

"Caleb," Remus said, his voice shaky with nervous anticipation for what he was about to do.

As soon as he turned around, Remus shot him once in the collarbone area. With only two shots left and no clue how to reload, Remus had to choke down the instincts to shoot again. The reflex to shoot became increasingly tempting as Caleb lurched forward, grabbing him by the throat.

"You no good piece of scum. I knew it was a mistake to trust a lily-livered dog," Caleb snarled, spit flying out to rain across Remus' face. Remus was afraid he had misjudged how long the epinephrine would last, or that Caleb had taken another shot when he wasn't looking, but then his grip on Remus' throat slowly started to slack. "Why?" Caleb demanded with a heavy breath.

"Because your plan was desperately stupid and would have gotten you killed," Remus stated. "Because Athena would not want your sacrifice."

Caleb's laugh was one reserved for when someone did something so astonishingly stupid that mere words could not cover it. "You killed her!" he shot at Remus just before his head slumped and sleep took him.

Remus took a deep breath and vehemently hoped he was nowhere near Caleb when he woke up. He reassured himself that Athena wouldn't want Caleb to sacrifice himself, and even if she did, Remus didn't want the man's death on his conscience. He leaned over and fished through Caleb's pockets, all but sure the unconscious man would suddenly grab him like you saw in a horror flick. His search paid off as he found a small box of tranquilizer darts in his coat pocket, and a container of injections with a clear liquid that Remus hoped was the epinephrine. Caleb suddenly groaned and Remus froze, but the man fell silent. It hit him hard that he had tranqed the only ally he had, and it was beyond tempting to just lie down and wait for the universe to bowl him over. Exiting the van, he walked over to Caleb's side and, with a grunt, grabbed Caleb's motionless body and started to drag him out. "*Athena, if you can hear me, know that I'm coming for you,*" he thought, trying to fill his mind with reassurance and confidence. "*I'm coming and I will save you!*"

Chapter 68

"Idiot," Athena said. She closed her eyes and a smile splashed across her face. "You hopeless idiot."

Mycheal tightened his grip on the gun that Payton had been kind enough to give back. "Ma'am?"

"Just talking to myself. You should see me when I start to argue with myself. I never win." Athena wriggled her hands to see how much leeway the handcuffs gave. "Could you have possibly have made them any tighter?"

"Be lucky no one thought to bring shackles," Mycheal said, and Athena laughed. Her eyes held a clarity that they hadn't held a minute ago, and they had lost the desperation that she'd tried to cover up with snide remarks and subtle threats. Whatever she had been dealing with was now over, which had to mean trouble, for they were now dealing with a thinking and clever Athena instead of the Athena who was making it up as she went along.

Athena smirked at him but made no comment.

"Any contact with the other van?" Froce was asking Herman over the radio, sounding as sour as Mycheal felt. Ms. Yang, the secretary for the bigshot Mr. Titanos, had called in a near-panic and demanded they treat Athena with the upmost delicacy. Not a hair on her head was to be harmed, which increased the difficulty of the mission, as Athena now knew she had a carte blanche to do whatever she wanted without the threat of death.

"No, sir." If they had been in contact, Herman would have mentioned it in the beginning, but Mycheal understood why Froce felt compelled to ask. It felt like they were pawns in some higher game, completely out of control of the situation and completely expendable.

"Fine, we're moving out. Tell Pandora's Box to send another squad and have them check out the last known location of Caleb's team. We'll use a different path home just to be on the safe side."

"Yes, sir."

"Well, Athena," Froce said, clipping the radio back on his belt. "I don't know what you did, but we can't get in contact with the other van, which leads me to assume they're all dead."

Athena matched Froce's stare. Before, she had been faking her indignation, but this time when she spoke, Mycheal heard sincere bitterness and anger."What do you want from me, Froce? Remorse?"

"It would be a start."

"You know if they don't kill me, they're going to lobotomize me? Take away what I value most all at once instead of little by little with the Ambrosia formula. My most hopeful scenario at the moment is a quick death, and you want me to shed a tear for my tormentors?"

"Caleb and you were friends!"

"Caleb and I were acquaintances," Athena said, her voice rising slightly. "I liked him more than I liked most of my other tormentors, true, but that doesn't change the fact the man would have put a bullet in me and not thought twice. Why is everything I do considered monstrous, and everything you people do considered necessary?"

"We protect the people from—"

"Lies!" Mycheal and Payton exchanged looks. "You made us! You can't claim to protect the world from creatures you create."

"Do you know how many people you killed?" Froce rose to the bait.

"You can't imagine how tired I am of having this conversation. Everyone I killed was trying to kill me or someone I cared for. I was six months old when I was admitted to Pandora's Box. What crimes did I commit then to get locked up and experimented upon?"

It was a good question, and Mycheal was secretly anxious to hear Froce's answer. But, instead, the man shook his head. "That wasn't my call."

Athena sized Froce up, her gaze scanning the environment for some type of advantage.

"Athena, don't do it!" Froce commanded.

Athena's gaze flicked back on Froce and her smile was reckless. Crazy even.

"Damn it, Athena!" Froce hissed, taking a step forward and pulling out his gun. "There's no way you can take us all. You know that!"

"Give me liberty or give me death!" Athena countered. She leaned forward on the couch and positioned her feet so that she could lunge forward.

"And what would dying accomplish?" Payton argued sharply. "No one here wants to kill you!" It was a blatant lie, and the fact that both Delmon and David's hands were drifting towards their guns made the statement almost comical. Athena gave Payton a withering look for treating her like an idiot, but Payton stubbornly continued. "Dying here is the same as giving up. It's a coward move and I know you're not a coward." Payton paused and then said, almost challengingly, "Are you?"

The tension was unbearable as they locked gazes, and Mycheal saw Payton try to hide her trembling hand. Athena was the first to blink and she smiled affably. "I'm not that far gone that I wish to die," she confessed.

"Then stand up!" Froce commanded. Mycheal saw Athena's shoulders stiffen in defiance at Froce's order, but she quickly suppressed it and, with an air of royalty, she stood on her feet, rocking back and forth on her heels until Froce told her to stop. "We're now going to escort you out. If you think about giving us trouble, then read my mind and know I won't hesitate to kill you." Athena rolled her eyes in an exaggerated fashion, but remained silent. "Payton, take the front. Delmon and I will cover the back. Mycheal and David will be at her sides. Move now before anything else inconveniences us."

"Yeah, because I really care about you being inconvenienced," Athena muttered under her breath, sounding like your average teenager. But she obeyed and started walking towards the door with Mycheal on one side and David on the other. "By the way, it was nothing personal."

It took a second for Mycheal to realize Athena was talking to him. "What?"

"Don't talk to the beast," David said, never once looking at him. "Lest you fall into its trap."

"He thinks I'm some type of demon," Athena said, answering Mycheal's unspoken question solemnly. With a straight face, she added, "And as every good God-fearing person knows, you deal with a demon not with an exorcism, but with a well-placed bullet to the head."

Mycheal succeeded in not laughing, but Athena read his thoughts and smiled for him. He now understood how being a telepath gave her an advantage

"It has its uses," Athena said airily.

Froce's radio crackled. "Sir, this is Herman Creed. We have confirmation on the other van. I repeat, we have confirmation on Caleb's van. It's heading our way now."

Payton breathed a sigh of relief. "That's good...right?" she asked hesitantly, as she realized no one else was rejoicing.

Froce clearly didn't share Payton's optimism, and asked, "Has the van made radio contact?"

"No, sir, even though we tried a couple of times."

They were inches from the door when Froce stopped them and cast Athena a furtive look. Her professionally blank face spoke volumes. "I want two of you to stop the van and confirm that it's actually Caleb's squad inside of it. The other two need to stay within the safety of our van. Contact me as soon as you get a confirmation."

"Yes, sir, is there anything we should be looking for?"

"Just looking for confirmation." He glanced out the window, straining his neck in a fruitless effort to see the van. The van being parked out of sight was supposed to be a disadvantage for Athena, not for them. "Who's in the van, Athena?" he asked, afraid that the boy really had spoken the truth about Athena calling for help.

"They're outside my telepathic range, so I don't know." She paused and looked up as if she was thinking deep thoughts. "Of course, if my telepathy *did* extend that far, I would lie and issue the same statement I just said a couple of seconds ago, so it's really a toss-up."

Once again, Mycheal fought the urge to laugh and Athena grinned at him, but before she could rat him out, Herman spoke over the radio again. "Sir, the van is not slowing down. Looks like its aiming to shoot past us." A second later, "Oh shit! It's on a collision course with us. I repeat, it aims to rams us!"

Chapter 69

"Okay, Athena, here I go," Remus thought as he crawled into the driver's seat to get behind the steering wheel. *"I hope you can hear my thoughts, because I hate to think I'm talking to myself. Or actually, thinking to myself...I suppose that's acceptable, lots of people think to themselves. Of course, they're not under the presumption that someone's picking up their thoughts, so I guess it's okay if I feel a little weirded out by this."*

He adjusted the mirror that didn't need to be adjusted just to forestall what he had to do next, but with Athena's life in danger, he didn't have any time to waste being cowardly, so he took out the syringes he had snatched from Caleb and stared at them with a good deal of trepidation. He'd always hated needles, and for the briefest of moments, wished Caleb was still conscious to administer the drugs.

"Craps!" he yelled as he stabbed himself with the needle and felt a jolt of pain go up his arm. "That bites!" He pushed down on the plunger, glad no one was there to see him behave like a wuss.

"Some savior I am, right, Athena?" Tossing the discarded needle aside, he started up the van and pulled onto the street. He had dumped Caleb on the side of the road, well within sight of anyone passing by. The police would soon be called, which would be a benefit...probably. Remus had a plan, but was constantly second-guessing himself as he stumbled ever closer to Athena. *"I really hope I can do this, because if I let you down and they capture you, I don't know if I can forgive myself."* He laughed as a thought struck him. *"Look at me, making it all about my problems when you're*

the one in mortal danger. I'm driving back to the house and I hope you're still there. If you can, stall them for me. Don't let them leave. Tell them you have to go to the bathroom or something. Hah, aren't I funny? Did I ever tell you about the time I threw up on the prettiest girl at school?"

He inched forward in the van until he was out of sight of Caleb's body before stopping to make arrangements for his grand plan, all the while keeping up the barrage of humorous stories to keep Athena's spirit up. Before the house could even come into view, Remus spotted a black van, identical to the one he was driving. They had hidden out of view of the house, but for what reason? Athena was a telepath and would know they were coming regardless. He stopped the van. Drumming his fingers on the steering wheel, he paused to speculate and to talk to Athena. *"I assume you're not in the van, which sucks because it puts a wrench in my plan. That's okay. Caleb said there were only two vans, but I forgot to ask him how many people were in this one. Probably should have done that before I knocked him out, right? On that note, he's not the type to hold a grudge and come after me, is he? It just seem like we're even now because he did hit me in the face a couple of times. This is probably a conversation we should have face to face. I'm moving out now and my heart is pounding because I know this is going to hurt...a lot. In case you haven't realized, I have a major aversion to pain. Continue to stall the people on your end."*

The streets were wide enough so that Remus could properly angle the vehicle, and after doing so, he slammed his foot on the gas pedal and the car rocketed off with a squeal. He kept his hands steady on the wheel as the other van grew larger and larger in his line of sight. As he drew nearer, he saw the driver in the other van gape at him, surprised that someone would do something so incredibly stupid, and Remus had a chance to laugh at his expression just before slamming into the side of him at 45 mph. The crash was enough to deploy his airbags, pounding him in the face. "Good times," he said faintly before passing out.

When he awoke a couple of seconds later, he discovered what could be a flaw in his plan.

"Raise your hands, slowly," a man ordered, pointing a gun at him through the window. He had a long gash on the forehead, and looked none too happy about it. "Unlock the door. "

Remus replayed the words in his mind. "How am I supposed to unlock the door if I have my hands up?"

"Don't be a smartass," the armed man snapped, sounding eerily like his father. "Unlock the door and then put your hands in the air."

Remus unlocked the van door and the man opened it and yanked him out. "What do you think you were doing?" he demanded. There was a vein pulsing in his head. Out of all the men who had tried to kill him thus far, this man was the youngest. His skin was a dark brown and he had a prominent scar running down his left cheek. Remus did him the honor of dubbing him Scarface.

"I'm sorry," Remus said, trying to sound petrified, which didn't take much effort. "I had to do it! The monsters...they forced me to do it. They said they would kill me if I didn't!" As he was babbling nonsense, he had a chance to look around. He must not have been out long for no one had moved the vans; they were still merged together by the collision to look like a slightly crooked T. "You have to help me or they'll kill me!"

Scarface wasn't expecting that, and he stared blankly at Remus until his partner showed up. In contrast with Scarface, his partner was old as dirt and gave every indication of keeling over in the next five minutes. Remus nicknamed him Dusty simply because he couldn't think of anything else at that moment.

"What's going on?" Dusty asked, giving Remus the mandatory scowl that everyone seemed to give him right before trying to put a bullet between his eyes. "Where's Caleb, and why is this idiot driving?"

Scarface shrugged uneasily. "I don't know. He's not being coherent. He said something about the monsters telling him to do it. Think he means Athena?"

"Don't know. Nothing about this day has made sense." To Remus, he said, "Who are these monsters?"

"Terrible beings," Remus answered, purposely being vague. "They told me they would kill me if I didn't follow their orders. They told me not to look in the back! They're monsters!" If Hollywood could have seen his performance, they would have gave him an Emmy on the spot.

"They?" Scarface said, sounding more and more nervous.

"Is he crazy, or are we talking multiple Residents?"

Dusty gave Remus a hard look. "He might be making it up. Hoping we won't kill him for his crimes."

Remus was about to ask what crimes had he committed, but caught himself in the nick of time. "I'm telling you the truth! The monster took out your men and forced me to drive here! Why else would I come to you, knowing you would kill me?"

"He's right. There's no way this wimp could have taken out a whole van of us," Scarface said. "Someone else had to have done it." To Remus, he said, "Are these monsters Residents? Are they like Athena?"

"They're monsters!" Remus exclaimed, explaining nothing. "They told me to drive the van and don't look in the back."

"What happened to the others? Did the monsters get them? Are they still alive?"

"I don't know. The monsters probably took them and are now doing monstrous things to them right now!"

Remus realized he'd taken it a step too far when Scarface hit him across the face. "Think this is a joke?"

Dusty's radio crackled. "Ryan, Froce wants to know what's happening."

Dusty unclipped his radio. "We got the situation under control. The kid seems to be terrified, but he could be making it up. No sign of the others, though we haven't checked the van."

"Hurry up. Froce wants to make sure it's safe before transporting Athena."

Remus felt a moment of relief. *"So you're still alive then. I need you buy to me a couple more minutes. I'm almost done out here."* His own confidence astounded him. Also, though scared, his heart was beating way too fast and sweat was pouring down his cheeks in waves. The adrenaline shot he'd taken. Remus cursed himself for being an idiot. The stimulant would protect him from the gas, but would cause him to be overly excited and anxious. He couldn't be sure that his plan to save Athena was plausible or a drug-induced hopeless dream, and the realization cast doubt in his mind.

"Okay then," Dusty said, putting up his radio. He walked towards the still open driver's door and glanced inside, his gaze pointed to the back. "I don't see anyone in the back, but someone could be hiding under all the canisters and equipment. Sangia, bring the wimp with you and go around. I'll approach on this end."

"Nooooo!" Remus wailed as Scarface got a firm hold on his arm. "You don't understand! The monsters will kill me!"

"Would you like it if we kill you now? Move it, kid!"

Remus complied, making a few more protesting sounds. The walk to the back of the van was more brutal than it should have been. Particularly because Scarface made it a point of shoving him every time it looked like Remus was slowing down. Whatever misgivings Remus had were gone by the time they reached their destination. Scarface reached for the door, hesitated, and then took a step back. "Open the door," Scarface ordered, and Remus heard the nervousness in his voice.

"You're going to regret it."

Scarface shoved him violently. "Open the door!"

Just my luck. My tormentor turns out to be my high school bully," Remus thought sourly, hoping Athena would get a chuckle from it. He grabbed the door handles, noted that Scarface had raised his gun, and with a twist, pulled the door open.

Dusty had all but made it to the backdoors and his hand tightened around his gun, but then relaxed as he saw Remus. Other than that, nothing happened.

"Stupid kid," Scarface muttered, shoving Remus out the way to get a better look. "You actually had me worried." He moved a couple things around. "There's a lot of stuff packed back here, Ryan. It's going to take forever to sort everything out. At first glance, nothing seems to be missing or out a place." Then with a frown, he added, "I hear something, though. A faint hissing noise." Remus watched with incredulity as he took another step, his back completely turned to Remus. Was he so little of a threat that he didn't even warrant anyone keeping tabs on him? *"The sheer arrogance!"*

"I hear it, too," Dusty said. "Not a clue what's causing it."

"Still doesn't answer the main question," Scarface said with a yawn. "What happened to Caleb and his team?"

"Not sure," Dusty said with a yawn of his own. "My best bet is another Resident. No one else..." Dusty froze in mid-yawn as the truth dawned on him. "It's the gas! That sleeping gas! It must have sprung a leak!"

As soon as Dusty finished his sentence, Remus charged into Scarface and slammed him, the front of his shoulder taking the majority of the blow. It would have been more impressive if Scarface had moved more than a few inches, and it did not help that Remus' shoulder now blazed with pain. Scarface turned around in drowsy confusion and clumsily fumbled for his gun, but Remus slapped the weapon from his hand.

"Not bad for a dumb kid," Remus gloated. "I guess this will teach you not to underestimate—" His words were cut short as Scarface struck him in the face, which just proved that gloating never led to good things. Remus stumbled back and launched his own attack. His fist connected with Scarface's abs. Damn! What were his abs made of? Remus did his best not to wince in pain as his throbbing hand told him he was an idiot. The next blow almost brought Remus to his knees. In a one-on-one fight, it was clear that Scarface would wipe the floor with him. Fortunately for Remus, he had the gas on his side and Scarface didn't think to call for backup.

Scarface fired off another punch and Remus dived out the way, landing rather painfully on the ground. He grabbed the gun that he had previously slapped out of Scarface's hand and pointed it straight up at him. Scarface froze in his tracks, his face a mask of rage. "Do you have the guts, kid? To take a life?"

Remus slowly got to his feet, his eyes never leaving Scarface. "Try me." For some reason, his squeaky voice and his shaking hands failed to be convincing.

"I don't think you do have the guts," Scarface snarled, and lunged at Remus, who waited until Scarface was inches from him before kicking him squarely in the balls. Even if Remus could have taken a life, there was no point to it. Scarface doubled over in pain, and Remus lifted the gun and slammed it on Scarface's head. He went out like a light, and Remus checked to make sure Dusty was out of the fight as well. Both men were sleeping peacefully and Remus maliciously wished them both nightmares of killer bunnies, clowns, and other disturbing images.

Dusty's radio buzzed. "Ryan, do you hear me? What's going on?" A moment of silence then in a more urgent tone, he said, "Ryan, answer me. What's going on?"

"In a couple of seconds, the people outside are going to

call the people inside and inform them of a problem." Remus walked to the back of the van to get the tranq gun, where he'd hidden it earlier. *"I don't know what you're doing, but whatever it is, keep it up. It's imperative that they not be tempted to leave...and don't get yourself killed."* He added, remembering Athena had the habit of over performing, *"Keep it simple."*

A door slam alerted Remus to another threat. Someone was coming to investigate. He held his breath and slowly crouched down so that he was nearer to the ground. He placed Scarface's gun under the van so that it wasn't easily accessible in the heat of battle and retrieved his tranq gun and the box of ammo from where he stashed it in the back of the van. As the sound of footprints drew steadily closer, his hand started to shake violently, and doubt began to enter his thoughts once again. Did he really think he could do this? Stop the bad guys and save the princess? A raven on a near-by branch seemed to disagree as it began to squawk. The footsteps drew nearer to the back. Any second, the man making the footsteps would see the outline of Scarface. Re-mus needed to tranquilize him before that happened. Remus held his breath and was about to make a move when a voice froze him.

"Lucas, come back. Froce wants us to wait inside the van."

"Then how the hell will we figure out what's going on?" Lucas yelled back, confused.

"No idea. It's not like the man shares the intimate details of his plans with me. Hurry up and come back before some-thing grabs you."

Remus peeked around the corner just in time to see the man named Lucas turn around and head back towards his van. In a flash of recklessness, Remus jumped out from be-hind the van and fired off a shot. Before he could even see where the shot landed, a sharp, stabbing pain exploded in his neck, and a second later, a raven flew by, circling around for another attack. Remus half-heartedly raised his gun, know-ing full well that he didn't have the aiming capabilities to shoot a flying target, but the raven veered off, landing fifteen feet to the side of him. Through his luck had always been universally bad, it had never stooped low enough to make him a target for birds. Had to be the work of another Resident. The raven seemed content to glare contemptuously at him, so Remus risked a glance from around the back of the van and saw the man named Lucas looking confused, his hand over the base of his neck where the dart had landed. He opened his mouth as if to yell, but then the light in his eyes dissipated and he slowly sank to the ground. Remus heard a flutter of wings and instantly shielded his face as the raven clawed for his eyes, its little feat clawing painfully at his hands.

"You know, I always did hate the Colonel," Remus informed it as he tried to improve on their relationship. When that failed, he raised the tranq gun again and the raven flew off, apparently believing Remus had the precise aim of a professional sniper. Landing on a tree, it let out a loud, baleful cry that was sure to attract attention if allowed to continue.

"Big Resident can't handle me by itself?" Remus asked shrewdly, a plan beginning to form. As discreetly as he could, Remus locked the safety on the gun.

The raven cut off its cry midway and, though it didn't seem possible, fixed Remus with a glare of indignation. Remus raised the gun and squeezed the trigger, but then frowned as nothing happened. The raven, sensing its chance, flew straight for Remus' eyes and the action revealed a very important lesson. A Resident might have astonishing powers, but might not have the intellect to go with the abilities. Remus covered his eyes with the tranq gun, waiting for the raven to draw nearer. When it was close enough for Remus to count the individual feathers covering its head, he released the safety that he had hit after shooting Lucas, and fired his last dart. At first, he thought he had missed as the raven continued to hurtle towards him. But then it dipped at the last second, slamming into Remus' chest instead of his face. By the time it fell to the ground, its little eyes were closed. It might have looked cute if it hadn't spent the last minute trying to tear out his eyes.

Remus released his breath and tried to control the shaking of his hands and the pounding of his heart. Amazingly enough, the driver had failed to notice the entire incident, the angle of the van shielding his actions, which gave Remus yet another foolhardy idea. Keeping his head down, Remus ran to where Lucas had fallen, all the while expecting someone to yell, "Stop, or I'll shoot!" Or worse, not even bother with a warning. He fished Lucas' keys out of the sleeping man's pocket and then spent a good minute figuring out how to reload the ammo in his tranq gun. It did not help that his hands were drenched in sweat and with every heartbeat, he thought death would claim him.

"You better still be alive, Athena, because I'd hate to do all this and not have anyone to boast to afterwards. Oh, and how awesome was I to take out that Resident?"

He crept around, using the bulk of the vehicles as cover, until he was at the back of the other van, the one where his next unexpected victim sat. Using the keys, Remus unlocked the doors and swung them open.

"Is that you, Lucas?" a voice called out from the driver's seat. An empty, narrow space separated the driver from Remus. It would not be long before the driver turned around and realized it was not Lucas he was speaking to.

Remus hopped in the back, slid past two canisters, and sprinted towards the front. His feet clanging against the floor of the van alerted the driver. Remus saw surprised eyes as the driver turned around in his seat. Remus fired, but he had no practice firing a gun while moving and the shot went wild. The face disappeared.

"Froce, it's the boy! He's attacking!"

Remus had almost covered the distance when the driver turned around again, a gun in his hand. Remus should have been terrified, and he was, but a strange calm was washing over him. He jumped to the left, behind the driver's seat, missing the first burst of bullets that sparked and ricocheted against the van walls. Remus fired blindly; another astounding miss, but it did make the driver duck back into the cover of his seat.

"What is he doing?" a voice demanded. It came from the radio.

Remus had reached the back of the driver's seat and his plan had been to try and shoot around the seat when a better idea came to him. He angled the tranq gun over the seat's head and fired the last tranquilizer into the gunman's leg. Success, but Remus had little time for elation as the gunman's hand reached up to grab his arm. He jerked back, managing to free himself, but falling back on his rump in the process.

"I've been hit!" the driver cursed before standing and

rounding the corner of his seat, stumbling towards Remus, gun in hand.

There was no way the gunman would miss at this distance and Remus could not get up in time to avoid the hail of bullets. It was over, but he had taken a decent chunk out of the enemy's forces. Maybe Athena could escape.

He lashed out with a feeble kick that connected but did nothing, the gunman not reacting at all. Instead, he continued to look down at Remus with an expression of outrage...not moving, not blinking. Just staring.

Remus slowly got to his feet, a theory springing into his mind. The radio in the front crackled and a different voice floated out. A feminine British voice.

"Glad we made it in time. You're a nice lad, you are." Remus heard the sound of a child cooing on the other end. "Now I'm technically breaking the rules, but what the hell? I'll be forgiven and I did want to pay you back for helping me out at the grocery store. Also, it was quite chivalrous how you tried to protect and save me at the hotel, but this is a one-time deal. Only the driver's mind has been suspended; everyone else is moving as normal, so if you have a plan, I'd say you get to it. They have orders not to kill Athena, but that doesn't mean they'll follow them."

Remus raced to the front and grabbed the radio. "Wait!"

The radio crackled again and an angry male voice roared out. "Who is this?"

A thump from behind and Remus turned his head to see that the driver had fallen to the ground, fast asleep. The voice had said it had paused only his mind, which meant the sedative from the tranquilizer still had ample time to work its way into his body.

"I said who is this?"

No time to dwell on what had happened.

Remus had brought the radio to his lips and thought on what to say. "This is Remus Sylvia and you have kidnapped a dear friend of mine."

Chapter 70

"Remus Sylvia, this is Tyrone Froce, the man in charge.

"Well, I have to say, sir, you're doing a bang up job." He grabbed an adrenaline shot and, with a grimace, stabbed himself with it, all too aware that, if not careful, the stuff could kill him.

"Now is not the time to be a smartass."

"If you only knew how many times I've heard that today."

"Who's helping you?"

"Helping me? So it's impossible that I defeated all of your people by my lonesome?"

"How many people are in there with you?"

Remus heard Froce start to reply when Athena's voice piped up in the background. "You better start taking this serious," she warned merrily. "I reckon you have about five seconds before he gets really angry."

So there were five men with her. Not too bad. He was hoping for two, but was expecting twenty.

"She's right," Tyrone said, oblivious to the message Athena had sent. "I ask again, how many people are helping you?"

"At the moment, none."

"Don't lie to me, kid."

"I'm telling the truth. Anyone who might have been helping me is long gone now."

"Fine, who was helping you?"

"I hardly see how that's any of your business."

"What happened to my men?"

"An excellent question." Remus could hear Athena laughing in the background and one of the soldiers telling her to shut up.

"Are they alive? Is anyone alive?"

It was impossible for Remus to be flippant when he heard the worry in his voice. Also, he would be less likely to kill Athena in anger if he knew his comrades were okay. "They're alive." Jumping out of the van, he rushed back to his own and prayed the collision had left it functioning.

"That's good," Tyrone said encouragingly. "Where are they?"

He didn't need to tell Tyrone, but saw no reason to withhold the information. "Tied up," Remus lied, not wanting Froce to figure out things too quickly. "About two miles down the road, behind a small shop. Someone will eventually find them and call the police."

Silence from the radio. It would be great if he could simply convince Tyrone to release Athena and then everyone go on their merry way. But then again, Tyrone was probably thinking on similar lines about him.

"If you surrender," Tyrone offered, confirming Remus' assumption, "and if my comrades are still alive like you say, I will do my best to make sure you live."

"Surrender and you'll get to live!" Remus countered, the adrenaline once again making him say reckless things

"Damn it, kid!" Tyrone screamed. "Do you really know what you're doing, or has Athena completely warped your mind?"

"You people attacked a hotel full of guests, and I'm the warped one?" Remus scoffed, almost itching for a fight. He heard Athena whistle in the background. Probably a message for him to calm down.

"This isn't a story, kid! This is reality. Decisions must be made for the greater good. You're asking how we could attack a hotel for the sake of this girl. That's like asking why the cops would attack a suburban home to uncover a nuclear weapon."

"Your analogy is weak. There's no way you can make a comparison of Athena and a nuclear weapon." Remus climbed into the front seat. Closing his eyes and praying to any deity that might be listening, he turned the key and sighed in relief as he heard the hum of the engine.

"You truly have no clue," Tyrone was saying, with a certainty that made Remus feel like he was missing something crucial. "At any rate, I don't wish to explain it to you. Unless you surrender immediately, I will kill Athena and be done with it."

The words hit Remus hard. "You can't kill her! You have orders not to."

"Now how would you know that?" Tyrone mused. "I'll disobey those orders if it means keeping the world safe."

"It's true," Athena said from the background. "He will kill me if he feels I'm too close to escaping."

Remus gripped the radio so hard that his knuckles turned white. "Look at her! She doesn't want to go out and spread mayhem and havoc. All she wants to do is escape and live free."

Tyrone was clearly unmoved. "She is perhaps the biggest danger that our world faces, and I won't allow her to roam free. Now surrender."

His belief in what he was doing was so absolute that mere argument was useless. Remus had a plan, but now it seemed too dangerous to implement. *"You caught that, Athena? I have a plan, but it might get you killed. What do I do?"*

Athena said, "Faith is not belief without proof, but trust without reservation."

It was obviously a message to him. Was she saying she trusted him? Had faith in him? This was the perfect time for the universe to pull the rug from underneath him.

"You kick the universe's ass!" Athena screamed.

"She's communicating with him," Tyrone yelled. "Shut her up!"

Remus heard a sickening crunch. *They hit her!* His rage began to boil. Screw the universe. He would save Athena.

"Are you going to surrender or not?" Tyrone asked.

"No," Remus said flatly. The next step was important; his whole plan hinged on his next words being believed. The house that Athena lay prisoner in came into view and Remus stopped the van directly in front of it. He was briefly worried that someone would spot him and open fire, but he saw no movements from within. They might not even know he was there.

There was a pause. "So, you don't care if we kill her."

"No, you're totally not the bastards here," Remus said, unable to resist the jab to Froce's integrity. When he didn't respond, Remus went on to say, "I like the girl, I really do. But not enough to sacrifice my own life in an attempt that will end in both of us dying."

"Then why are you lurking outside?" Of course they would have someone watching the streets in case someone showed up.

Remus fought the urge to duck. "Because I wanted to prove to you that I am leaving. See?" Remus sped off down the street and turned a corner.

Froce was unconvinced. "Yes, I saw you leave, but it's a minute walk from where we parked the van, and from what I understand, my driver is incapacitated. What's to stop you from swooping in as we attempt to move Athena?"

"Stop overanalyzing," Remus reproached, trying to put enough annoyance in his voice. "This is a fair deal. You have Athena. I have the money she left. Your men are safe and so is my brother." When he wasn't contradicted, Remus breathed a sigh of relief, certain that if his brother had been in danger, Froce would have mentioned it so he could use it against him. "I'll leave and you don't follow. Tell your masters that I know better than to try and go to the media with stories of Residents. Convince them to back off, will you?"

"I can try," Froce said, his words signifying a reluctant acceptance of Remus' deal. "Where would you go?"

The question was enough to surprise a laugh out of him. "You don't really expect me to tell you that."

"Guess not." There was something strange in Tyrone's voice. "I suppose I shouldn't have expected anything more from you."

"One last thing before I go," Remus said pleasantly. He paused for a second, knowing Athena knew his plan, and hoping that if she disagreed with it, she would say something to let him know. Dead silence, although that could also mean Athena wasn't in a position to speak. "I took the liberty of calling the police and directing them to your location. I called about two minutes ago, so I'm guessing you have...three minutes before they get here."

"Damn you!" Froce hissed angrily. "You're forcing my hand."

"I suppose I am," Remus agreed. "Sucks to be you right now. Goodbye, Tyrone Froce, and goodbye, Athena. I really wish things had ended differently." He put down the radio and took a long, ragged breath. He had preparations to make.

ChApteR 71

Payton's real name was Fortuna, goddess of luck and pristine Resident of Avalon. For the last three years of her life, she had been a spy at Pandora's Box, forced to hide her talents and abilities from those who would see them as proof she was a monster. During the beginning of her stint as a mole, she had been resentful of the assignment. Like most of Avalon, she had seen the humans as nothing more than barbaric, backward animals, desperate to cling to the top of the evolutionary chain where they clearly didn't belong, but as time progressed, she realized how complicated and diverse the species truly was. You had your standard pricks and pigs, those who most Residents believed represented humanity as a whole, but then you had your honest and noble men and women who strove to do the right thing in every circumstance. Using those terms alone still narrowed humanity to a couple of classifications when there was so much more to them. You had your desperate and your liars, your religious and your atheists. Those seeking redemption and those seeking fortune and fame, all of them reaching for a different goal. Unlike Avalon, in which all Residents were trying to achieve the exact same dream.

Mycheal coughed quietly and Payton left her speculation behind to focus on the task at hand. Events had unfolded quickly. Remus, the human whom Athena had taken a liking to, had somehow managed to defeat a small army of Pandora's Box operatives. Then, with victory so close, he'd suddenly decided to up and leave, but not before calling the police, which meant Tyrone Froce had to make a decision on whether to kill Athena and run, or try to drag the girl all the way to the waiting van. Froce was staring coldly at Athena, and Athena, almost by impulse, tried to hide behind Mycheal. Payton was surprised and unreasonably jealous at the same time. *"When did you appoint him your guardian?"* Either Athena hadn't gotten the message, or she was ignoring her, instead choosing to peek nervously at Froce from behind Mycheal's back.

"I had nothing to do with any of that," she said defensively. "Remus acted on his own accord and without instructions from me."

"What happened to our men?" Froce asked. His tone was quiet, but left no doubt the wrong answer would result in her death. Athena must have gotten the same feeling.

"There was a gas leak in the other van and your men were affected by the sleeping gas. Remus is a partial Resident, or a Resident Level One."

"Is that true?" Payton thought to her as Athena paused to let the words sink in.

"It's the truth," she said to Froce, who was looking skeptical. "I think he has immunity to certain forms of gasses and drugs...like me."

That certainly wasn't true. Payton had spent the majority of her life in Avalon, and knew no Class One Resident could display such an advanced ability.

"I've never heard of a Level One Resident displaying those abilities," Froce said, his voice accusing.

Athena shrugged helplessly. "I don't know what to tell you. If there is another Resident involved, they are shielding themselves."

Payton also knew that, besides herself and the small chance of Andraste, there wasn't another Resident helping Athena. It meant that the most likely answer was Athena had inside help. *"You have your own mole inside Pandora's Box? Someone feeding you help and information?"* Athena tilted her head slightly forward with a small sigh. An acknowledgement not only of Payton's words, but for the offer of help she had promised. *"Only if you promise not to kill a single one of my comrades on your way out,"* Payton thought, temporarily ignoring her failure of not knowing about Athena's saboteur.

Athena was young, and though massively intelligent, her emotions still ruled her actions and upon hearing the condition, she whipped her head towards Payton, her mouth open in surprise. Froce reacted to her sudden movement by taking a step towards her while Mycheal slid closer to Payton, driven by the unconscious need to protect. Payton made herself flinch nervously to divert suspicion away from herself.

"Athena," Froce warned, and the young girl, realizing how close she was to death, quickly raised her hands in the universal gesture of surrender.

"Listen, I agree..." Athena let the words hang in the air and Payton smiled to herself, confident that she and Athena had reached an accord. "That it looks suspicious, but I'm telling you this is all a huge misunderstanding. I just needed to get out for an hour or two. I was coming right back to Pandora's Box. Honest."

The emphasis on "out" was not lost on Payton. Her plan of escape must only be viable if they left the house. "Sir, we don't have time for this," Payton spoke up. "If what Remus said is true, we have mere minutes before the cops come. We need to head for the van, now."

"Are you stupid?" Delmon asked. "We need to waste her and run. There's no way I'm going to jail for kidnapping."

"So you'd rather go to jail for murder instead?" Payton enjoyed debating with humans. Each one had their own unique moral code and philosophical stand; it was fun to explore them, but right now she was pressed for time.

"At least we would be ridding the world of a great evil," David added his voice.

Froce held up a hand, ending the argument before it had a chance to escalate. "How did Remus take out our men outside?" As Froce stared at Athena, Payton carefully released her toxin into the air.

One of her talents was the ability to secrete a potent pheromone that made all who breathed it in drowsy and unresponsive. It wasn't as fast-acting as the sleeping gas, but enough of it could put a reasonable-sized man to sleep. During the trip to Athena, she had released the pheromone at regular intervals, the closed off space of the van making it more effective. Some of Remus' luck with dealing with Froce's men could be due to her pheromone's effect on decision-making skills.

"Your men were stupid," Athena was saying bluntly to Froce. "Unnaturally so. Two of them got too close to the van and fell under the effects of the gas, and the other two were taken out by Remus with a tranquilizer gun."

"Where would he find the tranquilizer gun?" Froce asked.

"He took it off one of the sleeping guards from the other squad."

"How would he know how to use it?" Froce asked.

"Sir...our time," Payton said impatiently. "If Remus did indeed call the police, then..."

"I know!" Froce snapped, and Payton redoubled her efforts with the pheromones, but as she did, she noticed herself growing tired. The downside with her pheromones was that as they were released, her own bloodstream was pumped with a toxin thaty weakened her for up to three days. "Listen up," Froce spoke up. "We will be escorting Athena back as planned. However, if she makes any type of threatening move, or if anything else deviates from the plan, you all have permission to shoot her without waiting for my order." Froce glared at Athena's scowling face. "That should keep you honest."

Athena protested. "You can't be serious. There are people in this room who would do anything to kill me." She pointedly looked at Delmon and David. "An untimely sneeze will end my life."

"In that case, I suggest not sneezing." Before Athena could waste more time stalling, he said, "We're moving now. Delmon, I now want you in front. Payton, take the rear."

Froce's opinion of her must not be high for him to reassign her to the back of the line, but it could have simply been a case of misguided chivalry. Humans were complicated like that.

"Our objectives are to reach the van and leave, which means we will be leaving men behind. If you have any objections, kindly stick them up your ass until we're safely back home. Delmon, please do us the courtesy of opening the door, and remember, Athena...no sneezing."

"He picked an odd time to discover his sense of humor," Athena whispered, sounding oddly proud of him. She was still sticking incredibly close to Mycheal, which meant any bullets that headed her way had a fair chance of hitting him as well.

"*Keep him safe, Athena,*" Payton warned. She had become fond of all humans, but had a particular soft spot for the grumpy soldier, and the thought of him dead left her physically ill.

"I promise to be on my best behavior," Athena said sincerely.

"Quiet," Froce ordered..

"Thank you."

Athena nodded. Payton had met Athena several times before at Pandora's Box, and had always found the young girl to be a deadly enigma. Polite, but ready to kill at a moment's notice, and intelligent enough to do so without getting caught or punished. She had always been kind towards Payton, but in hindsight, it could have been because she knew she was a Resident of Avalon.

Delmon opened the door, letting light stream into the house. He waited for a moment, but when nobody struck him dead, he started forward while everyone else piled out behind him. It was possibly the tensest situation imaginable. Athena was surrounded on all sides by men who had orders to kill her if they saw even the smallest hints of deceit. Added to that, they all expected at any moment to be attacked by a wave of Residents.

"Ole Macdonald had a farm," Athena sang softly, unable to help herself. "EE-I-EE-I..."

"Last time, Athena. Shut up."

In this small suburban area, where people were just beginning to wake up and start their day, four men and two women moving at a cautious yet brisk pace with guns poking out in every direction, making their way down the street to a very suspicious-looking black van, which most likely had a very large and impressive dent on it, would be instantly noticed. If anyone happened to wake up and look outside, they would no doubt rub their eyes, thinking it was an illusion. Once realizing that the apparitions in front of them were, in fact, real, they would reach for the phone and dial the police in a state of panic. If Remus hadn't called the police, someone would eventually.

"Did you know I was a Resident?" Payton thought out of curiosity.

"Yep, this is going well," Athena commented.

"Shut the hell up!" Delmon snapped, and Athena glowered at him.

When Payton was first contacted by Andraste to help

Athena escape, she had wondered what Avalon could possibly be thinking to risk her cover by helping this ordinary Resident. As far as Payton knew, Athena didn't have any super abilities, even counting her telepathy. She was recklessly brash and at times didn't appear to be completely stable, a common quality among Pandora's Box Residents. But as Payton thought about it, she realized how much it had taken for Athena to escape from Pandora's Box, defeat two of Ragnarok's teams, one of which had a powerful Resident, and remove two trackers from her body through violent and painful means. The fact that she did this with nothing but telepathy and ingenuity made it all the more impressive. Perhaps there was a place at Avalon for that type of creative out-of-the-box thinking.

They had just turned the corner without incident, the van clearly in sight, when Froce held up a hand, signaling everyone to stop.

"What is it?" Payton asked in exasperation, secretly wondering when Athena's plan was going to take place. "We're almost there!"

Froce ignored her. "Delmon, I want you to go ahead and check the van. I don't want any hidden surprises."

Delmon hesitated, but one look from Froce was all it took. "Yes, sir."

Payton persisted. "Sir, there's no way we could look any more suspicious. If the police came right now..."

"Then I would shoot Athena and we would all go to prison, where hopefully Pandora's Box has enough influence to get us off," Froce stated in a tone that suggested Payton was overly exaggerating the situation.

"You can tell he's been spending too much time with Caleb," Athena said in mock whisper to Mycheal.

"And what happens if the van has been compromised?" Payton asked.

"How do I help you?"

"Then we shoot Athena and take our chances on foot."

"Is there a scenario that doesn't get me shot?" Athena wondered, her spunk and insolence returning. "If someone could give me the key to getting out of here alive, I'd be grateful."

The message was easy. She needed her handcuffs unlocked, and while Payton had a key to accomplish the goal, a problem still presented itself. *"That's going to be tough to do without the others knowing,"* she thought regretfully. Her orders were clear—do what she could to help Athena, but not at the expense of her cover. Athena seemed to know that, but still didn't appear worried. Payton was almost eager to see what she had planned.

Delmon had reached the van and, with great trepidation, opened the door. When nothing leapt out at him, he carefully peered inside. "Sir, I found Herman." A moment passed. "He's still alive, sir. Seems to be just sleeping." Delmon backed out and Payton, using sharp eyes that only a Resident could possess, saw him blink away blurry tears and stifle a yawn.

"Interesting," she thought approvingly to Athena as she realized what Remus had done. *"But that alone won't grant you freedom. Froce will figure out what he did if he hasn't already."* Athena didn't comment and her air of confidence did not vanish.

Delmon went to the back of the van and opened up the double doors. "I see the others they're all here but sleeping. And I hear a hissing..." Delmon froze in mid-sentence and looked at Froce, panic in his eyes.

"Everyone back up," Froce commanded. The silky menace in his voice had returned. "Remus wasn't honest with me."

Athena shifted uncomfortably, looking less confident, and huddled, if possible, even closer to Mycheal. "I didn't do this, Tyrone."

"Do what?" Payton asked sharply, feigning ignorance while pretending to search for an unknown threat.

Mycheal watched Delmon try to stagger forward, away from the van. "The sleeping gas. He must have unscrewed the valves. The whole van has been exposed." He laughed humorlessly. "This is why you shouldn't try to be fancy with your equipment. There's no way we can reach the van now."

"You knew!" Froce accused Athena. "You knew one of the tanks was leaking."

"Froce, you're wrong!" Athena cried tearfully. But then a smile began to tug at her mouth as her tone became taunting. "You're wrong. I knew *all* the tanks were leaking."

"All..." Mycheal stuttered. Delmon collapsed on the ground and Mycheal started forward, but a warning from Froce made him halt. "Is that safe? Won't he and the others die from overexposure to the gas?"

"Oddly enough, no," Athena answered seriously. "The gas uses a lot of naturally occurring elements found in plants and wildlife. For a dose to be toxic, you would need to inhale about three times the amount of gas currently circulating within your fallen comrade's lungs." She stopped and frowned, as if trying to puzzle something out. "Am I making this up or telling the truth?" she wondered out loud. "Forgive me, I tell so many lies that it's sometimes hard to—"

There was no warning; no hint or small gesture that gave away Force's murderous intentions. Athena's telepathy had to be the only reason she lived that day. As Froce raised his pistol and pulled the trigger, Athena was already ducking and spinning to the left, towards Payton. Though she hid it well, Athena was still injured, her movements sluggish, and she was just barely quick enough to avoid the bullet. Froce redirected the gun, only to hesitate as Payton stepped in front of his target.

"We have orders to bring her in alive!" Payton roared at him, wishing she was at full strength so she could teach Froce a lesson about pointing guns at helpless prisoners.

"Move out the way," Froce ordered. When Payton didn't budge, Froce's expression became ugly. "I am ordering you to get the hell out of my way!" During the standoff, David was scanning the houses to see if anyone had heard the gunshot. Yes, Froce's gun was equipped with a silencer, but a common misconception was that a silencer blocked out the entire sound of a gun going off. In reality, it only changed the noise of a gunshot from a miniature explosion to that of a jackhammer. A bit more quiet, but definitely loud enough to be noticed in a suburban neighborhood.

"We. Have. Orders," Payton said slowly, spacing out the words for added effect. Mycheal, the man she had become infatuated with, was inching towards her, and she had no clue to what his intentions might be. The biggest problem with being a spy was the people you call friends could become your enemy in a matter of seconds.

"Our oath to protect civilization from what we created goes above Ms. Yang's orders to capture a valuable resource."

"You didn't create me," Athena retorted bitingly from behind Payton, reasonably angry at almost being killed. "Only gifted me with powers through inhumane means."

Froce didn't lower his gun, and Payton was beginning to expect he would shoot through her to get Athena. "It amounts to the same thing."

"It does not." Athena's voice was rising with desperation as Mycheal crept near enough to grab her. Things were not going her way, and as Payton stared into Froce's eyes, she realized there was a chance she wouldn't make it out alive either. At the very least, her cover was severely compromised. "Whatever they told you was a lie. I'm not a killer; I'm not the apocalypse, Tyrone. I'm a girl who had the bad luck of being experimented on by you people. You can't justify this?"

"No, I can't. What they did to you was an atrocity. But because of it, you're no longer fit to live in our world. It's not fair, Athena. I acknowledge it."

"That doesn't do me much good, does it?" Athena shot back. "I'm still dead!"

"I don't believe that you didn't know what happened to Caleb's team. I don't believe that one of the canisters just happened to spring a leak, and Remus just happened to be immune to the gas, and that he then proceeded to defeat four trained military men without anyone's assistance."

"It is hard to swallow," Athena admitted, still hidden behind Payton's back. Mycheal was right beside her and, when Payton met his gaze, he looked away. Her heart sank; he would not stand by her in defense of a Resident, which explained Athena's desperation. Any second, he would make his move and would force Athena to either fight or try to flee.

"Sir, we're being watched," David informed. "They're probably calling the police as we speak."

"He's lying!" Athena responded, indignant. "Trying to force you to make a decision! The police aren't coming."

"So Remus lied when he said he called the police," Froce concluded, and Athena fell silent, realizing her blunder while Payton sighed inwardly. Definitely still young and prone to outbursts.

"We went from twenty-five men to four, and without a vehicle, there's no chance we can take you alive and I don't believe you will go quietly. This is the only way...Ms. Trist!" Froce said loudly. "Believe me when I say that if you do not move, I will shoot through you!"

"He's telling the truth!" Athena said quickly. Payton didn't understand who Athena was talking to until she spotted Mycheal's face.

"Sir, you can't do this," Mycheal argued, not necessarily in defense of Athena, but in defense of Payton.

Froce froze and turned his head towards Mycheal, his eyes unreadable as he recalculated the odds. "Excuse me?"

Mycheal met his stare, unflinching. "We can't kill her. Not in cold blood...it's not right."

"All you people are so blinded by the demon's face!" David said, his hands trembling with rage as Athena's chances of survival increased. Only when Payton glanced at him did she realized his gun was pointing towards her and Athena. "If you don't have the faith to kill her, then allow me!"

"I assumed you had a plan!" Payton thought frantically. David would not hesitate to shoot.

"There will be no killing," Athena said gleefully, taking a step back so that David could shoot her without fear of hitting Payton. "Gentlemen...and lady," she said, tilting her head in Payton's direction. "It was close for a moment, but I'm afraid this is where I make my exit."

David, without preamble, started to fire and though Athena twisted away from his first two shots, the third one must have hit for Payton heard her gasp of pain, and she faltered. Froce rushed forward, roughly pushing Payton into Mycheal, who propped her up. Athena had to have known David would take a shot at her. What was the plan?

"Look out!" Mycheal screamed.

Payton snapped her neck to see the other van, the one Remus had driven off in, barreling towards them with no signs of stopping.

Chapter 72

The headlights grew brighter as the van roared towards them. Mycheal was going to die...flattened by a teenager who probably only received his license last year. At the last possible second, Athena, using her shoulder, shoved both him and Payton out of the way. The van screeched to a stop in the exact place where they'd once stood.

Mycheal landed on the pavement, his vision swimming, and when he sat up, he saw Athena lying on top of Payton. Scrambling to his feet, he rushed to stop her.

"Get off her!" he yelled, pulling Athena up by the arm.

The young girl glared at him like any teenager wrongfully accused of breaking curfew. "Idiot. I just saved her life. Yours too."

"From your boyfriend!"

Athena stretched lazily. "Remus? Naw, he's too squeamish to kill someone. At the most, you would have had some major booboos. Nothing more." It was as she stretched that it dawned on Mycheal that she was no longer handcuffed. As soon as the realization hit him, so did Athena.

The first hit was nothing more than a severe slap across the face that stung more than it hurt, but as Mycheal was reeling back, Athena kicked him three times on the side of his knee in rapid succession and Mycheal stumbled to all fours. He tried to get up, but a vicious kick from Athena sent him crashing back down.

"What are you doing?" he demanded, and she answered with another kick, this one directed for his temple, the sheer force of the blow making his head ring. He reached for his gun that he'd dropped a couple of feet away, but Athena stomped on his hand. For a brief second, he wondered why no one was helping him, then the answer came to him. The van had separated them. Athena had purposely pushed them to the right so the van could get between them, effectively making a temporary barrier. Still, he could hear Tyrone and David galloping around the van now, but their pace stalled as Athena's companion revved the engine, threatening to drive forward or backward and run over any man who was stupid enough to get in his direct path. Mycheal's hand reached out blindly and clasped the first thing he felt, a beer bottle. If he could get up, he could maybe take her out.

"Don't be stupid," Athena said, her tone devoid of kindness. She reached down, grabbed him by the shirt, and lifted him up on his feet with an inhuman strength she should not have possessed. "It takes more than a bottle to knock me out. Now let it go." Athena's eyes glittered menacingly as the bottle dropped to the ground. "I did warn you...back when we first met." Payton was still lying motionless on the pavement. Athena must have heard his thoughts. "She's alive. I knocked her out to steal her keys and unlock myself."

There were gunshots as someone tried to fire into the van, but Athena looked unconcerned. "Bulletproof," she explained. "Windows as well."

"You can't escape!"

"No?" "We'll see. Now the gunfire was a distraction for Remus and in just a second, David is going to come around the front and scream—"

"Don't move!" David screamed, coming around the front of the van.

Mycheal was spun around so that he faced David. Athena's arms wrapped themselves around his throat and began to tighten. "Good," she whispered into Mycheal's ears as David hesitated. "For all his talk on killing demons, he really is a coward and doesn't want to pull the trigger himself. Froce is trying to sneak around the back of the van so he can shoot me. Not very honorable, is he?" Taking one hand from around his throat, she knocked loudly on the van's door. "You doing okay, Remus?"

The window cracked open an inch and a nervous voice answered. "Just fine, thank you. However, there's a very loud and insistent man banging on the other side, firing bullets and demanding that I surrender, so if you could hurry along..."

"Give me a second."

"You're going to kill me, Athena," Mycheal thought angrily, knowing Athena would pick it up. *"I guess I was wrong. You are every bit the monster they claim you to be."*

To his surprise, her grip lessened...almost as if she was hesitating. For a brief second, Mycheal thought there might be hope...but then he felt a new tension enter her body and her grip retightened. "Damn it," she cursed under her breath. Mycheal didn't understand what happened until he saw the look in David's eyes.

"I won't do it!" he yelled with a twisted sense of pride. "I won't be responsible for the demon escaping. No sacrifice is too great to rid the world of this monster!" And that's when he fired his gun, point blank at Mycheal.

Athena cursed vehemently as she read David's intentions.

"No sacrifice is too great to rid the world of this monster!" David yelled, and Athena fought the urge to laugh. It sounded like he expected an audience to stand up and clap at his delivery of such a well-thought-out speech.

His gun went off, but Athena was already moving. She released Mycheal and shoved him forcefully out the way. Mycheal's head was slammed into the van before falling to the ground and staying there. Athena dived left, missing the spray of bullets intent on killing her. She rolled on the ground, gasping as her damaged shoulder hit the pavement, and grabbed the bottle Mycheal had picked up earlier before standing up.

David pointed the gun in her direction. Athena snapped her arm back and threw the bottle with all the skill of a professional baseball pitcher. The bottle's speed and force was enough to snap David's head back, and an even more fortunate surprise was when the bottle shattered, spraying David's face with shards of glass. The man fell screaming to the ground, and a quick mind check was all that was needed to know he had lost the will to fight.

There was no time to rest as Froce emerged from around

the back of the van, and though she was grateful to Remus, she wished he had the gumption to back the van up and hit him. For a long moment, they stared at each other, the distance between them no more than ten feet. With Athena's speed, she could maybe get to him before he killed her, but then again, she might not. "Let it go," she advised, hoping, for once, to take the peaceful way out. "It's over, Tyrone."

"You know I can't allow that."

"Look around!" Athena waited for Froce to assess his environment. Payton was still lying motionless on the ground where she'd pretended to be unconscious after having unlocked Athena's handcuffs. David was whimpering softly. Both hands clutched at his ruined face, shards of glass still embedded in his skin. Mycheal was stunned, but he would be up soon. "My friend, you have lost," Athena stated, hoping absolute confidence would unnerve him. "The only thing you can do now is avoid needless bloodshed." Force's thoughts were a jumble, but his determination didn't waver. "Don't make me kill you," Athena added quietly. She had made a promise to the Avalon mole, and she tried to always keep her promises.

"I'm prepared to die."

"What a coincidence! I am too. Difference is I'm prepared to die for the sake of freedom. What about you?"

Froce stared at her. The time of the attack was coming soon and there was nothing Athena could do to prevent it; her only chance was to stack the odds in her favor. "I'm ready to die to protect the innocent," Froce finally said, and Athena realized she was wrong. She could have convinced Froce to back off, but now the chance was gone and she had to continue playing the game.

"If you do not tell the truth about yourself, you cannot tell it about other people," Athena said, quoting Virginia Wolfe.

"And what does that mean?"

He would shoot during her answer in the hope to catch her unaware. He remembered her telepathy, but hoped she wasn't using it. *How naïve.* Athena prepared her next move. David, the religious nut, had managed to graze her with his last shot, but as far as wounds went, it was her least debilitating, the bullet only scraping her outer thigh. Her other injuries, though not completely healed, no longer greatly hampered her moves. She could escape Froce, but not without killing him.

"Horn!" Remus thought at her.

Oh, now that was an interesting plan. Riskier, but if pulled off correctly, she would keep her promise to Payton.

Athena bobbed her head up and down in agreement and then spoke to Froce. "If you really thought of me as a monster, you wouldn't have hesitated to kill me when I was sleeping. A moment ago, instead of rounding the corner with bullets blazing, you stopped to have this pleasant chat with me. The truth is you want me to kill you because you think you deserve it."

She wasn't being completely honest, but her words had enough truth in them to shock Froce into hesitating. That's when Remus pressed down on the van's horn, the loud, blaring noise causing Froce to jerk as he instinctively looked around for the new threat, and that's when Athena made her last desperate move. She ran...not towards Froce, which was what he expected...but instead towards the van.

"Catch me if you can!" she yelled with sheer giddiness. Froce managed to fire off a couple of shots, but Athena ignored him as best she could, even going as far as shutting down her telepathy so she could better concentrate. Just when it looked like she was in danger of plowing into the van, she leapt. She barely cleared it, landing on the roof, and she heard Froce running as he quickly figured out her plan. She rolled across the van's roof, the pain excruciating as her shoulder made contact with metal, but then she fell off, landing clumsily and without her usual grace.

"Hurry up!"

"You think?" Athena yelled sarcastically, opening the car door just as Froce came into view. The man's dedication was starting to grate on her nerves. He fired, but the open door acted as a shield. "Does he have to try so hard for employee of the month?" she demanded in great spirits, because she knew, without a doubt, she would escape.

"He's coming!" Remus yelled at her, not sharing her optimism.

Athena slid in. "I guess you better drive then." With an ear-splitting screech, Remus took off, but when Athena glanced forward, she had to laugh. "What are you doing? You're heading straight for a house!"

"Give me a second!"

"You must be the worst rescuer ever!"

"You're ungrateful! You know that?"

She laughed crazily as he spun the van expertly around and headed back in the direction of Froce. He shot her a concerned look. "Are you there, Athena?"

"You mean have I suffered a severe mental breakdown from which there's no return?" she clarified.

"Yes."

"Nope, I'm good." She rolled down the window an inch so she could scream at Froce. "Watch out or he'll run over you!" Remus would never have done such a thing, but Froce didn't know that, so the soldier leapt out of the way to avoid being crushed. As soon as he did, Remus slammed on the pedal and flew past him. "We did it!" Athena's gleeful laugh was cut short when the van bounced and then started to noticeably slow down. "What happened?"

Remus glanced out the mirror...it was so good to see him again. "What happened? You tempted the universe, that's what happened," he said sourly. "Your friend managed to hit both our back tires and now we're scraping the ground."

"Yikes!" Athena commented. "Well, keep on driving anyway."

"Yes, because I was really going to stop and call Triple A!" Remus snapped.

Athena let it slide, figuring he was allowed a couple of shots for saving her life, and also she didn't have the energy to peek in his mind to find out what Triple A was. "Where's the Thunderbird?"

There was a pause in which Remus caught up to her line of thinking. "Abandoned in a ditch. Has a few nice bullet-sized holes in it, thanks to your friends, but other than that, it should be drivable. Unless they took the keys from the ignition...then we're screwed."

Froce was only a dot on the horizon when they turned the corner and he disappeared completely from view. Athena smiled to herself, but unlike before, she refused to let herself relax until they were fifty miles away from the nearest agent of Pandora's Box, Ragnarok, or Avalon.

"We need to hurry to avoid the police."

"I was bluffing when I said I called them."

"I know, but the nice couple across from us wasn't. I'm

not in the mood to get this far and get captured by the police."

Remus sighed. "Yes, Athena."

Athena waited for a moment. "One more thing."

"Yes?"

She turned to him and gave him an awkward hug.

"I'm driving!" he yelped.

She ignored his complaints, tightening her hold and whispering, "Thank you."

Chapter 73

Maris stared at his last living son. "So that's it?"

"Yes, Father." Romulus' voice no longer held the careful respect that Maris was used to commanding.

Maris tapped his pen on the desk and stared hard at Romulus. This was usually the time when his son looked away, afraid to risk his father's ire, but Romulus stared back, his gaze just as hostile. Finally, a backbone was beginning to emerge. "You expect me not only to let you live outside my house, but pay for your apartment as well?"

"I do."

"And what makes you think I would agree to that?" Maris queried, leaning back in his custom-made cushioned chair, the most expensive thing in the room besides his desk.

"Because I'm holding all the cards. They want me...not you. If I asked, I'm sure they would gladly cut you off."

Romulus' words had multiple meanings. Though Maris felt pride in his son, his timing was terribly frustrating.

"Delilah will get to live with me as well," Romulus declared, growing bold as he thought he had Maris on the ropes.

Ah, well that was better. This arrangement was okay as long as Delilah was there to spy on him. "Fine, son. Whatever you want."

Romulus glared at his dad, surprised that he had given in so easily. "In that case, I'm going up to pack. Do I need to worry about hired gunmen following me up to my room?"

The joke was actually funny, and Maris waved his hand good-naturedly. "Not you, Romulus. You're the special one, not the screw-up." Romulus' fist clenched and Maris realized his anger stemmed from the death of his brother. Well hell, Maris missed him too, but it had to be done to protect the family. And in the end, Maris wasn't even involved in his other son's death. Remus did it to himself with his own stupidity. "Go upstairs and I'll find you a suitable place to stay."

"I already have a place in mind!" Romulus countered, and Maris' respect for him started to turn into irritation.

"If that's what you want."

Romulus, apparently realizing he was close to Maris' limit, retreated upstairs to pack, slamming the door behind him with unnecessary roughness.

While Romulus was packing, Maris made a few calls, and although he threatened all his informants with grisly and messy deaths, not one of them could tell him a thing about Pandora's Box. Annoying, but to be expected. If the local thug on the street could find information on the place, then it really wasn't a top secret organization. Still, no one was as clever and as adaptable as him and so when that stupid woman, Ms. Yang, came by to ensure Maris would accept her proposal, he had her followed. His thugs had eventually lost the trail, but Maris had a follow-up meeting with her and, this time, his thugs managed to follow her to where she stayed. Maris felt a thrill of excitement as he gazed at the new information and ordered his man, via text, to stay on Ms. Yang's trail and to report back everywhere she went. Here lay a new challenge. Something else that needed to be conquered. It would be hard, but with his superior intellect, he would pull it off.

Romulus reentered his office, without knocking, an action that greatly annoyed. "I'm done."

"Swell. It's going to take a day or two to get your place ready. I'm not magic after all. You should get some sleep. You been up the whole night, right? Don't worry about school."

"I'll be checking the room for bugs, so don't even try."

Maris slammed his fist on the desk. "It won't be bugged and you should consider yourself lucky that I'm generous enough to give you back your own room!"

Romulus stared at him and Maris was struck on how much he looked like his mother. "Do you regret what you did...to Remus? Do you feel any type of loss or any strong emotion, knowing our actions killed him?"

Maris pondered the question for a moment and then looked his son straight in the eye. "Not one bit."

When Romulus left, Maris poured himself a drink and took a pill for the migraine that was starting to creep up on him. His boy was dead, and he found he did miss him terribly, but he could never admit it in front of Romulus. It was never good to show emotions or appear weak, especially in front of his son and soon-to-be super soldier. His phone buzzed with a text. Maris glanced at it before spitting out his drink in horror. The text was a picture—a burnt up corpse with his mouth stretched wide as if it was still screaming in agony. Another text and, as Maris read it, his body trembled with rage and anticipation.

If you wanted my address, all you need do was ask. Thank you for the snack.

"It's breathtaking, isn't it?" Athena said serenely as the first rays of the sun peeked over the horizon. "I mean, I read books, but who could have imagined the sun would be this..."

"Wonderful?" Remus suggested. "Astounding, mind-blowing, spectacular?"

"Spectacular," Athena settled on, but then immediately second-guessed herself. "Though it makes it seem like a magician's trick."

She was sitting on top of the Thunderbird, her gaze completely focused on the sunrise. She had the same look of wonder on her face as she did when she was enthralled with the rain. Remus enjoyed watching her. Having seen it for most of his life, usually when trudging reluctantly to school, the sunrise would mean more to her than it would ever mean to him.

"We can only appreciate the miracle of a sunrise if we have waited in the darkness," she answered. "I've been waiting to see something like this for a very long time."

"Reading my mind again."

She smiled slightly. "Habit."

He didn't want to ruin this moment, but he had to. "Athena, we have to go. Eventually, they're going to find us."

"Just a couple more minutes," she pleaded instantly,

sounding like a child wanting to stay a little longer at Disney. "Please. I'm doing constant mind scans. No one will sneak up on us."

Upon finding the Thunderbird, they had traveled for a little while, but stopped when Athena caught first glance of the sun coming up. The smart thing would have been to leave and put as much distance from the bad guys as possible, but Remus found it hard to deny her.

"You pushover," she said with a laugh.

Remus sighed and turned his gaze on the sun. "Isn't this where the movie ends? The hero walking into the sunrise?"

She shook her head, causing her hair to wave. Remus found this a more breathtaking sight than any sunrise. "No, traditionally the hero walks into the sunset, because a sunset symbolizes the end. A sunrise symbolizes beginning."

They watched in silence for a couple more minutes. Remus didn't want to break the silence. He was at peace, standing beside Athena, and the sunrise was awesome.

Athena burst out laughing. "I'm sorry, did you just call the sunrise awesome?"

"You know, that telepathy could become annoying."

She shrugged. "What can you do?"

Remus shrugged, mimicking her actions. "Get used to it, I suppose. Unless that mess about being able to block your thoughts is true."

"In theory," Athena said flatly, and Remus' heart skipped a beat. Something was wrong. Athena might have reconsidered and decided to rescind her offer. She tore her gaze from the sunrise to look at him, her eyes unreadable. "I can't be sure and it will take a while."

"I have nothing better to do."

"I'm probably going to annoy you at least eighty percent of the time."

"You ever been to high school?"

There was a pause as she read his mind to get the reference. "I have no clue what to do next."

"So you had a plan up to now?" he asked.

"They might find us again."

"Then I kick their ass all over again."

She grinned. "You did a decent job." She studied the bruises on his face. "Although pissing off Caleb was a bad idea."

"You going to tell me about him?"

"Later." She stared at him and he matched her gaze. "I don't want you to end up a fool, Remus. There's a good chance sticking with me could get you killed."

"The fool is always beginning to live," he said, using one of her previous quotes against her. "I'm tired of always wondering 'what if,' Athena. This might be a mistake, and I might regret it later, but at least I'm making a decision instead of letting the universe make one for me."

She jumped off the car and walked up to him. "I can't be that girl, Remus."

"I never asked you to be. Stop being such a pain in the ass. Can I come or what?"

She blinked a couple of times before a smile broke across her face. "I'd be delighted!"

"Good," Remus said, relieved. He'd thought she might deny him the opportunity. "Now, we really need to go. There will be other sunrises."

Athena snapped a mocking salute. "Yes, sir!"

Remus smiled. He didn't know what would happen next, but he knew it wouldn't be boring.

Chapter 74

—Two weeks later

Caleb took another gulp of his beer as he flicked through channels in a futile attempt to find something both mind-numbing and interesting to watch. Two weeks had passed since Athena's miraculous escape. Two weeks he'd been sitting at home, wondering about his fate and contemplating his chances of living to retirement. No one, as of yet, had accused him of being a traitor, which was surprising in itself, for he was sure someone would have put two and two together by now and figured out he was the one who'd made Athena's escape possible, and who'd later on given Remus the tools needed to rescue the gal. Apparently, everyone's memory of the failed mission was fuzzy, and Caleb certainly wasn't volunteering any information. Was this a new power that Athena had neglected to mention, someone else involved in the game, or just a run of good luck.

He took another swig of his beer and jumped as a cell phone went off, instinctively reaching for the gun he'd kept with him ever since the suspension. He checked the cell phone and found the display was empty. No one was calling him. The ringing continued and Caleb leapt out of his seat, cursing himself for being slow. He stumbled towards his closet, and after two failed attempts, managed to open the doors. It was definitely time to cut back on the drinking. Tearing through boxes, he finally found the hidden phone underneath a picture of his ex-wife. "Hello?" he answered, out of breath. Damn, he needed to get in better shape. He resolved the hit the gym next week if he was still alive.

"Is this the grey bull?" an uncertain male voice asked. Not Remus and certainly not Athena.

"Who the hell is this?" Caleb growled, suspecting a trap from Pandora's Box. Grey bull was the code word, but Athena would not be foolish enough to give the number to some random bloke she didn't know. "One of you kids pranking my phone again?"

"What? No...I mean this could be a prank, but someone else..."

"Speak English, boy!" Caleb roared.

"Right. Look, this might sound stupid, but two weeks ago, I had my Thunderbird stolen from me by a freaky blond girl and a redheaded boy."

"I ain't the police, pal."

"I know...just hear me out. A week ago, I got an email telling me where I could find my car and to please not contact the police." Another pause. "It took me two days and I had to pass three states, but I found my Thunderbird exactly where the email said it would be."

"A real heartwarming story. Why the hell wouldn't you call the police?"

"I...the note mentioned some discrepancies about my marriage I'd rather remained secret."

"Uh-huh."

"It's when I was young and stupid; I've been with my wife for over forty years."

"Sure."

"I still don't know how she could have possibly known. As far as I know, I've never seen her in my life!"

"I'm sure you're going to eventually tell me what the hell this has to do with me."

"Right...sorry. Anyway, I found my Thunderbird, but not only that. I found five thousand dollars in the glove department along with a note."

"Did the note tell you to send the money to me?"

"What? No."

"Damn!"

"The note was an apology for stealing my car, and it said the money was mine to keep. It also asked a favor... It wanted me to call this number and deliver a message."

"Well you got this far," Caleb said gruffly when the other man fell silent. "Might as well finish what you started."

"It told me to tell whoever picked up that she appreciated everything you did, and she forgives you and hopes she has the chance to see you again one day."

"That's it?"

"Uhhh...yeah."

"Well that is mighty interesting, all right, but I have no clue what you're talking about. Thank you so much for wasting my time and don't you ever dare call this number again!"

He hung up before the tears started to flow, and he cursed himself for being such a pansy.

Epilogue

—A month later

The walls trembled with the force of the explosions, and Dr. Pluck felt the old fear returning. *Not again!*! Life had just settled down to its familiar routine, and now another Resident was trying to escape. Since Athena's departure, all the guards had been terminated under suspicion that one or more of them had helped Athena escape, and a fresh batch of guards had replaced them. With Athena gone, the change in the other Residents had been nothing short of miraculous. Since the month started, there had only been three minor injuries and no deaths—a feat that had never happened within Pandora's Box walls, and Dr. Pluck was prepared to believe that Athena had been the bad apple, influencing all the negative behavior.

Brian Tin, his new personal bodyguard, barged through the door. Brian was once a prominent Yakuza member until the organization tried to kill him and he fled to America at the age of 23. He had since become a mercenary-for-hire and was one of the best, if not most expensive, new employees now working at Pandora's Box. Dr. Pluck felt like his safety was well worth the extra money.

"Sir, I need you to stay down.

"What's happening?" he demanded, at the same time ducking underneath his desk. "What's going on?"

"A breakout, sir."

Dr. Pluck inhaled deeply. This wasn't a surprise, but it was still painful to hear. He still was unsure how he'd kept his position after Athena's escape, but he very much doubted his career could handle another one. Just as well, he had been making plans to leave Pandora's Box anyway. "Which one?"

Brian looked at him, and Dr. Pluck's heart rate trembled when he saw the naked fear on his face. "All of them, sir."

Dr. Pluck stared dumbly, unable to comprehend. "All of them," he repeated. "But that's impossible. The new security measures...."

"Were ineffective, sir."

"How did they escape?"

Brian Tin shrugged helplessly, but then something odd happened. He staggered back as if someone had hit him before placing a trembling hand to the side of his forehead.

"Brian?" Dr. Pluck asked with trepidation.

"They used a variety of methods," Brian said, and it took Dr. Pluck a moment to realize he was answering his earlier question. "Some of the doors just melted apart. Some of the security guards unlocked several of the doors. A few of the stronger Residents knocked their door down, and one of them simply walked through his door."

Dr. Pluck ground his teeth together and wished for a smoke. "They planned this. Those animals...this whole time they were playing nice, they planned this whole thing!"

"That assumption is correct."

"So what can we do to get the situation under control?" Dr. Pluck asked desperately.

"At this junction, no course of action will be effective," Brian said, too calm given the circumstance. "This is the end for Pandora's Box. We have been planning this for a very long time. Plotting your downfall. It was unreasonable for you to think you could keep us locked up for an indefinite period of time."

Dr. Pluck froze and studied Brian's face. His bodyguard's eyes, usually so intelligent, now had a vacant look to them, and his arms hung limply at his sides. "What's wrong with you?" the doctor demanded. "You're supposed to be protecting me!"

"Brian Tin's primary concern was himself," Brian said, speaking in the third person. "He wished to make a deal with my kind. In exchange for you, he would walk freely. An improbable plan, for few Residents would consider this deal, more likely choosing to kill you both. It is due to my actions that you are still alive."

"You're possessed!" Dr. Pluck gasped.

"Two humans, lacking in any Resident knowledge, realized this truth in considerably less time than it took for you, a supposed expert of our kind, to come to the same conclusion."

"Who am I talking to?" Dr. Pluck asked, his voice trembling. The possessed man had made no move to attack, which meant there was still a chance for Dr. Pluck to get out of this alive, and if he did, he swore he would never deal with Residents again.

"That resolution comes far too late," Brian Tin observed. Another mind reader. Brian Tin turned slowly around, walking toward the door, and it didn't take Dr. Pluck long to understand he was going to unlock the door and let whatever monster was waiting on the other side in with them.

"Stop!" Dr. Pluck yelled as Brian made the approach. "Brian Tin, I'm ordering you to stop!"

When it became clear that mere words weren't enough to stop him, Dr. Pluck grabbed the gun he now kept since Athena had escaped from the secret compartment in his desk. And though his hands were trembling and sweating badly, he managed to raise it and shoot Brian twice in the back. Brian stumbled forward as the bullets slammed into him, but amazingly enough, the man continued to walk. "Stop!" Dr. Pluck screamed, and fired twice more. Still, Brian, riddled with bullets, continued forward and unlocked the door.

"You may die," a soft voice said, and Brian immediately fell over.

Dr. Pluck stared as Selene, a Resident only four months younger than Athena, walked into his office. "What are you doing here?" he whispered, remembering belatedly that there were no guards or bars protecting him in case the Resident found him too belligerent and decided to adjust his attitude.

"I came to pay my respects," she said just as softly. Selene was a 16-year-old African American girl with black hair that extended to her shoulders. Her hair hid pointed ears that gave her the impression of being an elf. The other telltale sign she was a Resident was the slight glow her skin emitted. Barely noticeable during the daytime, it was plainly obvious at night.

Dr. Pluck pointed his pistol, his hand shaking from fear.

"Don't move!"

"If that arrangement will make you comfortable," she said affably, seemingly unconcerned. She looked around. "I have only been in this room as a prisoner. Freed from your tyranny, the room appears to be much bigger in stature."

"What's going on outside?" Dr. Pluck asked meekly. Selene's lack of any emotion was always disconcerting, but now, without protection, it seemed alien and unnatural. Perhaps it was a good thing. After all, if she didn't feel any emotions, then she would feel no need for vengeance.

"All your men are dead or dying. Two have made it past Pandora's Box perimeters alive, but are currently being hunted by several Residents. It is doubtful they will survive."

Dr. Pluck gawked. "All of them are going to die," he repeated dumbly.

Selene nodded while watching him with big, expressionless eyes. "It is likely this will be known as a massacre; the biggest incident in recorded Resident history."

"This is all Athena's fault," Dr. Pluck hissed. "This is her doing!"

"You give her too much credit." Selene strolled forward and Dr. Pluck tensed up. But all she did was take a seat in the empty chair across from Dr. Pluck. It was just like their previous sessions, except Selene wasn't chained to the floor. "We have been planning our exodus from Pandora's Box for some time now. Two years and nineteen days, if you wished for an exact count."

"If that was true, then why didn't Athena wait and escape with you?"

"Fair question," Selene complimented, and Dr. Pluck began to think he might make it out of this mess alive. Of all the Residents to corner him, Selene was perhaps the best choice. "Athena had been planning her escape for double that amount of time, approximately four years."

"Still, even if that's true, why not combine her plan with yours? It offers a better chance of escaping."

"Whether humans or Residents, Athena hates to follow a crowd. There are more reasons than that, but I do not see what relevance they play at this point." She paused. "Your last man has been killed. Most of the remaining Residents are leaving now."

"They won't get away with this!" Dr. Pluck snarled, making sure to differentiate Selene from the other Residents and hoping she would notice and be appreciative.

"Spouting off silly sayings is unbecoming," Selene stated, still not a hint of emotion in her tone or face. "However, you are undoubtedly right. Some of us will be stupid and get caught immediately. Some of us will die. Others will become the new monsters and horror stories of the next generation. Again, this has no relevance to your current situation."

She looked so relaxed in the chair that Dr. Pluck felt himself begin to relax too. "I thought you and Athena were friends. Why didn't you go with her?"

"A complicated situation that I have no wish to go into. We suffered tremendously at the hands of you and your masters; neither of us would be alive if not for the actions of the other one."

"A mutually beneficial relationship in which the two of you protected each other," Dr. Pluck concluded, his curiosity getting the better of him. He had thought the Residents too mentally unstable to effectively use teamwork.

"An accurate summation," Selene acknowledged. "However, your thoughts are flawed. Residents have been using teamwork ever since I can remember, the biggest example being the mass escape that is currently happening outside your door." As if emphasizing her point, a loud crash and the sound of maniacal laughter echoed from outside, Dr. Pluck flinching fearfully. Selene continued to watch him. "We even established a barter system in which favors are exchanged for future favors."

"Like what?" He was trying to keep her talking until help came.

"Most recently, I aided Athena in her escape, and in return for a future favor, she also saved you so that I could have this chance."

Dr. Pluck's heart had almost slowed down to normal, but at her statement, it sped up again and he tightened his hold on his pistol. "What do you mean?"

Selene stared solemnly at him. "She had a chance to kill you and yet she did not. Her hatred of you was known to all, and yet you never wondered why you were spared?"

Dr. Pluck recalled Athena's words. *"To be honest, Dr. Pluck, I doubt you'll live much longer."*

Dr. Pluck pointed the gun at Selene and pulled the trigger. Or at least, he attempted to. Try as he might, his finger would not squeeze down, and he almost cried as his arm lowered of its own volition.

Selene cocked her head, seemingly not upset by the fact he had just tried to kill her. "The last Resident has left the building. We're the only live bodies left in Pandora's Box, and your help is still fifteen minutes away."

"Listen," Dr. Pluck said faintly. "I'm sure we could work something out..."

She held up a hand, silencing him. "There are no deals to be made, no loopholes to exploit, no escape from your fate, Dr. Pluck." She stared at him, her gaze intensifying. "Take the gun and stick it in your mouth."

Dr. Pluck's arm immediately moved to comply, and his mouth opened so the pistol would fit securely inside. He felt the metallic taste of the gun as it rested on his tongue, and stared at Selene with desperate eyes.

"*Don't do this. I can help you! What do you want to do? I can make it happen.*"

"After I kill you, I plan to leave Pandora's Box before your backup arrives," Selene said, still in a mood to answer his questions. "Once I'm safely out of reach, I, more likely than not, will track Athena down and kill her."

As frantic as Dr. Pluck was, he was still a scientist and Selene's statement triggered another rush of curiosity. Why would Selene want Athena dead?

"It is a complicated matter," Selene answered. "And once again, it has no bearing on your situation. Pull the trigger, Dr. Pluck. It is time to end your existence." Dr. Pluck had no choice other than to comply.

About the Author

Wesley is a native of North Carolina and currently resides in Raleigh. He possesses a passion for writing and storytelling since his early childhood when he would create stories to amuse his brother. His dreams are often besieged by creatures and characters from far-away worlds. When not writing, he has long thought-provoking discussions with the voices in his head.